Killing Time
in Ocean City

Killing Time
in Ocean City

Jane Kelly

Plexus Publishing, Inc.
Medford, NJ

Third Printing, 2002

Published by: Plexus Publishing, Inc.
                 143 Old Marlton Pike
                 Medford, NJ 08055

Library of Congress Cataloging-in-Publication Data

Kelly, Jane, 1949-
    Killing Time in Ocean City / Jane Kelly.
        p.   cm.
    ISBN 0-937548-38-3 (hardcover)
    I. Title.
    PS3561.E39424k55   1997
    813'.54—dc21   97-31390
                                                         CIP

Price: $22.95 (hardcover)

Editors: Rhonda Forbes, Diane Zelley
Cover Design: Erica Oehler

To Rosemary,
Mark, and Frank

Chapter 1

"Why he doesn't look bad at all. Considering."

On his best days Donald K. Bascombe's image was not impressive but his appearance hadn't deteriorated as much as I'd expected. The body was his. I was certain. Even death couldn't wipe the perennial scowl off the executive's face. "I was afraid he'd be all gruesome and bloody but really, he looks pretty much like he's asleep. Not that I ever saw him sleep, mind you. Actually I never saw him lying down before but you know there's that thing when you lie on your back—your skin falls into place and you appear younger. Or so they say."

My words appeared to confuse Detective Dupuy, the young, stern, relentlessly humorless policewoman who, after awakening me at dawn, had dragged me into a swamp, forced me to identify my boss's body, and ignored all my attempts at female bonding.

I explained. "You know reclining on your back is like an instant facelift. Well, you wouldn't know. You're too young. Not too young to be a detective. Too young to need a facelift which technically I am too. But old DK here, he was getting to be that age and all, so lying down he appears somewhat better. Than he did standing up. Which is how I would see him. Always." I paused only briefly. "Are you going to stop me or let me babble all morning?"

1

Detective Dupuy's eyes accused me of being a dumb blonde. Strictly speaking, neither was true.

"For the record, Ms. Daniels. You are saying that this is the body of Donald K. Bascombe."

I completed a leisurely review of the reclining figure. Even with the traces of a frown on his face, Bascombe appeared as pleasant as I had ever seen him. His graying hair was neatly combed and his hands were folded in a fig leaf position I'd seen him adopt at all official functions, as if anyone would want to steal a peek at his crown jewels. His clothes were familiar from casual Fridays: khaki pants, brown leather belt, pink shirt. For some reason that was not explained to me, his feet were covered by a black tarp.

"Ms. Daniels. Is this D.K. Bascombe?"

"He looks so natural."

"Ms. Daniels." If the cop had any patience, she wasn't wasting it on me.

"Yes. Yes. It's Bascombe."

"Tag him and bag him." Detective Dupuy turned to the police officers who surrounded her and snapped the words as if she gave similar orders every day. I had the feeling she'd been waiting to give the command for her entire, albeit short, career.

Chapter 2

That day, my fourth at the Jersey shore, had gotten off to an inauspicious start. I was awakened by constant knocking on my suddenly and inexplicably wooden skull. Eventually, I figured out that my tapping co-workers had accompanied me on holiday only in my dreams. The knocking was real and occurring at the front door to the dilapidated but beachfront house I had rented in Ocean City, New Jersey.

Rising did not come easily, and not just because a steep incline lay between me and the edge of the aged mattress. Unless an intruder affixed a giant boulder to my head while I slept, I had gained quite a bit of weight overnight—all above my shoulders. If I weren't a social drinker who had traveled to the beach alone, I would have sworn that I had a hangover.

The banging persisted. Clad only in an oversized T-shirt, I staggered down the short hallway and flung open the door. The fist of a very tall man in very dark clothes slammed into my forehead which hadn't been feeling too well in the first place. I reeled backwards, slammed into the faux pine paneling, and slid to the floor while I wondered how a material that presented such a poor imitation of wood could offer such an accurate simulation of splinters.

Sprawled on the hard and grimy linoleum with no concern for modesty, or much else besides my head, I made no move to protect myself. Defense wasn't necessary. The intruder immediately grew kind and solicitous.

"I am so sorry, miss. Are you okay?"

I squinted at the man hovering over me. He was actually more of a boy in some sort of uniform or costume. "Why did you hit me?"

The youth, sputtering a protest that he hadn't mean to strike me, asked if I wanted to get off the floor and onto the couch.

"I don't think I can." His blow had little effect on my inability to rise but why share that information?

The young man appeared alarmed. "Let me help you up."

If I hadn't been injured before, I was by the time he yanked me to my feet.

"I can walk." I protested—falsely as it turned out. My uninvited guest guided me to the sofa, or to approximately two feet above the sofa, where he let me go. I plopped onto cushions that had felt considerably softer the day before. "Oh, the light!" I shielded my eyes from the glare of the sun that had barely cleared the horizon.

The kid, eager to placate me through whatever means possible, closed the curtains across the broad window. It wasn't his fault that the open weave hardly filtered the glare into a bearable glow. The only shade I got resulted from his standing guard over me. "Would you like a glass of water?"

His question made me realize that the same person who had attached a boulder to my head had apparently filled my mouth with sawdust. "That would be a good idea," I answered truthfully.

It was at that moment that I noticed Detective Dupuy. Her small, dark brown eyes peered from under heavy lids to study me with an intensity I found puzzling. She flashed something. It might have been a badge. She said she was a cop and I had no reason to doubt her. Who else would be up at that hour? Who else would wear that baggy navy blue pantsuit at any hour?

In clipped tones reminiscent of Dragnet reruns, the detective apologized for the overzealous behavior of Officer Timmy Borden, the summer intern she supervised—not closely enough if you asked me. She then explained why I had been awakened by the police. A crime had been committed in the neighborhood the night before.

"What kind of crime?" My question was delivered from the cover of an ice bag that the younger cop had created out of a baggie as inefficient at keeping water in as it was at keeping air out.

"Probably nothing but your neighbor is the victim."

Your neighbor. My memory made a sudden, although not complete, comeback. I remembered my neighbor.

"Which direction?" I asked even though I suspected we were not discussing an unauthorized occupant of the empty lot that bordered the south side of the house. I lifted the ice pack and stared at the detective.

"Guy next door." She pointed north. "Named Bascombe. Ever meet him?"

"Unfortunately."

"Not a good neighbor, eh?"

"Not a good boss."

Apparently, Detective Dupuy didn't place a lot of faith in coincidences. I spent the next half hour trying to explain my presence in the cottage next to the summer place my employer had purchased just months before. If I had not known that the house belonged to Bascombe, and I swore repeatedly that I had not, how had I discovered that he was staying next door?

The details of that realization were lost with the larger part of my memory but the overall feeling of depression was easily called to the surface. "At first, I felt certain that I was hallucinating. Who could believe it? I mean what could be worse than going on vacation and finding that your boss is next door?"

If the detective saw any irony in my situation, her expression didn't show it. "You don't like Mr. Bascombe?"

I didn't want to say that my boss Donald K. Bascombe was a lunatic. Well, yes, I did want to say that but given the circumstances blatant honesty didn't seem prudent. "Let's just say that I've never had a similar work experience."

The detective's eyes said, "Let's just say more."

I tried to keep the anger out of my voice as I described working for Donald "DK" Bascombe. The turnaround specialist had been introduced to Markshell Publications as a man of many talents, not one of which I had uncovered in the eleven months, two weeks, and three days that I worked for him. "Everything changed at Markshell over the year. The management. The culture. The products. Oh, and yes, the customers. They changed suppliers. Our sales were down by 40%. Our staff was cut by 50%. Our morale was reduced by 100%—largely due to the unique contributions of Donald K. Bascombe." Although I told the detective that Paul Markshell, founder of the firm, recruited Bascombe to bolster sagging profits, I didn't mention that hiring him was only one sign of senility demonstrated by the aging entrepreneur.

"Working with a company the size of Markshell was kind of a comedown for Bascombe. We only do, did, about $100 million. He usually destroyed much bigger outfits." The detective appeared to have no appreciation of business—or humor. I resorted to facts. I reviewed Bascombe's efforts over the past year: killing products, firing customers, and downsizing all departments. Had any of these approaches been supported by clear goals or logical decisions, the tactics might have worked. None of them were; none of them did. Markshell was on a downhill slide and Bascombe was greasing the track. "Bascombe's job was to get the company back on an uphill climb. He said he had a plan." I shrugged. "A secret plan, I guess."

I caught a trace of a smile on the young woman's face but the expression was fleeting. "Did you speak to him while you were here?"

"I ran into him on the beach." I volunteered quickly before the specifics of the meeting came to mind. The detective was waiting for more information. Her stare told me so.

"I ran into him. Literally." I laid the ice pack on my forehead as I recalled the day before when I had realized that what I had thought, what I had hoped, to be hallucinations turned out to be real.

"Ms. Daniels?" The detective's concerned tone brought me back to the present.

"Oh. Sorry." I adjusted the ice-filled baggie. "I don't feel well."

The detective shot an irritated glance in Officer Timmy's direction. Let her attribute my condition to the young officer's blow. Although the better part of my memory had departed on a separate vacation, I recalled a different variety of punch had created my problem.

Detective Dupuy made a great effort to sound sympathetic. "I know this is inconvenient for you but time is of the essence, and it is extremely important that we talk to everyone as quickly as possible."

"Of course." I feigned greater confusion than I felt as I fought to understand the underlying meaning of the detective's visit. "What was your question?" I laid the ice pack on the sofa cushion and massaged my temples to deflect blame for my hesitation onto my aching head.

"You were telling me you ran into Mr. Bascombe on the beach."

"Oh, yeah. I ran into him on the beach."

The policewoman stared at me. What else did she want to know? I had told her who, what, where, and, oh yeah, when. "Yesterday." I added.

"Was he alone?"

"Yes."

"Were you alone?"

"Yes."

"Did you speak?"

"Briefly."

The detective found me uncooperative. Her otherwise attractive features contorted to tell me so. If she wanted cooperation, couldn't she have waited until after breakfast? What time was it anyway?

"It's just after seven."

The detective's deep sigh prodded me to move on. Her expression told me that the interview was not going well. I embarked on a campaign to cooperate or at least to appear cooperative. "Would you like to know what he said?"

The detective tried, unsuccessfully, to hide her sarcasm. "That would be nice."

What could I tell her? Not the truth. Not if Bascombe turned out to be the victim of a heinous crime. "I don't really remember. I was riding a wave and I got all bumped around." I emphasized my statement with a swinging of shoulders and bobbing of head that proved disturbing to my stomach. "You can imagine my surprise when I stumbled in the shallow water and a man grabbed me. I don't mean grabbed me. I mean supported me. The guy turned out to be Mr. Bascombe."

"He was happy to see you?"

"No." I answered too quickly, too honestly. My tone asked her not to be ridiculous. "DK Bascombe was never happy to see any of his employees. In fact . . . " Another recovered memory snapped my mouth shut. I couldn't tell a cop about the comment I had overheard the night before. "In fact, he was never pleasant." A nice innocuous ending to my thought.

In retrospect, it does seem odd that based on what I had learned at the time I had already concluded that DK Bascombe was dead—murdered. My boss, however, was such a suitable candidate for violence that instinctively, I knew. Both that he was dead and that I should speak cautiously.

"How did you happen to choose Ocean City, Ms. Daniels? The rental records show you live in New York."

I didn't get her point. The city was less than three hours away. Good highways provided easy access. It wasn't as if I had traveled millions of light years from deep space. Maybe she didn't understand why I didn't stop at one of the towns that lined the northern Jersey coast—or maybe she just wished that I had.

I didn't tell Detective Dupuy that vacationing in Ocean City wasn't my idea but the brainchild of a recent significant other. Instead, I tried to ingratiate myself with the detective by stressing my local connections. I related happy memories of Ocean City from infancy through young adulthood. Lounging on the wide clean beaches (complimenting the municipality for its respect for the environment), strolling the safe boardwalk in the evening (acknowledging the city's concern for its guests), enjoying the amusements (crediting the town's ability to entertain). Apparently the detective had heard similar stories before. Or, maybe the early hour explained her yawn.

Detective Dupuy's reaction indicated a greater interest in my immediate rather than my distant past. Wasn't it amazing that after all these years I decided to return to Ocean City? And, that I rented the house next to my boss's? And, that I picked the same time as my boss to visit the beach resort?

What could I say? Yes, I thought the coincidence was amazing—not to mention disgusting, appalling, nauseating and a slew of other adjectives that, given my weakened physical condition and the absence of a thesaurus, eluded my grasp.

Detective Dupuy seemed to know a lot about me considering that her interest extended back only a few hours. The young policewoman wondered what had happened to the other tenant. The records showed that the house had been rented to Meg Daniels and one David Orlander, as she referred to him. Was I alone in the cottage?

I was surprised by the emotion welling in my heart, not to mention my stomach and my tear ducts. I explained that I had decided to go it alone—life, that is, not just the vacation—only three weeks before. "I can't believe I felt that guy was my soul mate. I mean if David had seen this house . . ." I shook my head. "He would have hated this place."

Despite, or possibly because of, its shortcomings, I believed the old building exuded charm. My ex would have viewed the house with very different eyes. David, who during his last three months as my companion had apparently been sneaking out for a series of personality transplants, had suddenly become the type who worried about what the neighbors thought. Living in the ramshackle cottage would have embarrassed him although he knew no one in Ocean City, had never visited the town before, and was unlikely to encounter the neighbors again. The fact that the cottage overlooked the beach would not have satisfied David's status quota.

The rickety building appealed to me for a reason other than its water view; the cottage was scheduled for demolition upon my departure. That fact not only put the beachfront property within my price range but guaranteed that I wouldn't have to clean when I left. The combination proved irresistible even if the house did demonstrate the worst use of space, paneling and linoleum that I had ever observed.

"The condition of the house wasn't why David decided to stay in the city," I clarified.

Did the detective's gaze soften or was I wearing her out with the story of my life?

"It's okay." I assured her. "Our relationship was ending anyway. I just like to have the last word."

"With Bascombe too?"

Detective Dupuy was beginning to annoy me.

Chapter 3

Detective Dupuy wanted to know a lot more about me than I believed necessary. She had a crime to solve. Why was she sitting in my living room probing for the embarrassingly mundane details of my solitary vacation? There appeared to be no end to her questions. When had I last seen Bascombe? What time had I gone to bed? Was I a light sleeper? Had I slept alone the night before? Officer Timmy didn't hide that he found the line of questioning amusing and my answers somewhat pathetic. I suspected that back at the station, he would learn about the merits of a poker face.

"Tell me, Ms. Daniels, your answer doesn't have to go any farther but . . ." Detective Dupuy hemmed and hawed only for effect, " . . . do you and Bascombe have a thing."

I laughed loudly. "Donald K. Bascombe and I most assuredly did not have a thing."

I chuckled as I emphasized the detective's choice of words. "As a matter of fact . . . " Again instinct silenced me. What if Bascombe had been murdered? A motive like overhearing news of my imminent firing would leave me facing twenty-five years to life. "As a matter of fact . . . ." I laughed lightly as I fought for a way to end the sentence. "As a matter of fact, I hardly knew him."

"But he's your boss?"

"He wasn't exactly outgoing." Shrugging took all my energy.

"Ms. Daniels, aren't you curious about what has happened to your boss?"

I realized the real answer, no, was inappropriate. I returned the ice pack to my head and spoke from under the cover of the plastic bag. "Of course I'm interested. I figured you couldn't talk about the case. Are you allowed to?" I lowered the ice-filled baggie to display an expression as eager as my hangover would permit. As I listened to the detective, I returned the dripping pack to its position on the growing lump.

Sometime during the previous night instead of keeping a scheduled appointment with his estranged wife, twenty-five miles north in Brigantine, Donald K. Bascombe had disappeared leaving behind signs of foul play. The cops weren't willing to tell me what those signs were.

"Maybe he got called back to the city." I shrugged.

The detective found the idea ludicrous, but didn't tell me why.

"Do you mind if we take a look around your house?"

"Why?" I moved quickly to override my first response. "I mean it's fine but why would you want to?"

The detective's smile was remarkable for its insincerity. "Just to get the layout of the area."

My limp wave granted permission to go through the entire place. I know the detective interpreted the gesture that way because she was careful to repeat her assumption to me.

I listed to the left and laid my head on a pillow that last demonstrated the properties of foam rubber during the Eisenhower administration, first term. In retrospect I understand that I should have paid attention as the cops rummaged through the house but I didn't.

"Ms. Daniels." The call came from Detective Dupuy. She was in the back bedroom, the one I used. "Could you join us, please?"

I doubted it but with effort I got to my feet and dragged myself down the hall. I let my body fall against the doorjamb and peered into the room. What were these cops doing? Certainly

12

not the laundry, although Detective Dupuy had my dirty wash in her hands.

"Can you explain what this is?"

I checked out the pile of cloth the detective held. "It's a bedspread." I identified the white chenille object. "It came with the house."

The detective's expression indicated she wanted to know more.

"It goes on top of that bed. Some people . . . ."

"Ms. Daniels." The detective was not impressed with my explanation. "What I want to know is why is this bedspread concealing a pile of bloody clothes?" Detective Dupuy held up a clump of black material.

"What bloody clothes?"

With a dramatic flourish, overdone given the situation, not to mention the size of the room, the detective unfurled my black leggings and tee shirt. I vaguely recalled stripping the clothes off and tossing them on the floor during the previous night. The garments weren't covered with blood at that point. It took me a moment to recall that they were drenched in strawberry daiquiris. "Those are not bloody clothes." I shuddered remembering the feel of icy liquid streaming down my back. "I spilled a drink." I didn't mention that the spill occurred after I had fallen asleep with a full pitcher of daiquiris—not the first of the evening and I suspected not the second. "Take them with you for all I care. You'll see."

Detective Dupuy indicated she would do that and Officer Timmy produced a plastic bag from a large black satchel that, undetected by me, he had carried into the bedroom.

The policewoman had more questions. Could I explain the overturned chair? Explain? I hadn't even noticed it. Was there a fight in my room last night? Not one I was involved in. Was I alone all evening? Absolutely. Of that I was sure.

The cop's interrogation was interrupted by a loud pounding. Officer Timmy, still guilty at striking me, offered to answer the door. Good thing, I don't think I could have covered the ten yards to the cottage's only entrance—although the cop's punch had little to do with my limitations.

"Wendy. We got a body. Three blocks south in the tall grass." Another young policeman, shorter, darker and cuter than Timmy Borden, had come to deliver the news.

"Whose?" Detective Dupuy asked casually as if on any given day several unidentified bodies materialized throughout the town.

"I'm betting on Bascombe. Six foot. Late fifties. Gray hair. Nice build. Khaki pants."

"Okay, okay. I'll come see for myself." Detective Dupuy stopped at the door and turned. She grew suddenly polite. "Ms. Daniels would you be kind enough to accompany us. I hate to impose but you could make the identification immediately. If the body is Bascombe's."

Now I admit I didn't care for Bascombe, but that didn't mean I wanted to see his dead body.

Detective Dupuy's request, despite the dulcet tones in which it was delivered, read more like a command. There was nothing to say but sure. I headed for the door, but Detective Dupuy stopped me with another request. I heeded her advice and put on some pants.

Chapter 4

And so I found myself wasting a summer day on a rickety milk carton provided for what the Ocean City police force defined as my comfort—although my personal definition of comfort included being more than fifteen feet from a corpse.

Alone on the stool, I watched the drama unfold before me and contemplated the implications of Bascombe's death. I didn't consider myself a serious suspect—a belief apparently not shared by Detective Dupuy. I reassured myself that she would come to see things my way. After all, I could rustle up witnesses. Okay, maybe not alibi witnesses. The details were sketchy, but I knew I had spent Monday evening at home alone.

Weren't character witnesses important? Many people could testify to my integrity. Of course, under oath they might be forced to describe my feelings toward Bascombe. Could witnesses use that kind of language in a courtroom? It didn't matter; I wasn't worried. There would be hairs and fibers. Before the lab work was finished, the cops would look at lots of casual suspects. After the test results came back, they would zero in on the real perpetrator, and my problems would be over.

Detective Dupuy emerged from a circle of blue uniforms and explained that she would like me to stop by the Ocean City police station and make a statement. Stop by was not said with a casual tone. I agreed to wait on my designated seat for an officer to fetch me.

Without a good-bye the detective headed down the makeshift path that we had navigated to reach Bascombe's body. She stopped short. "You know it's interesting." She turned towards me and assumed her best Colombo pose. "When you were identifying the body you spoke about Bascombe in the present tense."

I nodded and shrugged.

Her eyes bored into mine. "It's just odd because all morning you referred to him in past tense."

I understood her implications and attempted to hide my reaction. She seemed satisfied by the guilty expression on my face and didn't wait for an answer. Actually, I didn't have one.

While I contemplated my situation, I studied the buzz of activity surrounding me. Usually the only buzz in the overgrown area was from the mosquitoes and, in August, the green flies. I had never known a human to venture into the tall grass that lined the Great Egg Harbor Bay. If a local pilot had not joined the search at daybreak, Bascombe's body would have laid undetected until most vital evidence had been compromised if not destroyed. I overheard one of the cops say that.

I didn't even know it was possible to move through the thick growth, but that day the area was mobbed with more humans than insects. The cops must have hacked or beaten the thick stalks into submission before positioning a row of cardboard boxes to create a pathway. Thanks to that impromptu engineering feat, the grasslands were rendered passable.

The rest of the world had disappeared. Sitting among the tall fronds, I could see only grass, sky, and a bevy of seagulls anxious to determine the reason for the human invasion. The birds seemed as interested in the drama before me as I was. I didn't know what the gulls thought but I especially enjoyed the performance by the widow of DK Bascombe.

I first saw Caroline Bascombe when she flew down the improvised path. DK's wife, make that widow, swept down the uneven runway with great élan and despite the best efforts of the police to restrain her. "Donald. Donald." She called her husband's name although I knew by my eavesdropping that the cops had informed her that DK Bascombe was dead.

"Oh my God." She stopped at the damp edge of the temporary sidewalk—in time to save her white canvas espadrilles from the marsh. Falling back six inches, apparently to guarantee the cleanliness of her flowing flowered skirt, she fell to her knees. Miraculously, not a drop of mud found its way onto her clothing. The new widow was so despondent that she fell back on her heels but not so upset that she failed to take the time to lift her skirt. Still immaculate, Mrs. Bascombe set about weeping profusely for her poor dead husband—her words, not mine. As she leaned forward to verify that Donald K. was dead—my words not hers—she seemed suddenly more relaxed.

I surveyed the crowd of police. They all appeared to be buying her act. I wasn't. The first thing working against Mrs. Bascombe's credibility was her theatrical good looks. Although clothed in appropriate summer shore gear, her body, one of the few I had ever seen that could accurately be described as statuesque, cried out to be encased in red sequins. I suspected the leggy redhead would feel more at home on a stage in Vegas than at a PTA meeting. Her clothes were in sync with her husband's, but not with her hair, her makeup or the glint in her eyes. As I watched from my plastic perch, I decided that I had my suspect.

Despite great efforts to appear distraught, Mrs. Bascombe was strong enough to quiz the police about her husband's murder. I also benefited from the information.

How? Stabbed.

When? Last night. Tests would establish a more specific time.

Where? Uncertain but not there. The cops were fairly sure the body had been moved.

By whom? Suddenly I popped back into Detective Dupuy's mind. She glanced in my direction before telling Mrs. Bascombe that her husband had been killed by person or persons unknown. No murder weapon had been found.

Mrs. Bascombe was not oblivious to the cop's less than furtive glance in my direction. Her eyes narrowed as she scrutinized my image without, to my relief, meeting my gaze. What she saw didn't impress her but did puzzle her. She swept away, however, without asking any questions.

Forgotten again, I listened to the cops theorize that the killer probably believed DK had been finished off in his house. Most likely DK had come to and followed his assailant outside. That scenario explained a trail of blood that apparently ended under my window. How he had gotten into his current position was unknown and the source of much speculation. Especially given the feet thing. They neglected to mention what the feet thing was.

Chapter 5

Timmy Borden, visibly unhappy with his assignment as my escort, resurfaced to lead me out of the grasslands via the quickly deteriorating cardboard. Sections of the path surrendered to the swamp even as we crossed it. Much more graceful people than I am would have had difficulty negotiating the path. I felt that Officer Timmy's blatant impatience and implied ridicule were uncalled for. I was just about to tell him that when I heard the voice.

"Meg. Meg. Up here."

I squinted into the sun and spotted a long object waving from the back of a house that overlooked the tall grass. What the flapping item was, I had no idea. As the house provided my eyes with shade, I identified the object as the arm of Janet Gilbert. I had last seen that limb enfolded in the long, blue-wool sleeves of a uniform at Mount Saint Joseph Academy.

"Meg Daniels. It's you. I knew that was you." Janet called from the porch.

This was not the moment to encounter a voice from my past.

"You haven't changed a bit. You look wonderful."

Maybe I was wrong about the timing thing. "Janet, nice to see you."

Janet scurried down the steps from the deck that overlooked the grasslands as I fought my way out of them. Officer Timmy appeared perplexed. I sensed he didn't want me talking to Janet but couldn't produce a reason to stop me.

"Janet, you look great." I wasn't lying. I'd heard she'd had kids but her figure had bounced back completely. Her body seemed to have a better shape than it had in high school. Her nose definitely did.

Janet whispered as she kissed the air beside my right ear. "What is all this about? The cops just came to ask my husband some questions."

"Oh. My boss." I nodded towards the crime site. "The cops wanted me to ID the body."

"The body?" Although Janet's eyes grew wider than a natural reaction dictated, her concern was real.

"He was . . ."

"Dead." Officer Timmy cut me off. "There's been a terrible accident, ma'am." The young cop turned to me. Despite my understanding that we were on our way to the police station, he said, "Let me take you home."

"No. No. We'll take her home." Janet wrapped a protective arm around my waist.

Officer Timmy's sputtering constituted no match for Janet's exuberance. Before I, or more importantly the intern cop, knew what had happened I was on Janet Gilbert's porch sipping orange juice and ignoring scrambled eggs and bacon. Apparently, identifying a dead body, even the body of DK Bascombe, inhibited my appetite.

One thing I'll give Janet, she hadn't called me onto the deck simply to pump me about the crime. She turned her attention to Bascombe's murder only after filling me in on her life after high school, which began with a luncheon at Whitemarsh Country Club. She had the chicken.

Janet Gilbert was now Janet Maxwell. In terms of sophomore, not sophomoric, values, Janet had married well. Glenn Maxwell, who was then off chatting with the police, had been president of the student council, captain of the basketball team, and most likely to succeed at nearby LaSalle High School when Janet and I were at the Mount. Even my mother had been awed by the eighteen-year-old Glenn Maxwell's sophisticated appearance. "But," she had assured me, "he's not going to have that hair much longer." My mother was wrong. I observed Glenn in the driveway talking to Detective Dupuy. Glenn was still drop dead gorgeous with more than ample brown waves and a hairline that showed no signs of receding.

Janet and Glenn, it turned out, had gone to the senior prom (I knew that), broken up (I didn't know that), gone away to college (I knew that), and gotten reacquainted after graduation (I didn't know that). They married when Glenn graduated from law school and, as far as I could discern, were happy with two houses, two cars, two boats and two children. Their kids, a girl and a boy, aged eight and nine, excelled at multitudinous sports, played several instruments, and earned straight As. Apples apparently do not fall far from the tree—at least Glenn's branch.

Janet appeared to have no interest in my life since graduation. Not that I had that much to tell. College, pretty routine. First job, mostly boring. Graduate school, fairly standard. After that I had done a stint in London managing distribution for a U.S. publisher before joining Markshell in New York. I probably could have mustered interesting stories from my years in Europe, but Janet never inquired. Fifteen minutes passed before she asked me a question—one I never had the opportunity to answer because Glenn returned from his conference with the police and Janet redirected her attention his way.

The cops had told Glenn as little as possible. The word was out that a body had been found. No one had mentioned the word murder.

"The man was Meg's boss. She identified him." Janet made the announcement with pride. She turned to me. "How did your boss die?"

I told her what I had overheard.

"No one gets murdered here." She turned to Glenn with fear in her eyes. "What will this do to our property values?"

Glenn assured her that the mess, obviously the doing of out-of-towners, would blow over and be forgotten. He was impressed by the victim's status. Apparently, he assumed that a high class corpse indicated a high class killer. Murder didn't seem to bother Glenn as long as the perpetrator fit in.

If Janet is representative of the public, Bascombe's death would be forgotten quickly—a footnote to an otherwise successful season at the shore. She dropped the topic of murder and explained the history of the house, their decision to buy and their choice of location—the privacy provided by the only house jutting into the dense grasslands for three blocks. How would Janet feel after dark, sharing the west side of the street exclusively with a murder scene? She didn't seem worried.

"Do they know who killed him?" It was Glenn who brought the topic back to the body in the backyard.

"The cops have suspects." I neglected to mention that I was one of them.

"Why were you here with your boss?" At last my situation had caught Janet's attention.

"The police asked me to identify his body."

"No." Janet's interest piqued. "Why were you in Ocean City with your boss?"

"I wasn't."

Janet's face registered her confusion. I remembered that Janet had worn that same perplexed expression through four years of high school. I explained the events of the last few days—slowly and selectively.

"Oh," was Janet's sole response when I'd finished. She didn't believe me.

"Talk about bad luck." Glenn didn't believe me either.

Detective Dupuy's reaction to finding me eating breakfast on the Maxwell's deck didn't help my case—with the Maxwells or the detective. "Ms. Daniels. How convenient. You know these people?"

These people meant "the people who own the house where the body was found."

I shrugged. "I went to high school with Janet." I pointed to my former classmate; she dodged to the left.

Detective Dupuy tried to sound casual as she inquired about my relationship with the Maxwells. She didn't fool me, and she didn't fool the Maxwells. The couple made it abundantly clear they hadn't seen me in years until coincidence brought us together. As I said good-bye, I had the feeling that another fifteen years would pass before I would be invited into the home of Janet and Glenn Maxwell.

Chapter 6

By the time Officer Timmy Borden dropped me off behind my old house, the sun that had shone so brightly into my sleepy eyes that morning had disappeared behind a ceiling of dark gray clouds. The yellow crime scene tape stretching from Bascombe's house to my staircase added the only hint of sunshine to the setting.

I returned to the house without trepidation. It had not yet occurred to me to find my rental's proximity to a murder site frightening. Nor had I yet realized that, with many of the neighbors gone, the cottage was isolated. The lot to the south was empty except for a sign that indicated once I cleared out of town work would begin on two multi-unit buildings. Okay, my name wasn't posted, but the placard did explain that the cottage was doomed and once gone, the two lots would face development. Thanks to a Nor'easter that had blown along the coast in March, the house on the far side of the vacant lot hadn't been ready to host summer visitors; construction was in the final stages. Most of the homes lining the beach and the alley that ran parallel had emptied the night before when families packed up their cars and departed for work and school. The lone resident remaining was an octogenarian across the alley who used his cheerful facade to lure unsuspecting passers-by into discussions of the evils of beachfront development.

Despite these facts, the last thing I felt was alone. I climbed the stairs under the watchful eyes of strollers who, although feigning indifference to the only crime scene in town, suddenly favored the alley over the street and beach.

As I reached the stop of the stairs, I heard my name. The call came from a young woman in a tailored tan pantsuit who appeared not at all familiar. The severity with which her red bob clung to her head made her oversized features appear even larger. She was the only person I had seen since arriving at the shore who was less tan than I. The difference was that her pallor appeared to be carefully cultivated.

I didn't recognize the face; the woman was too young to be a classmate. Yet she seemed to know me.

"Miss Daniels, I hate to disturb you." She started up the stairs; I met her halfway. After pulling a pad from her large and over-stuffed handbag, she struggled to open first the pad and then the cap of the pen. A dozen jangling bracelets emphasized her difficulties.

In a pleasant but surprising baritone, the woman introduced herself as a reporter who wanted to ask me a few questions. Her wide blue eyes opened even wider with enthusiasm. "You must have seen something."

I explained that I had observed nothing related to the murder.

When I stared at her pad she belatedly attempted to note my response. The pen refused to write. Smiling at me encouragingly, she scoured her handbag for a another pen.

"You must have heard something, then." Her hand still dug in her bag.

Again, I noted that I had not.

"But you are right here, next door." She wanted to disarm me with her smile. I was in no mood to be charmed.

"I'd like to help you but I can contribute no information to the investigation." I turned.

"But you must know if Bascombe had visitors on his last day?"

I hesitated. Did I want to get into a discussion of Bascombe's last hours with the press? No way. "I really don't know anything."

I had climbed only one step when I heard her plaintive plea. "Look, I need a break. I can't go back without this information."

"I would really like to help you, Miss . . ." I paused to encourage her to fill in the blank but instead she resorted to begging.

"Look, lady, Ms. Daniels, I really need this story. If I go home without it, I will be in big trouble."

"But you did get the story." I smiled cautiously. "The story is that I did not see a thing."

With that I turned and abandoned the reporter who stood disappointed and disgruntled on my stairs. My mood wasn't much better than the newswoman's. I felt hungover, tired, and musclesore as I climbed the last steps to my cottage. Opening the door was an effort, but not as great an effort as it should have been. Hadn't I locked the door? Security would have been easy to forget when rushing out to ID a body, but wouldn't the cops have remembered? Wasn't that their job?

The cottage was an obvious target only to the most underachieving of burglars. Although the house, whose glory days had coincided with the Allied army's in France, sat on pilings that burrowed into the sand less than a hundred yards from the high tide mark, it didn't compare with the newer and more opulent neighboring structures. If the cottage's occupants had any money, the funds would have gone towards renovation.

I pushed the door open and called hello—as if a trespasser would respond, "Over here in the closet." After checking behind the door for signs of an interloper, I stepped across the threshold. I dropped my bag and moved towards the counter that separated the kitchen from the living room. Without a strategy for confronting an intruder crouched out of sight, I peeked behind the low wall. All I spotted were three strawberries that had eluded the blender but apparently not the soles of my feet.

I returned to the hallway and slid along the rough paneling towards the rear of the house. Across from the spare bedroom, I stopped. I had not entered the room, the least inviting in a house of inhospitable rooms, since I'd arrived. With the closed drapes blocking the afternoon's weak light, the bedroom appeared even less appealing than usual. I stepped across the hall and slammed my back against the open door which in turn slammed against the wall behind it. No one hid there.

I eyed the closet door. The closet could hide a small intruder—one who could be watching me through the louvered slats. After stooping to check under the bed, I slipped across the room and fought to open the warped door. It required my best effort to defeat the swollen wood but at last the door responded to my tugging. I peeked inside and sneezed. The closet was full, but only of mold.

The bathroom was the next stop along the hallway. Luckily the open shower curtain provided verification that no one lurked in the tub. I grabbed a tissue and, holding it to my nose, moved on quickly to the bedroom that I'd chosen to occupy. The room extended across the rear of the cottage offering a lovely view of Bascombe's siding on the north side, an empty lot on the south side, and a paved alley at the rear.

From the doorway, I could confirm that no one was under the bed—thanks to the police who had carted off my bedding. The only hiding place for an intruder was the tiny closet at the far end of the bedroom. Once more I sidled down a wall, this one full of more faux splinters than the last. With no plan if I confronted a trespasser, I flung open the closet door. Luckily, the tiny space stood empty—except for the mold. I sneezed five times in a row before I considered my next step.

I surveyed the bedroom. The bed was stripped. My suitcases lay open in a corner with the contents tossed carelessly on top as if the bags had been searched but failed to yield anything of interest. I'd done that. If an intruder had come along and replicated the search, I wouldn't have known. Likewise, I wouldn't have realized if the trespasser had rummaged through the items I'd left strewn across the top of the old bureau. What I could detect, however, was the presence of a gray substance. I found the powder on the bureau, the overturned chair, the windowsill. The cops. Of course. I had told them it was okay to look around. Apparently, "look around" had a different meaning for the cops than for me.

Suddenly, I realized why the police kept me at the station so long. They needed to conduct a thorough search of my place—including dusting for fingerprints. God, they had even checked the headboard of the old bed. Were they hoping to find Bascombe's fingerprints? The vision of how his prints might have gotten on my bed made me nauseated—and worried. What if Bascombe had an affair with last week's tenant? Last month's? Last season's? The housekeeping standards in the cottage weren't what I would term rigorous.

Full of fear I slumped onto the old mattress and confronted a greater terror. Who knew what unfriendly organisms lurked on the ticking? With effort I rose and wandered forward onto the porch avoiding boards that threatened to give way under my feet and planks that had already surrendered. I settled into an oversized, old-fashioned pine chair that had rocked visitors for decades.

The crowd on the beach thinned and then evaporated as a smattering of rain drops grew to a downpour. Parents grabbed children who were already wet and ran for home. The parent left behind inherited the job of collecting towels, toys, and coolers and piling them onto a stroller that was not designed for use in sand, let alone wet sand. As I watched the mommies and daddies struggle towards the path of planks that led from the beach, telltale splotches of red skin on their noses, legs and arms confirmed that the day had remained a glorious beach day as long as I remained at the police station. From what I could see, the weather was still nice over the Atlantic and in Philadelphia yet a black cloud hung over me. I took the weather personally!

Four days into my vacation, I felt appreciably worse than I had when I'd left the Markshell offices late on Friday night. I didn't look any better either. Too much stress, too little sleep, too much alcohol, too little sun—or perhaps too much sunscreen. On my seventieth birthday, I might be happy I had used PF9000, but the lack of color wasn't helping my appearance. And, my pallor wasn't lifting my mood.

Four days. Each one worse than the day before.

I'd arrived on Saturday and spent the remainder of the day, or of the sun before a late afternoon shower, getting settled. The entire time I moaned silently that I had to unpack the car myself—especially since most of the supplies had been purchased and packed by the missing David. The only social contact I had was the friendly octogenarian who offered to help me unload my bags—apparently in return for listening to his tirades about rampant and mindless development. I declined despite a desire to know how he planned to manage the rickety stairs with my bags and his walker. That night I'd fallen asleep on the couch, feeling lonely and exhausted and more than a little drunk on the rum that David had packed weeks before.

Sunday, a beautiful beach day on which I had applied copious amounts of sunscreen, had been marred by what I perceived as persistent hallucinations that DK Bascombe was in the vicinity. Everywhere I went I heard his voice or his laugh—a sound the humor-impaired Bascombe uttered only in response to others' humiliation. I left the beach with no tan and a severe case of paranoia. I passed the evening pretty much in the same fashion as the previous night—as far as I can remember.

Labor Day was the day that confirmed my worst fears. The holiday had begun with great promise. The sky was blue. The sand was warm. The surf was high. I read. I sunned. I slept. Repeatedly I enjoyed forays into the rough sea until the time I encountered Bascombe among the waves. After that the only thing I plunged into was depression—and a couple of pitchers of daiquiris.

Compared to Tuesday at the police station, however, Labor Day weekend had become the good old days. Or that was how I saw the time as I sat brooding on the porch. Not that the police had been abusive to me at the station. They had been very pleasant when they interviewed me—and when they finger-printed me. I didn't believe them for a moment when they said their actions would help clear me, but I knew that they would. After all, I was innocent.

Long after the last sunbather had left the beach, I remained curled up on the old rocker. I headed for the shower only when the sun reappeared, just in time to set. The pounding water cleared my brain as much as it cleaned my body. Why worry alone? Word of Bascombe's demise must have reached the office. Maybe Bascombe's killer had already been found. How would I know? No one could call me.

I had not anticipated that the absence of a telephone in the vacation home would be a problem. Cellular service had maintained a low priority on my to-do list during my three years with David, who never left home without a flip phone next to his ear. With David and cellular gone from my life and vacation, my only option was a phone booth. After waiting for a couple of giggling teenage girls to work their way through a long roster of boys to harass, I commandeered the pay phone on the corner of 34th and West to catch anyone working late at Markshell.

I didn't reach Lindy Sharpe, the person I most wanted to speak to, but I did reach Randall Wallace, the person I least wanted to speak to. Always the last to know no matter what the topic, Randall "Don't-Call-Me-Randy" Wallace seemed to enjoy being in the know. Assuming that since I was on vacation he knew more than I about Bascombe's murder, he took five minutes to convey what he knew (DK Bascombe was found murdered in Ocean City, New Jersey) and what he felt (Bascombe was a valued asset to the company who would be missed). I kept trying to interrupt, but the accounts payable supervisor was riding high on the excitement of having something to tell and someone to listen. Mercifully, the flow of Randall's praise of DK Bascombe was not punctuated by his usual attempts at puns. His comments usually missed the mark by such a wide margin that if he didn't stop to guffaw extravagantly, even the most attentive listener could not have identified them as jokes.

"Maybe he's just emotional." Lindy Sharpe's tone was strained when I finally persuaded Randall to relinquish the phone.

"Maybe he's just stupid." No other explanation for liking Bascombe existed in my eyes.

"Bascombe is dead, Meg. Can't you show a modicum of respect for him on this of all days?"

I deliberated my answer carefully. "No."

Lindy was the closest thing I had to a friend at Markshell. My feeling was that Lindy honestly believed she liked me. Our limited friendship was based on a common disdain for Bascombe— or at least it had been until her last comment.

"Boy, I never thought I'd side with Randall on anything. But at least his mourning is appropriate." Lindy's tone was accusatory. "And, Bascombe fired him."

"What?"

"Randall was let go. His head rolled along with two in marketing and four in editorial. Even though he was fired, he understands the human tragedy."

Tragedy? I asked silently.

"Okay, he was singing a different tune Friday when Bascombe gave him notice. Last week he was distraught. He arrived late today. I figured he wasn't coming at all but now he seems okay with leaving Markshell even though I heard he didn't score much severance."

I cringed. Had I been rescued from that same fate by Bascombe's timely, from my perspective, demise? Did others know? Were there rumors? I probed gently and generically. "Any other heads slated to roll?"

"Not that I'd heard of. Of course, it doesn't matter if I heard. If the person getting the ax knew . . . I think that makes a nice little motive."

I graduated from cringing to shuddering. Prefacing my question with a painfully phony laugh, I inquired. "Well, you haven't heard my name." I added "have you?" with a little too much urgency.

Lindy did not catch my serious tone. "When did you get lucky enough to earn a paid exit from this dump? No, Meg, you are gonna have to get yourself out of here."

I quizzed Lindy about the day's events at Markshell Publications. Who had made the announcement about Bascombe's death? Paul

Markshell—without tears in his eyes. Had any cops been to the office? Tomorrow. Were there suspects at Markshell?

"Suspects are all we have around here." Lindy sounded wistful as she continued. "Many of us could have and probably should have killed Bascombe. Frankly I don't think any of us did. I heard there was a divorce pending; the cops are considering that angle."

Not very closely from what I had observed in the marshlands that morning.

"Of course, I've also heard his murder was a mob hit, drug related, and retaliation for his early work in the CIA. I wouldn't put too much stock in the office gossip although you might to keep in touch as the week goes on. The quality of the information can only improve. Though why are you calling us? You're the one who's in Ocean City. What have you heard?"

"Who do I know here to fill me in?" When threatened, answer a question with a question.

Lindy reminded me of local newspapers. "You'll get better info. And, Meg, keep your eyes open. Bascombe could get murdered right under your nose and you would miss it."

My laughter was hardly convincing. I ended the conversation without divulging special knowledge of Bascombe's death.

Why had I chosen to be so secretive? I had nothing to hide. If I did, my memory was keeping the information from me. Would I speak more freely once I recalled the details of the night Bascombe died? Not if those details proved to be too painful. So far, each fact that came to the surface was more embarrassing than the one before.

I blamed my juvenile behavior on Bascombe. Seeing Bascombe always depressed me. Seeing Bascombe would have depressed Chuckles the Clown. The guy had a talent for contaminating the air around him. I remembered the dejected feeling I experienced trudging up from the beach on Monday and my efforts to elevate my mood. Those efforts involved at least two pitchers of strawberry daiquiris with more rum than fruit. Recalling my drinking was embarrassing enough. Remembering that between the first and second batch, I had changed into black leggings, turtleneck,

and sneakers in order to spy on Bascombe was far more humiliating both for the stupidity of the plan and the senselessness of
the attire. The memory of my costume, however, was not as mor-
tifying as recollecting that I had hidden on the floor under the
window to eavesdrop on Bascombe.

Thank God no one had seen me.

Chapter 7

I needed comfort. To me the best comfort food in Ocean City was available at Bob's at 14th and the boardwalk. I headed in that direction through dwindling throngs, but still throngs, of vacationers. As I hit the boardwalk, a wave of nostalgia washed over me. I had forgotten the sound of shoes on the boardwalk—a constant patter with no real rhythm. To me, the feet played a happy, nostalgic tune.

Retired seniors, families with young children, and groups of kids who didn't report back to school by Labor Day contributed to the beat. Each group I passed appeared happier, healthier, and tanner than the group before. I felt conspicuous. Four days and the only color I'd gotten was black and blue—courtesy of Officer Timmy Borden's fist.

I set out to find out if Bob's still served what I craved—or at least if Bob's still served. Would my old haunt be there? It was—plus some. Bob's needed the extra space; I was only one of many seeking comfort in the restaurant that night. After checking the menu to confirm that the basics hadn't changed—it had only been fifteen years—I requested a cheeseburger with raw onion and french fries from a quintessential example of the pretty, hip and inevitably tan college girls that had been taking orders at

Bob's since my youth. Since I hadn't seen milkshakes on the menu, I asked if they still made them.

"I don't think we ever did." She smiled politely and walked away.

Was I wrong? Memory told me black and white milkshakes were a staple of my diet when I dined often at Bob's. Were my fond memories of my youth all as distorted as my recollection of those milkshakes? I was contemplating my days in Ocean City and watching the steady flow of people down the boardwalk when I heard my name called with great excitement. The woman from whose mouth the sound emanated had many children bearing a startling resemblance to her in tow. No one in the group looked at all familiar to me.

"Meg Daniels. Don't pretend you don't remember me."

I did not pretend.

"After all those summers we sat together on the beach."

My blank expression still involved no pretense.

"I was just wondering the other day what happened to you and my mother said, 'Lisette, don't be an idiot, you remember that Meg never married so she moved away to work in Europe.'"

That wasn't how I remembered the story of my life, but I was more interested in placing the woman's face than in correcting her version of my history. Lisette. Lisette. Had I ever known a Lisette?

"You remember," she wrapped her arm around the neck of a child apparently selected at random from the crowd clustered around her. The girl, about six years old, struggled to elude the grasp. I understood how she felt. "My mother always called me Lisette. Why I don't know. If she liked the name so much, she shouldn't have used Lisette as a middle name."

I smiled and nodded, but whatever my mouth tried to hide, my eyes conspired to reveal.

"You remember my mother, don't you. She used to sit on the 24th Street beach every afternoon with Mrs. O'Donnell, Mrs. Bernardi, and Lucy Stanwyck."

I recognized not one of the names. I had begun to think that the woman had the wrong Meg Daniels when she asked about my old boyfriend, Tom Kennedy.

Immediately, I recognized Suzanne Lisette Rossiter. The bitch. Her question was not a casual one. What she said was "Have you ever heard what happened to Tom Kennedy?" What she meant was "You remember that Tom Kennedy dumped you for me, don't you?"

I said, "Little Tommy Kennedy. Gosh, I haven't thought of him in years." I meant, "I have moved on with my life and have better things to do than sit around and moan because a guy who appealed to my seventeen-year-old hormones found your pheromones more attractive."

My statement was true. Tom hadn't entered my mind in years. Why then had her mention of his name inspired a quick flight of butterflies through my stomach? Tom Kennedy would not interest the thirty-three-year-old woman I'd become. I'd moved on. I was certain Tom had too—as had his well-sculpted muscles, smooth tan, and sun-bleached curls. I hoped.

I was happy to see the years had not been kind to Susan Lisette Rossiter. Although her body was still lithe, she appeared to have gained quite a bit of weight—all in her face. Her pixie hairdo accentuated her problem and her protruding ears. Without waiting for an invitation that would not have been forthcoming, Suzanne Lisette Rossiter slipped onto the bench across from me and sent the children off to create traffic obstructions on the boardwalk.

"Are they all yours?"

"Yep. Five children in six years. Barry Lynchon, you remember him from the basketball team at Judge, kept me busy." She giggled in that conspiratorial yet condescending way that girls who became sexually active at an early age adapted to indicate that they were part of a great mystery. Unfortunately, some, like Suzanne, forgot to drop the tone as the rest of us were let in on the secret.

I studied the mob of screeching Rossiter-Lynchon children careening across the boardwalk. "They're very cute."

Suzanne caught the hint of surprise I let seep into my voice. Being nasty to my usually nasty classmate felt good. My mind told me to feel ashamed; I didn't.

Across the aisle another solo diner, the only one I'd spotted, fought his way into a booth beating out four sixteen-year-old boys for the privilege of listening to Suzanne and me trading thinly veiled insults. The attractive male in his mid-thirties did his best to pretend he wasn't eavesdropping. With his back to the boardwalk and his order placed, he had little to watch except my reaction to Suzanne's stories. Not that he could avoid hearing them himself. Suzanne's voice was unaccountably shrill. "So, I couldn't believe it. I mean there I was feeling sick and I was still having brilliant ideas."

Hidden from Suzanne's view the man across the aisle grimaced. The stranger's amusement became evident at the inane comments that flowed from Suzanne's lips. Eventually he and I reacted in unison. I tried to evade his gaze but his were hard eyes to avoid, more green than gray, set off by a deep tan that made his silky ash blonde hair appear even lighter.

Suzanne continued with the recitation of her accomplishments. I nodded at her and made feeble efforts to convert laughter into polite smiles. When I glanced in the stranger's direction, he rolled his eyes.

Suzanne paused to note the arrival of my burger and fries. "I admire you for not watching your weight." Before I could say that I admired her for not having her ears pinned, she had plunged into another story about her achievements. Across the aisle, the handsome man shook his head.

Suzanne described a brief but illustrious career as I bit into my cheeseburger.

"I mean after only five years I felt I had reached the peak of my career. You would have been so impressed by all the honors I earned."

I was more impressed by the man in the next booth. The handsome stranger and I appeared to be about the same age and to share a common dislike for Suzanne Lisette Rossiter. I bet there was more to the guy than a pretty exterior, although the Roman nose, firm jaw, and fine physique were sufficient to hold my attention.

I was thrilled when the Rossiter-Lynchon kids protested in mass that they needed to hit the road for school in Philadelphia the next day. Reluctantly, Suzanne bid me farewell. With a quick kiss of the air to the left of my ear, she spouted off her address and told me to keep in touch. I didn't even bother adding the information to my memory bank to avoid the annoyance of deleting the data later.

As I waved good-bye to the Rossiter-Lynchon gang disappearing onto the boardwalk, I glanced at the stranger. His laughing eyes were eager to meet mine. "You did not make that any easier." I worked to make my smile warm with a touch of flirtatiousness.

He shrugged. "You were very discreet, although if she had let you open your mouth I have no idea how you might have reacted." He leaned forward as if inviting further conversation. I replicated the motion.

"I felt myself slipping. When she first insulted me, I responded in kind. I should be ashamed. I sank to . . ."

Suddenly my words were blocked by a body, female and rather impressive.

"Andy Beck, I just saw you from the boardwalk. What a great coincidence."

Great for her—definitely not great for me and, I suspected as I peeked around her buns of steel to check out the man's face, not that great for Andy Beck.

"Charlene, I thought you had gone back to the city." I read in his tone that he had hoped she had. The woman, young to me—in her early twenties, didn't read the same message into his words.

"Nope. I'm staying through the weekend."

I considered the glance that the unknown Andy shot me, an apology. With wide eyes that expressed both puzzlement and anger, the young woman followed his glance.

"Thanks for the moral support." I grabbed my check and headed for the cashier. I had hoped that by providing an opportunity for conversation with the handsome Andy Beck, that Suzanne Lisette Rossiter had inadvertently found a way to compensate for stealing Tom Kennedy. I was wrong. Andy, the handsome stranger, remained locked in conversation as I pocketed my change, although I swore I felt his eyes follow me as I merged into the crowd on the boardwalk.

Chapter 8

As I pulled down the alley, I eyed the parking available under the house. I'd avoided the covered space all weekend. The car was a rental, and I wanted to verify that the agreement covered damage by building collapse. Until I confirmed that I was insured, I felt better leaving the Taurus in the safety of the open air.

An infrequent driver like most New Yorkers, I had no ritual for exiting a vehicle. I could never remember where my purse was, which knob turned off the lights, or which handle opened the door. I was invariably wrong—as I was that night. The darkness didn't help. I had only the motion sensitive lights from the other houses to rely on. The lamps that had turned on as I drove by, clicked off one by one as I worked to get organized.

Finally, headlights off, windshield wipers motionless, gearshift in park with keys and purse in hand, I climbed out of the car into the darkness of a cloudy night. The silence was broken only by the soothing sounds of breakers hitting the beach. A cool breeze curled around the corner of the house. Others might find the chill premature, but I loved it. I threw my head back and stared into the dark sky. Stars never seen from the bright streets of Manhattan dotted the black canvas. I took a deep breath and vowed to relax. I was on vacation. The time to enjoy my time off had come.

And, apparently gone. Behind me, I heard a crunching noise—the sound of feet on gravel. The feet were not mine. Neither was the hand that covered my mouth.

"I don't want to hurt you. All I want is a little information."

I had no hope of escaping the strong grip that pinned both my arms to my sides. I stood still and waited for further instructions.

"What did you tell the cops?" The hissing voice was male.

"Nothing." I murmured through the large but smooth-skinned hand.

"Don't stonewall me. I want an answer. You must have told them something."

"I knew nothing." Through his hand the words sounded more like IEW NNNNNNG. In anticipation of the police report, I memorized the salient features of my attacker. A keen intelligence wasn't one of them. It took three more rounds of incoherent mumbling before he understood that he would have to remove his hand before he could get an answer. "I told them my name, my address and that I'd only seen Bascombe once."

"And . . . ?" The jerk on my hair was unnecessary. I was cooperating.

"What else could I have told them? I don't know anything about Bascombe's murder."

"But I bet you know where it is."

I didn't even know what "it" was. Before I could point that out, however, a light came on across the alley. Then another. Without warning or explanation, I was flung forward on the ground. My hands and knees hit the gravel. I crawled across the yard forcing my sore palms and knees to repeat the painful experience of meeting the gravel surface.

"Run." A male voice yelled the command—to me I believed.

Still inching towards the house, I twisted my neck to glance over my shoulder. In the shadows of my driveway, two figures were involved in a scuffle. The voice had emanated from one of them, as it did again.

"Now. Run."

Convinced that the command was meant for me, I leapt to my feet with an unexpected ease and ran—up the stairs and into the house. Once inside, I fumbled with the bolt. As weak as the lock was, the rusty hardware would slow down an intruder. With the deadbolt in place, I dashed from room to room slamming windows down. Where shades and locks remained, I closed and fastened. I ran to the one light I had left burning and snapped it off. Feeling no more safe in darkness, I slipped onto the floor and tried to catch my breath. Fear, not exertion, was responsible for the difficulty I had bringing my breathing into a regular rhythm. Heart still racing, I crawled down the hallway on knees dotted with pebbles towards the window that overlooked the scuffle.

"Ouch." I'd overshot the window and bumped into the chair that I had finally righted only hours before. Once more it lost its precarious balance and fell to the floor. Outside I heard the muffled sounds of the ongoing confrontation. I raised my head until my eyes could peer between the windowsill and the bottom of the shade. The action had moved out of the range of the motion sensors; my neighbors lights had gone out. The scuffling figures were hidden in darkness.

Silently, I cursed my laziness. Without a cellular phone, I was trapped in a phone-free environment while a fight between two unknown parties determined my fate. Suddenly, I detected a glow growing brighter on the south side of the house. I crawled to the window that faced the alley and pushed my nose against the pane. One of the parties was fleeing down the alley setting off the motion sensitive lights at home after home. All I could make out was the form of a very fit male with enough hair that the wind rustled his flowing strands as he fled.

I slipped to the cold linoleum and sat shaking. I waited for the winner to knock on my door. I hoped the good guy had emerged victorious—if one of the players was a good guy. How would I identify a good guy anyway? A person who bothered to knock?

Crouched under the window I waited. And waited. And waited. Nothing happened. From my seat on the grimy floor I could watch the hallway and the door. I expected a knock; there was no sound. I envisioned the handle jiggling; there was no action.

I climbed onto my knees and peered out the window. The night was still. Without activity the lights guarding my neighbors' properties had again gone dark. I cracked the window and held my ear next to the opening. No sounds disturbed the calm. Was I really alone?

I considered my options. I had no phone. I feared going outside for help. I was trapped. Hours passed before I fell asleep on the sandy linoleum.

Chapter 9

As the sun cleared the ocean, its light reached just far enough into the bedroom to awaken me. The heat was oppressive. A quick check reminded me that I had slept with the windows pulled tightly shut. Only the one above my head was open a crack. With great effort, I climbed to my feet and pushed up the sash. The morning air was cool and eager to rush into the room. I felt revived as the breeze washed around me.

A night on the floor contributed little to my sense of well-being or to my appearance. For the second day in a row, the old mirror in the bedroom offered no consolation. The bruise above my eyes was a shade of purple that would never be called lush. The circles around my eyes were deep and dark and neatly accessorized with a gash that extended from the perimeter of the bag under my left eye to my jawline. The dent bore an uncanny resemblance to a crack in the linoleum. Some people grow to resemble their pets. I was growing to resemble my rental property.

Slowly the memories from the night before returned, and I understood my dilemma. Another vacation day and there I was —awake at dawn, feeling beat, with things to do that I would rather not.

I approached the window cautiously. The alley appeared quiet. In the first week after Labor Day fewer visitors would be making their way to the beach, but I had only a short wait until the first sunbather trudged by, toting a beach chair in her left hand. Only then did I feel safe enough to head for the pay phone, although I doubted the septuagenarian who held a cane in her right hand would have been much help had trouble ensued.

The police came quickly. Two male officers in uniform. I recognized neither of the faces. Neither of them appeared to know me by sight or reputation. Without undue emotion or energy, they took my statement before heading out to investigate the crime scene. Within five minutes they returned with my purse and Markshell security pass. My small wallet was tucked neatly into the side-pocket of the handbag. I took the occasion to hook the keys for my rentals, car and house, on the small key ring attached.

It wasn't until Detective Dupuy arrived that my story was called into question. Why hadn't I notified the cops sooner? Why was my handbag found safe and sound in the front seat of my rental car? Why was nothing stolen? Why was my security pass for Markshell Publications found wedged against the side of the house? Why didn't the hero who allegedly saved me stick around or call the police? Why didn't I have any bruises to prove that I had been mugged?

Happy for a question to which I had a response, I showed the detective my scratched knees and hands. She was unimpressed. "You could have fallen."

"I explained what happened. I told you what he said."

"Very convenient, wouldn't you say?"

"What do you mean?"

"Now you're a victim like your boss."

"Yes. That's true. I am."

Detective Dupuy found that comment amusing. "You don't have phone service in this house, do you?" From her pocket she produced a small piece of equipment. "Keep this with you at all times. If the intruder comes back, press this button." She pointed to the only button on the beeper. "Pressing the button lets us know there is a problem."

"I've fallen and I can't get up?"

"Pretty much the same concept."

Did this mean the policewoman believed my story?

"I don't imagine you'll be needing to use it."

Guess not.

"I'll make sure a cruiser drives by every so often to check that it's quiet."

Maybe she did.

"Why aren't you watching Bascombe's house anyway?" I went on the offensive.

"A little late, don't you think?"

I didn't remind the detective that the perp always returns to the scene of the crime. I was willing to bet that was what happened the night before. The young cop saw the situation differently. She didn't like me. Didn't trust me. How could she possibly think that I, an upstanding citizen with no, okay make that little, interaction with law enforcement, would suddenly graduate from a problem with speed limits to murder?

Sure, I had hated Donald K. Bascombe. Anyone with a triple digit IQ would. He personified everything that was wrong with business, America and American business. Sure, I was happy he was dead, but I hadn't told her that. Sure, I suspected he was about to fire me but that was another piece of information I hadn't shared. Detective Dupuy had no reason to view me so harshly. Obviously, I reassured myself, she was a poor judge of character.

"Donald K. Bascombe certainly was a bastard." The cop offered the assessment without prompting.

I'd have to rethink that judgment issue. "Why do you say that?" My emphasis was on the word "you." I wasn't disputing her conclusions, just questioning how she arrived at them.

"I didn't have to be Sherlock Holmes to figure out that guy had a lot of enemies. You were only one of many." I protested being added to an enemies list but the detective continued without heeding my objections. "You must know a little about these people."

Now I got it. Scare the witness into believing she is a suspect so she'll rat on others. What kind of person did Detective Dupuy think I was?

"Who?" I asked eager to divert attention from myself.

"Bish Winston."

Bish Winston had been the head of sales at Markshell until nine months before, when he had been unceremoniously dumped by Bascombe. I was sure he despised Bascombe, but I couldn't testify to any personal knowledge of that hatred.

"John Mancotti."

John Mancotti had been on the fast track until Bascombe shunted him off into a middle management position in administration. I had heard John was bitter. He claimed he'd been reduced to a party planner, but again I couldn't testify to his feelings, although I could confirm that he gave great parties.

Detective Dupuy mentioned six more names—ex-employees about whom I knew little. "Don't you suspect anyone I know well?" I asked eager to direct attention elsewhere.

"How about Randy Wallace?"

"Don't call him Randy."

"Why?"

"He doesn't like it. We call him Randall Don't-Call-Me-Randy Wallace."

"What happens if you call him Randy?" Detective Dupuy inquired seriously.

"Maybe Bascombe knows." I laughed. Detective Dupuy didn't.

"You don't suspect Randall Wallace, do you? When I called the office I spoke to him. He was one of the few true mourners for Bascombe."

"What about David Orlander?"

A shock shot through me from head to toe. "My David Orlander?"

The detective nodded. "It's not a particularly common name."

I pondered my position. David had dumped me three weeks before, and there I sat with the ability to implicate him in the murder of his former boss, a man for whom he openly expressed hatred. What a temptation. I considered my options. The high road? The low road? The detective waited while I pondered my decision.

I chose a middle path. "David wasn't crazy about Bascombe. Markshell recruited him from a secure job but not too much later Bascombe came. DK gave him a hard time. David only stayed two years, less than a year working for Bascombe. He considered working for DK a living hell and a roadblock in an otherwise successful career. By the end of his tenure, he was bitter. He used to say that meeting me was the one good point about working at Markshell." The smile I attempted came out rueful. "I doubt that he says that anymore."

Detective Dupuy was excellent at nonverbal communication. I understood from the expression on her face that my testimony was veering towards a place she had no desire to visit.

I tried sticking to business but kept finding personal notes creeping into my story. "David oversaw all the budgets. I had to work with him on the marketing budget. We went together over two years. Two years and then he began staying out late. You know the signs. I guess I overreacted. He said he wanted space. I suggested a two bedroom with den and told him to get out. I think . . ."

"Ms. Daniels." Detective Dupuy's expression reminded me she hadn't come about the demise of my relationship.

"David didn't kill DK. Trust me. If anyone wants to punish David right now I am the one, and I can tell you he didn't do it."

"You were with him when the murder occurred?"

"No. I've told you I was here alone."

"So he could have murdered Bascombe."

"I will not say that." Mentally, I added, "So you can take my quote to David and get him to implicate me."

"Was Bascombe ever physically abusive to any of his employees." Detective Dupuy's question shocked me.

"He didn't have to be. He was so adept at verbal abuse that he kept most employees in constant pain."

For the first time, the detective's eyes met mine. "I'm serious."

"So am I."

"You never heard that he hit anyone. Pushed anyone. Kicked anyone."

"Bascombe knew a move like that would cost him his job—and possibly some money. Bascombe did not like to lose money. Personal funds that is. He didn't seem to care how must the company lost."

Detective Dupuy liked the topic. "Do you know much about the company's finances?"

"Not really." I had no idea why I was protecting David, but I didn't tell the cop how he relished revealing confidential information at intimate moments. Actually, I should have known that was a danger sign but at the time his behavior seemed normal. Probably because David loved two things most in life—money and sex. Why wouldn't he think of them together?

The detective was talking again. "If Orlander worked with budgets, he had a clear picture of the financial status of the company." Detective Dupuy's statement was really a question.

"Sure. I wouldn't know how bad things were if David weren't indiscreet."

Given David's indiscretion, Detective Dupuy wondered if I had heard any juicy rumors about Bascombe. "I'm one of those people who is always the last to know." I paused before asking with a shock. "Was there something I should have known?" Even as I asked, I realized that I had never listened to David's financial pillow talk.

"Nothing specific to you. You didn't hear about any hanky-panky?"

My face contorted. "The idea of Bascombe involved in hanky-panky is pretty repulsive." I shook my head to chase the image.

"I was thinking of financial hanky-panky."

"Bascombe?" I mulled over the possibility. "He wouldn't be above it but I never heard. I think David would have known . . ." In reaction to the poorly suppressed excitement in the cop's eyes, I let the sentence trail off without a conclusion. "David and I were close. He told me everything and he never mentioned a word about financial wrong doing."

"Did he tell you about Laurie Gold?"

Detective Dupuy was really getting on my nerves.

Chapter 10

When the cops had gone I didn't contemplate Bascombe's murder or my ruined vacation. I couldn't get my mind off Detective Dupuy's comment about Laurie Gold. I hadn't asked her to elaborate. I didn't have to; I knew. I never wanted to admit it, but I knew. About two months before, Laurie Gold, accounts receivable supervisor at Markshell, developed a keen interest in David. She used the excuse of business questions to telephone him at his new job and then at home.

I suspected there was more to the calls than David admitted. Detecting the guilt in his voice was easy. My guess was that he mentioned Laurie's calls just for the opportunity to say her name aloud. I knew my suspicions were justified the first time I heard her thin but perky voice on our home phone. Denial, however, was the easiest reaction. I waited to confront David until the signs were too obvious to ignore; it was not a particularly long time. Nor did much time pass between that confrontation and David's departure. My companion of almost three years donated no more than five minutes to denials before he started packing.

While I watched other late season vacationers frolicking in the surf and sand, a full hour of my dwindling holiday slipped through my fingers. No more, I vowed. No more dwelling on failed romance. No more talk of murder. So what if my name appeared on the suspect list? Lots of names did. Detective Dupuy had confirmed that. I had been given no indication that I had made the short list. I would enjoy my vacation, knowing that the truth would come out and I would be exonerated.

Okay, so I couldn't remember every event of the night of Bascombe's death, but I knew myself. I could not commit murder. I had not committed murder. I would enjoy the rest of my vacation. I would return to my job. Okay, I would return to my job if I had a job. I told myself to relax. I couldn't control the situation. If I lost my job, I'd deal with the predicament. I wasn't going to worry. I leapt out of my chair. I was on vacation. I was ready to focus on sunscreen and the fine art of applying it.

When the beach towel finally lay slanted on the sand in just the right position and the suntan lotion was applied in a reduced SPF, I lowered my tired frame carefully. I surveyed the damage to my body since my vacation began. One bruise over the left eye, courtesy of Officer Timmy Borden. Multitudinous cuts and scratches on my knees thanks to my unknown assailant. An array of aching muscles from nights spent, at least partially, on the floor. If I maintained this pace, I'd be going home in an ambulance.

Time to start my recovery. I closed my eyes and enjoyed the psychedelic show of sunbeams trying to penetrate my eyelids. The sound of the waves, gentler than those over the weekend, lulled me towards sleep. I released an audible sigh of relief. At last I could forget about Bascombe, David, and my assorted aches and pains.

"Is this a bad time?"

It would have been if the words had been uttered by anyone other than the man who cast the shadow across my tanning surface.

"I know my behavior may seem pushy. You probably don't even remember me. It was you, wasn't it? In Bob's last night."

With a hand poised above my eyes to block the sun I surveyed the source of the voice from the tip of his toes to the top of his blond locks. Yes, I do remember you, I said silently in a tone too revealing to use in the vocal version of the sentence. I remembered the square jaw, the silky hair, and especially the coolly penetrating eyes he revealed as he slipped off his sunglasses.

"I hope you don't mind, but I was running on the beach and I saw you getting settled. I said to myself . . . I mean our meeting was sort of awkward . . . I mean at Bob's . . . my friend . . ."

"No problem." I helped Andy—I remembered the handsome stranger's name—out of his verbal impasse. Even with my hand above my eyes, I squinted as I tried to maintain eye contact with the stranger who in jogging shorts disclosed a body as impressive as his face.

"Are you here on vacation?"

I frowned, not from lack of interest in the hunk who loomed above me, but from surprise. The incredibly cute guy was making small talk with me. "Yes," I answered quickly as I saw his expression mirror my frown.

"Do you come here every year?" He smiled broadly as if his trite question brought the nature of his interest into the open.

"Actually . . ." Carefully arranging all body parts in as flattering a position as possible, I lifted myself onto one elbow. "I haven't been here . . ."

"Andy." The excitement in the voice was unmistakable. The body that accompanied the voice was also unmistakable. The details of the figure that had inserted itself between Andy and me at Bob's were now available for view. The woman who interrupted our second conversation, as she had our first, appeared to be wearing a single strip of fluorescent orange that covered only the most critical of her private parts before splitting and tying over each shoulder. With no position available between Andy and me, the woman wrapped an arm around his waist and pressed her unclothed side against his shorts.

Hers was not a force that I could compete with, even if I had chosen swimwear more exotic than a black tank suit. I smiled ruefully and resigned myself to losing the handsome stranger's attention once more. "Thanks for saying hello." I laid back on my towel.

The man appeared nonplussed and (was it wishful thinking?), a little annoyed by the woman's attention. I stole another glance at her body. Wishful thinking, definitely.

Charlene, as I recalled her name, led Andy off to take advantage of the unusual coincidence. "Sid and Debbie are over there." She waved eagerly with one hand and dragged Andy through the sand with the other. "I can't believe it's you. You never come this far uptown—and when did you get on a health kick?"

Was losing a second opportunity a cruel trick of fate, or was the woman stalking Andy? No matter. The odds of running into the handsome guy a third time seemed as thin as his companion's upper thighs. As I watched him cross the sand, and I did watch him cross the sand, I felt as if I were watching the end of a movie, a sad movie, the final scene—the one where the hero hops a freight, rides out of Dodge, flies off to war. There will be other handsome strangers, I reassured myself.

I hadn't been in the habit of lying to myself before I'd started on vacation.

Chapter II

I climbed the old stairs to my house carefully. At the top, I shook the sand out of my beach towel and laid it across the railing. That was when I saw it. The car. A red convertible. Sitting in the alley but not in a parking space. The car's roof was up and the small windows made it hard to see inside, but I could detect a figure in the front seat. Sure, the driver faced the other way. But, I knew. The eyes were watching me.

I hurried into the house and locked the door. Crouched on the linoleum, I kept watch. The car never moved; the driver never turned. Yet, I knew. I was definitely under surveillance. By the cops? By my assailant? I kept my surveillant under surveillance.

Eventually I realized that even those under surveillance have to take showers. While chasing the trickle provided by the fifty-year-old plumbing, I became distracted by my search for signs of a tan. My skin appeared to be sun resistant. Subscribing to the principle that a watched pot never boils, I covered my paleness under a long-sleeved shirt and ankle-length skirt. As I fastened the last button, I checked the window. The car was gone. Or had the red convertible simply moved to another vantage point? Had I imagined its purpose? Had I imagined the car?

Given my recent activities, I realized a drink was the last thing I needed. I was pouring orange juice when I heard the knock at the door. I stood, glass and bottle suspended in mid-air, and stared at the thin wooden slab. Who would be visiting me? No one I had invited, of that I was sure. I remained paralyzed in the kitchen. My visitor was tenacious. The banging continued. I massaged the lump on my forehead as I recalled the last time I had responded to persistent knocking.

I dragged an old aluminum dining chair across the linoleum without concern for scratches. I positioned the relic from a 1950's kitchen in front of the door and climbed on the seat to peek through the small diamond of yellow beveled glass that served, as similar designs had for many doors of that decade, no useful purpose. My visitor didn't observe me peering down at him. I leapt from the seat, kicked the chair aside and flung open the door.

Andy blushed sheepishly. "I hope you don't think I'm a maniac or anything, but I saw you when you went home from the beach."

I smiled but waited for him to continue.

"I felt really bad . . . I mean every time I tried to say something to you, Charlene . . . did you notice Charlene?'

"Charlene is kind of hard not to notice."

Andy seemed encouraged by both my words and the smile that accompanied them. "Anyway I wanted to offer an apology . . . for all the interruptions."

"That isn't really necessary."

"Well . . ." He allowed a sheepish expression to creep across his face. "I hoped . . . maybe I could make it up to you . . . maybe we could get a bite or something."

I hesitated before I blurted out, "Now?"

"Well, if you're not busy."

Busy. Busy didn't exactly describe my vacation when I wasn't identifying bodies or undergoing police interrogation. Afraid to sound overanxious, I sputtered. "Well . . . I mean . . . I was just . . ."

"I'm sorry. This is too pushy. I knew it was too weird." He said the words but made no effort to leave or free my eyes from his relentless gaze.

"No. No. Not weird. I can . . . sure . . . in a couple of minutes." I took a deep breath. "Would you like to come in?"

His smile was broad, disarming and, I hoped, sincere. "That sounds good. By the way, my name's Andy. Andy Beck."

I didn't admit I knew. "Meg." I introduced myself. "Meg Daniels."

Andy slipped by me into the narrow hallway and took the two steps necessary to move into the living room. I studied the man with prurient eyes as he traversed the space. If he had a physical flaw, it wasn't evident from that angle. His clothes were basic but tasteful. He'd changed from his beachwear into worn jeans and a casual shirt, both neatly ironed. His shoes suggested he spent times boating. When Andy turned, he framed himself in the picture window with the beach as backdrop. It made a pretty shot.

"Nice place."

I took umbrage at the two words which I interpreted as criticism of the old cottage. I grew suddenly defensive on behalf of the architectural anachronism. I viewed the living room with eyes that admired the care that had been taken in renovating the room, even if the vision was forty years old. There was a day when gold flecked linoleum was the latest thing and faux pine paneling represented the height of chic. Well, the height of convenience anyway. The room said more about the owner's sensibility for hospitality than their sense of style. Over the past few days, I had fantasized about the recently deceased couple. I saw them young and in love. Middle-aged with grandchildren. Old and alone except for their memories.

As Andy continued, I detected no trace of sarcasm in his tone. "When I come into a house like this, and there aren't many in town anymore, I can't help concocting stories. So much history." Andy was verbalizing my thoughts.

I watched with suspicion as Andy studied the details of the decor. "See how the pictures are positioned." He moved close to the hand-painted seascapes that I had failed to notice in five days. "Someone positioned these scenes so that when the sun rises over the ocean, the light appears to shine right into the frame."

His eyes moved to a large, dark and heavy forest scene in a large, dark and heavy frame. "Well, everyone makes mistakes." He shrugged. "Maybe that painting was a gift."

Not from a friend, I speculated. The dreary painting tucked in the corner near the kitchen was a monstrosity. Whoever and whatever Andy Beck was, the guy had good aesthetic sense.

He turned and gazed across the beach. "The cottage was apparently renovated in the fifties, but the building is older. At least the late thirties. I'm surprised a bulldozer didn't get to this house years ago. The owners must have loved this place. Did you know them?"

"No."

"Maybe the husband fought in World War II. Maybe he was in the European theater. His wife might have sat for hours staring across the ocean." Suddenly, Andy shifted gears. "Sorry." When he turned he seemed startled by the puzzled expression on my face. "End-of-season nostalgia. I get it every year."

I averted my eyes from his as I nodded. Was this guy for real? Why not assume that he was on the up and up until he proved otherwise? After all, I had no plans for that night and no prospects for many nights. Much later, when I told friends I'd offered him a seat and a glass of wine, they found my behavior careless. Why? It wasn't as if I'd invited a stranger into my home. We sat on the porch. He on an old aluminum glider and I on the old wooden rocker. Plus, I had the beeper Detective Dupuy had given me. Somewhere. Inside the house.

"What's with the crime scene tape next door?" His hair swung gracefully as he nodded towards the Bascombe residence.

"Apparently there was a murder."

"Apparently?" Andy seemed amused.

"Well, the guy is dead and it's unlikely he stabbed himself in the back."

"Actually, I saw the story in today's paper." He chuckled. "I think the press is trying to downplay the story."

How could a newspaper downplay the only murder in town? I hoped by not mentioning a bunch of names—like mine. "What did the article say?" I asked naively.

"Just the facts. Visitor died. Body found. Family notified. No local involvement."

"Any suspects?" I asked a bit too eagerly.

"Not that I recall. I'm surprised you didn't run out and buy a copy of the paper."

I shrugged.

"Did you see it?"

"The paper?"

"No. The murder."

I shook my head. "I must have slept through it. They said the whole thing happened outside my window."

"They?"

"The cops."

"So they interviewed you?"

"Boy, did they. Woke me at dawn and then made me sit at the station all day." I didn't mention my trip into the tall grass.

He nodded knowingly. "You didn't see anything?"

"*Nada.*"

"You mean to tell me there was a murder next door, and you didn't wake up."

"What can I say? I'm a heavy sleeper."

"This block seems to be full, or rather empty, of the back-to-school crowd. I didn't notice a lot of people around. You must have been one of the few, if not the only, potential witness. The cops must have been disappointed if you really observed nothing."

"I haven't any idea what other witnesses were around. I guess the best possibility is the old guy who sits on his porch all day in that tiny cabin down the alley. Rupert P. Downie. The only time he ever speaks to me he raves about the new construction. Did you know that development is an unthinking parasitic virus that has attached itself to this town? Mr. Downie will tell you all about the problem." I sighed. "No matter what you say, he curses the construction. 'Nice day.' 'Would be if you could see past the construction.' 'Looks like rain.' 'Always rains since they started the construction.' I think you could probably stab a man in front of him. Just don't try hammering a two-by-four."

"Did you ever meet the guy?"

"Mr. Downie?" I sounded confused.

"No, the victim."

"Oh, yeah." I took a long drink of wine. "I'd met him." My tone told the whole story.

"Bad neighbor?" Andy asked.

"Bad boss." I answered in parody of my conversation with Detective Dupuy.

"Why did you go on vacation with your boss?" Andy sounded both amazed and confused.

"That's what the cops asked. Do I look like the kind of woman who would go on vacation with her boss?"

"What does that kind of woman look like?"

"Not a thing like me."

Bascombe's murder provided a basis for conversation with the man I didn't know. And, Andy seemed interested. I let him in on the secret that I was the one who identified the body. He seemed more than willing to listen. With an apparently friendly ear to tell about my experiences at the police station, I went through the types of questions they'd asked—repeatedly—always returning to my relationship with DK Bascombe. Nonetheless, the self-portrait I painted was one of a witness. It's hard enough to meet men when you're not a murder suspect.

I referred only once to a possible role on the wrong side of the law. "The cops left me in the small waiting room, which believe me is a misnomer. There is no actual furniture—just surfaces you can sit on but not comfortably. At first I was mad, but then when I realized they were leaving me unattended within ten feet of an unlocked door . . . well, then I felt pretty happy."

"That is significant." Andy sounded extremely solemn.

In an effort to lighten the tone of the conversation, I related a bit of celebrity gossip. "All in all it was a boring day. The Ocean City police station doesn't attract many criminals. The only interesting visitor arrived when I was changing position for the 157th time. An extremely familiar face came in on top of a body that struck me as surprisingly short. I knew him from somewhere."

"An old school friend?"

"Too old. Besides my father never let me near a school with boys. I kept seeing this guy behind a desk but not at any place I had worked. That was, however, how I envisioned him." I explained that it had taken me more than five minutes to realize the desk was visible every night at 7 P.M. in my living room on Channel 3 in New York. The man with the imposing presence was the national news anchor for the NTS network, Richard Rothman. Andy didn't seem as surprised as I did. "I couldn't hear what he said. Not a word. For a man whose voice was his bread and butter, Richard Rothman was hard to understand. Whatever he said, however, got him right inside. I was surprised."

"That they let him in?"

"No. What surprised me was that Rothman has the voice and demeanor of a towering figure yet at five-six, I was definitely taller."

"Do you know why he was at the station?"

I shook my head. "I don't think Bascombe was big enough news. I read once that Rothman has a house somewhere at the Jersey shore. Maybe he got a parking ticket."

My efforts to divert the conversation in Andy's direction failed. He acted more interested in me. I enjoyed his attempt at winning me over—after all I was on the rebound. Why he was making the effort I had no idea, but I had to admit he was good. He hung on my every word. As he watched me speak about my life, my job, and my vacation, a slight smile turned the corner of his lips as if he found being with me somehow amusing and enjoyable. I didn't know why. At that point, I wasn't finding my life, job, or vacation amusing or enjoyable.

Andy didn't just look at me; he peered into me. I found myself blushing and averting my eyes but always turning back for one more fix of his misty green-eyed stare.

"Can I ask you a personal question?"

I turned to him with a quizzical expression and found myself lost in his eyes. I knew that I would answer.

"I don't want you to take offense, but I felt you might need to talk about it."

My expression changed from quizzical to baffled.

"I mean you told me about the murder and how you accidentally ended up next door to your boss."

I nodded.

"I know you want to be discreet but that's a pretty far fetched story. Were you and he . . .?" He left the question hanging in the air.

"What?" I played more confused than I was.

"Well, I believed maybe you and he . . . are you feeling pain because of his death?"

He really thought it. He believed that I'd been involved with Bascombe. I didn't mean to yelp and laugh but I did. "It's obvious you never met the guy or even saw him . . ."

Andy resurrected his sheepish expression. "You're here alone and . . ."

"It wasn't even my idea to come to Ocean City. My ex-boyfriend said he wanted to learn more about my past. Since I came to OC as a kid, he wanted to vacation here. But then our relationship changed." I moved quickly to direct the discussion away from David. "Bascombe and me." I chuckled. "Andy, if you knew Bascombe, I'd never forgive you for asking that question."

His green-gray eyes narrowed as he gazed out at the ocean. In the encroaching darkness, the eyes appeared as dark as the sea, yet when he smiled in my direction they grew pale like jade. I blushed.

Andy and I did not go to dinner that night. We never left the porch except for more wine and a blanket as night encroached. I stayed in my chair, and he stayed in his. The only intimacy that passed between us was verbal. By the time he left, the guy had heard my whole life history. As I walked him to the door, I realized how little I knew about him beyond his taste in music (eclectic), books (history and biography), and films (no musicals).

As he approached the battered door, Andy retrieved a small piece of white paper from the floor. "What's this? Lela Silver? Did you drop this?" He scanned the card before turning it over to me.

I glanced at the business card briefly. It bore the logo of the local paper and a handwritten note to call. "Oh, it must be that reporter's. Some young newswoman stopped by to ask me about the murder. She seemed pretty upset I didn't see anything. She wants a scoop."

"Well, my bet is that she missed her chance. I don't think the paper is going to feature the murder. The sooner forgotten, the better."

"I feel pretty much the same way."

Andy's eyes narrowed even as his smile broadened. "I can imagine," he said. "Good night."

Chapter 12

For me, first thing in the morning came after ten thirty. I didn't know if I slept late because of the strength of the evening's wine or the weakness of the morning's sun. I awoke on the couch under the blanket that had covered Andy the previous night. Did the police intend to return my linens? Would they wash them? I wasn't about to approach them. I would simply wait.

Another day, a new beginning. I was naively optimistic as I checked the mirror. The face peering back at me was notable not just for its pallor but for the bruise on the forehead—by then a shade of yellow not often selected by those perusing fabric swatches. What annoyed me most was the trace of a goofy grin that hovered around the corner of my lips? And the humming. I caught myself singing a World War II love song as I wandered into the bedroom. I hadn't even realized I'd memorized every word to "I'll Be Seeing You" until I was repeating the chorus.

A glance out the window silenced me. I leapt back. Once more the car occupied its spot. The red convertible with the black top sat at the end of the alley, half invading the driveway of one of the vacation homes that had been abandoned for the winter. By the profile of the baseball cap, I could tell the head in the driver's seat was turned slightly. The occupant could read the paper while detecting any motion on the sole staircase that led to my cottage.

In the daylight I felt more angry than afraid. Enough of captivity. If the driver was a cop, he should just come inside. If the person was a criminal . . . well, if he were a criminal, I should know. And, I would. I traded the long skirt from the night before for a pair of black leggings more appropriate for spy work. I didn't consider that they were designed for cat burglars operating against dark roofs at night, not marketing executives operating against white sand in broad daylight.

I checked the window where the watcher still relaxed in his car. To surprise him, I couldn't exit via the steps. I hatched a plan. I would lower myself from the porch, sneak around the next two houses and run in front of the car while he watched my cottage in the rearview mirror. That wouldn't work. I'd circle two houses on the other side and sneak up behind the car but on the right side where he wouldn't see me. That wouldn't work. I decided to get to street level and figure out the situation. If I had to wait all day for an opportunity, I would. I had to find out who the guy was and what he was up to. The mission set my adrenaline pumping.

The first step was to climb down from the porch. Not a problem to more athletic people. In my case, problem hardly described the dilemma. As far as natural ability went, I lacked only coordination, strength, and endurance. There was, however, a further complication. It wasn't that I didn't stay in shape; I simply had lower standards of what "in shape" meant.

I slipped onto the porch and out of the car's range of vision. Peeking over the railing, I calculated the distance to the sand to be nine feet at a minimum. Too far to jump—at least onto knees that had been less than supportive since my fall, with a six-foot china closet, from a U-Haul truck. I studied the porch frame. If I climbed over the railing and dangled from the studs, I could reduce the drop to under five feet. I hesitated even though I saw no other way.

I knelt on the floor and stuck my head under the lowest rail. Slowly, I lowered my head over the side to check if I had escaped the driver's line of vision. I didn't expect my body to follow but my body had no interest in my intentions. First, I felt my hips rotating above my head. If there were a way to stop the forward motion, I couldn't think of it. Next, the weight of my legs kicked in. My feet brushed the bottom of the railing before passing over my head. I had time to notice that my chest was moving perilously close to my chin when the weight of my feet headed for the ground flipped me over. Before I came up with a counteraction, I found myself standing upright in the sand. I checked if all my body parts still moved. Surprisingly, they did. Better than before. The fall had served as an instant massage.

Although I had successfully left the cottage undetected, I was still without a plan, without a weapon and, I would realize later, without keys. The weapon I could do something about. I sneaked between the remaining wooden slats that mostly failed to hide the open space under the house. The majority of the thin weathered poles had long since succumbed to the perils of the beachfront location, but enough remained to hide me from the driver as well as to snag my clothing. I had a growing hole in the spandex covering my right thigh and a slit across the back of my shirt as I crept into the shower and twisted the nozzle from the hose. Armed with a useless piece of cold metal, I faced a decision— picking a direction for the approach. If I chose to move north, I would have to cross his line of vision. If I headed south, he would see me in his mirror. I took a chance his eyes were glued to his rearview mirror.

No one was home at the house where DK Bascombe had died to notice my slipping past the yellow crime scene tape and into the dunes. I bent over and ran along the fence. The next house had been abandoned at the beginning of the school year although a collection of beach chairs and bicycles told me to expect the family for the weekend. Once I cleared the second house, I got to my feet quickly; but not as quickly as I fell back to the ground. I sat amidst the dune grass and pulled a nasty round burr from my right foot. After checking my left foot, I set out again.

I ignored the stares of a five-year-old boy who believed he was hidden behind a plant on the second floor balcony of the quadruplex next door. With my back against the wall of the rental property, I edged towards the rear of the building and a view of the alley where the driver sat—apparently without much fear of being observed. I stuck my head around the side of the structure for a quick peek. I determined that the driver's eyes were trained on the side view mirror and my place—their focus was hard to identify under the dark glasses and baseball cap. I surveyed the situation. If I wanted to cross the driveway, this wasn't the spot. Behind the building to the north, an overgrown garden offered cover. After circling the second quadruplex, I tiptoed over the sparse grass mixed in with the gravel behind the garden and then ran across the alley. I moved quickly from the cover of a row of empty trash cans to the cover of five squat pine trees. With any luck, the man had been watching my cottage and missed my action.

I cut between two houses to Central Avenue and ran down the street in front of five more. Slipping along the side of a red brick house, I was lucky to find that the occupants appeared to have left for the beach—if not for the summer. When I reached the rear of the building, I realized which cut-through I had taken. Behind the house, sitting flush against the alley, stood the house where Rupert P. Downie spent hours rocking on the porch and greeting passers-by noisily. If he spotted me, my cover was blown.

I crossed the back yard and tiptoed past the tiny building, straining to determine if the octogenarian was at his post. As I passed the kitchen window, I turned. Two bright blue eyes set among high bones and deep wrinkles were studying me intently. The tan and grizzled face with its sharp features contorted into a scowl belonged to the old man.

Rupert P. Downie stood at his kitchen sink doing the dishes. I flashed him a tentative smile and raised a finger to my lips. He mimicked my action and said "shshsh" in a tone loud enough to wake the dead. "Good girl. There was a day it wasn't necessary to sneak down tiny little alleys. Stop the development." He whispered loudly. I nodded in agreement and moved on to the end of the wall. I couldn't see the car. Apparently the driver had taken Rupert P. Downie's habits into account when selecting a position.

When I moved behind a wooden structure designed to camouflage trash cans, I saw the car and its occupant were still in position. The back of the baseball cap faced me. As I had suspected, the man watched his right side mirror and in it my cottage across the alley.

I gripped the hose nozzle tightly, took a deep breath, and charged. I suppressed the desire to yelp as I hopped over burrs and pebbles on the way to the car. Shoes would have made a fine addition to my gear, but it was too late to reconsider. Despite my footwear problem, I arrived at the car undetected and stuck the cold metal in the man's neck. "Who are you and why are you watching me?"

The uninvited visitor let out a deep sigh and folded his newspaper before he spoke. "I assume the cold metal cylinder I feel in my neck is the miniature flashlight you carry in your handbag. I suggest you drop it because the cold metal in my hand is a 45, fully loaded and ready to fire."

"It's a gun."

"It is not a gun." His right hand came around and grabbed the cylinder from mine. "That is a good way to get killed."

By opening his door, he pushed me out of his way. I was protesting but even I could find no meaning in my noises. Finally, I stared up into his sunglasses and uttered my first coherent sound. "Why are you here?"

He slipped off his shades to reveal those cool, green-gray eyes. "Just keeping an eye on you."

"You're a cop!" I exclaimed with shock, anger and disappointment.

"No. I am not a cop." Andy Beck sounded bored not defensive.

"Why are you here?" I answered my own question. "You killed Bascombe didn't you. I told you I didn't see a thing but you had to be sure. What are you going to do? Kill me too?"

"Maggie."

"No one calls me Maggie. My name is Meg."

"Meg is too button-down for you. I'll call you Maggie. Maggie," he repeated defiantly, "let me see if I've got this right. I killed Bascombe, then because I think you witnessed my crime, I introduce myself to you and the next day park at the murder scene in the hopes that my presence will jar your memory and lead to my identification, arrest, and conviction. That's your conclusion?"

"You're twisting my words . . ."

"Forget it, Maggie, I did not kill Bascombe. I had no motive to kill him. I simply want to find the person who did."

"Why?"

"I'm a private detective."

"You never told me that."

"You never asked."

"I didn't?" I was certain I had asked Andy what he did for a living. Not telling me was at best a lie of omission. Surprisingly, what I was feeling wasn't anger. The morning's smile had been driven from my face by disappointment and humiliation. I had believed a handsome stranger was interested in me. Well, he was, but not for the reasons I'd hoped.

"How can you stand here and face me after you deceived me last night? You talked to me under false, or at least incomplete pretenses, and then you sneak around watching me."

"It's what I do for a living." He answered without guile or guilt.

"That's a disgusting way to make a living."

"Well, I couldn't really come back this morning and ask you for another date. I would have appeared overanxious." Andy spoke with a cool logic that denied the underlying deceit of the situation.

He handed me a business card. On it, I saw his name, occupation, and phone number, but no address. "Why? Are you going to send me a letter?" He responded to my inquiry with a heavy helping of sarcasm.

"Why watch me?" I gazed in his eyes which despite the day's events still struck me as incredibly seductive. If you had to be watched, these were the eyes to be watched by. Not that I was happy to be under surveillance.

Andy's smile revealed his impressive array of dental work. "Isn't your remark a bit disingenuous? You know you're a suspect in a murder, and you wonder why I am watching you?"

"You should be out looking for the real killers."

Andy leaned back on the hood of his car. "Actually, I prefer watching you."

Andy seemed surprised by the sneer with which I responded. "Turn on all the charm you have Mr. Beck. I can't help you at all, because I don't know who the killers are." I started for my house.

"Then how do you know there is more than one?"

I stopped and frowned. "I didn't say there was more than one."

"You said killers. You used the plural. Twice."

He was right. I had said killers twice. Why? Had I heard something? Was the identity of two killers locked in my brain? Would the memory be recovered thirty years in the future? More importantly, would the secrets held in my memory constitute a reason to kill me?

Then it hit me. "Wait a minute. You knew I kept a flashlight in my handbag. You were there two nights ago." I thought for a moment before concluding he had to be the good guy. "You pulled that thug off of me. You put my wallet in my bag and hid it in my car."

"I know. As you said, I was there." The PI shrugged modestly. "No need to thank me."

"I'm not thanking you. You could have stuck around so that the police wouldn't think I invented the whole episode."

Again, a shrug. "I didn't think if I waltzed up to your door you would have opened it."

He was right, but his behavior still made no sense to me. "Why did you save my life one night, charm me the next, and then return to watch me?"

"It's obvious." To him, maybe. I was confused. "I wanted information. I still do."

"Why come to me? Why not ask the cops?"

"PIs don't like cops. And, vice versa."
The way I felt, I wouldn't have argued with either side.

Chapter 13

My friends often ask why, after I discovered Andy had lied to and spied on me, I invited him into my home. My decision had less to do with his looks and charm than the picklocks he carried. Plus, this was a man who ironed his jeans. I found it hard to see how anyone so well-groomed could be dangerous.

After Andy picked the lock, it seemed ungracious to ask him to leave. Plus, after observing the ease with which the PI gained access to my house, I realized that if he had been interested in killing me, I would have been dead already.

After a long series of questions, and an equally long series of beers, Andy admitted that he wasn't exactly working on the Bascombe murder case. PI Beck, as I then called Andy, had been following DK Bascombe for an unspecified period of time. I tried to cajole him into specifying but he wouldn't. All he would say is that the Bascombes were headed for divorce court and he was gathering evidence for Mrs. Bascombe's case.

"I don't know the finer points of the legal system, but it seems to me that if Bascombe is dead, continuing with the divorce would be overkill—no pun intended."

"Well, there are financial considerations—a will to contest."

"If you were tailing Bascombe, why didn't you witness the murder."

Andy glanced away and blushed. "I was momentarily sidetracked onto a different leg of the investigation."

"Why did Mrs. Bascombe hire a PI anyway?"

"The breakup was acrimonious."

"Bitter? Didn't seem that way the other night."

Until that moment, I had not recalled what I overheard only hours before Bascombe died. I could not explain how the thought resurfaced just then. I would not explain how I had happened to be sitting in the dark at the window of a silent apartment eavesdropping on a rather enthusiastic romantic interlude. "I could not help but overhear" was my story. I was sticking to it. The PI smiled skeptically at the position of the chairs and the window that faced an entrance to the Bascombe porch.

"I'm talking very enthusiastic. Apparently Bascombe had a side that few of us got to see."

Andy regarded me with amusement. "And you assumed his partner was his wife? Are you sure you live in the big city?"

"He was having an affair?" I asked naively.

The PI indicated I should add an "s." Apparently DK Bascombe was leading a much happier life than his facial expressions indicated.

"You're sure Mrs. Bascombe wasn't the person I heard."

"Not in the past three years, according to what she told me."

Andy was disappointed that I couldn't describe Bascombe's partner. I told him I had only seen the Bascombe children—two blondes—a girl and a boy.

"They were here? Who brought them?"

"They drove themselves—separately."

Again, Andy found my observations amusing.

"They weren't his kids, were they?" I was embarrassed to ask.

"How drunk were you?"

Given how that night had ended, I considered Andy's question dangerous to answer—at least truthfully. I changed the subject. "If he were having lots of affairs, it seems obvious that his wife killed him."

The PI dismissed my assertion that Mrs. Bascombe had murdered her husband. "Besides you said there were two killers."

I shook my head. "I didn't see a thing. Maybe I was dreaming." Monday had been a rough night for me. "I only remember the end of my dreams, but I know they had been going on all night."

"What did you remember?"

I explained my confusion when I believed the cops knocking on my door were two of my co-workers banging on my head.

Andy was interested in their names.

"You would convict Laurie Gold and John Mancotti on the basis that I dreamt about them. I don't think the case would hold up in court. Besides, I am telling you it was the wife. It usually is."

Andy Beck had a gaze that seemed to stare right through me.

"On television." I added nervously.

His narrowed eyes oozed amusement and invited conspiracy. "Look Maggie, I appreciate this innocent posture, but if you for one minute think that I believe this naive act . . ." He shook his head and chuckled. "No one is this naive."

I lowered my eyes to hide my embarrassment. "Apparently, I am."

"Oh, Maggie, you are good. Really, good. The averted eyes. The blushing. You play naive convincingly." He reached to set his beer bottle on a coaster despite the badly scarred table surface. He leaned close. "You want me to believe that you just happened to rent the apartment next to the house your boss bought. I checked. You rented your place one month after he bought that house. You know what that says to me, Maggie. It says you planned to be near him. And since Bascombe ended up murdered, you know what that says to the cops?"

I raised my eyes and stared into his.

"Premeditation, Maggie. Now, say I'm a cop and I look at the corpse and I look at the time line, you know what I see? Maybe

I see professional rivalry. Maybe I see a jilted lover. But I see one thing perfectly clearly. I see premeditation. Can you argue with that?" The PI attempted to gauge my fear level.

I met his question with only a blank stare. Mine was an honest reaction. I hadn't even considered protesting the assertion that I murdered Bascombe. I was still grappling with the idea that anyone could believe I could have an affair with that man.

"Now look, Maggie. I don't know you, but I've been watching you. I don't think you killed Bascombe."

"Thanks."

Andy ignored my sarcastic tone. "Oh, I did at first. It was so obvious. When the cops didn't arrest you, I wondered why. Then it hit me. You couldn't have killed Bascombe alone. Bascombe was a big man. Sure, you could have stabbed him. The autopsy is consistent with a two-phase stab wound. You could inflict a shallow wound. The perp might have pushed the blade further in or Bascombe might have fallen backwards and done the deed himself. So you could have easily handled that part."

"You saw the autopsy?" I interrupted.

"Not the final or I'd know the answer about the fatal wound." He resumed his evaluation of my culpability. "You couldn't have moved him into that grass—especially keeping him that clean."

"I could have dragged him in a sheet." I protested suddenly insulted by being dismissed as an incompetent.

"Maggie, you should be arguing the other side." He shook his head with exaggerated disgust. "The appropriate answer would have been that you couldn't move him at all, let alone load him into your car—especially since there's no evidence in the vehicle."

"How would you know?"

"Even down the shore, Maggie, you might want to lock up overnight."

I was annoyed by the prospect of Andy going through my personal possessions or personal rentals. "No one calls me Maggie."

"Well, that makes me different, doesn't it?"

I should have hated this guy. My head was perfectly clear on the issue. Some of my other body parts were more indecisive. I watched our interactions with amazed detachment.

"Anyway, once I decided you couldn't have committed the crime alone, I began watching. To see who came by. But your only visitors roughed you up. So I decided no, Maggie isn't the killer. Maggie is a possible victim. Maggie knows too much."

"I'm not naive enough to think you are here to protect me."

"I don't think you're naive at all, Maggie. I said you act naive. I think you and Bascombe were lovers." Suddenly he regarded me with surprise and concern. "You look sick. Are you okay?"

"How could you think that I would be involved . . ." I couldn't even finish the thought. "Do you think that I am that desperate? Sure, David dumped me, but to tell you the truth, I sort of forced his hand. I mean I didn't need any guy hanging around if he wasn't sure. I wouldn't have to stoop . . . to Bascombe. That arrogant, pig-headed, arrogant, stupid, idiotic, arrogant . . ."

When I glanced in PI Beck's direction, I saw that his arms were raised in surrender. When I took a breath, he interrupted. "Okay, okay. Maybe you weren't having an affair with Bascombe. But if you weren't, how the hell did you wind up in the house next door."

"I've told everyone. Luck. Bad luck, but luck. My being next door was a coincidence."

PI Beck's face indicated limited belief in coincidences.

"The police believed me."

"You know, Maggie, I hate to cast a pall on your vacation but my guess is that the police did not believe you. They just do not have enough to arrest you. Yet."

"I haven't heard a word of suspicion from them." What did this guy know anyway?

"Maggie, trust me, they have an eye on you. They don't have any physical evidence but until the finger points at someone else . . ." The PI let the possibility hang in the air and stared at me as I mulled over the information. "If I were you, I'd be work-

ing damn hard to put another suspect in front of that finger."
His tone changed to solicitous. "Who would have wanted to kill
DK Bascombe?"

The answer was clear to me. "Anyone who ever met him." I
walked to the window to watch the sunbathers and swimmers.

"When you make that statement, I hear you saying you could
have done it."

I turned to face the PI. "If I were capable of murder, DK
Bascombe would have been my first victim. I would like to
point out, however, that I am not capable of killing anyone."

"Anyone is, under the right circumstances."

"I was never on the debating team. Let's drop it. I am not a
suspect."

"Right now you may be the only suspect."

I yelped as I dropped onto the sofa. I had forgotten the pain
of flopping on cushions that old. "If I am the prime suspect, why
aren't the cops following me?"

"Who says they aren't?"

I shrugged. "That's true. I wouldn't spot the cops. They would
be a lot better at surveillance than you are."

"Go ahead. Ridicule me. But if I were you, I would think real
hard about who could have killed DK Bascombe."

"The entire case will revolve around hair, skin, and fibers, right?
Why should I worry?"

"Because from what I hear the cops aren't having much luck
with hair, skin, and fibers."

"All the tests aren't back, right?"

"Maybe not but from what I hear the medical examiner
found no skin under Bascombe's nails. The cops found no
prints in his house—which is really odd. I mean no prints. Not
even Bascombe's."

"No hair?"

Andy shook his head.

"No fibers?"

"None that can be matched."

"You're telling me that the murderer went into that house, killed Bascombe, wiped off all the prints, and left no physical evidence."

"Actually, the cops aren't certain where it all happened. He was stabbed in the house but the rest . . . "

"What rest?"

"The rest the cops are being a bit cagey about."

I considered the suspects Detective Dupuy had mentioned. David. Randall Wallace. John Mancotti. Bish Winston and other ex-employees who had moved onto better lives. "I can't think of a soul who would have killed Bascombe—unless wishing counts."

"Think hard, Maggie." The PI slid onto an old vinyl ottoman at my feet. "I can help you. Trust me. We can work together. I can help you."

I lifted my eyes and gazed into those penetrating green-gray orbs. Advantage Beck. I was hooked.

Chapter 14

A mong the things that were hard to explain to the police as well as my friends, was why I played detective with Andy Beck. Hell, it was hard for me to explain my behavior to myself—at least when the PI wasn't nearby to fix me with one of his penetrating, somewhat mocking and totally endearing gazes. When he was with me, I found myself following his orders—for example, jumping in his car to go visit Caroline Bascombe.

I warned Andy that Mrs. Bascombe might recognize me from the crime scene.

"She wanted to know if you are having an affair with her husband."

"Great. So you're dragging me along to visit her! Why? So she can quiz me about my affair with DK?"

"No. I told her you denied any romantic relationship."

"You couldn't tell her flat out that I was not having an affair with her husband?"

"That would have been subjective. I only deal in facts."

"Right."

Andy caught the sarcasm in my voice. "What's wrong?" He scrutinized my contorted features.

"You were following Bascombe. You must be some PI if you concluded that I was having affair with Bascombe."

"You worked with him. You moved in next door. What was I supposed to think?"

I asked if he had ever seen Bascombe and me together.

"I thought you were clever."

"Trust me, I'm not." I shook my head with disgust. "Thinking I am a murderer is one thing, but suspecting me of having an affair with Bascombe . . ." I punctuated the sentence with a shudder.

"Well, he was having an affair with someone at work."

Andy found my shock amusing. "I didn't know anyone could stand DK." I assured Andy that I couldn't.

"Somebody could. Somebody you worked with. I can't believe you don't know."

"I don't know. Tell me."

"I don't know either."

"And you call yourself a PI?"

Andy explained he had enough for a divorce case even without identifying the new flame which he described as "the hot one." Not that he hadn't tried. "This one was new. Brand new."

"How can you not know who the hot one is?"

Andy mumbled something about giving him the slip and watching his old girlfriend.

"Well, she's a likely suspect. The old girlfriend."

"Not really. That's who I was with when Bascombe bought it."

"Good timing, Andy."

We rode in silence. I considered the candidates for the hot one but didn't have any suggestions. Everyone knew how I felt about Bascombe. Why would a woman confide in me that she was having an affair with a man I despised?

To reach Brigantine, we headed for Atlantic City. To the passengers in the cars and buses headed to the gambling mecca, billboards promised cheap food and big stars. None of the signs promised to withdraw the gamblers' life savings. Not that a warning could have deterred those seeking their fortunes at the tables and machines of Atlantic City. However, a traffic jam could slow them down. Andy cut around the backup and headed for a high bridge.

"Where is Bascombe's house?" I asked as we crossed over the span to Brigantine.

"Over there." Andy threw a casual wave in the direction of the town.

I glanced over and saw that Brigantine had grown well over 100% since my last visit. Based on Andy's description, thousands of houses could have belonged to Bascombe. My recollection of Brigantine was of a rustic community with magnificent dunes. We'd never spent much time in the town because of my father's assertion that Brigantine was home to too many green flies. Apparently, he had once been bitten on the Brigantine beach. In his mind that bite translated into infestation. What we drove through on our way to the Bascombe's was a well-manicured upper-middle-class suburb that hardly appeared to play the welcoming host for insects.

The house that Caroline Bascombe held full title to in light of her husband's death reflected, like several nearby homes, an intrusion by modern architecture and big money into an otherwise typical suburban neighborhood. The tall white structure was full of odd angles and set on an even odder angle on an indeterminately shaped lot. A black Mercedes sat in the driveway; the tail of a bright red Porsche peeked out from behind a sharp corner of the building.

If the Bascombes were seeking privacy, they had chosen the wrong architect. The house included more glass than wall—a design feature that a woman with Caroline Bascombe's housekeeping abilities should have rethought.

"Do you think the house has been ransacked?" I pulled on Andy's arm to stop his advancement towards the door.

Andy peered through the window before asking, "What makes you ask that?"

I waved an arm in the direction of the glass wall. "Look in there."

He shrugged. "I didn't figure you were into housekeeping."

"I'm not. David used to say that I believed Martha Stewart was the anti-Christ."

"Funny guy."

"Not really but he was perceptive. However," I paused for emphasis, "even I can see that this place is a mess."

Andy ignored my warnings and pressed the doorbell. We waited for a response. None was forthcoming.

"You know this woman might be dangerous." I had not dismissed Caroline Bascombe as a suspect in her husband's murder.

Andy met my comment with a cynical sneer. "Right. She decided to kill him, so she hired me to tail him in the hopes of having a witness." He pressed the button again.

I didn't point out that he hadn't witnessed the murder. Had Caroline arranged that? What a great plan!

Andy rang the bell a third time before we heard the high-pitched voice of Caroline Bascombe singing a welcome. "Andrew." She grabbed Andy's face in two hands with long fingers further elongated by lengthy red nails. When I first saw Mrs. Bascombe at the crime scene, I had sensed that she was tall but I didn't realize how tall until I saw her lean down to plant a kiss on each of Andy's cheeks. Andy was close to six feet tall. "I was thrilled when you called." I noticed that if she had eschewed the four-inch heels she might have been staring Andy in the eye.

Seeing Caroline Bascombe, I understood the condition of her house. Spending so much time on hair, makeup, and wardrobe would leave few opportunities for housekeeping. I speculated that Caroline Bascombe was considerably more comfortable in the tight black jumpsuit she wore that day than in the preppy attire she had worn to the crime scene. I didn't imagine that she had selected black to show respect for the dead as much as to contrast with her pale white skin and brashly colored makeup of which she had applied generous portions.

Andy's protest that he hated to intrude at a time like this was met with befuddlement. "Oh, you mean because we have to get off to the funeral. We're leaving in a couple of hours. That reminds me. Kids. Kids." She clapped her hands and peered towards a loft overlooking the hall and living room. "It might be a good idea to clean up. Kids? Kids?" When no answer was forthcoming, she shrugged and waved Andy and me into the main room. Mumbling about Donald's artistic aspirations, which she labeled pathetic, she pulled several canvases off the white leather couch and told us to make ourselves comfortable. She tossed the paintings against a glass wall. The landscapes were visible only to those outside the house. So much for sentimental value.

The odd angles of the building's design, the overabundance of windows, and the proximity to the ocean made me feel that we had landed on a remote and uninhabited island. Only the noise of sunbathers rising over the heavy brush of the dunes betrayed the location of the house in a heavily populated area.

DK's widow studied me intently as Andy made the introductions. I was presented to Mrs. Bascombe as Maggie. "You were the . . ."

I nodded to acknowledge my presence at the crime scene before she finished.

"You worked with Donald."

I couldn't tell whether her comment was a question or a statement. I answered with a pursed lip sneer and a nod.

"I can tell you were crazy about him." Mrs. Bascombe knew how to let sarcasm drip off her words.

Beside me I felt Andy relax.

"Well . . . " I glanced toward the loft where the unseen Bascombe children played.

"Don't worry about the kids. They're not his. Those two are probably as happy as anyone to see Donald go." With a high heel pump, she kicked a pile of laundry, apparently clean, out of her way and settled into a modern contraption of white leather straps strung on asymmetrical chrome bars. "You can say anything bad about Donald to me, Maggie." She crossed her legs, neatly wrapping one ankle around the other, and leaned forward as if to coach gossip from me.

"Maggie didn't seem to like DK very much," said Andy.

I frowned at Andy's speaking for me.

"Smart girl. From what I hear, all the ladies at Markshell weren't so smart. You weren't one of Donald's . . ."

The horror on my face confirmed for Mrs. Bascombe that I had never been involved with her husband.

"No." She dragged the word out as she let a smile creep across her dramatic features. "I didn't think so. I was rather confused as to why you had ID'ed the body."

Caroline Bascombe leaned back as I told my story, complete with recollection of perceived hallucinations that were revealed to be real events. I related how DK had kept me from falling into the waves.

"Didn't DK love to strut that body of his!" Caroline Bascombe sounded almost sentimental. "He had some physique. Too bad we didn't have kids. My genes with his. I am no slouch in that area myself." I would be the last to contest that assertion.

"Of course, they might have gotten his personality, which between you and me, was really weird." She shook her head. "But he took care of me and the kids. What the hell am I saying. He bought me, and I was not cheap. Make that inexpensive. First husband." She paused to set the theme. "He ran off with God knows whom or even what and left me penniless—with a lifestyle that I couldn't sustain for more than a month—and I lasted that long only because he died just after Christmas and the collection agencies were too busy to get to me. DK's interest was the answer to my prayers. I mean the guy almost drooled the first time he saw . . . well, let's just say the first time . . . which was no more than an hour after I heard how much money he had made in his latest takeover or buyout or whatever it was he did. But Andrew has heard all this."

I had the feeling that Mrs. Bascombe wanted to reminisce about her late husband. Despite her bravado, her freedom, and her financial gain, I detected a trace of sadness—probably more for what might have been than for what actually was.

"Well, let's celebrate. Want a drink?" She slapped her hands on the arms of her chair and leaned forward to indicate she was anxious to serve.

Andy declined; I asked for a soft drink.

I followed Mrs. Bascombe past a wet bar, which she declared empty, through a dining room equally disheveled as the living area, and into an immaculate kitchen. As she draped herself theatrically across a bright white counter, I gasped—not at her pose but at the city skyline behind her. Atlantic City had never looked better or bigger.

Mrs. Bascombe threw a glance over her shoulder. "Donald liked to watch his money. What can I get you?" As she burrowed through a huge chrome refrigerator for the coke I requested, she continued to speak. I couldn't hear whether her words concerned DK and his gambling habits or the supplies in the refrigerator. "*Voilà!*" She emerged successful with a coke in her hand.

"I never use this room." She waived the can at a spotless array of chrome appliances and glass front cabinets as her high heels click-clacked across a floor so clean a human would be happy to eat off it. "I mean if God had wanted us to cook our food would He have invented takeout?"

"I don't think God invented takeout." Andy had followed us and was leaning against the doorjamb.

"Of course He did, sweetie. God handles everything. That's why DK is dead. Everyone said he deserved it, and he got it."

While Caroline struggled to free the cubes from a plastic ice cube tray—she apparently did not realize she had an automatic ice maker—I gestured to Andy to pursue that topic. If we were visiting on a murder investigation, we weren't going to get a better opportunity than that one. Andy shook his head vehemently.

"You two are cute together." I turned to find Caroline observing our interaction. "Are you two . . .?" She arched her eyebrow considerably higher than I deemed possible. Everything about Caroline Bascombe was arch—and long. Her legs, her nails, the time it took her to get ice cubes into a glass. "Andrew, honey. You're a sweety. If I weren't involved, I'd give you a tumble myself, but the reason I'm glad you dropped by is I had something I wanted to tell you. You're fired." She said the words with a broad but tight smile as she passed me the soda.

"Caroline, no. I am so close."

No one paid attention to the quizzical expression on my face. Close to what?

Caroline busied herself disposing of the coke can. She never glanced Andy's way as she spoke. "Andrew. I have enough money. Richard's wealthy. This was all about revenge and now that Donald is dead, don't you think revenge is overkill, no pun intended." Caroline threw back her head and projected a soprano laugh towards the ceiling.

"But it's your money." Andy protested.

Caroline's eyes met Andy's. "Perhaps not from what you've told me and I am certainly not going to put out my hard-earned money to service the abstract interests of justice." The laugh that accompanied this statement was in alto.

The PI's eyes weren't the only part of his anatomy begging. "Caroline, my fee isn't important. It's the challenge, the opportunity to complete something . . ."

"Andrew, you're a charming guy." Caroline turned to me with a wry smile. "Isn't he charming?"

"Charming." I repeated without an ounce of sincerity. I cursed myself for swallowing Andy's lies—whatever they were.

"Yes, Andrew, you are a charmer." Finally, Caroline got to her next point. "But you are as transparent as saran wrap." She glanced at me for agreement.

"Saran wrap." I muttered wondering what was going on, how she knew, and why I had so much trouble seeing through clear plastic film.

"Andrew," Caroline knew how to play a line, taking her time planting her hands on a center island and leaning forward before she spoke. She captured the PI's gaze with hers. "Andrew, you are interested in one thing only. Your cut. I understand that. Three days ago I would have killed for money." She slapped her fingertips over her lips and released an exaggerated "Oops. Now that was an unfortunate choice of words." Her smile at the irony of her remark persisted as she talked to Andy. "Andrew, I don't need the money. You do. Go ahead. Go for it. All of it. But

I'm not paying you. Now if you'll excuse me, I have to pull an outfit together for the gala event. I suppose I have to wear black."

"You're damn right you'll wear black."

I glanced towards the door and saw Richard Rothman, network news anchor and recent visitor to the Ocean City police station, standing beyond the screen in a bathing costume that included matching trunks and terry cloth jacket with color-coordinated flip flops. That the colors were royal blue, turquoise, and orange rendered the outfit even less attractive. On the bright side, the getup probably looked as good on Rothman as it ever would. The newsman's muscular physique surprised me. The anchorman was compactly yet powerfully built. Rothman rinsed off his feet, slid open the screen, and stepped onto the kitchen floor depositing tiny puddles of wet sand on its immaculate surface. Caroline Bascombe did not appear to notice, let alone mind.

"Andy, nice to see you." The anchorman bounced across the room so that his height varied greatly depending on whether he was airborne or landlocked. He shook Andy's hand vigorously and warmly. "Guess you're glad this is all over."

"Hello." Rothman covered the kitchen in three steps and took my hand. "I'm Richard Rothman. We haven't met. I recognize you from the police station."

"Maggie Daniels, Richard Rothman." I didn't correct Andy. I found the possibility that Rothman would be calling me anything again rather remote. Meg. Maggie. What did it matter?

"Maggie. Nice to meet you. Thank you for helping the police." Rothman thought I had helped the cops. Only the police could have told him that. The tension was just slipping from my body when he added, "I'm sure they'll clear your name quickly."

Chapter 15

"**A**ndy what was *that* about?" *That* was our visit to Caroline Bascombe's.

"You heard." Andy worked his way through traffic towards the bridge from Brigantine to Atlantic City.

"Sure, I heard that you knew Richard Rothman, something you chose not to share with me when I mentioned seeing him."

"I couldn't discuss a case."

"This is no longer a case. You were fired. Tell me what's going on."

"You heard."

Andy was right. I had heard—but none of the information made sense to me.

"You asked her to keep you on. Whatever you were working on, it wasn't the divorce."

"I was working on the divorce but . . ." He hemmed and hawed for twenty seconds before adding, "from a particular perspective." Claiming client privilege, he refused to define that perspective.

"Andy I am not a complete dope. You were after money. Bascombe's dead. You can tell me. What is the story?"

Andy, however, knew how to keep a secret. He didn't respond to nagging. He didn't respond to flattery. He didn't respond to flirtation, but that might have been because I am really bad at flirting.

"At least you can tell me why you had to drag me along."

I refused to believe his first claim, that he liked my company. I put no more credence in his second explanation that it was beneficial for me to know Caroline Bascombe. When he mumbled his third reason, I found one I could believe.

"It was a litmus test?"

"Women always know."

I had told Andy repeatedly that I had not been involved with my boss, yet he believed my claim only after watching Caroline Bascombe and me interact.

"Is that why you ran back to say good-bye? To check my story out?" I found it odd that their farewell included a long gaze in my direction. "What did she say?"

"She said, 'No way.'"

"Any particular reason?"

"Well, for one thing she believed you were too smart."

His tone warned me I might not find the other reason as flattering.

"What else?"

After an exaggerated display of hemming and hawing, he indicated that DK would have found certain parts of my anatomy too small.

"They are not that small." My inflection was devoid of defensiveness. "It's what I'm wearing."

I glanced at Andy in time to see him blush. He let the conversation dwindle to an awkward silence which I, true to form, filled.

"I can't . . . you believed that I could . . . " I shuddered but not from the breeze in the convertible. "I told you . . . thinking I am a murderer is one thing but believing I would have an affair with that man . . . " I shook my head. "You'd better take me home."

"Look, Maggie, if we are going to work together, I had to know."

I was screaming into the wind as we pulled onto the highway, "Who said we are working together? And, my name is not Maggie. Besides, I think it's pretty obvious who killed Bascombe."

"Tell me." Andy's smile mocked me but his direct tone told me he was really interested.

"Caroline is having an affair with Richard Rothman. That's obvious."

"So?"

"So, they needed DK out of the way."

"Divorce, remember?"

"Mrs. Bascombe wanted it all."

"Richard Rothman could buy and sell DK a hundred times over."

I recited the names of celebrities the general public thought wealthy who had ended up bankrupt.

"Richard Rothman is not the kind of man who squanders his money. You can tell that by looking at him."

"If I judged him just by looking at him, I wouldn't expect to find him with Caroline Bascombe."

"What's that mean?"

"She's a mite theatrical wouldn't you say."

"And you don't think there's a fine line between television news and entertainment." Andy broadsided me with social commentary. "Not to mention, if you compare their heights you'll note that he is always eye-level with two of her more salient strong points."

I folded my arms across my chest and stared at the blur of pine trees.

Andy continued his protest. "Look, they didn't do it. I know these people. The killer, or killers, remain at large."

Between exit 38 and exit 30 of the Garden State Parkway, Andy presented his case for Caroline and Rothman's innocence, my role as a suspect, and our common interest. He wanted me to believe his motives. He wanted to catch a murderer. I needed to prove I wasn't that person.

I ignored his assessment of my needs and addressed his efforts. "You are not after a murderer, Andy. I'm not sure what you are after, but it has nothing to do with the murder."

"I think it does. Maybe we can learn more at the funeral."

"Funeral?"

"I thought I could drive you to Bascombe's funeral."

"Yeah, I didn't understand how they can have the funeral already? Shouldn't they be checking out his body or something?"

"A knife wound in the back is pretty clear-cut. No pun intended. I haven't noted popular demand to keep DK Bascombe around. The whole family is anxious to get him into the ground and out of their hair. So what do you say, we could drive to New York tonight."

"I am not interrupting my vacation to go to DK Bascombe's funeral."

"All the other suspects will attend."

"I'm not a suspect."

In response, the PI only chuckled.

"It's true. Detective Dupuy asked me about a lot of other people."

"And you don't think she asked them about you?"

I changed tacks. "Those other suspects won't go to the funeral. Trust me. None of them liked him any more than I did."

"All the more reason to go and put a nice little patina on your relationship with Bascombe."

"No one would expect me to interrupt my vacation to go to my boss's funeral."

"Not if you were in Tahiti." Andy had an answer for everything. "If I wanted to keep my job after a shakeup I would be at the funeral networking like hell."

"Andy, you claim you are helping me, but I am mature enough to make my own decisions, and I have made one. I am not going to Bascombe's funeral."

Chapter 16

A ndy picked me at 5 P.M. and we headed north to New
York for Bascombe's funeral. I wasn't sure how Andy
had worn me down or how he had wheedled an invitation to spend the night in my apartment. "We can go tonight and
stay at your place." He had presented the idea as a given.

"Whoa," had been my response. Inviting a marginally shady
character onto my porch in a quiet little beach town was one
thing; having him spend the night in my apartment in New York
was another.

"I can sleep on the couch."

"I sleep on the couch." I had lied. "It's an efficiency."

Andy volunteered to sleep on the floor. I confessed. I had a bedroom, a bed and a sleep sofa. I agreed to let Andy use the latter.

After four failed starts—Andy's convertible, he informed me,
was an early Mustang and doing incredibly well for a car that
had passed its twentieth birthday—Andy and I headed north to
Bascombe's funeral.

After Andy dropped me and his bag in front of my brown-
stone on the Upper West Side, I sat on the steps and waited for
his return, less to mark the correct spot than to avoid carrying

his heavy duffel up three flights of stairs. What had he packed for an overnight trip to a funeral?

As I watched Andy approach with a long and confident stride, I was amazed by how easily the boy who declared himself small-town fit in on the streets of New York. My subconscious had been hoping that by appearing hopelessly naive and out-of-place the PI would lose all his appeal. But he didn't. Not as he walked down the street towards me. Not as he guided me down crowded blocks of Columbus. Not as he maneuvered the intricacies of ordering at a less than hospitable restaurant. For a guy who described himself as sort of a hick, Andy was surprisingly suave. And for a man who defined his role as an investigative partner, surprisingly attentive.

"Why did you hate Bascombe so much?" Andy waited until the main course to turn the topic to business.

"Hate? Hate is a strong word. I didn't really hate him. He didn't have that big of an impact on my life. Well, okay, he did. So I guess . . . when he was acting up . . . yeah maybe I did hate him."

Great. I'd just stated that I hated the murder victim. "I don't suppose you're wearing a wire, are you?"

"One thing you never have to worry about with me is collusion with the cops." Andy stared at me as he took a long sip of wine. "Plus, I thought you had nothing to hide."

"I don't. I just don't want to go on the record with my feelings about Bascombe."

"Off the record. I repeat my question. Why did you hate him?"

I sighed. It was hard to describe working for DK Bascombe. Almost anything I said would have made me sound paranoid rather than making Bascombe sound sadistic.

"Well?" Andy was growing impatient.

"Bascombe played mind games—not just with me—with everyone. He would tell you to do something, order you actually, and then belittle you in public for following orders."

"And if you didn't follow orders?"

"Same response. He'd berate you in public for not doing whatever it was well enough. Of course, if you implemented your plan well, he hated you, too, because he hadn't done it. No idea was good unless it was his. This guy, Bishop Winston, came up with a good plan shortly before he left. Bascombe told him he was stupid, fired him, and a month later resurrected the idea as his. At that point he considered the plan brilliant."

"Was he fair with money?"

"He'd dangle rewards. He'd pit one employee against the other. Neither employee would ever see a dime. Cash flow would interfere."

"So the company had cash flow problems."

"According to Bascombe anyway. The problem got worse after he came. We're having problems with suppliers because of our payment record."

Andy's entrée was almost finished. My plate remained full as I criticized Bascombe's style and substance. When I at last dug into my penne arrabiatta, I knew that my arguments had not been persuasive. To understand Bascombe's abusiveness, one had to experience it. "It loses a lot in the translation."

As we walked to my apartment I noticed that Andy's hand brushed mine casually on an average of twice a block. An accident? It was no accident that mine was always in position awaiting his touch. Was my behavior stupid? Rash? Incomprehensible? I thought so, but the realization didn't stop me. It didn't even slow me down.

Sure, I noticed that when the PI described his varied interests, he always omitted key information that would provide a glimpse under his surface. Of course, I understood that Andy was personable, charming, but above all, secretive—a characteristic he hid well through his loquacious demeanor. My brain was functioning on all cylinders. My emotions, however, were operating independently.

The toughest part of the evening was climbing the three flights to my apartment without appearing to struggle for breath. I suspected my breathlessness was caused more by the PI's presence that the forty-seven steps. Andy handled the three flights easily. I guess I didn't take his breath away.

Was I nuts? I barely knew this man and yet he was about to enter my apartment and enjoy the hospitality to whatever level he requested. Did he realize that? If he did, he didn't let on. He launched into a nighttime routine laying out his clothes for the next day, making up the sofa bed and asking to use the bathroom. Maybe Andy wasn't ready to make the stupid mistake I was. I visualized his friend Charlene in the orange bathing suit and understood that perhaps I didn't measure up. Less than five percent of the population did.

While Andy busied himself with bedtime activities, I wandered into the tiny bedroom to mimic his activities. Picking appropriate nightwear was difficult unless I knew Andy's intent. My interests didn't count. I wasn't about to throw myself at this man if he didn't appreciate me. My eyes flipped from silk to flannel and back again. Without making a decision, I flopped onto the bed exasperated. When I rolled over onto my stomach, I noticed the first sign. Someone had made my bed more neatly than I ever had. I had a philosophical objection to making beds at all, let alone with the precision this one had been made. I sat bolt upright and surveyed the room. The signs were subtle but many.

People often mistook me for sloppy. At home or in the office they assumed, because they did not understand the pattern, that my things were carelessly strewn. Not so. Everything had a place, and I knew the location. As I scanned the room, I saw many violations. I began to examine each surface, each drawer.

"Something wrong?"

I was working so intently that I hadn't heard Andy approach but not so intently that I didn't notice that he had chosen baggy and nondescript sweatpants and a white T-shirt for sleepwear. I didn't care. Romance was no longer in my game plan either.

"Someone's been in here."

"I'm assuming that's a statement, not an accusation."

I stared at Andy with a perplexed expression. I had never considered that he might be the intruder. "Why would I suspect you?"

"I am practically a stranger whom you invited into your home."

"I think I've got bigger problems with uninvited guests." I explained my suspicions.

"Maybe Mr. Right returned for his things."

I shook my head. David had departed with all his worldly possessions to emphasize that he would not be coming back. "Someone uninvited was in here and went through all my stuff." I recited for him all the articles that I had found moved.

"Is anything missing?"

Again, I shook my head. "Not that I can identify."

"We should call the police."

"Yeah, right. They'll rush right over for this case."

"Sorry. Forgot where I was." He sat on the bed beside me—for comfort not for proximity. Whatever electricity that had been generated earlier had been turned off either by me or events, I didn't know which.

"So, who do you think your visitor was? I think given that cash and jewelry is still here we should rule out your standard second story man. Did you check for signs of forced entry?"

Andy took charge of the case. His conclusion was that the intruder had gained access with a key. He wasn't happy to learn how many keys were outstanding.

"I let people stay here. Do you know what hotel rooms cost in this city?"

He didn't care. "Tomorrow after the funeral we change the locks."

"But I want to get back . . ."

His withering glance cut me off, ". . . after we change the locks."

I slumped on the edge of the bed. Once more he sat beside me, but his mind was on business. "Now let's talk about why this happened? Do you think the break-in had anything to do with Bascombe's murder?"

"I don't have anything to do with Bascombe's murder." I shouted the word "I."

"Okay. Okay. Calm down." He patted my clenched fist. "Relax. Even if you aren't involved . . ." The glance I shot in his direction compelled him to interject, "and I don't think you are, someone may not know that. Just like the police found out that you were next door, so might the perpetrator."

"Do you think the cops were in here?"

Andy's answer was definite. "Not without a warrant. Not those cops. They don't break the law."

I shrugged. "Well, that's all I can think of—that the cops broke in to see if I was hiding something."

"Or to plant something." Andy was suddenly energized.

I didn't understand.

"The intruder might have looked around while they were in here, but that might not be why they were in here. Start checking around again. See if anyone put something in your apartment."

Andy seemed more than happy to help me search. It was 1 A.M. by the time I found what I was looking for. The paper was in a file on my desk. "Why did the intruder think the cops would ever find this?" I held the paper by the corner.

"Cops are good at that. Trust me they would have found it. Check your hard drive. I'm sure the perp printed it here and left a copy."

"I'm surprised he didn't save the document in a directory called 'murder.plan.'" When I reviewed the list of files on my hard drive, the file name designed to attract the cops attention was easy to spot "Bascombe.itn." The document contained details of Bascombe's Labor Day plans as well as a split infinitive. "Well, this certainly would have cleared me. I never split an infinitive."

"Right." Andy leaned over my shoulder to see the screen. "No jury would have convicted. Check the date and time on that document." Andy's shoulder brushed mine as he monitored the action. I tried to hide any reaction; he did not appear to have one. "The perp had a leisurely time. Looked through all your stuff, browsed your hard drive, and, assuming I am correct, took the time to reset the calendar and date on this computer to create the document."

I flipped over to check the date and time. The document had supposedly been created two weeks before I left for vacation. I pulled up my calendar. "Aha! I was home that night. That document was not created when the clock indicates." When I smiled at the PI, I detected the slightest hint of skepticism in his eyes.

"Well, let's get that letter bagged. I'll take it for evidence."

"You're going to give that to the cops?"

"You think I'm stupid, don't you? No, I am not going to give the letter to the cops. I am going to call in a favor and see if there are traceable prints on this letter. What we find may help us, but in case it doesn't, don't clean until we know we won't need to check for prints."

"Not a problem."

As I watched the PI search the kitchen for a plastic bag and take custody of the letter, my face contorted with concern. Was I making a terrible mistake?

"Don't worry." Andy didn't understand that his possession of the incriminating document had put the worried expression on my face. "Everything will be okay." His lips brushed my forehead lightly. He hesitated before pulling away and suggesting that we get a good night's sleep. I smiled wanly and disappeared into my bedroom. I was not enjoying my vacation.

Chapter 17

Having his funeral at a mortuary that buried the rich and famous represented the pinnacle of social achievement for DK Bascombe. Too bad he had to miss the big event. The establishment's staff chose a variety of stances and expressions to indicate their boredom as we made our way past them. To get into Bascombe's memorial service all you had to do was act like a mourner—although in truth most of the guests were suppressing grins. There were no swarms of swooning teenagers to restrain as there had been six months earlier when the mortuary buried the lead singer of a heavy metal band. No crowds trying to get a peek at friends bidding a centenarian movie star farewell. The security staff, each with the face and physique of an aspiring actor, suppressed yawns.

In the lobby, I saw many familiar faces in a much larger sea of unfamiliar faces. As Andy and I fought our way through the crowd, I spotted Lindy Sharpe standing with Suzanne Wing from marketing. The two women were watching our approach with a mixture of surprise, curiosity, and, most blatantly, envy. As I got closer, they regarded me with the awe reserved for the winner of the lottery or the Nobel prize. I earned the look for having Andy in tow. I glanced at the PI. He had cleaned up nicely for the funeral. He demonstrated no show of wealth but apparently didn't skimp on clothes—at least dress ones. I was willing to bet his sport coat was Italian. With the nattily cut pants, his appearance stacked up against any of the high price suits with whom we mingled.

"Nice to meet you." Lindy elbowed Suzanne out of the way to greet Andy with a toss of her strawberry blonde curls and more enthusiasm than I deemed appropriate. After all, I could tell by the expression on her face she believed Andy was my romantic interest. "Well, Meg, my dear, you appear to be having an enjoyable and fruitful vacation." Lindy vamped for Andy's benefit.

"Appearances can be deceiving." I warned my co-worker.

"But not always." Andy added jovially. He flashed his best smile at Lindy as I worked to discern the meaning of his words.

"You're from Ocean City?" Lindy focused on Andy's remarkable eyes. Her grin was exaggerated; her behavior, almost manic. She thrust her right leg forward to guarantee that Andy took note of her shapely limbs.

The PI failed to notice. He simply nodded in answer to her question.

Lindy shifted her weight to thrust her pelvis forward. "And that's where you met our Meg?" Lindy was pouring on the charm.

This time Andy smiled and nodded my way.

"Nice work." Lindy murmured in my direction before adding in full voice, "Are you guys going inside?" She nodded towards the room where Bascombe's body lay for viewing. Lindy's question was an invitation delivered with more enthusiasm to Andy than to me.

"Yes." "No." Andy and I answered simultaneously. I in the negative; he in the positive.

"Come on, Maggie. You went to all the trouble of putting on a black suit. Let's go inside." Andy gestured for Lindy to precede us and grabbed my arm to provide heavy-handed direction. I had no good reason to resist except an unflappable faith in the certainty that I would say or do something stupid—which is odd because death is no stranger in my life—to the extent that there's no one left who has to invite me to Christmas dinner. Yet I'd never felt comfortable around death. Or mourners.

I never regretted going inside even if Detective Dupuy did toss a number of dirty looks and meaningful comments my way when she saw me with Andy. Enduring the cop's skepticism and disapproval was worth it just to see Caroline Bascombe in action. The widow should have charged admission.

Caroline's funeral clothes consisted of a black satin suit with a tight skirt that covered the top 25% of her thighs. Sheer black stockings stretched from that point to four-inch stiletto heels. The jacket with braid-trimmed peplum emphasized her tiny waist. She'd chosen a hat that would take her from mourning to evening—a narrow slit of satin adorned with netting and a single feather. The widow looked happy. She looked beautiful. She looked like a hooker. An extremely successful hooker.

Even though I suspected he had made all the arrangements, I questioned the appropriateness of Richard Rothman's attendance. After all, Caroline and DK were still married and technically Rothman was the widow's date. Not that anyone knew that. The anchorman had positioned himself across the room from Caroline—but he never took his eyes off her. On his face, I detected a combination of love, horror, and fear.

With Andy at the helm we sailed toward the front of the room. The PI appeared anxious to see DK Bascombe in his coffin. I was anxious, too, but in a more figurative sense. Andy was literally in a hurry. A garish display of flowers told me that someone had either died or won the Kentucky Derby. The sweet aroma was suffocating. Who on earth had sent all the floral displays? I couldn't imagine that DK had that many friends. I moved close enough to verify that at least three of the arrangements were from Markshell suppliers. That made sense.

Andy joined the receiving line but I kept moving. I did sneak a peek at DK Bascombe in his blue silk-lined casket. The quick glance confirmed that, even after several days dead, DK looked nasty. But better than he had in a while. Blue was his color. I found an inconspicuous spot and a pillar to lean on while I watched the activities.

"I wish Caroline could calm down a little."

I was surprised to find Richard Rothman at my side. His eyes were on Caroline, but he was talking to me. What possessed the newsman to confide in me? Although I wanted to reply "Anyone would be happy to get rid of the worst husband on record," I chose words more in keeping with the occasion. "She's had a shock."

"She's elated and you know it. I know it and I believe Detective Dupuy knows it."

I had to agree that every attendee with a triple digit IQ knew it; only the minister appeared surprised and shocked by the realization.

Rothman turned his body towards mine and whispered in my ear. I enjoyed the feel of his $2,000 suit on my bare lower arm. Across the room, I watched Lindy's puzzled expression. How in five days had I not only picked up a handsome stranger but had come to be on intimate terms with a celebrity who the previous year had been voted the most trusted man in America? "I'm relieved this episode is over. I saw no need for the divorce to be messy. Caroline can be extremely vindictive. I used to think she was unemotional but that was until I watched her try to screw DK. Not that he didn't deserve it. That man put her through hell. He enjoyed humiliating her."

"He enjoyed humiliating everyone."

"Were you having an affair with him?" He asked matter-of-factly.

"No." I spoke too loudly. Several mourners turned to stare; Detective Dupuy was one of them.

"He was having an affair with someone at Markshell. Caroline thinks that's how it started."

I didn't ask what "it" was. Again, I professed that I was not Bascombe's partner in the affair and had no idea who was. "I mean . . ." I shuddered at the idea.

John Mancotti, Markshell's head of administration, was working his way towards us through the crowd. I had last seen John in my dreams shortly before Detective Dupuy and Officer Timmy

Borden had awakened me. John had been one of the parties knocking on my skull.

John made a point of being impeccably attired for every occasion. Bascombe's funeral was no exception. John had managed to tone down every hot style and color of the season so that his outfit offered a subdued version of the latest *GQ* cover suitable for mourning. He had done the same thing with his usually brilliant smile.

I attributed John's approach to a desire to meet Richard Rothman; he had never been particularly interested in spending time with me. On the rare occasion he was forced to meet with me, John always missed eye contact by five degrees. The effect was disconcerting. I always kept glancing over my shoulder to see who was behind me. Usually, no one was. The day of the funeral Richard Rothman occupied the spot.

"Meg." John made eye contact with Richard Rothman as he grabbed my hand. "How good of you to suspend your vacation plans."

My antenna went up. How did he know that I had interrupted my vacation? Did he keep track of everyone in the company or did he have a special interest in my case? Who was I kidding? Of course everyone at Markshell had a special interest in my case. Did I think that because I had not shared the details of my vacation, my run-ins with Bascombe both dead and alive, remained a secret? Were they eyeing me now as a suspect? I surveyed the room and found more than a few eyes focused on me. Me or Richard Rothman? I didn't know.

I surmised that John Mancotti had been talking to me during my reflections because he stared at me as if he expected a response. "I'm sorry, John. I'm a little distracted."

Richard Rothman saved the moment by politely introducing himself and just as politely excusing himself, leaving me alone with John. Oddly enough, John did not seem to mind.

"Meg, I heard all about it." He leaned closer than I found appropriate or desirable, "I never knew you and DK were . . ."

"Were what?"

"You know . . . involved."

"You're kidding, right?"

Apparently he wasn't because he continued comforting me in a soft voice. "I feel for you. I do. I understand that if you were involved, you would have no one to talk to . . ." John grasped my hand and squeezed. I peered into his eyes and for the first time they were making contact with mine. "I know it's hard when you lose someone . . ." With that, a hand dragged John, still under the impression that I was Bascombe's lover, away from my side and into the crowd.

Lindy took advantage of my freedom to sidle up to me. "What's this with you and Richard Rothman. You have been making some interesting friends on vacation." Her smile did not cover the strain on her face.

"It's been an unusual week." I chose understatement.

"Meg." Lindy gazed over my shouldered as she gathered her thoughts. "You and Bascombe weren't . . ."

I didn't let Lindy finish the thought. "You weren't going to ask me if was romantically involved with Bascombe, were you?"

Her eyes were tear-filled as she nodded.

"I'll forgive you for asking."

"I'm sorry." She dabbed at her eyes with a tissue. "I just would have felt so betrayed." She attempted to change the mood of the conversation. "How have you been spending your time? You certainly have a great tan."

I ignored her sarcasm. "I've been busy."

Lindy eyed Andy and said only two words, "I see."

I gazed across the room where the PI was involved in deep conversation with a tall blond man in a tan linen suit inappropriate after Labor Day. My hormones did a dance. My reaction wasn't to the blond, although he was quite capable of stirring female hormones. My chemical makeup was responding to Andy.

"Lucky girl." Lindy watched as Andy moved towards the back of the room. She made her excuses and, ample breasts thrust forward, took long strides in the same direction.

John Mancotti, free of business constraints, worked his way back to my side. As he stared into my eyes I realized for the first time how handsome he was. His deep brown eyes struck me as much more attractive when focused on mine. "I hope all this hasn't been too traumatic for you." He wrapped an arm around my waist. I might have learned why I was in his grip, but an inappropriately spirited contretemps erupted across the hall and John, in his role of meeting planner, had to investigate leaving me free to suffer the attentions of Bish Winston, Markshell's former vice president of marketing.

The term loosey-goosey could have been coined to describe Bishop. His long limbs dangled from their sockets in conflicting directions. The effect was that of a string puppet manipulated by a hyperactive two-year-old. His loose gait carried Bishop in my direction. "Meg, Honey Bunny." The name was in no way indicative of our relationship. Bish had similar names for all the employees of Markshell—at least the women.

The crowd recoiled from Bishop as he loped across the room. Only Bishop would think, or rather not think, to smoke in the presence of a corpse. He took a deep drag on his cigarette as his last step delivered him to my side. He was still exhaling when he leaned down to kiss me. I grimaced and averted my lips so that his smoke wafted by my ear.

"So somebody finally blew the stupid shit away. 'Bout time. I'm surprised someone didn't take care of that oversized mother-er a long time ago."

I eyed the crowd nervously. Who could overhear Bishop's comments? The short list included those who couldn't. "No one blew him away, Bish. He was stabbed."

"Shoot him. Stab him. I don't care. Just do him. Yahoo!" I jumped at Bishop's rebel call. "No one deserved it more than that carpetbagging bastard."

I glanced in Detective Dupuy's direction and noted she was moving closer. Her eyes never turned in our direction, but we were obviously the target of her maneuvers.

Bishop leaned down conspiratorially. "Now I hear you were right there when the happy event took place. Don't tell me I have you to thank for this?"

I shot a glance toward Detective Dupuy and met her eyes straight on. Whether or not the detective heard Bishop depended on the acuity of her hearing. The policewoman was young; she didn't miss the words. But even if she had, she did not miss the tone.

"Bishop." I said through gritted teeth. "We are being watched, and, no matter how much we think it's a joke, the members of the law enforcement establishment aren't laughing."

Bishop hovered over me. He had me trapped. "Where?" He flung his head from left to right.

"Anywhere." I couldn't guarantee that no one in closer proximity than Detective Dupuy was listening to our conversation.

"Well, shit. Anyone who knows us knows we wouldn't hurt a fly . . . even a disgusting insect like DK Bascombe."

"They don't know us, Bishop."

"Hell." He straightened. I relaxed in response. "You don't seem like no homicidal maniac." His comment attracted stares from nearby mourners.

"How kind of you to notice." I said sweetly. "I try not to." I lowered my voice. "I suggest you do the same."

"I try. I try." He waved his cigarette. "Hell, where are the ashtrays?" He surveyed the room. "Sorry, honey. I got to get rid of this butt. I'll see you at the cemetery. I want to make sure they put that little shit in the ground." He winked. At 6'6", Bishop was one of the few who could accurately call DK a little shit.

The crowd had created a space around Bishop and me. The nearby mourners eyed Bishop with reactions from disgust to amusement. Only one reaction concerned me. Detective Dupuy did not appear amused.

"Who was that?" Andy's tone told me he really wanted to ask, "What was that?"

"Bishop Winston. He was the sales VP who got demoted and finally tossed out when Markshell brought Bascombe in. Likely candidate, isn't he?"

Andy shrugged. "If I were he, I would have killed Markshell not Bascombe. Plus, do you think that guy could pull off a murder? He could barely pull off getting to the door."

Brains might not have been his long suit, but Bishop had the brute strength. "I just don't think he could do anything quietly. If Bishop had done it, he would have awakened me."

Andy sighed. "If you were a light sleeper, Ms. Daniels, we would be a lot better off."

Andy wandered off in search of whatever he hoped to find at the funeral, leaving me to fend off the greetings of more co-workers who, since the murder, had developed a sudden interest in me.

Even Randall "Don't-Call-Me-Randy" Wallace sought out my company. Randall, who possessed all the traits of a classic computer nerd without any of the technical ability, worked in accounting. Randall carried no more than 150 pounds on the 6'6" frame that he reduced by inches by hunching over. His hollowed out face and oversized glasses made his eyes protrude even more than nature dictated, which was plenty. Given that he shaved his head weekly, it was unlikely the world would ever know the color of his hair. The total effect was that of a human caught forever in the process of transmogrifying into a fly.

"Meg." Randall stretched my name into three syllables all enunciated through his nose. "I heard what happened to you in Ocean City. It must have been terrible." Randall gave each word and each syllable within each word equal accent. His lack of emphasis made him hard to understand.

"It was not really a problem."

"But it's so terrible about Mr. Bascombe. I heard you were right next door and that your window overlooked the crime scene. Did you see the murder?"

"Randall, if I saw the murder, I would have mentioned it."

"You mean you didn't see a thing."

I shook my head.

"You must have heard something."

Again, I shook my head.

"That's hard to believe."

"Yeah, so I've been told."

Randall studied me with a thoughtful expression I had learned was reserved for murder suspects. Then, he changed the subject. "You know, Meg, when you come back from vacation we won't be seeing each other any more."

"Really, Randall?" I had seen Randall once a month, at most.

"You've been away. You don't know. Yesterday was my last day at Markshell. I've been downsized. Don't you hate that word? Downsized." He let the word hang in the air for a minute as he contemplated its full meaning. "I never believed corporate cutbacks could affect me, but here I am being cut back like an overgrown bush." He chuckled quietly but still too loudly to be appropriate for the setting. Randall believed he had made a pun. "I thought I was too valuable. But I guess in this day and age no one is too valuable. Or at least no one is seen as valuable." He pursed his lips and nodded. "But I don't hold a grudge against Bascombe. I even bought a new suit to show there were no hard feelings."

I felt angry but not at Randall. Who had sold him the ridiculous suit he was wearing? Cheap material. Bad cut. Hideous color. Although I didn't really like Randall, I deplored the idea of someone taking advantage of him. Of course, this was Randall. Maybe he genuinely liked the outfit. He seemed content.

"As a matter of fact, now I can see that this was the best thing that ever happened to me. You'll see."

Now Randall had my interest. "What do you mean, I'll see?" I reacted so violently that Randall jumped.

"Nothing."

I immediately regretted frightening Randall, but what had he heard? I wanted to know.

"Nothing about you. About me. You'll see that I am going to do well. I am sure of it. This is the best thing that ever happened to me. That's why I came today. I mean DK Bascombe had to do what he did. He was a businessman. Maybe a better one than we all suspected."

Randall continued talking, I think his conversation was about how much Bascombe would be missed, which to my mind was not at all. I didn't hear a thing he said. Laurie Gold was in the room.

I strained to see if David had accompanied his new lover to the funeral, but I didn't see him among the crowd. Laurie was alone and networking furiously. I watched her with a combination of awe and disgust as she moved from guest to guest. Laurie was all in black. Black suit, black hose, black cell phone. Repeatedly, she glanced in my direction without making eye contact. She knew that I was watching her. She knew that I knew she knew. She also knew that I knew that she knew that I knew. She must have realized that someone had hit me with the news about her and David. Why else would she appear so interested in me? I chuckled. What would Laurie think if she knew it was the cops who had told me about her affair with David?

After verifying that I noted her popularity, Laurie elbowed her way through the crowd. She dismissed Randall with a single glance. "Meg, I heard you were nearby when the murder happened. DK's death is such a shock, isn't it? Last Friday he was at work. Just being DK, you know. DK was always so full of life." She paused for effect. Her eyes were wide with excitement but they almost always were. "I cannot believe that this happened to our DK." I had yet to say anything, but Laurie had yet to notice. "I just can't imagine who would hurt DK. He was respected in the community and the industry and in the company."

Where did Laurie get her information?

She gazed off into the distance, in the increasingly crowded room that meant the back of a very long and very expensive man's suit. "We won't see the likes of him again."

"I sure hope not." I mumbled.

Laurie appeared puzzled. She opened her mouth to ask another question. I didn't find out what it was because John Mancotti appeared at my side to tell me that Paul Markshell, the owner of Markshell Publications, wanted to see me.

Chapter 18

"What did Markshell want?" Andy pressured me for information as we rode in a cab towards my office. The PI had insisted on the visit to the Markshell headquarters before we met the locksmith at my apartment. He wanted to check for planted evidence. I had smiled at the suggestion as if I believed Andy did everything for my own good. I hated to admit it, but I needed his help—no matter what his motives. If someone had made the effort to hide false evidence in my home, why leave my office untouched? I felt safer having Andy make the discovery than the cops—if they hadn't already.

Andy repeated his question. "What did Markshell want?'

"It's always hard to tell with that guy." Most attributed the entrepreneur's unpredictable and inappropriate behavior to encroaching senility. I bet that was what the assembled mourners believed when Markshell opened the eulogy with the acknowledgment that most of the attendees probably hadn't liked DK. "Hell, I didn't like him much myself. DK wasn't a likeable guy. Being liked, however, was not what DK Bascombe was all about." Such wise words! Just how senile was Markshell? If the stories were true, the founder of Markshell Publications had been acting in an eccentric way since his late twenties.

"What did he say exactly?"

That was also hard to tell. Markshell's monologue rambled as his voice rose and fell in cadences unrelated to the meaning of his words. "The one thing I could get is that he's giving me a bonus for finding the body."

"You didn't find the body."

"Try telling that to Markshell." I had explained that I had simply identified Bascombe after his corpse was spotted through an air search. "Good work, girl," he had responded. "I think he believes I was flying the plane that located Bascombe's body."

"Did you tell him you weren't?"

I turned and stared at Andy who was monitoring the taxi driver's skills nervously. "Andy, why would I protest too much? I attempted to clarify. If the man wants to give me a couple thousand bucks, why should I protest? He can afford it. I deserve a reward for enduring Bascombe all these months."

Andy shrugged and nodded in agreement before my words struck him. "Thousands?"

"That was a word he used."

"One thousand?"

"Put an 's' at the end."

"Maggie, don't make me jump through hoops. What did Markshell think your finding Bascombe's body was worth?"

"Around ten thousand dollars. He said I spared the family a lot of pain. I think Markshell likes Caroline Bascombe."

Andy flashed a cynical grin. "I think Markshell likes Caroline's breasts. He never took his eyes off them. Even when he was speaking."

"Too bad. If he had glanced up, he might have glimpsed the grin that showed just how much she loved his eulogy."

Andy sat silently for four blocks before exclaiming, "I can't believe he gave you that money. Boy, everyone was wasting their sympathy on you today."

I ignored his first comment. "What do you mean 'everyone,' 'sympathy'?"

"Everyone was feeling sorry for you—being caught in such an embarrassing situation and all."

My eyes challenged him to go on.

"They feel bad if you really cared for the guy . . ."

"Wait a minute." I cut him off. "Give me the executive summary on this topic."

He cleared his throat. "It seems that in the course of questioning the employees at Markshell, Detective Dupuy created the impression that you and Bascombe . . ."

"Everyone would think that was ridiculous." I dismissed the idea easily.

"No." His voice attempted a calming effect. "Everyone would think that they were stupid to have missed it. And then, they would recall incidents that they would now see differently. Maybe, how obvious that you protested too much—always claiming to hate Bascombe and all."

I stared at the PI with disbelief. "Let me see if I understand this correctly. Choice one: I was in love with the guy and was only pretending to hate him as a cover. Choice two: I really hated the guy and killed him. Either way I lose."

Andy sighed. "Though choice one is not a capital crime and carries no prison sentence. I'd go with that scenario."

"What about the truth?" I protested.

"Truth has very little to do with the U.S. legal system. You watch TV. You know that." Andy dug in his wallet for cab fare. "For me, it's deductible."

The taxi dumped us in front of the old building that housed Markshell Publications. It was depressing enough that I was walking into the office on a vacation day. Now I knew that I was walking in as a marked woman. Killer or whore.

"They all think whore." Andy tried to be encouraging.

At the twin glass doors I slid my security pass into the slot. Andy pushed on the heavy metal handle. "Try again." I did. He pushed. We were still on the sidewalk.

I felt a sick feeling in the pit of my stomach. I had been fired, and no one even had the decency to tell me. I only found out because my passkey didn't work. I was about to break the news to Andy when John Mancotti hopped out of a limo behind us.

"That thing acting up again?" He shook his head. "I'll take care of it after this funeral furor is over. I'll get you a new card." He grabbed the security pass from my hand. "I've got to grab some stuff for the after funeral party. You guys coming?" He smiled at me encouragingly.

"No, gotta get back on vacation."

"Well, have a good time. We'll talk." John made meaningful eye contact before he disappeared into an elevator leaving Andy and me in the lobby.

"It never occurred to him we were going up?" Andy surveyed the lobby and realized the elevators were the only form of egress.

"Nothing ever occurs to John that isn't completely about John."

I pressed the button to recall the elevator. From viewing the lobby and the reception area, Andy gained an appreciation of the role of image at Markshell—minimal. I led Andy down the long narrow hallway to my workspace.

"I can see you didn't pick your office to suck up to Bascombe."

I started to agree. "Wait, how do you know where Bascombe's office was?"

"You assumed I only handled the investigation in Ocean City. You underestimate me, Ms. Daniels. I am a big-time PI. I can even cross state lines." He stopped at the door with a perplexed expression on his face. "Not locked?"

"Never seemed necessary."

The PI did not complete a roll of his eyes. Instead, he shrugged and murmured, "I see."

"Checking this place out will be easy because I straightened up before I left."

Andy cleared his throat meaningfully.

"Really. I did." I protested.

I began the search for planted evidence at my computer. Nothing. My in box. Nothing. My out box. Nothing. I grew bored as I went through my drawers. Andy settled onto the battered visitor's chair next to my desk and watched over my shoulder.

"We've been here twenty minutes and at least thirty people have passed down this hallway. Several repeats but still a lot of traffic. Is that typical?"

"Probably slow because of the number of people at the funeral." I ignored the PI as he reached past me into the drawer.

"Maggie, what are these?" The PI held a set of keys aloft.

"My extra set of house keys." I answered absentmindedly.

"Here in your unlocked desk? In your unlocked office?"

I got his point. "How could I anticipate that someone would want . . . I mean I never dreamt . . . I . . . ."

The detective asked for an envelope and dropped my keys inside. "Unlikely because of the rough surfaces but maybe we'll find some prints."

Andy sat lost in thought for several minutes. "The person who planted that letter in your apartment probably got the keys out of your desk. My guess is that the culprit did not put anything here. The person couldn't afford to get caught digging around in your drawers. Plus it would be easy to claim evidence was planted in an office. To get to your desk for your keys, however, the person must work here, right? Would former employees have access?"

I shook my head. "Not unless they had inside help. The first thing HR does when you get fired, is kill your keycard. You saw how upset I got downstairs." I waived a memo in his face. "Invitation to strategic planning in three weeks. Guess I have a job."

"Why did you think you were losing your job anyway?"

I blushed thinking of the night Bascombe died. I always did.

"The day Bascombe died, I ran into him on the beach. When he asked where I was staying, I pointed to the cottage and he said, 'How unfortunate.'"

"And based on that comment, you thought that you were getting fired?"

"There's more." This was the part I dreaded talking about. "I happened to . . . uh . . . I was . . . I had . . . put myself in a position where I could hear Bascombe speaking to one of his guests. It was the woman. I overheard him say that he hated it when one of them was around. You should have heard the way he said 'them.'"

"And based on that . . . ?"

I shook my head. "There's more. When he said he hated having one of them around, the woman said, and I quote, 'But Pooksie, you said that one isn't going to be around much longer.'" I imitated the woman's deep tones.

"But it wasn't you." Andy lapsed into thought.

I continued the search while the PI contemplated my remark.

"I considered the idea that the person targeted you when they heard you were in Ocean City, but that doesn't hold water. For example, I was in the area but I had an alibi." In response to my twisted features, he added. "I was with Bascombe's old girlfriend. I told you that." Why did the thought of Andy with Bascombe's ex make me jealous? Luckily the PI had looked away and didn't catch my reaction. He continued hypothesizing. "If the perp tried pinning the murder on me, she could have ruined the plan. You were alone. The person who planted the fake evidence, whom we have to assume is the killer, had to know that you were alone that night. If they didn't, there would be no point in planting the evidence."

I blushed. Some details of the evening still eluded my memory, but I recalled enough embarrassing behavior to fear the story coming out in court.

"Meg. Are you okay?" Had my expression frightened Andy into using my real name?

"It's kind of scary, don't you think? A person seeing what you're doing in the privacy of your own home."

"You don't remember anything?"

I went over it once more. "I went home from the beach. Got drunk. Sat in the dark. Somehow or other got into the bedroom and fell asleep."

"What about your dreams?"

"You know, you can never remember the early parts. I recall the end when I thought John Mancotti and Laurie Gold were banging on my head. I know other people had been in the dream earlier but who they were . . ." I sat lost in thought. "I think Larry Fortensky might have been there."

"Larry Fortensky?"

"Elizabeth Taylor's seventh husband. Or eighth if you count Richard Burton twice."

"I hadn't thought of targeting Larry in this investigation."

I couldn't argue with Andy on that point.

"Do you think Larry represents your ex, David?"

My eyes lit up. "Good assumption, Andy. Let's go with it. I'll try to envision David killing Bascombe." I sat back in my chair and closed my eyes. "Maybe Laurie was cheering him on. That would make her an accomplice, wouldn't it?" I visualized Laurie in orange prison gear. A smile curled the corners of my lips; orange was not her color.

"But why was Laurie with John, not David?"

I opened my eyes and leaned forward, elbows on my desk. "Actually, I think Laurie and John were squabbling. They were hitting me for different reasons." I paused. "Andy, I don't think the answer is in my dreams. If my subconscious ever knew the identity of the killer or killers, I think the solution was in that part of the dream that gets lost when you wake up."

"Maybe we could try hypnosis."

I checked for traces of a grin on the PI's face but found none. Andy was one relentless private investigator.

Detective Dupuy was arriving at Markshell as Andy and I stepped off the elevator. I guess she wasn't invited to the post-funeral party. She took a long hard look at Andy and then turned to me. "Can I see you for a minute, Ms. Daniels."

"Please call me Meg."

"Ms. Daniels, I'd like to ask you a question." She didn't wait for my agreement. "How did you come to know Andy Beck."

"I . . . I . . . I just met him. On the boardwalk. On the beach."

"Before or after DK Bascombe was murdered?"

"After. Long after."

The detective's smile was rueful. I guess it did sound silly. Bascombe had died only four days before.

"Well." The young woman released a quick but deep sigh. "I see."

Whatever it was she saw, I didn't see, but I was willing to bet it didn't look good for me.

Chapter 19

I had mixed feelings about bringing Andy to the one social event of my vacation. The cons were numerous. First of all, I barely knew him. Well, that was the big negative. That and the possibility that another guest at the party would know him. On the plus side, he had just driven me from New York. He wanted to buy me dinner. He looked gorgeous. My brain lined up on one side of the issue; my body on the other. In the end, my hormones won and I asked the detective to accompany me.

I issued the invitation just north of Long Beach Island as we headed south on the Garden State Parkway. Before then, there was little opportunity. Andy may not have found a lot of answers at the funeral, but he sure did walk away with a lot of questions about Markshell and the people who worked there.

Bish Winston. My feeling was Bascombe needed him out because Bish was the one person who knew what was going on everywhere in the company. He saw through Bascombe right away and might have successfully exposed him. By firing Bish, Bascombe paid him the ultimate compliment.

John Mancotti. Until Andy asked, I hadn't realized that I had no feelings about John Mancotti. Sure he had been shafted by Bascombe but who hadn't? And John used his new job after demotion to introduce a fitness center into the company—largely for his own personal use. Luckily for him, Bascombe's vanity played right into his plan. Once it opened, the two spent more time working out than simply working—although never together. John deserved no more sympathy than anyone else—and probably less. Because of an obviously supercilious attitude, John was somewhat annoying but like a fly. He was the ultimate lightweight. I believed he got where he was because he dressed well and had great hair. The way his silky strands wafted in a breeze was the one thing that I liked about John.

Randall Wallace. It was easy to apply names to Randall. Loser. Weirdo. Wimp. Even though he had been fired, he still had to say nice things about Bascombe. If I'd already been fired, there would be no way I would show up at the funeral. Especially in a new suit. Even the horrid green one Randall had chosen.

After mumbling that it was hard to believe that was a new suit, Andy moved onto Laurie Gold. My emotions came to the fore when describing Laurie. Andy caught on immediately.

"Why does she bother you so much?"

"She really doesn't." Andy let my response sit until I burst out. "That's not it. I hate her because she is a conniving little opportunist. She has been since the day she walked in the door." My tone remained animated as I described the business-related reasons I disliked David's new love. Although Laurie was a lower level than I was, she was a Bascombe hire. "She was new regime and treated the rest of us as if we were idiots." I didn't mention that a few of us were. "And Bascombe. She sucked up to him pretty well but, hold onto your boots, I am about to utter a positive phrase about DK Bascombe. I think he saw through her. I mean he used her, but I never felt that he liked her. Her stupid machinations flattered him, but I think he looked down on her for them."

"Machinations?"

"Little things. She ran everywhere but wouldn't accomplish anything when she arrived. She would stop talking to you midsentence and rush to Bascombe's side when he walked in. She would engineer running into him accidentally, even on week-ends. She even finagled an office next to his. Of course, no one else wanted it. For a couple of reasons. Number one, its proximity to Bascombe. And, number two, the space was horrid. Small, dark, with only a sliver of a window. But taking that office gave her face time with the big B."

"Does she have big breasts?"

I recalled our meeting with Caroline Bascombe.

"Not big enough. If they were, wouldn't you have noticed?"

Andy shrugged. "Nope. I did not find her at all attractive."

It was at that moment that I invited Andy to accompany me to a cocktail party in Ocean City. After all, we were already dressed for the occasion. I'd never seen Andy so well pulled together, and my black suit carried me easily from funeral to cocktails.

The occasion was an annual event that I generally missed—cocktails at the home of my little sister from high school. At the Mount, each junior was assigned a freshman to help get acclimated. I took the responsibility more seriously than most. Twenty years later, and I was still watching out for Sally Giancarlo—now Digby. Actually, Sally was doing just fine, but we checked in on each other once a year—usually by phone. Even though I knew Sally long, I didn't know her deep. At that point, we had little in common except a mutual devotion to the lunacy of maintaining the relationship of honorary big sister.

Conversation was often strained but not that night. Sally broached the topic of the murder. Once I explained that I was staying next door to the crime scene, I became the center of attention. When I mentioned that the victim had been my boss, the crowd grew even larger. No one was attaching a negative connotation to my story.

"I met the guy a couple of times." Sally's husband Burt did not sound impressed. "He was pretty much of a phony if you asked me. Always throwing cash around. You know the type. The kind who makes a lot of $9,000 purchases."

I didn't know the type, but I made a note to learn about it. I asked as soon as Sally and Burt went to greet new arrivals. Andy explained. "IRS tracks transactions of $10,000 or more. It's easy to spot those who are moving a lot of cash they don't want anyone to know about. By anyone, I mean the IRS."

"Did you know that about Bascombe?" I asked Andy.

"I can't say I am surprised." He gazed over my shoulder. "They have a nice house here."

Andy was right. Burt and Sally's house sat on an inlet with direct egress to Egg Harbor Bay. Two boats—one sailboat, one motorboat—sat at the dock. The evening was young enough to see that the house took advantage of both the light and the view.

"What does Burt do?"

"He's an art dealer on the Main Line."

Andy's only response was hmmmm.

Ever the conscientious hostess, Sally introduced us to the guests as they arrived until we were swept away from the entrance by a group anxious to discuss the crime. Given my role in the murder, we were the toast of the party. I grew comfortable with the role. I was surprised that Andy squirmed under the attention.

"Oh, oh." We were an hour into the party when I heard Andy's exclamation.

I didn't want to hear oh, oh. "What does that mean?" I awaited his answer with trepidation.

"I just saw someone I know, er . . . knew."

"Will this person be happy to see you?" I knew the answer before I asked.

"Not really." His tone told me his answer constituted a gross understatement.

"I was afraid of this." I mumbled. "Does this person see you?"

"Not yet."

"Is this situation serious enough that we should consider leaving?"

Andy swallowed hard. "I think disappearing would be an excellent idea."

"Let's go." I started to turn.

"Not via the door. He just came in."

Andy and I worked our way through the crowd and onto the deck. Our popularity presented a problem; our progress was blocked by well-meaning and pleasant guests eager to hear about Bascombe's murder. I watched Andy as he watched the door. I took my cues from the urgency painted on his face.

"It has been so nice talking to you. I need to get another drink. I'll be right back." I smiled warmly and backed away from Sally's aunt in response to Andy's tug on my skirt. "At least tell me whom I am avoiding." I spoke through gritted teeth.

"Check the living room. See the silver-haired guy with the great tan."

I saw five silver-haired guys with great tans. "You've got to give me more."

"He had on a blue blazer."

We were now down to three candidates.

"His wife is an overdone blonde bimbo in a hideous green outfit."

"Oh, oh!" I hadn't seen the couple approach from the left.

"Beck, is that you?"

Slowly Andy rotated on his heels. Ninety degrees and he was nose to nose with a silver-haired man with a great tan and a wife with too much of everything, hair, jewelry, makeup and a noxious shade of green.

"Charles. Nice to see you."

The other man gripped his beer so tightly I expected the bottle to burst. My guess was that more than the hideous green remark, which he had clearly heard, was bothering him.

"I'd like you to meet my . . . date . . . Meg Daniels. Meg went to high school with Sally."

The subtext of Andy's remark stressed that his date's ties to our hostess were too close for Charles to do something rash.

"Sure, I remember Charles." I reached across Andy for a handshake. Charles did not even see my extended hand.

The next three minutes passed quickly. Charles made the first, but not smart, move. Seeing Andy in action made me realize the PI could take care of himself, although I sensed he didn't want to. Andy was holding back and urging Charles to cool off as the altercation moved from the dock to the cockpit of the sailboat and back to the dock. Physically, Charles was not much of a match for the well-toned PI. I suspected that Charles's idea of a sporting activity was a hearty game of chess followed by a vigorous football match—watched on wide-screen TV while eating popcorn, drinking beer, and reclining on his favorite chair.

The entire party held its collective breath as Charles's jabs drove Andy towards the edge of the deck. Exhorting Charles to calm down, the woman in green trailed the pugilistic duo along the dock. For her efforts she was awarded with a tumble into the bay. Her fall was purely accidental, but that wasn't how Charles saw it. It wasn't long before he and Andy plunged into the water at the end of the dock.

Charles wasn't much of a swimmer. Luckily it was high tide and Charles had to devote his efforts to returning himself and his wife to dry land. Andy disappeared around the stern of the Digby boats. Casually, I sauntered to the port side where I saw him gesture that he would ride the tide out. He swam away with a strong stroke. Forty yards down the inlet, he paused to throw his shoes and car keys onto the lawn next door.

No one seemed to care when, hanging perilously above the inlet waters, I slipped around the end of a cyclone fence onto the neighbor's property. The guests, gathered around the dripping Charles and his equally wet wife, never saw me scoop up Andy's shoes and keys and run behind the adjoining house. The elderly couple sitting on the screened-in patio of the spacious ranch house noticed but didn't seem to care. They smiled brightly and waved as I ran past them to Andy's car.

The old Mustang started on my third try. Without meaning to, I sent the neighborhood children scurrying on their bikes and rollerblades as I burnt rubber screeching away from the curb. A low profile was not in the cards for me that night. I cruised several blocks before I found a dripping Andy at the end of the next cul-de-sac. "Sorry, I didn't exactly know which way the tide would be heading when it goes out."

"I can't believe this. I just had this jacket cleaned." Andy made a squishing noise as he plunked into the passenger's seat. "This would have to happen when I'm wearing my go to meeting/wedding/funeral outfit." He wiggled out of his jacket. "Thank God I left my wallet in the glove compartment."

"Your nose is bleeding." I pulled a tissue out of my handbag.

Andy had a bloody nose, but I had a bloodied reputation. How could I have anticipated that Sally's brother Charles would cheat on his wife—that his wife would hire Andy to gather evidence of his infidelity—that the photographic proof would result in alimony payments that would break the bank account of a far richer man?

"Technically, I was on the right side." Andy defended himself.

"That's very reassuring." I wiped blood from the detective's upper lip.

"Doesn't that matter to you?" He was more amazed than indignant.

I considered my answer carefully. "Andy, I'm just not used to being with people who are involved in so much . . ." I groped for a word.

"Excitement?" Andy asked eagerly.

"Violence." I countered.

"Hey, he was the violent one. I did my job. I didn't blow his cover in there. He did."

I watched the detective with affectionate amusement. I detected an innocent quality about the man. Despite his job and the fight. As I wiped the last drop of blood from his lip, he grasped my wrist. "Give me a chance. I'm not such a bad guy."

Nervously, I pulled my hand away. "Well, you'd better drop me off and head home to get out of those wet clothes."

"Actually, I could do that at your house."

Did he mean . . . ? I stole a glance to gauge his expression. He meant . . . .

I attempted to keep a blank expression on my face as I turned away. I didn't want to reveal what a good idea I thought that . . .

what he meant . . . was. For one thing, I barely knew Andy. And, what I did know about him couldn't truthfully be called positive.

"Is there a problem?" Andy spoke to the back of my head.

"Well, actually, there is just one little thing." I didn't have to explain the full range of my doubts. "We discussed your alibi, remember?" Nervously, I glanced in his direction.

Andy made no attempt to hide his irritation. "Don't tell me we're going to start this again. I told you I didn't kill Bascombe."

"No. No. That's not my problem." I took a deep breath. "You said that you were with Bascombe's old girlfriend."

"Yeah?" Andy didn't get my point.

"Well, when you say you were with her. I mean we don't know exactly when Bascombe died. His murder could have happened any time that night. Were you with her all night?"

"Yes. I was with her all night." Andy mimicked my meaningful pronunciation of the word "with."

"And previously, she was with Bascombe."

"Yes." Again he mocked my emphasis on the word "with." "But Bascombe had broken it off two or three weeks before. She was depressed . . ."

"You don't owe me an explanation." I interrupted the PI.

"Then what? Is this a health thing? Because if this is a health thing I can assure you . . . "

Again, I interrupted. "No. It's not a health thing." I searched for the right phrase. "It's an icky thing."

"An icky thing?" He sounded puzzled, disbelieving, and exasperated. "I'm not familiar with icky things."

"Well, you know, first Bascombe. Then you. If we . . ."

Andy sat in the passenger's seat shaking his head. "I can't believe this. I feel as if I'm back in high school." I glanced over to catch him massaging his temples. "Why don't you drive to your place, and I'll drive myself home from there." He slumped into the seat and didn't speak until we made the right into my alley.

"Don't you make left turns?" His tone contained elements of disbelief.

"Not onto Central, Asbury or West except at 29th, 15th . . . you know the lights. It's hard to see past the parked cars. So I go right, left, right, right and right. It's just the same."

"Maybe in your eyes." He forced a faux smile.

As I opened the driver's door, he clutched my arm. "Can I ask you one thing?"

"Sure." I answered in my most perky tone.

"This icky thing. Is it permanent or does it fade?"

I shrugged my shoulders. "I think the icky thing can fade. I've had it before and it ended. Eventually."

"Any idea how long it took?" Andy's smile was returning as was the glint in his eye.

"More than fifteen minutes," which was the length of time it had taken to drive to my cottage.

"So it could be gone tomorrow?"

Again I shrugged. "Could be."

"Is there anything you can take . . . a cure?"

He had finally made me laugh, but not relent.

Chapter 20

As dusk grew heavy, I noted an influx of visitors to the crime scene next door. From my perch on the porch, it was impossible to miss sightseers who approached from the beach. I could hear giggling tourists walking between the houses. The intruders apparently believed that the encroaching night was dark enough to hide them (which it wasn't) and light enough to provide a good look at the crime scene (which it wasn't).

"Where do they think they are, Noah's ark?" I asked myself with some bitterness. A trip to Bascombe's house had apparently replaced a trip to lover's lane. Giggles and grunts rose from areas across the dunes. I would have felt like a voyeur, but I couldn't see anything. Not that I would have felt guilty if I had observed any romantic interludes. If the night visitors wanted privacy, they could go elsewhere. I'd paid for this view of the moon on the water and, damn it, I was going to enjoy it—even if the half moon did a poor job of projecting light.

Actually, I found solace in the presence of citizens who, with the exception of violating the curfew on the beach, were law-abiding. There was safety in numbers. I'd scoffed at the beeper Detective Dupuy had given me. At first. I'd told my attacker exactly what I'd told the cops, so I didn't expect him to return. However, I was learning to expect the unexpected.

Nonetheless, I was still shocked when I spotted Janet and Glenn Maxwell. The couple had emerged from the dunes into the light thrown by intruders savvy, or possibly audacious, enough to carry flashlights. "Janet. Glenn." I stood at the railing and waved enthusiastically. The couple turned my way slowly and lifted their arms to wave even more slowly. Given the look in their eyes when we last parted, I didn't find their reaction surprising. "Do you want to come up?" Again, I got caught by the unexpected. They said yes.

Glenn and Janet entered the cottage tentatively. I wasn't sure if the couple was afraid of the old structure or me. After all, the last time I'd seen them I was leaving their house with the cops.

"So how are you enjoying your vacation?" Janet opened the conversation in a nervous tone.

"You'll need a drink to get you through that story." Unexpectedly, they agreed and waited on the porch while I made gin and tonics. When I joined them, the twosome was huddled at the railing peeking into Bascombe's house. I heard Glenn mumbling something about locks.

"Sorry. I know we're acting like tourists. Things like this just don't happen around here. We thought we would come over and take a look." Janet giggled nervously as she took both glasses from my hand and served Glenn.

"Well, if you didn't come by, you'd be one of the few. There's a pretty steady stream of sightseers."

Janet and Glenn settled on the glider only after testing to make sure the aged piece of furniture was reliable. Janet released a sharp yelp as the seat slid under her.

"Isn't this place great?" I asked knowing full well that they hated the cottage. "I only got this house because it's going to be torn down after I leave. A shame, don't you think."

"You sound like one of your neighbors, Rupert P. Downie." Glenn took a swig of his drink.

"I know. I've met him. He's always telling me about the downside of development. Quite a character."

Glenn's tone was stern. "I can tell you fell for his charming eccentric act. Trust me. He knows exactly what he is doing. He slows down every step towards progress this town makes."

"Glenn." I was relieved when Janet interrupted. "Don't get so excited." Janet seemed embarrassed as she faced me. "Glenn finds Mr. Downie annoying, to say the least. He gave us trouble when we wanted to build our house. He is kind of a busybody."

"That I understand."

"So," Glenn regained control of the conversation. "What have you learned about the murder?"

I shrugged. "Not much. If the cops have any leads, they aren't telling me."

"Do they have any idea about the motive?" Glenn leaned forward.

"None that I know of, but they are not about to share any information with me."

"Have they mentioned Downie?"

I laughed out loud. "Downie? Bascombe was over six feet tall. How could an old geezer like Downie kill him and move him behind your house?"

Glenn remained emphatic. "He had motive and opportunity."

I was still chuckling. "Maybe, but he sure comes up a bit short on means."

Glenn answered with a harrumph that indicated disagreement. Janet worked hard at soothing over the tension by asking about my vacation. After deleting the embarrassing incidents from the account, there was very little to tell. An uneasy silence descended on the porch. Glenn filled it.

"Who owns this place?"

I shrugged. "I have no idea. I just know whoever it is owns the lot next door as well." I pointed to the open space to the south. "I found that out from the sign that's posted." I launched into my explanation of how happy I was that I wouldn't have to clean. Glenn was not amused. Janet's husband might have retained his drop-dead looks, but somewhere between high school and that night, he lost his sense of humor. I was relieved the couple decided to leave after one drink.

My sleep that night was a repeat of the restless night Bascombe was murdered—although I did my dreaming on the sofa. John Mancotti and Laurie Gold returned. Both remained mute when I beseeched them to tell me why they were knocking on my head. This time, however, they stopped knocking without turning into Ocean City police officers. David showed up but the purpose of his visit was never clear. I was running away from him when I awoke. And that was when I saw it.

It wasn't moonlight. It wasn't a headlight. It wasn't a security light. The beam on my living room ceiling was coming directly from the north—Bascombe's house. I froze. The light didn't. It played on the plaster ceiling. I considered two possibilities. Maybe the light came from the flashlight of thrill-seeking kids who had broken in to see their first crime scene. I liked that scenario. Maybe the light came from the flashlight of the killer returning to the scene of the crime. That scenario didn't please me.

I wanted to reach for my beeper. I would have if I had known where it was. Once again I was a captive in my house. The light made a few more laps around the ceiling and then disappeared. I felt relief until I thought of the second floor of Bascombe's house. As the building was structured, from the window in my living room I could peer, and had peered, down into Bascombe's living area. Likewise, from Bascombe's second floor anyone could peek into the only floor of my house.

I grabbed my pillow and comforter and jumped behind the sofa. Just in time. The light was playing on the south wall of the cottage. I watched the beam dance across the wall and into the kitchen. This would teach me to clean the counter. Huddled tight in my comforter I gazed up at the light as it crossed above my head. What was the strong beam searching for?

Whatever the light sought, it did not find. The room fell dark. Still, I remained on the floor. Enough moonlight was filtered through the curtains that any motion on my part could be detected. So, I didn't move. Apparently not even after drifting off to sleep. When the sun awoke me, I found myself in the same rigid position I'd hidden in. Still on the floor, I stretched out and dozed off.

I intended to call Detective Dupuy, but I forgot about it when once again I was awakened by knocking. This time dawn had long since passed. "Who died this time?" I muttered as I dragged myself to my feet and staggered to the door.

I started to open the deadlock but stopped. In deference to recent history I asked who was calling. The answer was "me." It took a few seconds to realize that "me" was Andy. When I opened the door he charged past me waving his arms frantically.

"She's gone?"

"Who's gone?"

"Caroline. She's missing."

"How did you arrive at this conclusion?"

Andy wandered into the kitchen; his eyes searched the countertops. "Where's your coffee maker?"

"Don't drink coffee."

"Everyone drinks coffee."

"Clearly you're wrong on that one." I didn't add that I thought he was wrong about Caroline Bascombe as well. "Have a coke." To his horrified expression, I answered, "It's sugar and caffeine. I'll heat it up if that would make you feel better."

Andy stalked out of the kitchen and began pacing the living room. "She's gone. Vanished."

We'd seen Caroline less than 24 hours before. In my opinion, Andy was jumping to conclusions. "Maybe she didn't come back to the shore. She only buried her husband yesterday."

"She told me she would be back."

"She changed her mind."

"No. She's in trouble. You should see her house. It's a mess."

I had seen her house. Who would know if the Bascombe domicile had been ransacked?

"The place was searched. I mean top to bottom. Drawers dumped. Closets emptied."

"Andy how did you get into Caroline's house?"

He met my eyes; a stricken expression covered his face. "Door was open."

"Andy, I think you better sit down and start at the beginning."

Andy perched on the edge of a dining chair. He bounced his legs as he spoke. At the funeral, Andy had approached Caroline and asked if he could meet with her. She had instructed him to come to her house at 9 A.M.

"Caroline Bascombe was going to be awake and receiving visitors at 9 A.M.?"

"She's a morning person."

"Sure doesn't look like one." I shook my head.

Andy inquired as to what a morning person looked like, but I encouraged him to get on with his story.

"Anyway, she agreed to see me."

"Why?" I was genuinely perplexed.

"Confidential or I would tell you."

I held up both hands to call a timeout. "You were working on her divorce. Her husband is dead. I heard Caroline Bascombe fire you. I don't believe she wanted to be your client anymore. Face it." The guy could not take a hint.

"So?"

"So! What will it take for you to give up on this job? Unless you haven't told me the entire story. Of course," I managed to add sarcasm to the act of clearing my throat, "I can't believe after you've been so honest with me that you could ever mislead me."

Andy gazed off into space searching for an appropriate follow-up. Finally, he spoke. "Maggie, divorces are complicated. Sometimes there are financial considerations. I found something out I had to tell Caroline."

I stared at him. He was telling the truth, just not the entire truth. I told him to go on with his description of the morning's events.

Andy had arrived at Caroline Bascombe's house in Brigantine shortly before 9 A.M. to find the house in disarray. Worried at the disorder he saw through the window, he had checked the entire place. "Every inch had been searched. Caroline wasn't there."

"The kids?"

"They were going to stay with Caroline's mother for the next few weeks to go to school. But Caroline was going to remain in Brigantine. She told me."

Andy was sincerely alarmed. Why, I could not figure. "Maybe she is with Rothman."

"I called him first. He's still in New York. He confirmed that she was supposed to be in Brigantine."

"Andy, maybe he lied. Maybe she didn't want to see you."

"So she agreed to meet me and then trashed the entire house? Right." He leapt out of the chair and went to the picture window. I don't think he saw the smattering of sunbathers squeezing the last weekends out of the summer. He shook his head. "Something is wrong. I can feel it."

Why had he come to me with the news? Did he suspect I might be involved? Why? How? Andy turned and answered the question I had not voiced. "I came here because I needed to talk to someone. I am worried. I need a sounding board."

"Maybe you should call the police."

He hesitated before answering that Rothman asked him not to do so. "He's on his way down. He'll take care of it." Andy began to pace the small room.

"If you need a sounding board. Why don't you sit down and sound off." But Andy didn't want a sounding board. He wanted company. I busied myself in the kitchen while he paced. He was still pacing when I settled on the couch with a breakfast of coke and Tastykakes—Butterscotch Krimpets. Finally, he sat at the opposite end of the old sofa. "I bet her disappearance has to do with Bucky." He turned his gaze in my direction. "That's disgusting." He nodded at my breakfast.

"Want one?" I offered cheerily.

His answer was totally non-verbal: a grimace. "I think we should go see Bucky."

"We?"

"I thought we were partners." Andy feigned surprise.

"If we were partners, I think I would know who Bucky is."

Chapter 21

On the ride Andy had filled me in. We were headed to the club where Caroline Bascombe had practiced tennis and other more rudimentary skills with Bucky Whitelaw until three weeks before. Officially Bucky was a pro at tennis. Apparently, there were other services he provided at a professional level. Andy had confirmed that Bucky supplemented his income substantially using skills that his female clients, with time to kill and husbands who spent the week in the city, found very attractive—as they did the tennis pro himself.

"Andy, if you were investigating DK's indiscretions, how did you happen to end up so well-versed in Caroline's extracurricular activities?"

Andy swallowed before reciting his standard disclaimer. "Maggie, divorces are complicated." Thus, he concluded his remarks on the topic.

The resort where Bucky Whitelaw served as tennis pro was considered elite. The architect had used Corinthian columns and Doric trim to convince the guests that they were housed in an antebellum southern mansion. The stately building sat amongst well manicured lawns and carefully tended gardens. Technically, once the resort had been taken over by a national conglomerate, the facilities were open to the general public. The members of the general public who chose to visit, however, bore an uncanny resemble to the former club members and to each other.

Young men, the kind who date waitresses at Bob's, rushed out to great the lean, the tan, and the blonde and to relieve them of their Mercedes, Range Rovers, and BMWs and the luggage within them. The guests then moved, unencumbered, up a wide red carpet into the opulence of a center hall that could have been lifted from one of the great houses of England two centuries before. I envisioned my little cottage on the beach. Although the accommodations suited me fine, I suspected I could adjust to the obsequious service at the Seacrest Country Club.

While I admired the general physical and sartorial splendor of the arriving guests, Andy got directions to Bucky Whitelaw from the concierge. He spent five minutes with the young blonde and a map before fetching me from the seat I'd taken near the door.

We followed a series of paths through lush green gardens and eventually emerged in a wide open area that the grounds crew apparently never located.

The green clay appeared absolutely emerald compared to the yellow grass across which were strewn small, squat, square, stark white buildings. My guess was that when the time came to build the tennis facilities no one had clued the architect in on either the purpose of the property or the style of the other buildings. In contrast to the gracious edifices that fronted the road, the structures offered minimum style, few amenities, and no shade.

I was fearing sunstroke when a smiling, silver-haired player in tennis whites that revealed a body most eighteen-year-old boys would envy, directed us down another sun-drenched path along the side of a clay tennis court. Bucky was just finishing a tennis lesson when we arrived. When I saw him, I remembered the tennis pro from the funeral. I bet most of the female attendees would have memories of the blonde in the tan linen suit. Although I didn't consider Bucky my type, I could understand his appeal. The man who walked across the court to greet us could have been sent by central casting.

Bucky didn't behave as if he had anything to hide. "Yoah." He pointed happily, if somewhat extravagantly, in our direction as Andy and I approached him. In his tennis whites, which like his preternaturally bright teeth and sun-bleached blonde hair, showed off his competition level tan, Bucky looked every inch the tennis pro. The arm he had wrapped around a middle-aged student completed the image. Bucky might have been sleazy, but he certainly was good-natured.

"Andy Beck, right? Caroline Bascombe introduced us at the funeral. Nice to see you under happier circumstances. Here for lessons?"

Andy was not an avid consumer of Bucky's services or his nice guy routine. He shook the tennis pro's hand hastily and indicated that he was here on business. Bucky was obviously disappointed that Andy was not a revenue source but quickly complied with the PI's request to talk. Bucky's student agreed to wait in a small cabana bar while her teacher met with Andy. I wandered to a hot wooden bench. I could gauge Bucky's reaction only from visual cues.

Bucky appeared dismissive of Andy's initial comments. Did he, like I, wonder how anyone would know if the Bascombe homestead had been ransacked? As the PI continued, however, I could tell by the narrowing of Bucky's eyes that he was buying into Andy's theory. He ran his hand through his thick golden locks and searched the ground with his eyes as if he would find the answers to Andy's questions there. Apparently, he didn't because his final gesture was a shrug of the shoulders combined with a wave of his arms to indicate he couldn't help. He appeared to regret that he couldn't.

"I don't believe him." Andy muttered as he led me to the parking lot. "He says that except for the funeral he hasn't seen Caroline in the past three weeks. Oddly enough, however, he has seen DK Bascombe. He was here with one of the . . . nice young women who help the guests who check in unaccompanied."

Why was Andy being so delicate? "Hooker?"

"Call girl."

"I knew Bascombe could afford a hooker; I had no idea he could afford a call girl."

"Bascombe could afford quite a lot, believe me."

I was flabbergasted that Andy was sharing what could be considered information. I was just as flabbergasted when Andy asked me if I would like to date Bucky Whitelaw. "Bucky isn't telling the truth. You could get close to him."

"Me?" I checked out my leggings and oversized T-shirt. "I don't think I'm the type."

"We may have to clean you up a bit. Make that sleaze you up a bit. How do you feel about looking cheap? I mean sexy."

He meant cheap but I didn't quibble. "You don't think I project a sexy image?"

Andy had a quick answer. "I'm more discriminating than Bucky. He responds to a more obvious appeal."

Looking back, I can't explain why I said yes. I hated dating—even people I liked and I saw no indication that I would be forming a special bond with Bucky. Unless Andy got his way.

Andy dropped me at the Hamilton Mall on Route 40 with instructions to think sexy. "And don't forget to hit the makeup counter. I'll be back in an hour."

He was asking a lot in 60 minutes. Not only did I have to outfit myself in clothes I hardly knew existed, I had to overcome twelve years of Catholic education before I could plunk down my credit card. And, Andy offered no assistance.

"Where are you headed?"

"I can't put all my eggs in the Bucky basket," was his only answer as the old Mustang pulled away from the curb.

In search of a slightly sleazy image, I ventured into a store whose marketing strategy was targeted at those born fifteen years after me. The store was heavily stocked with size twos and fours. I headed for the tens where I pulled a number of items apparently intended to be worn as dresses from the rack. I had never even tried on a similar getup. Without Andy's instructions I never would have touched the garments, but there I was carrying them towards the dressing room.

Small curtained stalls shared a common mirror before which preternaturally pretty teenagers primped and preened. With great difficulty and little success, I held the curtain closed as I maneuvered into the clothes. I decided that women look good in spandex because of the workout required to get in and out of the dress. After struggling through several outfits, I decided on sleazy simplicity. I found the image in two dresses. One black. One pink. Both tight. I suspected I looked pretty good in them but couldn't tell because a cluster of teenage girls taking advantage of the end-of-season swimsuit sale were vying for position in front of the common mirror. I watched for the area to clear.

"Can I, like, help you?" A perky voice punctuated by gum chewing came through the curtains.

I glanced up from studying the way the spandex clung to my hip bones to see the face of a wide-eyed high schooler framed in the curtain. "Awesome. I didn't think that dress would look good on anyone so old."

"Thanks." I muttered without conviction.

"You need shoes." She chirped and disappeared. Demonstrating lightening speed she reappeared with a pair of pumps supported by three-inch heels. "I can always guess the size," she said proudly before I sent her back to get a pair two sizes larger.

Once the shoes were on, I had run out of excuses for staying in the tiny booth. The main area of the dressing room was empty. I stepped in front of the mirror. I looked hot. Or at least I thought so. I didn't voice my opinion because I knew the salesgirl would not believe that anyone over thirty could look or feel hot. I felt myself vamping. Discreetly, I hoped. I balanced on the toes of the high heeled pumps to study myself from all sides. The spandex clung to all the right spots—at least the few it covered. The total length of the dress was approximately twenty-six inches from shoulder to mid-thigh. In the context of the occasion, my opinion was that I looked great.

The only decision was whether to get the dress in hot pink or black. I leaned towards black, but pink seemed more appropriate for shore wear. I was debating the issue with myself when I heard the voice.

"Meg? Meg Daniels? Is that you?"

In the mirror, I spotted a familiar face over my right shoulder.

"Debbie?" I turned enthusiastically. "Debbie Simpson?"

"McNamara now. But yes I was Debbie Simpson. I couldn't believe that was you." Her eyes took in my outfit. "What are you doing here?"

"Oh . . . I need . . . kind of a costume . . . it's a long story. What are you . . .?"

At that moment, a tow-head preteen popped out of a small dressing room. With dismay, I noted that the girl wore the dress I had on except in a size two. And in pink. I immediately decided on the black.

"Meg, I want you to meet my daughter Stacy. This is Meg. I went to high school with her."

Her mother's news had little impact on Stacy. Her only interest was the dress that clung to her tiny body. "Mom, don't you love it."

"No way, Stacy. That dress is not appropriate for tonight's party. You look like a hook . . ." She glanced in my direction as she bit off the word.

"It's okay. Remember, I'm in costume today. I kind of want to look like a hooker."

Debbie's eyes grew round.

"It's a joke." I smiled broadly. "The outfit. I don't usually dress this way."

Even as I said the words, I could envision Debbie at the next class reunion. "You know I saw Meg Daniels in this teeny-bopper store . . ." Before she could finish the sentence, Janet Maxwell would jump in with the tale of how I murdered my boss. "Do you think he was her pimp?" I imagined Debbie asking. Then Sally could chirp up and relate the story of the fight at her party. "I bet that guy was her pimp." They would all agree.

My former classmate's voice brought me back to the present. "I can't wait to tell the girls I ran into you."

Her tone told me she wouldn't wait long.

Chapter 22

After Andy dropped me off at the house, I realized that I
had forgotten to eat lunch. Could I eat and expect to
squeeze into my costume for Bucky hunting? A perusal of
the high carbohydrate foods I'd brought with me convinced me
that if I was going to eat, I should walk down to the shopping
area at 34th Street and see what low calorie refreshments the
stores had to offer.

As I came down the steps, I spotted Mr. Downie out of the
corner of my eye. Risking a lecture on the unthinking virus of
development that was contaminating the town, his words, I
walked down the alley.

"Hello, young lady." He called cheerfully.

"How are you today, Mr. Downie?"

"Not like the old days, you know. Used to be a man didn't
have to see around duplexes, and triplexes, and all these plex-
es to see God's ocean."

I should have gone the other way.

"Did your visitor find you this morning?"

"Andy, with the red convertible?"

"No. No. The other fellow with the scooter. Young chap. Tall.
Baseball cap." He leaned forward and rested his arms on his

walker. His tone was conspiratorial. "Between you and me I think a pretty lady like you could do better."

"Are you sure he wanted me?"

"Parked under your house. Went up. I guess he knocked. Waited on the beach for a while. Came back and sat on your steps. Was still sitting there when I went in to have my lunch. Always eat at the same time. Every day like clockwork."

"That reminds me." I made a great show of checking my watch. "I've got to get to the store."

"If he returns, should I tell him you'll be right back?"

That was a hard question to answer. I had no idea who would have visited me—especially on a motor scooter. "Sure." I answered reluctantly. Whoever the visitor was, he hadn't been acting secretive. "Sure. I'm just going to the store."

That, however, turned out not to be true. I was at 34th and Wesley when I heard my name. "Yoah, Meg, honey." The booming voice was unmistakable. I searched for the source. "Over here." The door of a maroon sedan opened and Bishop Winston's silver hair appeared above the roof of the car. Bishop slammed the roof with his entire arm. "Haul that ass over here, honey. I'll take you for a ride."

"Where?" Despite a lack of interest in an outing with the former Markshell employee, my feet, motivated by a desire to quiet Bishop who was blocking traffic, were propelling me toward the sedan. A horn blared from the minivan behind Bishop's car.

"Hurry it up, honey. Things are getting ugly out here." Bishop reached down and flicked the locks. I grabbed the handle and yanked the passenger door open.

"What are you doing here, Bishop?" I asked as I settled into a plush leather seat. "Nice . . ."

"It's a rental." Bishop flashed a broad smile and reached over to pat my knee. I was surprised. Not because of Bishop's inappropriate gesture. He did similar things all the time. Just not to me.

"Where are we going?"

"Why honey, you name the spot." His voice deepened. "Your place?"

"You ought to be careful, Bishop. I might say yes."

"That's why I ask. See I saved you from the rain." Bishop flipped a switch but the wipers failed to brush the drops from the windshield.

"I think you turned your lights on." I worried about where Bishop had consumed lunch as I reached for my seat belt.

"Well, it's getting damn dark anyway." Bishop chose another switch and the wipers began to sweep back and forth before us. His hand grasped at the dashboard again. A minute later the lighter popped out. Bishop pulled a half-smoked cigarette from the ashtray and relit it. "You don't mind, do you, Meg, honey. You're not one of those old fuddy-duddies." He slapped my knee energetically.

"Where are we going and what are you doing here?"

"Here I am, right?"

Hardly an answer but typical Bishop conversation. "Why?" I added quickly, "I'm not complaining. Just curious."

My former coworker headed west, out of Ocean City. "Didn't have nowhere else I had to be. I am living the life of Riley these days. 'Member? No job. No wife. No house." I knew that his house had gone with his wife and his wife had gone after his six-figure income disappeared. Bishop's smile turned lecherous. "You sure look good, Meg, honey." He laid his hand on my knee. His cigarette ash threatened my leggings.

"Your ash."

"No really. I know you never think so, but you look good."

"Bishop, I said your ash." I emphasized the H. "It's going to fall."

Bishop glanced down at his hand. "Oh shit. Sorry." He flicked the ash in the direction of the ashtray. It fell among others on the gray carpet.

"Where are we going?" According to my calculations, I had now asked this question three times.

"I'll buy you lunch. A nice lunch." Minutes later we turned into the parking lot of the Tuckahoe Inn.

"My parents used to bring me here at least once every vacation. It seems so funny, we would bring dressy clothes on vacation. This year . . ." I glanced in Bishop's direction and let the sentence trail off. He was climbing out of the car.

As I followed Bishop into the restaurant, I peppered him with variations on the same question. Why was he in Ocean City? His answers ranged from "just in the neighborhood" to "visiting friends" to "wanted to see where the old shit bought it." I judged the last answer to be closest to the truth.

When the waitress asked for our order, I elected myself designated driver and ordered a Coke. Bishop ordered a double scotch, neat. I was relatively certain the drink was not his first of the day.

"So how long are you staying?"

Bishop grew suddenly pensive. "I don't know. I think I'll stick around for a while." Bishop's eyes met mine. I had never seen the playboy sad before. He attempted a smile. "Meg, honey. Can you keep a secret?" He didn't wait for an answer. "Ah, sure. Hell, you can. I know it." He leaned forward as the waitress slipped his drink in front of him and took my food order. Bishop passed on solid refreshment. Apparently, he was going to drink his lunch.

Bishop stared into the amber liquid as he spoke. He listed even more towards me until our elbows met. "Meg, honey, you ever been in love?"

"Not requited." I responded offhandedly as I sucked on my straw. I glanced up in time to see Bishop wipe a disappointed expression off his face. Before I could get the conversation back on the path he had chosen, Bishop leaned back in his chair, enjoyed another long drink of scotch and lapsed into his familiar persona.

"So Bishop, who do you think killed DK?" I leaned forward to take advantage of the cozy atmosphere.

Bishop positioned his face inches from mine. "Didn't you?"

I sat back. "Seriously, Bish. Do you think the killer is someone from Markshell?"

"I told you the truth. If any of us did it, I'd suspect the one who mouthed off the most. And that, pretty lady, is you."

"Noooooo." I jammed the straw in my mouth and stared at Bishop. He didn't recant. I slammed my drink down and leaned forward. "You mean it."

"I sure as hell do. When I heard the news, I said to myself 'Old Meg finally did it. That little shit finally pushed her 'round the bend.'"

"Why me?" I was incredulous.

"Well, for one thing you were the only person next door at the time."

"Exactly. I was next door—not in his house."

"Who the hell else ever told the bastard off?"

"You. For one."

"Yeah. But I got out of his slimy little clutches. I'm a free man. You were still caught in his web."

"No one else agrees with you." I sounded sure. But then the force in my voice weakened. "Do they?"

"Honey. I ain't said a word to nobody. Never will. If you cut the old boy down to size, more power to you." Bishop raised his glass in a toast and drained the liquid, holding the tumbler aloft until the last drop fell into his mouth.

"Bishop." My voice was soft. "Can I confide in you?"

Bishop leaned forward until our elbows touched again. "Anything."

I spaced my words for emphasis. "I didn't do it."

Bishop stared at me as I elaborated. "I would love to be the cult hero who killed DK, but I would also like to live my life outside a jail cell. Or just live my life." My thoughts turned to the electric chair. I laid my hand on his arm. "Please believe me."

Bishop patted my hand. "If you say so, I believe you. You might be a little high-strung, but you're no liar."

"High-strung!" I recoiled from Bishop as I screeched.

"Just because I couldn't live in his fantasy world. Just because I insisted on truth. I'm sick of hearing that I was high-strung and emotional because I wouldn't let that weaselly little bastard tell me black was white." I lowered my voice and my eyes to avoid the glances from the diners at the next table.

"Hey, kid. Calm down." Bishop pulled away from me as he patted my shoulder. "You must be under a lot of stress. I believe you. I do." He trained his teasing eyes on me and slid his body toward mine. "I'll tell you what I'll do. I'll have another scotch and then you ask me again. I bet I still believe you." Bishop waved his arm at the waitress.

"Honey, how 'bout you get us a couple more of these libations we're drinking over here."

"I suppose you have an airtight alibi." I sighed.

In response, Bishop raised both his eyebrows.

"You're being so smug, I figured you're covered."

He shrugged. "I figure other people got a lot bigger problems. Like you. Location. Location. Location."

"Purely coincidental."

He feigned spitting his scotch across the room.

"What?"

"Don't put on a naive act with me, Meg honey. I know the drill."

"What are you talking about?" Okay, I understood what he meant but wanted him to spell out his thoughts.

"You could choose a vacation spot anywhere in the world. Think of the variety of states in this country—even the variety of beach towns in this state—the variety of beaches in this town. Do I need to continue?"

"Coincidence. Sheer coincidence."

"So let's consider the number of weeks in a year . . ."

"Bish. Can it. I get your point, but I am telling you I ended up in that house simply by luck—very bad luck. It wasn't even my idea to come to Ocean City. David was the one . . ."

"David Orlander?"

"You didn't know I was seeing him?"

Bish was sputtering, but I didn't care. I was too busy defending my position. It was bad enough that I had to defend myself to the cops—but to friends and co-workers!

"So you and Bascombe were not romantically involved. Okay, I'll buy that story." His tone was not convincing. "You must have seen him around. What were his last days like?"

I explained what little I knew—including the news that he went out with a bang with a woman who was not his wife. "I couldn't help overhearing," I explained weakly. Bishop was disappointed I didn't know who the woman was but interested when I indicated it was no one from Markshell.

"I heard he was having it off with someone at the office. No one from the office came by?" How did Bishop know the gossip when I didn't? He hadn't worked at the company for almost a year.

"Not that I saw. I heard the rumor, but I never heard the person's name. Sorry to disappoint you. I can't point the finger at anyone."

What was with Bishop anyway? He should have given up on Markshell a year ago. Moved on. Started over. I let the topic drop. Bishop didn't. All through the main course, mine—Bish drank his lunch—he again quizzed me about Bascombe's last day. I didn't have much to say. The conversation grew tediously repetitive. Bishop didn't seem to notice but then again he didn't seem to notice much.

The rain had stopped and the streets were already dry when I drove Bishop's rental car to the Port'O'Call where he was spending the weekend. As I slipped out of the driver's seat I blocked Bishop from climbing in. "Bish. I'm worried about your driving. Go inside and take a nap first. Then eat something before you go out."

Bishop cut my concerns off with a bear hug. His words seemed to come through his stomach that pressed against my ear. "You worry about me. Thank you. I don't think anyone ever does. She doesn't. I worry about her." He sighed. "I promise I won't drive."

My attempts to escape failed. Bishop had me pinned in position. A full minute passed before he released me.

Chapter 23

When a cheerful taxi driver dropped me at my cottage, I noticed a dark sedan parked in Bascombe's driveway. I hadn't noted any activity around the house since the initial onslaught of police and technicians, and I still didn't see any action as I climbed the steps. It wasn't until I was relaxing on my porch that I heard the voice.

I'd taken a bag of potato chips, basic, and a can of coke, classic, with me. Apparently, evolution has gifted seagulls with the ability to detect tearing foil at five hundred yards. Most of the flock that responded to the call of my opening bag clustered on the dune in front of the cottage, executing traditional gull maneuvers and waiting for a stray potato chip to fall their way. A single proactive gull took a position on the far corner of my porch railing. He pretended to ignore me.

"Don't play coy with me. I know why you came."

The gull turned his tail on me and stared at the vacant lot next door. I crinkled the bag. The gull rotated to catch the action. Realizing I was watching, the bird again feigned indifference.

"Two can play this game." I stared in the opposite direction at the Atlantic City skyline.

Out of the corner of my eye, I saw the bird sauntering ever so casually down the railing in my direction. I turned. That bird could stop on a dime. Once again he feigned fascination with the view.

"If you would just be straightforward and ask for a chip, I might give you one." I was talking to the bird but it was a human who answered.

"Do that and you'll never get rid of him." Detective Dupuy spoke to me from Bascombe's porch.

"Hi." I answered cheerfully in the hopes of putting our relationship on a social level. "Think my social life needs work?" I nodded towards the seagull who was hightailing it down the railing. "I couldn't even hold his interest."

"Ms. Daniels." Her opening indicated there was nothing social about our intercourse. "Have you seen anyone suspicious around here?" I found it impossible to read the expression in the detective's small, deep-set eyes.

"Nope." I shrugged my eyebrows with my shoulders.

"We had reports of people sneaking around here."

My thoughts turned to the call I had meant to make that morning. In light of Andy's visit, I'd forgotten about reporting the previous night's visitors. Should I admit I'd seen the light? Wouldn't the detective wonder why I hadn't used my beeper. "I've seen curiosity seekers walking by, but I haven't seen anyone going inside or anything. Not that I've been watching." I wasn't lying. I simply chose my words carefully. I had not seen anyone going in.

"I've heard that there have been Markshell people in town." Detective Dupuy was studying me without ever making eye contact.

The woman didn't miss much. "Makes sense." No reason to single out Bish Winston. Her silent stare told me she wanted more information. "Coming here is like visiting a shrine." I regretted that analogy right away.

"Was Bascombe's height ever an issue?"

There was a question with no meaning—and no answer. "I don't understand."

"Did people make fun of him for being tall?"

"I knew he was well over six foot, but I never paid that much attention to his height. I mean it wasn't like we ever danced or anything." I smiled. Detective Dupuy didn't. "There were a lot of taller people, men, at Markshell. Bish Winston was taller. If he ever stood up straight, Randall Wallace would be taller." I strained to think of others. I couldn't.

"So you never heard anyone mention his height as a problem."

"Hardly."

Detective Dupuy shifted gears. "You know something has been bothering me." I recognized the detective's Columbo pose. "Do you have any idea if Bascombe was ever in your cottage?"

"How would I know? I guess he could have been—if he knew other tenants. I didn't invite him."

Her only response was an elongated period of nodding and a wistful gaze out to sea.

"Have you made any progress in solving the crime?" Expressing interest seemed appropriate.

She smirked. "No. Have you?"

What did that mean?

"It's hard not to notice that you are working with Andy Beck."

"Working? No, not working. Hanging out. You know."

"Oh yeah. I know." She packed her words with meaning. I wondered what it was.

Chapter 24

"I knew you had something." Andy held open the door to his convertible as I slipped onto the front seat—and I do mean slipped. I wasn't used to three-inch heels. The detective eyed my form-fitting black sheath with admiration. "Now *that* will get the job done." He glanced at my upper arms. "Although you could use some work on those delts."

I displayed a limited smile as I pulled a black denim jacket over the dress. And the delts.

"I like the makeup." Andy nodded encouragingly as he climbed into the driver's seat. "You should wear that stuff all the time."

I didn't explain the main reason I wore makeup was to cover the bruise on my forehead that, although fading, was far from invisible. Or, that I had just as much makeup on my knees to cover my miscellaneous scratches and bruises.

"And, you must know how I feel about the hair."

I fluffed my curls nervously. I'd invested a lot of time in tangling the strands. Mine was a well-thought out disguise—and I did think of my outfit as a disguise.

Andy eyed me from head to toe. "Great packaging. You know if you had done this earlier maybe that guy of yours . . ." Andy realized he had stepped off a cliff. "I mean . . . " He stopped reviewing my appearance and put the car in gear.

As we drove, Andy kept his eyes on the road. I watched the wind rustle his hair. The strands were like silk and made a fine complement to his aristocratic profile. I couldn't remember a time I had been driven by such a looker.

He glanced my way. "What?"

I shrugged. "Nothing."

He grew nervous under my gaze and, after clearing his throat, explained his hopes for the evening's activities. "The way I see it, you just come on to the guy . . ."

"Andy. Wait. Don't get your hopes up. I don't know how to come on to my boyfriends let alone a stranger . . ." I shook my head. "If this is a singles joint, there are going to be lots of hot young things running around showing lots more of much better bodies . . ."

"They couldn't show too much more." Was that a hint of disapproval mixed with the admiration?

"Trust me, Andy. The competition will be tough."

"So." Andy cut me off. "You've got maturity on your side."

I fixed Andy with a disbelieving stare. "Yeah. Right. My experience with men is they can hardly wait to get to the mature woman."

"A woman who matured like you . . ." Andy finished his sentence with a whistle.

Despite my brief acquaintance with Andy, I realized arguing would be futile. "I saw Detective Dupuy today."

"Oh." Andy's interest was focused on passing a pickup truck loaded, illegally I suspected, with high school boys in jackets festooned with varsity letters.

"She asked me about my working with you."

"Oh." Now he was focused on moving back into the right lane.

"I got the impression you two had worked together. Before."

The smile that curled his lips was better described as a smirk. "It's small town," was his only, enigmatic, answer.

When we pulled into the parking lot of the Waterfront, Andy eschewed valet parking. "Not good if we have to make a fast getaway."

"Why would we need to make a fast getaway?"

Andy sounded exasperated as he steered the car to a far corner of the parking lot. "What if you and Bucky drive off and I have to follow?"

"I do not intend to go riding into the night with Bucky Whitelaw."

Andy released a deep sigh.

"Okay, I'll see what happens." With effort, I climbed out of the car, slamming the door behind me. "Let's get this over with."

"I'll meet you inside. Bucky can know that we're acquainted, but I don't want him to think that we . . . you know."

After ten minutes of animated discussion, I agreed to walk into the bar first—and alone. Andy promised to join me five minutes later. I wasn't happy but had despaired of ever winning the argument.

"You'll be fine in there alone. Just relax." The detective gave me a pat on the backside. "Strip off that jacket and let me see you sell it."

I took a few steps and turned to gauge his reaction. His furrowed brow suggested I'd failed the test. I tried again and struck my version of a seductive pose. He shook his head. "It's not that kind of crowd anyway. Just get in there."

In my heels, crossing the parking lot slowly and cautiously was my only alternative. Even though it was evening, I was suffering from the heat. And humidity. Why else was I sweating? I wiped my brow, took a deep breath, and stepped inside the restaurant.

As I walked past the host's desk towards the bar, I was conscious of the number of eyes directed my way. Not necessarily a compliment. It wasn't that I looked good; I looked unfamiliar and somewhat out of place. Literally. I had veered in the wrong direction. I was headed for the dining room where elderly couples and happy families were dining. The bar scene, for which I had obviously dressed, was to my right.

I didn't focus my gaze; the less I saw the better. What I could see was thirty feet of dance floor, empty, that separated me from the bar. Praying that the surface wasn't slippery, I set out across the room. My gaze was glued to my feet. I tried to saunter, but I appeared to teeter. Nonetheless, my unsteady gait carried me to the only available stool at the far end of the bar. I released an audible sigh as I slipped onto the shiny wood surface. The dress's smooth material almost slipped off the other side. I grabbed ahold of the bar and attempted to appear in control.

I wanted a coke but feared Andy's reaction when he found me drinking soda pop. Hardly the image for a seductress. I asked the handsome bartender, who was twenty-two, tops, for a Margarita. "Got it, ma'am" was his response. Ma'am. I bristled as I peeked over my shoulder to survey the assemblage.

Andy was right about the crowd. It was one—and Bucky, resplendent in an evening version of tennis whites, was part of it. Except for the dance floor, the Waterfront was jammed. Despite the blaring music, no one had time to dance. They were too busy keeping the decibel level high with talk of career, golf, and real estate prices.

I was right about the crowd as well, except for the scantily clad part. The women were young, fit, and pretty but were not flaunting their sexual personae. Since I was, Bucky Whitelaw ensconced in a group of admiring women, noticed me when he scanned my quadrant of the crowd. I averted my eyes and squirmed uncomfortably at his attentions. When I glanced in his direction again, they were no longer mine. His gaze was riveted on a petite brunette barely out of her teens.

I breathed a sigh of relief as the bartender slipped a glass in front of me. Something to focus on. I feigned overwhelming interest in the ice cubes and watched the crowd. I gulped the sour liquid. The drink seemed to help. I even stopped sweating. Surreptitiously I checked out the room full of blonde hair, clear skin, and white teeth. Suddenly, amidst the sea of blondes, I spotted a familiar golden shade—Clairol 103. I dropped all pretense and strained to check the hair out. As I suspected, the head sat on top of the body that belonged to Laurie Gold. My co-worker. David's current flame. She hadn't seen me.

I forgot my drink and my mission entirely. I couldn't take my eyes off the young woman. Physically I could understand what David saw in the 25-year-old. It didn't take a genius to figure that angle. Laurie was young, perky, and aggressively blond. And, totally vapid. But, I didn't think David counted mental attributes when scoring. I could only see Laurie's profile but I could tell she appeared happy and excited; she usually did. Laurie's eyes always sparkled—whether she was greeting a man or woman; friend or enemy; good news or bad. To tell the truth, I don't think she could tell the difference. Except between men and women. That fine point she had down cold.

The stricken expression on Laurie's face when she saw me warned me that David had accompanied her. My breathing became heavy; I started to perspire again. I couldn't stop the flush that rose from my neck across my face.

"Don't start without Bucky." I heard Andy's voice in my ear before I felt the sleeve of his sports jacket brush my bare arm.

I didn't turn to face the PI. "David is here."

Andy curled the left side of his mouth up to accentuate his incredulous expression. "Your David?"

"Apparently not anymore." I sniffed.

"Where?" Andy followed my gaze.

"I haven't seen him yet."

"Hey, you didn't run this psychic stuff by me before I hooked up with you. I didn't want you running amok based on intuition . . ."

"Andy. Shut up." I faced the PI for the first time. "Look to my left. About six people. A young blonde in turquoise. Got her?"

"Yeah. Turquoise's not her color."

I appreciated the support. "Laurie Gold. You remember her from the funeral. She's the . . ."

"Bitch." He filled in helpfully.

"As you would say, with whom my boyfriend is keeping company."

"Which I would never say . . . ." He interrupted. "Besides you said you dumped him."

"He didn't have to recover so fast."

"So you didn't mean it when you dumped him."

"Of course, I meant it." I spoke through gritted teeth.

"Then why are we talking about him?"

"Just because I didn't want to be with him doesn't mean it's okay for me to see him with somebody else."

"That's what it should mean. Someone gives me walking papers, I figure I'm pretty much free as a bird."

"Well, I'm not ready to see him yet." I silenced Andy with an icy stare and explained. "I could tell by the expression on her face that he's here—though God alone knows why. He's never been here before. Watch for a fortyish man. Blondish brown hair. Short. Hair that is. He's tall. Good looking. Conservative."

"That could be any guy here."

"Mole over right lip."

"Bingo. We've got contact. And he sees you." Andy laid his elbow on the bar and leaned close. "Do you want me to kill him?"

"Very thoughtful but a tad excessive."

"Maggie, do you want to go? All bets are off. You wanna go, we're out of here."

"No. It's ridiculous." My two hands clutched the glass so strongly, I feared the stem would snap. "I have to see him some-time." I stared at my drink.

Andy glanced to his left. "It's gonna be soon."

"Excuse me, fellow." I recognized David's voice. Why hadn't I ever realized how nasal his tone was. "I want to talk to my Meg."

Andy took a step forward to protect me from David. "I think that's up to Meg."

I stared over my shoulder into Andy's deep green eyes. They were soft and comforting. I nodded. "It's okay."

Andy shrugged, glared at David, and moved away. I saw him nestle up to the bar three stools down. He ordered a bottle of beer and monitored my situation closely.

I spun my barstool to face my ex. I tried to identify his weak points but was disappointed. He looked great. A little tired, as he did whenever he put in too many hours at the office or downed too many beers, but great. His blue oxford cloth shirt accentuated the brightness in his matching eyes. He had loosened his tie—just slightly—as he did every night when he arrived home. I softened at the memory until I realized the tie was new—and not his usual selection. I imagined Laurie had helped him change his image—after three weeks. I felt my body stiffen.

"I didn't think you'd be here. Why . . .?" David sounded gentle—as if he didn't want to hurt me.

"Why would I have canceled my vacation just because you couldn't go?"

"I mean here in this building. You don't really like bars . . . ."

I shook my head. "It's a long story." I glanced in Laurie's direction. All I discerned was a blob of aqua. "I heard about you and Laurie."

"Trust me, Meg. That happened a long time after we . . ."

I raised my right eyebrow. "We broke up three weeks ago."

I tried to spin my stool away from him; it moved about twenty degrees of the circle before my leg jammed into the next chair. "So," I took a deep breath. "How are things?" I kept my tone crisp.

"Fine. You look . . ." He eyed me from head to toe. "You look great." He rested his Italian loafer on the footrest that ran along the bar. His knee nudged between my legs. I was trapped. I could only escape mentally. I concentrated on memories of how he had hurt me. It wasn't difficult; those emotions lay close to the surface.

"Why didn't you ever call me?"

I couldn't believe David had the nerve to sound hurt.

"If you wanted to talk to me, you shouldn't have moved." I plastered on a hard expression but understood why David had expected a call. Some protest would seem logical. But I had made none. I hadn't called David for a variety of reasons: I was afraid to hear the truth; I didn't want to give him the satisfaction;

and, worst of all, I didn't miss him. I did miss the David who had disappeared months before. But that's another story.

"Can I call you?" David worked to infuse his words with significance.

Over David's shoulder I noticed that Laurie watched us closely. For her benefit, I smiled at her new boyfriend. "Of course, we have to talk." I didn't mean it.

I turned back to the bar and David returned to Laurie. Immediately, Andy was at my side. "I still think you ought to let me kill him. The offer stands." Andy glared after David.

I smiled ruefully at my drink. "Thanks. I'll think about it."

Andy dropped his beer on the bar. "Come on. Let's go. We'll do this some other way."

"No. I came to do a job. And I'm going to do it. I caught Bucky's attention when I walked in. Let me see if I can hold it." I guzzled my drink.

Andy smiled gently. "Now that you're rid of bozo, you'll be seducing lots of guys. Go ahead. The practice won't hurt." Andy gave me the once over. In response, I moved to a more seductive posture. "Don't worry. You look great."

"Any last minute advice?"

Andy wanted me to notice his furtive glance at my cleavage. "I think you'll do okay."

I slipped off my barstool and, steering clear of Laurie and David, wove my way through the crowd. I took a position beside the men's room and waited. Either Bucky Whitelaw didn't drink much or he had a gigantic bladder. I had collected four business cards from bigger drinkers with weaker kidneys before he passed. He feigned interest in the floor, but I noticed his gaze travel from my toes to my chest.

I waited until he had completed his business in the rest room and was on his way back to the bar before I stopped him. I only had one shot. I didn't want to waste it on a man in a hurry.

"Remember me?"

Bucky Whitelaw clearly didn't but just as clearly wished he could. "Help me." He laid one arm along the wall beside me. I was trapped between his arm and a pay phone; given the muscles in his forearms I realized I wouldn't be moving until Bucky decided I should. I would have had a better shot at dislodging the telephone.

I spoke while Bucky evaluated me like a new purchase. "Today at the club. Andy Beck introduced us. He was looking for Caroline Bascombe." I watched closely to catch Bucky's reaction. His only reaction was to my decolletage. I squeezed my upper arms against my sides to guarantee that my cleavage was impressive enough to hold his interest.

"You're Andy's . . ." His eyes finished the sentence.

"No." I shook my head making sure to tousle my tangled locks as I did.

"You're a friend of Caroline's?"

"Not really." I pulled out all my seductive powers for the next sentence. "Not that close." Let him think, "not so close that I'd pass up a good thing." I lowered my head and peered up at Bucky trying to remember if overhead light hid or accentuated the circles under my eyes.

Bucky relaxed his body towards mine. I leaned against the wall and stuck my pelvis forward. "I'm sorry." He hit his head to acknowledge what a dumb cluck he was. "I don't remember your name."

"Maggie." I extended my hand, but not very far. Bucky was practically on top of me. "Maggie Daniels."

"Well, Maggie. I certainly can't believe I forgot you." He moved his body closer. He wouldn't forget me again—at least in the near future.

"I hope Caroline is okay." I studied Bucky's face for signs of alarm. I detected none.

"I'm sure she is." Bucky's stare told me he was a breast man—and not a very discreet one.

"You don't know where Caroline is, do you?" I sounded teasing.

"No. I don't keep track of my pupils." Bucky was not the least bit distracted from seduction by my mention of Caroline Bascombe. "Will I be seeing you at the club again soon?"

"I don't know. I was with Andy."

"Well, I'll tell you what, Maggie." Overuse of first name. Sign of a lech or a good salesman. Maybe Bucky only wanted to sell me tennis lessons. "Why don't you give me a call next time you're at the club? Maybe I could help you. Good stroking is important, you know."

I knew. I bet it was a lesson most of Bucky's students learned.

I tried not to look askance at the ardent, if insincere, suitor. I couldn't believe his garbage lines worked. Nonetheless, I let Bucky think they did. "Maybe Caroline Bascombe will invite me."

"I hope so." Bucky leered. I peered into the tennis pro's eyes and saw no reaction to the name.

"Here." He flicked a piece of heavy paper in my direction with a deft move. I virtually cooed as I accepted the business card with his color photo in a racket shaped frame. I caressed the raised print meaningfully. I considered tucking the card down my dress. I stopped short with it laying on my bare chest. "We don't have to restrict our activities to the court, do we?" This was the most audacious I had ever been with a man. I was shocked; he responded in a positive fashion. Someday I'd have to try these tactics with a man I actually liked.

Bucky's eyes sparkled as leaned close. "I don't believe in restrictions."

I smiled and did a thing with my shoulders that even I didn't understand. Yet the motion came naturally and Bucky seemed to know what my movement meant. "Me neither. Or procrastination."

Bucky appeared frantic as he glanced at his watch. "Oh, Maggie, there is nothing I would rather . . . You have got to believe me." He was extremely convincing. "But I have a prior appointment. I would cancel if I could, but I can't."

"That's all right." I flirted outrageously. "There will be other opportunities."

"I'll make sure of it." Bucky's breath was hot in my ear. He backed away from me with his index finger extended in a pistol pointing position that I was supposed to find alluring. I curled my fingertips into a delicate wave and adjusted the position of my hips meaningfully. Was I getting good at this?

Bucky made a quick stop at the bar and guzzled the end of a beer. After a furtive wave in my direction, he headed for the exit. Only after the heavy wooden door slammed behind him did I return to Andy's side. "He dumped me for a prior engagement." I tried to tell Andy about Bucky's lack of interest in Caroline Bascombe, but he cut me off.

"Tell me in the car." Was his first statement. "Let's see where little Bucky is headed."

Chapter 25

A ndy pointed out the White Cherokee that Bucky drove as we ran to his convertible. Well, Andy was running. I was hobbling in my high heels. By the time I climbed into the passenger's seat, Andy had the roof up, the engine running, and the car in gear. His wheels squealed as we set off in pursuit of Caroline Bascombe's tennis pro/lover.

We caught up with Bucky as he rounded the Somers Point circle. For an old car, the Mustang provided excellent service—once it started.

"Don't you ever worry that you should have a newer car . . . if you're going to be chasing people all over the place."

"Number one, I don't do a lot of chasing people all over the place. Number two, this car is great for surveillance. Notice the rear window is glass. All these years and it never fogged up or clouded over."

"Andy, I love the car but as far as surveillance goes, don't you think people spot you pretty easily in a red convertible that's over twenty years old? Even I made you."

"No matter what, I am going to be in a red convertible. As long as this one runs, I'll be in this red convertible. Sentimental value. My uncle gave me this car when he got married. He might have moved on to a Volvo, but he passed the torch to me."

I didn't ask for a full definition of carrying the torch. "Well, the car is certainly comfortable." In those days when the designer said bucket seats, he meant bucket. I settled in for the chase.

Andy followed Bucky at a discrete distance down Route 9 and then west and north on two dark, but regularly traveled roads. Bucky steered his white Jeep Cherokee deep into the Pinelands of New Jersey. In most cases, a Jeep would have looked good in these surroundings. In the case of Bucky's automobile, there was a catch. The vehicle was adorned with gold detail of the heaviest kind. All the trim, the hub caps and a heavy step bar were gold—suitable for the chariot of a yuppie pimp.

I still believed Andy's fears about Caroline Bascombe's well-being were unfounded but I had to admit that if I wanted to hide someone, I would choose an area like the one Bucky sped towards. With its dark and heavy forest and thicket, there was no way around it, the Pinelands was one spooky area. According to local legend, the Pines were home to the Jersey Devil, a supernatural entity identified only by the evidence of the havoc the creature wreaked. I didn't believe in the Jersey Devil. Nonetheless, I hoped that Andy didn't ask me to get out of the car and venture into the woods. Just because I didn't accept the devil myth didn't mean I was deaf to the stories of bizarre events in the Pines. The legend got its start somewhere.

Bucky made a right down another two-lane road. Andy hesitated. He pulled onto the shoulder and waited before following. When he turned we caught sight of Bucky's lights a thousand yards ahead. Without signaling, Bucky's vehicle veered suddenly onto the left shoulder. We saw the Jeep's lights go out. By the time we reached the car, the tennis pro had disappeared inside a tiny white cottage that represented an incredible mismatch of design and environment. Everything about the Jersey Pinelands is dark, heavy, foreboding. In contrast the cottage Bucky visited was light and airy. The tiny structure did not even appear regulation size. The building resembled an oversized dollhouse surrounded by a picket fence that would not discourage any intruders over three feet tall.

Andy passed the house and pulled onto the shoulder 100 yards beyond. He flipped off the lights. We sat in the darkness in silence. He used the same technique, watching in a side view mirror, that he had utilized when he had me under surveillance. It didn't take long for that job to become boring. At least to me. Andy had the practiced patience of a professional.

I had no idea what would happen next but was afraid to ask in the quiet of the night. The silence was broken only by the rush of the wind through the Pines. If I hadn't been on the look-out for the Jersey Devil, I might have dozed off.

When the time for action arrived, Andy let me know via hand signal.

The PI slipped out of the driver's side; I slipped out of the passenger's side. He ran across the road; I ran across the road. He dived into the bushes; I dived into the bushes. The only difference was I dived into a pine tree head first. Andy stopped and crouched beside me. "While you're down there, check for signs of Jimmy Hoffa."

"Very funny, Andy." I ignored the helping hand he extended.

Andy and I circled the property to the rear of the house and then approached the fence. Once on the soft grass, I kicked off my high heels. I tiptoed to the low fencing with fear. In the short skirt, the pointed white slats appeared more threatening than quaint—and taller than they had from the car. Andy's extra six inches carried him across the pointy barrier without trepidation. I stepped over the fence gingerly.

The night was clear but a half moon did little to light it. I followed Andy across the lawn towards the dark house. It didn't occur to me that our activities might be illegal; I'm not sure the realization would have slowed me down. This, I assured myself, was adventure.

Suddenly, the back of the cottage was ablaze. Light flooded the lawn. Good thing. Andy and I had been headed for a small swimming pool. Andy grabbed the hem of my dress and pulled me down beside him on the ground. One of my black pumps rolled across the grass and wedged next to the cement path encircling the pool. I ignored the wayward shoe and concentrated on peering through the multitudinous windows. Spying wasn't hard. Apparently, the home's owners didn't believe in drapes, although they did believe in florals. Lights illuminated an array of pink and green flowers—on sofas, on lampshades, on walls. What appeared to be a dismembered blonde head floated through the floral sea. I realized it belonged to a giggling blonde in a flowered robe. Apparently, she and Bucky were playing a game of adult hide and seek. Bucky's fly was already open.

"Yoah." Andy's coarse whisper drew my attention from the activities in the room. He waved for me to follow him to what little cover the lawn offered: a lone pine tree. We settled on our knees and peeked around opposite corners of the bush. Inside, Bucky tore the flimsy robe from the laughing woman revealing the first things about the cottage that were not small. Beside me, Andy gasped and then quickly cleared his throat to cover his outburst.

Inside, the couple was progressing in an animated but fairly standard manner. Andy took advantage of the twosome's concentration to run in a crouched position towards the house. Despite a strong conviction that we should be going the other way, I followed him. We settled under a window in a space between a hedge, sticky, and the siding, cold. I leaned against the wall while Andy knelt and watched the proceedings inside. Suddenly he shrank down and flattened himself against the wall. With his left arm he held me in a similar position. I knew why when a door to my right flew open and the giggling couple, now naked, rushed down the path and into the pool. They shrieked loudly as their bare skin hit the water. The night was warm, but their screams told me the water wasn't.

Fearing that the twosome would feel my gaze, I pulled my legs against my chest and buried my head in my knees. Andy had no such fear. When I rolled my head to the right to glance at the PI, I saw his eyes were wide and his head was bobbing with the action he watched through the heavy branches. I contented myself with audio surveillance. While I listened to what sounded like a happy event, I contemplated life behind bars. I was positive we were going to get caught.

Suddenly, I sensed Andy freeze. I glanced at the pool. Bucky was helping the woman climb the ladder. I couldn't avert my eyes. I had never seen a body like the female form in front of me—at least without a staple in the navel.

The couple settled on the plank suspended over the water. The giggles involved into a more intense sound as the twosome used the diving board in an innovative and energy saving manner. I knew without checking that Andy's eyes, like mine, were riveted on Bucky and his lover. I became conscious of Andy's chest expanding and deflating. Watching the spectacle may not have made me like the tennis pro any better, but the experience fully explained the Bucky Whitelaw phenomenon. As a smooth glow of sweat glistened on his perfect lats, I watched his rhythmic motions with admiration. Such events were not within my realm of experience.

As the blonde-haired beauty's cries of ecstasy became uncontrollable, and to my mind a little unbelievable, I looked away into a short pine tree. Luckily, Bucky wasn't much for postcoital intimacy—I hadn't expected he would be. Complaining of the nighttime chill, Bucky lifted his apparently satisfied lover easily and carried her inside. Soon the strains of Pagliacci pierced the walls of the tiny house. Motionless in the bushes, Andy and I listened for five minutes.

Eventually I understood that the familiar gesture Andy was using meant that the couple were at it again. I surmised that he wanted me to stay put while he checked the other rooms in the house. Numb with fear, and excitement, I fantasized about prison life until I heard the shuffle of Andy's hands and knees. With a shake of his head he indicated that he'd found no sign of Caroline Bascombe in the tiny house. I interpreted his nod as a signal to follow him toward the fence we had come over.

I crept behind Andy through the bushes, across an immense expanse of lawn, over the picket fence, and into the pine woods. We picked our way through the trees until we discerned the silhouette of Andy's vehicle on the road ahead.

"Will you be quiet?" Andy sounded impatient with the yelps of pain I tried to suppress.

"It hurts."

"Put on your shoes."

"I can't."

"If it's going to hurt less . . ."

"No. I mean I can't." I hissed in Andy's ear. "I dropped one by the pool."

"What?" Andy's one word told me he didn't consider my conduct professional. He didn't take into consideration that investigating was not my profession.

"You pulled me. I dropped one shoe."

He glared at me.

"It rolled out of reach. Over by the pool."

Andy retrieved the high-heeled pump without incident and led me to the convertible. Without speaking, we climbed into our respective seats.

"It was your idea that I wear high heels." I broke the silence.

Andy seemed more pensive than angry. "They're at it again."

I sighed. We sat for a moment in silence.

"You ever done it, you know, like that?" I detected not a touch of lechery in his voice.

"You mean with such wild abandon?"

"Yeah."

"Not lately. But I can vaguely recollect the feeling."

"Me, too." Andy turned over the engine and pulled the convertible onto the road. "Me, too." I began to believe that Andy had an introspective side.

Chapter 26

Andy and I rode to Ocean City in silence. When I hopped out of the car—I had abandoned the high heels—Andy asked me to slow down. "I'd better see you in."

He didn't say a word as he followed me up the steps. At the top of the staircase, he took my tiny wallet with the keys attached and opened the door. "Let me just make sure no one is inside." I waited in the darkened living room listening to the surf while Andy swept the apartment for intruders. After pronouncing the cottage clean, he still seemed reluctant to leave.

"Would you like a drink?"

Andy's eyes didn't meet mine. "No, I should go." He headed for the door. He stopped with his hand on the handle.

"Andy, is something wrong?" I asked. I did wonder if something was bothering the detective. More importantly, however, I wondered if he really wanted to leave. I didn't want him to leave. I suspected he didn't want to.

"No, no. Nothing's wrong." He didn't open the door.

Was I reading his intentions correctly? If he wanted to stay, he was fully capable of making the first move. I regretted mentioning the icky thing, but I had said the icky feeling could disappear by Saturday. Still, he stood with his hand on the door handle. There was only one explanation; Andy had no interest. "Well, thanks for seeing me home." I knew my tone was dismissive.

Andy sighed. "No problem." It seemed that he opened and then closed the door with one gesture. He was still on the inside.

The PI made his intentions, the same ones I had suspected, known with great urgency. With lips locked we staggered down the hallway bouncing from wall to wall. In frustration, Andy carried me the last few feet and dropped me onto the old mattress. I felt the jagged springs in my back. Under other circumstances, I might have protested.

"Sheets?" His single word did not constitute a demand but rather a question.

"Cops." I stole a moment of freedom for my lips to reply.

"Hmmm." He indicated he understood.

By the time I heard the knocking on the door, I was down to one item of clothing and that was one more than Andy.

"Ignore it." Andy minimized the interruption. I didn't protest. The person at the door, however, did. The knocking grew increasingly loud. Even when the action elevated to pounding, Andy and I were both willing to overlook the commotion. By the time the shouting started, the sound was more of a hammering. "I know you're in there, Meg. It's me. It's David. Open up."

I recognized David's voice but didn't care. Apparently Andy did.

"Forget him." I yanked the PI back towards me.

"No. This isn't right." He staggered out of bed and pulled on his jeans. "Not this way."

"This way is fine." I reassured him. Any way would have been fine. "Don't go."

"I saw you tonight. You have to talk to him."

Andy retrieved his shirt from the foot of the bed, his jacket from the door handle and his shoes from the floor in the hallway.

"You can't leave now. How can you leave now?" Lacking the time to struggle into the tight dress, I grabbed an oversized T-shirt and followed him to the entrance in time to see the expression on David's face when Andy flung open the door and swept by him barefoot and naked from the waist up.

David was sputtering in outrage. "What . . . who . . .?"

"Cut the act, David." I turned and, leaving the door open, flipped on the lights in the living room. "You might as well tell me what you came for." My hiss mixed amazement, disgust, and pure hatred.

I plunked on the sofa and pointed at a stiff kitchen chair. David ignored my finger and sank into the fifties version of a club chair across from me. Given the style, he didn't sink very far.

I briefly considered running to the bedroom for more clothes. Why? David had seen me in much less and found resisting my charms easy enough.

My ex-boyfriend was more interested in Andy than in whatever had brought him to my door.

"He's just a friend."

"I saw him at the bar. You picked him up tonight. Meg, I know that you're feeling vulnerable but really."

"Really what?"

"I mean . . . someone you hardly know."

"I know him David. What do you want?"

"Who is he?"

"You don't know him. He's local."

David's mind was still on Andy, but he did change the subject. "This place really is a dump."

"David, that's not a smart opening when you drop in unexpectedly in the middle of the night. And, I am sure you didn't drop by to check out the house. Why are you here?"

"I just thought we should talk."

I didn't have my watch on but I knew the little hand had moved way past twelve. "Now?"

"Why not? I'm here. You're here."

"What do you want to talk about?" My tone was challenging.

"Well, for one thing, how about this mess with Bascombe?"

He might as well have said, "How about those Mets?" I leaned forward on my chair. "Let me see if I have this right. You drop in on me in the middle of the night, at a most inopportune moment I might add, to chat with me about current events?"

David ignored my sarcasm. "Meg, this is not just a current event. Think of the irony of his murder for us. All the times we said we said we wanted to kill the old bastard, and now someone did."

"If I recall correctly, David, you were the one who specifically expressed a desire to kill the guy." I was always conscious of the possibility of wires and bugs.

"Did you tell the police that?" David sounded apprehensive.

"Yeah, right. I told Detective Dupuy that you are definitely the type to stab a man in the back."

That time David caught the irony on my tone.

The irony was gone from my voice as I continued. "Well, metaphorically, you are capable. Literally? No way."

David was so gratified that I didn't suspect him of murder that he ignored my insult.

"Why are you in Ocean City anyway?" My fully contorted features emphasized my puzzlement.

"Laurie . . . " With horror he realized he had mentioned the dreaded name. He cleared his throat and stuttered before presenting a full sentence. "Laurie has a cousin with a condo down here."

"How convenient."

"What does that mean?" The guy was overly defensive.

I shrugged. "Idle comment. What else do you want to talk about?" My tone conveyed my message clearly. I thought the conversation was over.

"Well," David was undeterred, "why don't you tell me about your vacation?"

"You're kidding."

Apparently not, because David assumed the posture of an active listener. He learned the pose at a seminar.

I started to describe the weather, the beach . . . anything but my encounters with Bascombe. David interrupted. "Meg, there are more interesting aspects to your vacation."

"You mean Bascombe?" I asked ingenuously.

"Of course." David tried to sound jovial. I'd heard him use the same insincere tone on his bosses in the past.

In the hopes that he would leave once he heard about Bascombe, I related my standard story about the hallucinations, the encounter on the beach, and the visit by the police. I neglected to relate the humiliating details of my espionage efforts or to mention the threat to my job that I'd overheard. The omissions didn't matter. David was interested in Bascombe and the cops, not me. I answered his questions with marked impatience, but still he did not offer to leave. He was particularly interested in Bascombe's visitors during the last hours of his life.

"David, what is this about? Why are you so interested?"

David hung his head and studied his hands. I did too and noticed that they were far better manicured than when we were together. Laurie really had the guy under control. Finally, he raised his head. He had painted a pained expression across his face. "I don't know how to handle this, Meg. I want us to be friends. I guess my efforts are clumsy."

I didn't believe him, but as long as he had opened the topic of our relationship I had a question. "David, why Laurie?"

This time the pained expression on his face was genuine. "I didn't mean to hurt you." His pause was long enough that I filled the conversational void.

"I never nagged, did I?"

He shook his head.

"Sniped? Criticized?"

He continued to shake his head.

"So? Why did you walk? Walk! Why did you run?" The dispassionate sound of my voice surprised even me.

"I can't explain it." David was struggling for words. "You were always great. And, we had fun. Lots of fun. Laurie does nag and criticize. Yet . . . "

I braced myself.

"She just wanted me so darn much. And, what she was offering was so inappropriate. So, not me. I couldn't resist."

I understood. I really did.

Chapter 27

"I can't believe it." Andy pushed past me and flopped on the couch as if there was no more natural way for the day to begin. "You know the person who put stuff in your apartment?" I nodded. "Well, they've been taking stuff out of mine."

"No." I filled my voice with the requisite amounts of both shock and indignation.

"I just spent the morning with my insurance guy. The place is a mess."

"Where is that place?" I pumped. Andy had never alluded to a permanent domicile.

"Hardly matters now, does it? I moved into the Port'O'Call. Insurance pays."

"For a robbery?"

"It wasn't just a burglary. They ripped everything apart. I can't live there. Insurance has to pay. It's only for a couple of days."

Was that the only reason Andy had come? To tell me about the theft.

The PI grabbed a magazine from the cushion beside him and started flipping through the pages. "So," he asked with a forced casualness, "how did your visit with David go? I didn't know whether or not I should stop by this morning. I was afraid I might run into him." He kept his eyes on the pages, but I was willing to bet he couldn't describe anything he had read.

"No. Stopping by was fine." I waited to see how far his questioning would go.

"He left early, eh?" He turned a few pages impatiently.

"In a way."

Andy kept his eyes on the pages.

"He only stayed about fifteen minutes."

The PI kept flipping pages; now he was starting again from the back of the book. "What did he want?"

"Who ever knows with David?" I sighed. "I think he needed to work out some sort of guilt he felt. His departure was as enigmatic as his arrival. Want something to drink?"

"No. No." The PI threw the magazine back where he found it and got to his feet. "I thought I'd go out for breakfast." Somehow or other I got the impression that I had been invited along. At any rate, the PI seemed content when, in my uniform of leggings and oversized shirt, I climbed into his convertible beside him.

"Have you heard yet about the prints on the memo in my apartment?"

The PI's face clouded over. "Oh, gosh. I just remembered something." Andy slapped his forehead with an exaggerated gesture. "Do you mind if we stop by the hotel? I have to pick something up."

I knew that I was blushing. Andy wanted to pick up where we left off when David arrived. What else would explain stopping at the hotel? What would I do if my assumption were right? What would I do if my assumption were wrong?

I mumbled a few noncommittal words as I pondered my predicament. Things had appeared much less complicated in the dark. The night before I had known what I wanted, but in the light of day my intellect kicked in. I knew little about Andy and what I did know, except his physical attributes, was at best perplexing. He had lied before. Okay, he claimed client privilege, but his motives seemed muddled. I was lost in those thoughts when I heard Andy's door slam.

"Coming?" The PI was smiling down at me.

"You bet." I hopped out of my side of the car a little too eagerly—my intellect defeated by my hormones.

Andy led me down 13th Street and onto the boardwalk. "Easier than going into the lot," he explained although I hadn't asked why he had eschewed the free parking offered by the hotel.

On the patio that faced the boardwalk, a wedding was in full swing. A bride and groom, multiple attendants including flower girl, and assorted guests, covered the deck. "Maybe we should use the other entrance."

"Not yet." Andy stopped and positioned himself across the boardwalk from the hotel's front door. "I asked a friend to meet me here."

"Even though you didn't know you would be here?"

"That's part of what I forgot."

Andy was making no sense. My romantic instincts were fading fast, and a familiar feeling of distrust was working its way into my heart and head. I took a position three feet down the metal railing from Andy and watched the wedding. So far the groom had committed. I had no reason to doubt the bride would follow suit.

Suddenly the PI bolted for the hotel entrance waving that I follow. "I can't wait for him," he mumbled but didn't explain who "he" was as he led the way behind the wedding and through a lobby suddenly filled with departing guests and their luggage. I had trouble keeping up with the PI as he maneuvered through the crowded lobby and leapt into an elevator just as its door was closing. He flashed his pearly whites to assuage the annoyance of the couple who thought they had the lift to themselves, their four children, ten pieces of luggage and assorted Big Wheels, strollers and wagons. Apparently, they were staying through Christmas.

When we stopped on four, Andy tapped his finger on the Open Door button as the family dutifully unloaded their equipment. As soon as the last oversized plastic wheel cleared the elevator's threshold, the PI slammed a fist onto the Close Door button.

The disarming smile Andy flashed in my direction had the opposite effect. I'm sure my contorted features told him that. He threw his head back and watched the floor number display anxiously as we headed for the top. As soon as there was enough space between the opening doors, Andy rushed out. My romantic theory was completely blown. If he was in such a hurry to get me into his room, why had he forgotten me?

I followed Andy around a corner and caught up with him as he pulled a keycard from his pocket. When he opened the door and moved aside to let me enter first, I pretended I didn't see his hand slide the Do Not Disturb sign onto the knob. Although that move said romance to me, as I stepped inside, I didn't know what to expect.

I'd lived in studio apartments smaller than the room Andy let me into. "This is great. I can't believe your insurance company puts you up in here."

"I have a good agent."

"Must be if he works Sundays."

Andy was more interested in opening and closing drawers than in my appraisal of his insurance plan. Or in me. I guess I had been wrong about his flip-flopping romantic intentions. I experienced disappointment and relief simultaneously.

I checked out the room. The space was bright and as neatly maintained as the PI was groomed but contaminated by a stale smell. "I think the last guest was a smoker. We should open the window."

"No. No." Andy waved me away from the sliding glass doors. "We'll be out of here in no time. Just relax."

Eliminating the king size bed, I surveyed the seating possibilities. I had the choice of a club chair, ottoman, or love seat. I hesitated before choosing the last. "Is this a sofa bed?"

Andy seemed startled by my question. "How would I know? Why would I check?" He was speaking to himself as much as to me.

While he rummaged, I strolled over to the window. Below me, a patchwork of brightly colored towels dotted the beach for as far as the eye could see. Once more, last minute vacationers enjoyed the September sun without me. Above the waves, a one-engine plane dragged a banner inviting the sunbathers to happy hour. A wave of nostalgia washed over me. The medium had remained the same, even if the message had changed.

Andy's attention to the search was total.

"Can I help you?"

"No."

"What are you looking for?"

"My address book."

How could someone so neat lose his address book in a space so small? I didn't ask. Talking to Andy while he was busy was useless. "I'll wait on the balcony."

"No. No." Andy covered the distance between us in two steps and grabbed my shoulders from behind. "I didn't mean to say you couldn't help. I was distracted. I didn't mean to hurt your feelings."

"I wasn't hurt." I didn't mention that I was annoyed.

"I can't find my pink oxford cloth shirt. You could search for that." He offered the job as a consolation prize.

"You're wearing it."

He appeared startled before he smiled. "I have two."

I didn't spot a pink shirt but located a pair of jeans between the wall and the bed. As I held them up, I heard Andy's voice over my shoulder. "Got to take them to the Laundromat."

I displayed the pants. "My guess is that they've already run through the wash a few too many times—enough that they would now fit a five-foot-two size four."

"Old girlfriend—days ago."

"You said you moved in this morning."

Andy kept searching—for whatever he was looking for and for an explanation. "It isn't what you think. I haven't had a woman in this room."

That I believed. "Andy. This isn't your room is it?" I wandered to another corner where I found a full ashtray. I'd never seen the PI smoke.

Andy accelerated his search and promised to explain later.

"Andy whose room are we in?"

Again, he promised to explain—later.

"I'm out of here." I headed for the door. "Andy, if I am not mistaken, you just involved me in the commission of a felony."

"You're overstating the facts."

I stopped at the hallway. "Breaking and entering is not a felony?"

"Entering. No breaking. I had a key."

I didn't want to know how he got it. "That makes my crime a semi-felony? I don't think those kind of offenses are in the law books. I'm out of here."

Two things aborted my exit. I paused when Andy exclaimed "I've got it." I remained still when I heard the knock at the door. Two knocks actually. I turned towards Andy. His eyes stared at the entry as if they could hold the door shut. The sound of the lock clicking open disproved that theory.

Andy rushed across the room, pushed me backward onto the bed and threw his weight on top of me. I was too terrified to protest. In a grand motion, he gathered my hair into his hands and pushed the strands over my face leaving only my lips exposed. He hid those with his lips. My eyes stared wide open at his through clumps of blonde curls. The door was opening. Could the person hear my heartbeat? I didn't see how they couldn't. Slowly, as if embarrassed and reluctant and embarrassed by his reluctance, Andy raised his eyes, lifted his head, and smiled. "Would you mind . . ."

"I'll come back. I'll come back." The female voice retreated.

The next sound I heard was the door falling shut. Every muscle in my body relaxed.

"Housekeeping. Nothing to worry about." He sighed. "Now, this is better." Andy nestled his suddenly relaxed body into all the appropriate resting places on mine. He smiled down at me. "We handled that pretty neatly, didn't we?" His eyes searched mine for an invitation that wasn't forthcoming.

"Get me out of here." My well measured pronouncement crept through gritted teeth.

"But the housekeeper will never believe we finished our business so quickly."

"Yes. Oh yes. Oh yes." I groaned. "Yes. Yes. Yes." The final yes was the definitive one. "Now she will. Let's go."

Andy let me push him from atop me. He grabbed a small brown book, apparently the object he was seeking, and followed me into the hall. The housekeeper, now working two doors away, blushed modestly as we said hello. "Sorry." She pointed to the "Do Not Disturb" sign that had fallen to the floor.

Andy wrapped an arm around me as we headed for the elevator. For effect, he let his hand slip down to caress the seat of my leggings. For effect, I acted receptive. "Ooooh." I giggled as I slipped around the corner. Knowing that the maid could still see us in the mirror, I stood on tiptoe to plant a kiss on Andy's cheek. Holding my lips close to his ear, I whispered, "Do that again and the hand comes off."

I saw in his eyes that he believed me.

Chapter 28

"Come on. You never had so much fun."

I leaned across the table at the Chatterbox and smiled with as much insincerity as I could muster. "Riding waves, fun. Rollerblading, fun. Bicycling, fun. Felonies, not fun. Got it." I snapped a piece of bacon for emphasis.

"Maggie, you are too uptight. Crimes are only crimes when there is criminal intent." He leaned back and casually shoveled a forkful of home fries into his mouth.

"Your point?" I took a bite of English muffin.

"We had no criminal intent." He chased the yolk of his egg across the plate.

"I had no criminal intent." I waved toasted muffin at Andy.

"Neither did I." The egg found its way into his mouth.

"You took something."

Andy wiped his lips with his napkin and carefully returned it to his lap before he spoke. "Maggie, I can't tell you everything, client confidentiality and all, but you must believe me, what I did today was in the service of the law."

"Whose law?"

Andy shrugged. He had nothing to say.

"Can you at least tell me whose room we were in?"

"It's better you don't know."

"If they report that something is missing . . ." I shook my head. I didn't want to carry the thought to its logical conclusion. How many surfaces I had touched? Were my prints on file anywhere? Of course, I had given them voluntarily to the Ocean City police. To clear myself. Good idea.

"All I did was borrow the guy's calendar. I want to check out a few things. Call a couple of his friends. If he misses it, he'll think he left it somewhere else. I'll copy the information I need and drop the book back in his car. Don't sweat it."

"Do you happen to know the statute of limitations on this particular crime?"

"Give it a rest, will you." He was begging for peace. "I had my reasons. Maybe Caroline was in that hotel room. I had to find out."

"You never heard of house phones?"

"Like she could answer."

"What makes you so sure she's in trouble?"

"I feel it, Maggie. I feel it."

"Andy." I expressed my worst fear. "Were we in Bish Winston's room? I told you about seeing him."

"I told you. It's better you don't know."

"For God's sake, Andy, I worked with the guy. What would have happened if he had come in? Don't you think he might mention to my colleagues that I moonlight as a second story man."

"Woman." Suddenly, Andy was the picture of political correctness. "Besides he wasn't coming back. He had a tennis lesson with Bucky Whitelaw."

"Bish knows Bucky?"

"Aha. I told you I had reason to be suspicious."

"Andy, why would Bish Winston of all people hide Caroline, voluntarily or involuntarily?"

"I don't know." Andy's face assumed an appearance I'd seen before—usually right before I uncovered one of his deceptions.

"They weren't . . . " I let a hand gesture finish the sentence.

The PI offered an emphatic shake of the head.

"Andy, you must have a reason to suspect Bish."

Andy snickered. "Bish is just one of those people who you have to suspect."

The next voice I heard was sickeningly sweet. "Andy. I can't believe my luck in running into you."

I glanced up to find the most extraordinary face smiling warmly at Andy. The woman had shiny black hair, glistening blue eyes, and glowing porcelain skin. I didn't even want to think about the teeth. What was with the guy? First, we had been interrupted by the perfect body. Now, we were being interrupted by the perfect face. And they both had an interest in Andy. Did this happen every time he ate in a restaurant?

"Lela. Nice to see you. You remember Meg Daniels."

Lela maintained a warm expression. "No. Ms. Daniels never called me back." She extended her hand. "Lela Silver. I visited and left a card. Can't say I blame you for not responding. I never quite trust witnesses who are too anxious to talk to the press. Of course, if you want to . . ."

"Sorry, but I don't know a thing."

The woman redirected her smile towards Andy. "How about you, Andy? I know you were knee-deep in this one."

"Which is more than I can say for you guys. How come you aren't all over this story? The last update I caught was on page seven and that was the day after the murder."

Lela shrugged. "Not much local involvement, so no local interest. New York didn't stick with the story after the first report. It isn't like anything I write will get picked up on the wire. I'm better off hanging out in Atlantic City waiting for a scandal to envelop some poor contestant in the Miss America pageant." Lela smoothly ended the conversation. She left the impression she had better places to go and bigger things to do.

"She's not the reporter I talked to. I feel kind of bad I never called her."

"Never worry about Lela. If she had needed you, she would have gotten you." His voice had the weariness of one who had learned the hard way. He grew contemplative.

To snap him out of his suddenly serious mood, I changed the subject. "I never came in here when I was a kid. Only the cool kids ate here."

"Most restaurants don't have admissions standards." Andy appeared amused.

"I'm from New York. There they do," I offered by way of explanation.

"You're not in New York. Anyway, weren't you cool?"

I shrugged. "Who feels cool at sixteen?"

"I did."

I eyed him suspiciously.

"You seem cool enough now. Definitely cool enough for the Chatterbox." A wry smile twisted the corners of his lips as he surveyed the crowd. Our nearest neighbors, two retired couples in polyester, a workman in overalls and a patrolman in uniform who gave no sign of arresting me for my recent offense.

"Were you really cool?" I turned the conversation in his direction.

"Incredibly. Hip, happening, and all the rest of it." His smile was softer than usual. "I peaked early. Before my eighteenth birthday. Trust me, that is not good."

The list of Andy's cool deeds was fairly long and would have impressed any sixteen-year-old. "Surfed. Very cool. Football. Baseball. Too short for basketball. Student council. Studied just enough get into a good college. Smoked just enough weed to be cool but not enough to get classified as a pothead."

"So, what else have you done except be a private investigator."

Andy eyed me with amusement the root of which I did not understand. "I was a cop. Summers. Like Timmy Borden." I hoped he wasn't exactly like Timmy Borden. "Full-time for two years after I got out of school." He hesitated before he added, "Then a PI."

"And this is what you do, you know, all the time."

"Yeah. This is what I do."

I nodded and chewed.

"You seem perplexed."

"No. No. I just never met a PI before."

Andy leaned back, pushed his breakfast away, and laid his napkin beside the plate. "That's not what is going on here."

"No?"

"No."

My stare urged him to explain.

"What's going on here is that you realize that you went to bed with . . ."

"Almost." I interrupted. "Almost went to bed with."

"Fine. You almost went to bed with someone who has a job that you, the happy corporate worker, look down on as sleazy."

"I do not." Even as the words escaped my lips, I realized I was lying. I did think his job was sleazy. Fun but sleazy.

"You devour those damn mystery novels I saw in your house, but you never want to deal with a real PI. Ever since I met you, you've been watching for the gimmick."

"I have not." I hesitated. What did he mean? "What gimmick?"

"The thing that would make me acceptable. The Ph.D. in French literature that says I'm different."

"You have a Ph.D. in French literature?"

"Of course not. I dropped out of college. I am not slumming. This is what I do. To you, this is all a lark. To me, this is a life. I'm not hiding anything. I don't have an Ivy League degree, the ability to read Sanskrit or any other dead language. I have not lived with primitive tribes and fought to save the rain forest. I haven't climbed Everest or the corporate ladder. I never abandoned a lucrative career for the low life. I am an ordinary guy." He grabbed the check. "Only much cuter." Without waiting for my response or my money, he headed for the cashier. "Meet me in the car. We've got work to do."

I climbed out of the booth and made my way to Andy's old convertible. "What you said in there. You're probably right." I nodded sheepishly as I slipped into the passenger seat. "But can I ask you one thing?"

"Sure." His tone was kind.

"Does your family have like gobs of money so you can do whatever you want?"

Andy chose not to verbalize his reaction. Instead he slammed his foot onto the gas pedal and jerked out of the space. We were headed for Atlantic City.

Chapter 29

I didn't mind investigating crime in Ocean City—after all there weren't any criminals to speak of in town. But the word "city" in Atlantic City was more significant. The difference produced an anxiety that I didn't want to admit to Andy.

"What happens when we get to Atlantic City? You must have a plan."

Andy admitted easily that he had none. "I just need to nose around a little about Bascombe's gambling debts."

"Didn't you cover that in your earlier investigation? You know, the one about those financial considerations surrounding a divorce." Sarcasm dripped from each word.

Andy didn't take the bait. He answered calmly. "I made some inquiries, but the situation might have changed."

"Well, you're alone on this one. I'm trying to cut back to one felony a day."

"I'm not planning any crimes during our visit."

"Sure." I folded my arms across my chest. "And when you don't commit those crimes, just remember you are on your own."

Andy shrugged. "No problem."

"I'll be safe and sound in the lobby and if I see the cops hauling you off to jail, it's the first time I ever laid eyes on you."

"I've always worked alone. I'll be okay."

"I mean I am not even coming to bail you out. Got it."

Andy took a deep breath. "Maggie." He paused until he had my full attention. "I understand. I am happy for the company on the ride."

I studied the detective carefully. I didn't swallow his explanation for bringing me along for the ride. I just couldn't identify another reason.

We found our way through the neighborhood known as the Gardens and across the Ocean Drive bridge towards Longport, the southernmost of the towns that shared the barrier island with Atlantic City.

A large residence on the bay stirred my memory. "I remember a family that lived in that house." I pointed at a three-story structure festooned with decks and docks. A collection of power and sail boats were moored along side of the house. "I knew the middle son, Jake. Actually, I had a terrible crush on him." I recalled a jovial family of boisterous boys. Visiting the house was like visiting the whirling dervishes in Turkey, not that I had done that yet. "That's probably the father." I pointed to a distant figure puttering on one of the many porches.

"Maggie, I think that would be your buddy Jake."

"He couldn't be. He looks so respectable . . . so grown up . . . so bald." My voice sounded shocked and wistful.

I could accept the high rises and the condominiums. I couldn't handle my friends growing older—or that the log cabin was gone. "Remember the log cabin?"

Andy did. "It was in the movie *Atlantic City*. I loved seeing the interior. I always wondered what it was like inside."

The old log cabin sat at the tip of the island that housed Atlantic City, Ventnor, Margate, and Longport. Now I couldn't even find the point. "You can't even see the spot where the cabin stood."

I was growing more nostalgic by the mile. I had plenty of time. I glanced from Andy to the speedometer and back. "You're not exactly burning up the road." My statement was pronounced with surprise not criticism.

"Prior relationship with the local constabulary."

Why had I even wondered?

The drive to Atlantic City carried me down memory lane—actually many memory lanes. I had forgotten how wide the streets were and how palatial the homes that lined the Ocean Drive in Margate. At least the street seemed to be an elegant boulevard until we had to pass one of the big buses. "What happened to jitneys?"

Andy didn't know. "What were jitneys anyway?"

"I think they were just little buses. I don't even know if there was a charge. I only came here when I was really little. My mother paid." Andy felt that little buses still ferried passengers up and down the island.

"I hope so. I hate it when they change everything."

Andy snickered. "You've been away from this island for fifteen years or more. I suspect a few things have changed. Haven't you changed?"

"That's different. I'm supposed to change."

I pressured a reluctant Andy into taking a detour past Lucy "The Only Elephant in the World You Can Walk Through and Come Out Alive." Visiting Margate's six-story elephant-shaped building had been one of the highlights of any visit with my grandmother in neighboring Ventnor. A valiant campaign had been mounted to save Lucy. The least we could do was support the effort.

"Why would I want to walk through an elephant and come out alive?" Andy was acting depressingly practical. "Maggie, as enjoyable as this cruising is, I have work to do."

I had forgotten. I'd begun to think we were on a date. We were on a mission.

As we drove north, the street names became more and more familiar and not all from the Monopoly board. I'd spent happy summer days visiting my grandmother in a boarding house in Ventnor that even then had seemed to be the product of another era. I gazed down the street where, thinking back, we enjoyed a lifestyle seen now only on PBS series. "It's gone. And the house where Kathy and Karen lived. That was the best cottage." My tone hinted at the size of the twenty-room structure. "On a rainy day, it was really spooky. All dark wood and darker hiding places. I can't believe they tore it down and built a motel."

"Fifteen years, Maggie. Time marches on."

Maybe so, but I didn't have to be happy about the changes. "Look at Atlantic City," I screeched.

"Maggie, changes to Atlantic City you had to read about in the paper. Plus, if I'm not mistaken we drove by here on the way to Brigantine. Not to mention that you can see the skyline from your porch."

Andy's exasperation was well founded. I barely remembered Atlantic City before the big old beachfront hotels had been demolished to make way for the big new beachfront hotels with casinos. Atlantic City without slot machines was only a vague memory.

When we parked in a lot a block behind the row of casinos, I pulled a $20 bill and my driver's license from my wallet and shoved them in the pocket of my shirt.

"What are you doing?"

Andy stared as I jammed my handbag into his glove compartment. "Does this lock?"

"Yeah."

"Well, lock it."

Andy didn't think that leaving my money and credit cards locked in his convertible was the safest approach, but I assured him that it was. Ever since I had shoved $100 and the name of a long shot into a co-worker's hand at the dog races in Florida, I worried about a problem with gambling. Especially after she brought $700 in winnings to the sales meeting the next day. I held the door to the glove compartment as Andy turned the lock.

"We don't have time to do a lot of gambling." Andy groused.

"Good. I only brought $20. I don't want to get carried away."

"No offense," Andy cleared his throat, "but you don't seem like the type to get carried away."

Following Andy down the boardwalk gave me another opportunity to question why I was with this man. One glimpse of the elegantly prominent nose, the smooth, tan skin, and the muted green eyes confirmed the reason. I had taken leave of my senses.

But so had many of the folks who strolled the boardwalk that day. Actually, the ones who strolled had regained their senses. It was the ones who rushed from casino to casino who might be losing their senses, along with lots of cash—mostly quarters.

Rushing to keep up with Andy, I barely had time to study the beach—the one thing that had not changed. The expanse of sand was still wide and white. And the Atlantic Ocean? The ocean was allowed to change. Daily. Hourly.

I caught up with Andy at the entrance to the hotel. When I followed him inside, I found myself in the netherworld between the light of day and the perpetual night of the casino. Andy held open another door. Stepping into the gambling hall was like falling into a pinball machine. To me, the noise that should sound celestial to compulsive gamblers sounded hellish. Maybe my problem wasn't as critical as I imagined. The combination of racket and enforced nighttime was overwhelming and confusing. My pace must have slowed because Andy turned to urge me on. Then, he plunged down an aisle between flashing lights and clanging bells.

It was as we passed through the second row of $1 slot machines that I saw him. The blond curls and deep tan were not what differentiated him from thousands of other residents near the beach. What stopped me in my tracks was his profile. A nose, classically Roman until the last centimeters, suddenly took a dive towards a jaw that jutted with rare acuity towards the man's oversized nostrils. His was a profile that one was not apt to forget—although I had until the moment I saw him standing near the cashier's cage.

The only way to stop Andy was to grab his leather belt. He appeared pleasantly surprised to find my hand in the top of his pants. I withdrew my fingers quickly.

"See that guy over there." I pointed to the man who was engaged in animated conversation with an equally blonde woman with a tray of change half-hidden under her more than ample breasts. "That guy is the one I thought was Bascombe's kid."

Andy chuckled. "That guy is Miguel O'Shea."

"Miguel O'Shea?" I asked stupefied both by the name and Andy's knowledge of it.

"No one you would know. No one I am proud to know. An underachieving hustler who hangs out around the casinos until the management sizes him up. He's always on the verge of making an unscheduled exit. It's just a matter of timing. Do you recognize the woman with him?"

I studied the woman, tiny except for her breasts. Cascading blond curls hid most of her face. "I couldn't recognize my own sister in that wig."

"I didn't know you had a sister."

"It's a figure of speech."

It was the woman who caught sight of us and appeared shocked to see us. "Who is she?" Under the impression that it was Andy who worried her, I asked the PI.

"I've never seen her before."

"She recognized us."

"Maybe you, not me."

I doubted that the woman knew me but couldn't see her face clearly. What was clear was that she was worried. She scurried off with her change tray swinging from side to side. I thought about following her, but Andy had taken off after Miguel. The two were moving in the opposite direction. I set out in hot pursuit. I came close to losing sight of the PI in the sea of gamblers and machines. Luckily, I noticed his pink shirt disappear out an exit. When I pushed through the set of glass doors, I discovered Andy and Miguel involved in an intense but not friendly conversation.

"Look man. I ain't got nothing to do with no murder." Miguel defied the laws of physics by jamming his hands into the pockets of his tight black jeans. He bounced on the toes of heavy leather motorcycle boots.

"But you were going to rip him off." Andy appeared suddenly powerful—looming over Miguel who was basically the same size.

"Okay. Okay." Miguel raised his hands in surrender. "I mighta had some plans." The guy waved a cigarette at us as if to ask did we mind if he smoked. I read Andy's nod to mean he minded. Miguel read the action as a go ahead. He lit up.

"Look man if you promise to leave me alone I'll tell you everything you need to know." He puffed nervously on his cigarette without inhaling. If I have to put up with a cloud of cigarette smoke, I at least want the smoker to inhale. I did not, however, share that thought with Miguel.

"I didn't do nothing illegal, you know." Miguel continued.

"Ever hear of conspiracy, Miguel? You conspired with your friend Ella to defraud Mr. Bascombe."

"But we didn't go through with it."

"Only because the guy died. I have a witness who can put you at the scene of the murder."

Miguel's gaze shifted immediately to me.

"I mighta been at his house that night . . . but when I left he was alive."

Andy smirked. "If you were there . . . ."

"We didn't do nuthin' illegal." As Miguel's nervousness increased so did his New York accent.

Andy was playing good cop. "The police won't see it that way but I can. You tell me the truth, I mean the whole truth and the story stays between you and me. You mess with me, Miguel, and I go to the cops." Although Andy hadn't touched Miguel, he seemed to have a hold on the man. Miguel made no attempt to get away. He spilled his guts.

Miguel's story sounded true to me. What did I know? I had believed Andy was staying at the Port'O'Call.

Miguel and his girlfriend Ella's plan had been a simple one; the couple had stumbled upon the opportunity. Ella, the tiny but buxom blonde with the change tray, had been seeing Bascombe over the course of the summer. She met him at the casino and, in Miguel's words, knew a good thing when she saw it. "She never asks for money but on occasion people like to give her a little something—helps out with expenses you know. She ain't no pro you know. She has a career you know."

"Really," I interrupted. "In what?" I asked earnestly.

Miguel seemed confused by my question. He groped for an answer before coming up with, "Finance."

I nodded. An elderly woman in a lime-green polyester pant-suit chose that moment to open the door to the casino. Over Miguel's shoulder I could see Ella working—making change.

Under Andy's stare, Miguel explained Bascombe's proclivity for pillow talk. By mid-July the couple learned that Bascombe had been skimming money from the company where he worked. By the first of August they knew that much of that money was kept in cash to hide the funds from the IRS and his wife. By mid-August they realized that Bascombe was worried about moving the money before hurricane season. That revelation led them to the house in Ocean City repeatedly—including the night of the murder. "But I swear to you, man, when we left Bascombe's house, he was alive. Why he and Ella even, you know, so I could check around."

"What about the money?"

"It ain't in that house, man. I blasted through that place. The money ain't there."

I was happy I had trailed along with Andy. The trip to Atlantic City provided me with answers. I met the person who attacked me. I identified the woman I naively assumed was Mrs. Bascombe. I gained insight into Andy's motives.

Andy was less satisfied with the results of our visit. He wasn't finished with Miguel. "Why should I believe you?"

"Look man, you can make me. No way I lie to you."

Andy insisted that Miguel provide him with a way to keep in touch. Miguel wrote down the numbers of two phones and a beeper. Real? They might have been since Miguel begged Andy to keep his name away from the cops. "I'll tell you anything I can. You just call me." The sun blinded us momentarily as Miguel pushed open a set of double doors to the boardwalk. He broke into a run as soon as his feet hit the wood.

"What a lucky coincidence, eh?" I was proud of my role in identifying Miguel.

Andy shrugged. "Bascombe hung out at this casino. He probably knows lots of the characters around here. If only we knew who his other cronies were."

I felt deflated. "At least, we found out who mugged me."

"Miguel?" Andy sounded incredulous. "No way. I would have recognized Miguel."

"In the dark?"

"At a distance of six inches?"

Andy had me on that point.

"I never worry that the guy who mugged me will reappear. Do you think I should?"

"He hasn't been back, has he?"

I shrugged. "Not to my house."

"What does that mean?"

I explained the flashlight beam intrusion of two nights before.

"Why didn't you mention the episode to me? Did you call the cops?"

I shook my head. "In the morning I wasn't sure that I hadn't dreamt the entire thing." That was half of the truth. I didn't explain that I had forgotten the episode.

"What about that alert necklace Detective Dupuy gave you?"

I mumbled. "I'd better find it."

"What?" Andy was asking because he had heard.

"I know I put it somewhere safe. I'll find it."

"I suggest that you do."

Chapter 30

I followed Andy into the casino but no farther. "You are on your own."

The PI's expression told me that I had made that point clear—possibly on one of the twenty previous occasions I had mentioned it. That same expression encouraged me not to broach the topic again. "I'll meet you here when I am done." His tone was dismissive.

Andy headed for the hotel lobby in search of his nameless source; I went in search of big bucks. I had a theory. If a supreme being wanted to bestow large sums of money on me, I needed to provide the avenue. I had pursued this theory on many occasions. In each instance, I reached two possible conclusions. One, there is no God. Two, there is a God, but He has no interest in bestowing money on me. Nonetheless, the crowds of gamblers had barely closed behind Andy before I was making change.

I sought out Ella, Miguel's girlfriend, to get eighty quarters and another look. When I handed her the twenty-dollar bill, the young woman went on with her work as if nothing unusual were taking place. Then, she glanced up. Suddenly, she grew flushed and obviously jittery. Her enormous blue eyes grew even bigger. As she wiped her brow with the back of her hand, an impressive collection of gold bracelets betrayed that her hands shook. Why did I cause her so much discomfort? I had no time to ponder the question. Andy might return before I had made my fortune.

I sped around the floor in search of video poker. Finding the machines among the slots and gaming tables was one thing. Finding an open station was another. Apparently, I had arrived immediately after a senior citizens group from Harrisburg. A large and lucky senior citizens group. I thought no member would ever lose, but at last a tanned and fit gentlemen, out of luck and quarters, retired from the game. I was ruthless in my pursuit of the seat. The woman in the pink pantsuit didn't have to be on the bus for hours; my time was limited.

Eagerly, okay maniacally, I pumped quarters into the slot and slammed the appropriate buttons. I loved the clatter of coins hitting the metal trays. I would have loved the sound more at my own resolutely silent station. Recalling the advice of a friend's father—who routinely returned from Atlantic City with a bulging wallet—I played the maximum of five coins. After four minutes I had confirmed my earlier findings. If there were a divine being, that divine being had no interest in bestowing huge sums of cash on me. Only moments after Andy vanished into the bowels of the hotel, I was waiting for him in the lobby with an empty cup and dirty hands—and not a quarter to my name.

Suddenly, I doubted the wisdom of leaving my bag in Andy's car. What if he abandoned me? What if the car were stolen? What if my next roll of coins had proven to be the lucky one? I was contemplating how to raise cash when the elevator doors opened and Andy rushed out. At the same moment, I noted an attractive man in a shiny suit noting Andy. He watched the PI with narrowed eyes that didn't say "Andy Beck. How nice to see him here."

I considered pretending Andy was a stranger. Before I reached a decision, Andy took my arm. "Let's get out of here." I thought his was a excellent idea.

Back in the casino, Andy suggested a stop at the blackjack table. "Well, that depends," I peeked over my shoulder. The gentlemen in the tasteless suit was still with us but he was no longer alone. "Andy, do you have any," I chose my words carefully, "enemies at this casino?" The PI didn't issue an immediate denial. A bad sign.

"Why do you ask?" Andy's eyes followed the tip of my finger as I pointed over my shoulder. His reaction to what he saw was answer enough.

"Meet me on the boardwalk." He gave me a shove and a command. "Now. Go." I didn't have to be told twice.

Andy strode in the opposite direction with confident, purposeful strides.

Hidden by the tall machines, I zigzagged through the maze of light and noise. I had no idea in which direction the boardwalk lay. The casino might have been loud, but the noise was no match for the pounding of my heart. In the center of a long row, I stopped and turned expecting to see silk-suited men in pursuit. No one followed me. I checked out the gamblers. Pumping coins into those slots occupied all their interest. No one cared about me.

When I leaned back to exhale a deep breath, I caught sight of the mirrored balls hanging from the ceiling. In addition to the long column of reflecting glass down the center, the balls were positioned all over the casino. If anyone wanted to watch me, they could. On camera. Or in person. There was no point in running. I pursued a slow, if not leisurely, search for the right exit.

Finding the boardwalk was not difficult. Finding Andy was easy. I didn't arrive in time to see the silk-suited men throw him onto his back; Andy described the episode later. I arrived in time to see the outcome. A small crowd had gathered slightly apart from the PI who lay sprawled on the wooden slats. I sauntered over to the PI who, apparently unhurt and not particularly embarrassed, had pulled himself into a sitting position and was brushing off his pink shirt to the entertainment of tourists on the busy boardwalk.

"I assume you knew those guys."

The PI nodded and inspected his jeans for rips.

"I assume they are the reason you are seated here."

The PI nodded once more.

"I assume the danger is over."

The PI nodded and extended a hand. "Could you stop with the twenty questions and help me up?"

I grasped Andy's hand. I had lifted his rear two feet off the ground when I heard my name. The sight of Lisa Merriweather made me lose my grip. I saw Lisa's face contort at the same time I heard Andy's grunt and the small crowd's gasp.

"Oh sorry." I knelt this time and, with exaggerated motions, mounted a concentrated effort to help Andy to his feet, less to help him than to extricate myself from this increasingly embarrassing situation.

Andy spoke through gritted teeth. "Luckily, I didn't have any pride to begin with or more than my rear end would be hurting."

"We saw . . ." Lisa was at my left as Andy popped up on my right.

"I didn't . . ." I smiled at Lisa.

"Those men were terrible." Lisa's voice was full of righteous indignation. "I mean they didn't have to kick you when you were already down."

I glanced at Lisa as she extended an arm across me towards Andy. "I'm Lisa Merriweather Margulies. I went to school with Meg. I didn't realize she had married."

What Lisa's tone said is that she hadn't realized that I had married a man who would be forcefully ejected from an Atlantic City casino. I sensed a strange tone of admiration in her voice.

"You're married?" Andy asked with amusement as he brushed himself off.

"This isn't my husband." I said with more force that I'd anticipated.

Lisa's eyes searched the crowd as if my husband were hiding from the spectacle his wife was creating.

"Don't bother looking. You won't find him in the crowd." I brought her attention back to our little group.

Lisa stared at Andy with wide eyes. The PI extended his hand. "I'm Andy Beck, a colleague of Meg's." I guess he used my real name to guarantee that Lisa knew the same Meg Daniels from her graduating class was the person caught in the embarrassing situation.

"Oh." Lisa's voice was ripe with misunderstanding. "What does your husband think?"

In my haste to clarify my relationship with Andy I forgot to mention that I didn't have one. "Andy and I are business associates. He's in law enforcement."

"Really?" Lisa's comment was not rhetorical. She didn't believe me. Why? Two weeks before, everyone believed every word I uttered.

Luckily Andy took charge. "I guess you didn't realize that Meg was in law enforcement. Well, officially she's not, but on occasion we bring in experts to help us on particular cases. Meg is one of those experts." Andy's smile would have charmed a tougher case than Lisa.

"Oh." Lisa accepted Andy's word, although her expression told me she doubted my expertise.

"I hope you don't mind if we don't say more. You know . . ." Andy nodded towards the casino.

Lisa nodded in agreement and, utilizing an overly cute cliché, locked her lips.

"Well, Lisa," I changed the subject, "what have you been doing since high school?"

With another cute gesture Lisa unlocked her lips and told us in great detail about her life since high school. Andy listened with the most insincere display of interest that I had ever witnessed. I kept my eye on the casino door. Five minutes had gone by and Lisa wasn't even married yet, although I knew that story lay ahead since she had pointed across the boardwalk to the spot where her husband and three daughters leaned against the railing and regarded our group with barely disguised horror.

If Lisa had overcome her fear of associating with disreputable characters, her family had not.

Out of the corner of my eye, I saw the sun reflecting off the surface of a shiny gray material. The suit in front of the door was the same one I'd spotted in the casino. The man inside stared in our direction in what I interpreted as a warning to move on. Lisa was disappointed, but Andy was relieved when I suddenly remembered an appointment downtown. I didn't even know if Atlantic City had a downtown. Either the city did, or Lisa didn't realize it didn't. She took a breath and Andy used that opportunity to say how happy he was to meet her and that he hoped they'd meet again. Seeing how smoothly he lied to Lisa should have given me pause, but at the moment, given the circumstances, I admired the skill.

Chapter 31

"I can't wait to see the alumnae news." I injected a high level of reproach into my voice.

Andy pasted a skeptical expression on his face. "Are you kidding? I charmed her so solidly that she has long since forgotten that I was on the ground when I first met her."

"Lisa is only one of my problems. I left Sally's party in disgrace. Debbie Simpson thinks that I'm a hooker. And Janet Maxwell thinks I killed my boss/lover."

"Do you know everyone in this area?"

"Apparently. Although I never see anyone when I'm behaving normally. But then again I haven't been doing much of that."

"Meg?"

It was impossible. I could not be hearing my name again.

"Meg Daniels!"

For the first time, I saw not the face of a high school chum but rather the ungainly countenance of the dullest man at Markshell Publications. Randall "Don't-call-me-Randy" Wallace loped across the boardwalk with a little old lady in tow.

"Meg." Randall whined.

"Randall." I attempted to sound enthusiastic. "How nice to see you." Luckily, Randall's interpersonal skills were limited. I think he believed me.

Randall bore an uncanny resemblance to the woman he had in tow—except for the eighteen-inch difference in their heights and the fact the distaff member of the party actually had hair. If Randall hadn't been standing beside her, I would have sworn the woman was Randall in a bad wig—kneeling.

"Oh," the woman needed thirty seconds to enunciate the single syllable, "you work for my Randall."

"With, Mommy." Randall corrected the woman who had, with the apparent exception of a height gene, produced a son in her exact image. "Meg works with me. Or I should say worked with me."

"I thought you said she worked for you." Randall's mother placed an emphasis on the preposition that Randall found embarrassing. He argued semantics while she conducted a head to toe inspection of me and then Andy. Neither of us met her standards. Since Randall did, I wasn't worried.

"I guess you can tell. I brought my mom to Atlantic City."

"Yes, I am Randall's mommy." The woman exclaimed with inexplicable pride. "I am so proud of my Randall for getting out of that dead-end job. Staying in a rut may be okay for some people . . . "

Why was she staring at me?

"But my Randall!" She stood on tiptoe to tweak Randall's cheek. She could reach his face only because he was, as usual, hunched over. "He knows how to take charge." As Randall's mother went on to heap praise upon her son, she revealed a talent for denigrating comments disguised as a compliments. I began to understand Randall's personality—or lack thereof. Mrs. Wallace had enough personality for the entire family. Not good personality but personality. Her excesses had smothered Randall and threatened to smother Andy and me on the boardwalk. "My Randall was mistreated by that vicious Mr. Bascombe. He got exactly what he deserved, that one. Don't you think?" She didn't wait for an answer. "But with the settlement and all, I think Randall will do just fine. He is such a good boy. He's talented. So bright. Even as a boy . . . "

Suddenly, Randall transformed before our eyes. "Mother, Meg knows me. You don't have to sell me to Meg. She is my colleague and knows exactly how competent I am."

Competent wasn't a word I would have chosen but why quibble? I was fascinated by the transformed Randall. The Randall who stood up to his mother. Literally. He actually pulled his frame to its full six feet, six inches. I gazed up at a new Randall, a Randall who exuded confidence—and who wasn't sniffling.

With his mother silenced, Randall focused his attention on me. "I think that being downsized was the best thing that ever happened to me. The company was quite generous. I am taking advantage of this opportunity to enjoy myself." When he smiled, I noticed that his teeth had been cleaned; that treatment couldn't have been an easy job for the most determined of dental professionals. "Are you enjoying your vacation, Meg? I understand you are still in Ocean City."

"Yes. Yes." I was floored by Randall's show of interpersonal skills. He's actually made small talk. Generally, Randall answered questions but posed none. The accounting clerk, now free of Markshell, was a new man—or would be if we could do something about his clothes.

"Well, I hope you enjoy your vacation. I just wanted to say hello. I'm taking my mother out to lunch. Her brother owns a restaurant out on Route 40." He took his mother's arm. Just as Andy and I turned to go, he added a statement that despite his new demeanor I still considered a threat. "Maybe I'll drop by and see you in Ocean City. Maybe we could drive out to my Uncle Jim's for dinner. I could take you out to the inn." He guffawed.

By Randall's standards, that was a pretty good pun. I smiled only because I wasn't worried that Randall would show up on my doorstep. He never asked for my Ocean City address.

"Who's next?" Andy asked sarcastically as we bade farewell to the Wallaces.

"I couldn't possibly know anyone else in town." I flashed a quizzical look in the PI's direction. "How come we never run into anyone you know? You live around here."

"Those guys at the casino knew me."

"Right." I nodded.

"You're probably not interested, but that was another case where I was on the right side."

I thought of the men who had accosted the PI. "I certainly hope so."

Andy chuckled. I didn't.

Without further interruptions, we found our way to the parking lot and Andy's convertible. I now understood his choice of lots; the exit provided a fast shot to the main drag out of town. Even though it did not appear that we were being followed, Andy made record time.

Chapter 32

"**A**ndy, do you realize that after listening to you and Miguel, I know that you've been lying to me?" I pitched my voice above the wind as we headed down the Garden State Parkway in Andy's convertible.

"Not lying. I couldn't tell you about the money. I told you about client privilege."

"Andy, I heard Caroline Bascombe fire you. You're doing this on your own. You are searching for money Bascombe stole. You are using me."

"Not using you." Anxiety crept into Andy's voice. "What we are doing here is mutually beneficial."

"Right." My single word spoke volumes.

To the consternation of a church van tailgating us, Andy jammed on the breaks and screeched to an abrupt halt on the shoulder of the road. He spun in his seat to face me. "I will admit it. I want the money."

"Which is not yours . . . "

"I want my cut. That's all." Andy interrupted my interruption. "I may want the money, but it just so happens that my finding the money will help you. Bascombe's death has to be tied to the cash. When I find it . . ."

"Andy, what makes you so sure you are going to find the money and what you find will be cash."

"It's cash." He spoke with confidence. "That much I determined before I was fired. And," he paused for emphasis, "this murder is tied to the missing millions."

"Millions?"

"At least one million. Bascombe told his wife he lost a lot of money gambling, but he never lost a dime. He gambled on occasion and when he did . . . he won. Today, I confirmed that trend continued until he died. The other day after I dropped you off at the mall, I checked out the Atlantic City race track. He won there, too. Plus, gambling wasn't his only source of cash. Bascombe would skim cash from the company. He liked to convert the money into any easily liquidated asset. That's why your friend Sally's husband met him. He bought artwork. Cash transactions under the $10,000 mark. With the divorce, however, Caroline would get a hefty share of his assets. Bascombe wasn't about to give his money away. So he kept cash and hid it."

"How can you know this for sure?"

"I told you. I . . . talked to . . . his old girlfriend."

"If she knew where the money was, she'd be the most likely suspect."

"She knew about the money but not where it was. Plus, I told you, I was with her at the time of the murder. I'm her alibi."

I spoke very slowly. "And she's yours?"

Andy suppressed his first surge of anger. "I guess turnabout is fair play. I suspect you; you suspect me."

I sat in silence. Did I really suspect Andy? Why not? If money turned out to be the motive for this murder, he certainly expressed enough interest in the missing cash.

"Come on." Andy had been waiting for me to tell him suspecting him was a crazy notion. "You don't believe that I . . . . Lots of people know about the money. You better believe that's why David had you book this vacation. And why Laurie Gold suddenly developed the hots for David. He worked in accounting.

She took over parts of his job. Suddenly they are down here together hitting the bars. Give me a break.

"And how do you explain your sudden popularity with the gang from Markshell? Why do you think Bish Winston had to see the town where Bascombe bought it? Do you think it's a coincidence that suddenly he wants tennis lessons from the coach of the missing widow? Do you really think that the aggressively asexual Randall Wallace suddenly has the urge to take you to dinner? Maggie, they are all over town looking for that money. And they all believe that you are the key."

"Don't make me sound like an idiot because I didn't figure this out. Maybe if you had told me the whole story I would have seen things differently. Or been more help."

Andy made no defense.

I crossed my arms and sat back in my seat. I needed time to think. Right then Andy topped my list of suspects—along with the widow. I had never completely written off Caroline Bascombe. I saw only one reason for Mrs. Bascombe to call off the search for the cash. She already had it. And if she had the cash, she had come by it by killing her husband. That was why she had to disappear.

Andy's tone was earnest. "Maggie, I want to accomplish three things. First, I want to make sure that Caroline Bascombe is safe. Second, I want to catch Bascombe's murderer and guarantee that your name is cleared. Third, I want to find the money."

"And then?"

"I don't understand your question."

"What will you do with the money?" Implicit in my tone was the accusation that to keep it would be a crime.

"Maggie, we've got three things on our to-do list. Let's not worry about adding things."

"If you steal the money, I become an accomplice."

Andy put the car in drive and watched in his side mirror for a break in traffic. "Maggie, Maggie, Maggie. You worry too much."

Not nearly enough, I thought to myself as he pulled onto the highway. What was I doing? I'd broken the law. Okay, it was unintentional, but I didn't know if the jury would take that into account. Just riding around with Andy, in a red convertible no less—in case the local cops missed me—cast suspicion on me. I was behaving like a crazy woman. I envisioned my essay "What I Did on My Summer Vacation" or "How to Ruin Your Life in Ten Easy Steps." I had to be firm. No more investigations. No more break-ins. Sad as I was, no more partnership.

When we pulled into my driveway, Andy opened his car door. "I don't remember inviting you in." Even I was surprised by the rancor in my tone. My words stopped the PI with his grip on the handle and one leg out of the car. "How many times can you lie to me and expect me to go along with your little adventure?" I slammed the passenger door and stalked up the old staircase.

Once inside I waited for the PI's knock—and apology. In vain. Andy was gone.

Chapter 33

Apparently David was not gone.

"David, why are you here?" I was surprised, and disappointed, to find that David not Andy had knocked on my door.

"I'm going back to the city tonight."

I supposed that was an answer—but not to the question I had asked.

"Can I come in?"

"Why?" It was an honest question.

"Meg, I'm looking for closure." He said the phrase like a line in a play.

I searched for a flip response. Finding none, I invited him in but drew the line at offering him a drink. After watching him take the few steps to the living room, I suspected he had already had plenty of liquid refreshment. Turning to face me required David's undivided attention.

My ex-boyfriend's face betrayed a strain I had never seen before—even when he was working for Bascombe. Lines I'd never noticed framed his mouth and delineated his eyes. David was headed for forty but that night he looked like he was well past the milestone. Somehow I felt the pain of losing me was not responsible for his transformation—although I would have enjoyed thinking it was.

"Meg, I don't know how to say this." David stared at his hands as he wrung them. "Meg."

"That's me." I filled the conversational void with questionable grammar.

"Meg. I know that we never discussed what was happening with Bascombe. Maybe I should have told you."

I stood facing him with my arms folded across my chest. "Maybe you should tell me now." I had no idea what he was talking about. Was Andy right? Was David referring to the money?

"I mean, Meg, you were here and Bascombe . . . I mean you must know . . . I mean nothing was in his house . . . nothing is in his wife's house . . . you are the logical one."

Using the word "logical" in that mishmash of a thought took real nerve. "What is your point?"

If he was talking about the money I wanted him to come right out and say it.

Courage seemed to surge through David. He spoke with assurance but not clarity. "Meg, don't hold out on me. I know what I want, and I think I deserve my share or . . . I don't want to hurt you."

All my questions about his earlier comments were lost in my rage at his last words. "You don't care about me. Don't come in here saying you didn't want to hurt me. Get out. Now. Get out."

David didn't leave. Instead, he flopped onto the old sofa. He eyed the seating with disdain. "I just can't believe this dump."

"You mentioned that before David. Are you drunk?" I sounded surprised because David was always far too controlled to allow himself to become inebriated.

"Maybe." His tone was unappealingly coy.

"David, you have to leave."

"Why? Is Mr. Right coming over?"

As if on cue, I heard a knock. Who now? Andy, I discovered as I opened the door. He peered past me towards David, by then reclining on the couch.

"I'm sorry. I didn't know . . . " He pivoted quickly to head back down the steps.

"David was just leaving."

"No, I wasn't." David yelled across the room.

"Yes, he was."

"No, I wasn't."

"Yes, you were."

Andy shifted his weight from foot to foot in time with our ripostes. Going. Staying. Going. Staying. I resisted meeting Andy's eyes but eventually gave in to his stare. My eyes beseeched him to help me get rid of David.

The conversation remained repetitious, but David's protests grew weaker and weaker as Andy moved into position in front of him. Although the two men were similar in size, Andy loomed over David and seemed the far larger figure. Andy must have had thirty pounds on David, all muscle. Plus, he had another advantage. He was sober.

"I'm going. I'm going." Suddenly David appeared sober, too. An illusion? He pushed himself onto his feet, but there was no guarantee he would stay on them. He waved a finger in my direction. "I can't save you." When his eyes met mine, I saw a familiar expression that David used frequently to convey hostility, self-pity, and arrogance all in a single glance. "If you want to go slumming . . . "

With a quick gesture Andy pinned David's arm behind his back. Andy's other hand contracted into a fist that I ran to his side and unclenched. "Don't. He'll sue you. David is always looking to make a killing . . . but not through any effort of his own."

David spat a few names descriptive of his contempt for women in general and me in particular as Andy propelled him through the door and down the steps. "I'll be back." David shouted over his, and Andy's, shoulders. He didn't hear me tell him not to bother.

I waited at the top of the steps for Andy to reappear. He did three minutes later. "He says he walked so I let him go—after I escorted him to the end of the alley."

"Thank you. I could have gotten rid of him, but it would have taken me considerably longer."

Andy stood halfway up the flight of steps. I blocked the head of the staircase and stared down at the PI.

"I stopped by because I wanted to apologize. Meg, using you never entered my mind. Running around like this is fun for me." He sneaked peeks in my direction as he spoke. "More fun when you're along. Sometimes I just don't think things through." He shot a last plaintive glance in my direction.

"Apology accepted. I really appreciate your taking the time to stop by. Your timing was especially good."

Andy stared at me expectantly. I hesitated before thanking him again and stepping inside. I shut the door behind me.

Chapter 34

After leaving time for Andy to vacate the neighborhood, I headed for the beach. As I trudged through the sand the waves to my left were low and few and far between. Big rollers formed at a distance but instead of crashing forward the white foam sank down the back of the wave like a surfer waiting for a better ride. Perhaps the lethargic ocean was saving its energy for the big show that was expected later in the week. By eavesdropping, I discovered that a hurricane was hesitating off South Florida. Weathermen were watching to see if the storm would break loose and head up the East Coast.

I moved closer to the water for the comfort of a harder surface. Once all my efforts weren't going into making headway, I was able to think.

How could I be mad at Andy? It wasn't as if I had believed the PI was being completely honest. That was part of his charm. Part of the excitement. Even I couldn't figure out why I was so upset. It wasn't as if I suddenly decided Andy was an inappropriate partner. His inappropriateness was what made him so appealing. Satisfied with the answer, I reversed direction.

Maybe the question should have been how could I get mad at Andy now?

I wasn't sure how far I had walked when I reached a conclusion. I wasn't mad at Andy for what he was. I was mad at Andy for letting me see it. Once he and I both knew that he had lied to me, I had to reject him. If I didn't, we would both know that I was a fool. I'd already known. Lost in thought, I let out a deep sigh.

The old cottage was in sight when I asked myself the next question. "Why? Why did I have to reject him?" I continued past the cottage.

I hiked ten blocks before I came up with an answer. I didn't have to reject Andy. I'd played the game every bit as much as he did. The answer was to get everything out in the open. If I ever saw the PI again. If he would talk to me. If he hadn't gotten angry and delivered the evidence he found planted in my apartment to the cops.

Tired from my extended stroll and my extensive soul searching, I sank onto the sand. In front of me, two teenaged girls searched for rides on waves that lacked the strength to carry them. Failure was a given, but the teens didn't seem to care. They giggled happily as wave after wave rolled to shore without them. As I monitored the two girls' attempts, I reminisced about my own late afternoons in the surf. I liked the beach best after the crowd had departed. I did in my teens. I did in my thirties. At last I felt relaxed.

Suddenly, a familiar form moved into my line of vision. "Bishop." I called with more excitement than my sentiments dictated.

The jogger swiveled his head but kept moving.

"Over here, Bishop." I waved both arms. Only after Bishop stopped running and started struggling up the beach did I recall my visit to his hotel room. By the time Bishop plopped on the beach beside me, my face was red with embarrassment. I hoped the flush could pass for sunburn.

"Thank heavens you're here, Honey Bunny." He struggled to enunciate the words between gasps. He took a deep breath before continuing. "I thought I was gonna have to keep up this running thing." He felt in the shallow pockets of his jogging shorts. "You gotta cigarette, Honey Bunny?"

"I don't smoke. What's up with the running? For a second I believed you were on a health kick."

"For a second I was. But now I am outta sight."

"Of?"

"The young lady with whom I keep company."

I recalled the jeans on the floor of his hotel room.

"She thinks I should be in better shape."

I thought of the ashtray overflowing with cigarette butts. "And she lets you smoke?"

"I smoke after she leaves. On the porch."

"Well, then you should do a better job of emptying your ashtrays." I froze. Would Bishop question my knowledge?

"You're right. That rental car is a sty."

The sigh of relief I released was unfortunately loud. Bishop, still laboring to control his own breathing, didn't notice.

"So is your new love the reason you're hanging around at the shore?"

"She's been working down here for a while. Look at how much fun those two are having." I noted the ease with which Bishop changed the topic of conversation to the two girls wrestling with the raft.

"Are you staying at the shore long?" I would not be diverted from my line of questioning.

"Not sure. Hotel is pretty booked up." He changed the subject yet again. "I stopped by to see you earlier today."

"How come?" I spoke over the guffaw Bishop let loose as the girls toppled backward off another wave.

"I had a little time on my hands. The young lady works during the day. So I thought we could have lunch." Bishop and I had lunched together only once in our lives—on the previous day. Was he establishing a daily routine? "We should keep in touch." He paused before adding. "You'll have to send me your address. I can't seem to locate my address book."

Was my blush deepening? Had Bishop associated me with the disappearance of his address book? I studied his face. He was watching the teenagers. He wasn't looking for a reaction to his comment.

"I hate it when that happens. I do it all the time."

Bishop was still watching the would-be surfers as he answered. "Really odd for me to lose something that important. I don't forget things. For a guy who walks around dressed like a slob, I am surprisingly neat at home."

I agreed but couldn't admit having enough information to judge. Guilt was rendering me tongue-tied. Luckily, Bishop became talkative on the topic of our getting together. I eyed him suspiciously and recalled Andy's assertion. Was Bishop's sudden interest in my friendship an outgrowth of his interest in Bascombe's missing booty?

"So whatta ya say we have lunch tomorrow."

"I . . . eh . . . well . . ." Finally I just spat out the words. "Bishop, I know about the money." Fearing for my safety, I added quickly. "Not where it is but that it exists."

"What money?" Bishop's demeanor was casual.

"Bishop, don't be coy."

"I think you're the one being coy, Honey Bunny."

"You don't know?"

Bishop's face was blank.

"You really don't know." I made a statement.

"Don't think I do, Honey Bunny. But I sure do like money. What is the story?"

It was too late to back away from the topic. "Well, there were rumors that Bascombe hid quite a bit of cash, some stolen from Markshell."

"Where?"

"If I knew that, Bishop, I'd be a wealthy woman."

Bishop didn't pursue the topic, but his eyes narrowed as he watched the teenagers abandon rafting. "They would be better off coming back tomorrow." Suddenly, Bishop leapt to his feet and waved. A voluptuous young woman in running clothes as revealing as any bathing suit jogged along the water's edge. When she spotted Bishop, a smile erupted on her face. I thought she was going to run up the beach to join us. When she saw me, however, she hesitated. With arm gestures she encouraged Bishop to join her. "Gotta go. Looks like I got busted goofing off."

"Stop by anytime." I called after Bishop as he jogged off trailing the blonde ponytail. I assumed it belonged to his new girlfriend. The woman had a figure that could fill the jeans I'd found on the floor—very well.

He responded with a wave over his shoulder. Although he raced to join the woman, he hadn't caught up by the time they passed out of sight.

The sun was close to the western horizon when I arrived home laden with seashells. Classic shells. Long skinny shells. Shells that had been recently vacated by snails. Watching for additions to the collection, I didn't glance up at my cottage until I was almost ready to cross the dunes and slip through the fence. Luckily I did or I would have walked right into Randall Wallace. Since he seemed to be both in the process of leaving my driveway and experiencing an extremely bad mood, I decided to keep my presence a secret.

Hiding was easy. For the benefit of no one in particular, I feigned exhaustion and settled onto the seaward side of a dune. I peeked around the mound of sand concealing myself in the tall grass. Randall was kicking a large motorcycle with a vengeance. Eventually, the bike toppled. Apparently, the fall convinced Randall he had punished the Harley Davidson sufficiently. He reached down and with one arm yanked the bike upright. At his height, throwing his leg over the seat required little agility. He was still angry as he jumped on the starter. I was relieved to hear him roar off.

I was left with many questions. Why was Randall in my driveway? Was he the young fellow on a scooter that Rupert P. Downie had mentioned? Did he really think he looked good in the wildly printed orange cotton trousers he was wearing? Had Randall come to visit? If so, why? How had he found me? And, what made him so angry? More importantly, would he be back? If so, would he still be angry? Those questions were only the top of my list. I had more.

I doubted that Randall had been to my cottage before. Even with his fading eyesight, Downie could have told the difference between a scooter and 650 pounds of Harley. Even if his eyes failed, certainly his ears could have clarified the difference. Couldn't they?

As the roar of Randall's motorcycle moved out of hearing range, I became conscious of eyes watching me. I stood and rotated 360 degrees but saw no one looking my way. Nor did I see any familiar faces. I stared at the vast expanse of glass that formed the front of Bascombe's house. Without lights, I couldn't see inside. Was an intruder in the house watching me? I shuddered. I considered calling Detective Dupuy. To report what? A case of the jitters? I shook my head to chase the feeling and headed home.

Chapter 35

Since I was no longer spending my time investigating, I turned my attention to vacation activities. With the addition of my denim jacket and walking shoes, I was ready for a walk on the boardwalk—an invariable tradition. I planned to hit the fudge shop, come home and eat half a pound of vanilla. This plan was not an outgrowth of depression. I'd been looking forward to eating myself silly on Copper Kettle vanilla since mid-March.

I walked to the end of the boardwalk at 23rd Street and started my stroll down the boards. As I made my way towards the center of town, I waited to hear the sound of a supposedly familiar voice and see the face of a long lost friend. I saw no one—and I assume no one saw me. Of course. Nothing embarrassing happened. If a humiliating situation had arisen, I bet old classmates would have crawled out from under the boardwalk like teenagers before curfew.

I did, however, encounter one problem. The Copper Kettle fudge shop was no more. No more crowds gathered around the window. No more handsome college students stirring the sugary concoction. No more sugary concoction. I stared at the building as if willing the business to reopen. I was sure I had the right spot. Just to be sure I covered a few more blocks. No Copper Kettle. More change! Was there no end to the changes? I remembered Andy's reaction to my conservatism. I could change. I would change. Steel's and Laura's offered vanilla. I bought enough of each brand to conduct a taste test—and to put me into a coma.

As I carried my fudge-packed bag down the boardwalk, I smiled at familiar sites. Gift shops. Amusements. Miniature golf. And, skee ball. I loved skee ball. In the age of electronic games, the few skee ball machines extant had been pushed into dark corners of modern arcades. The tame wooden runways and old mechanical scoreboards paled next to the lights and sounds of modern games. Yet as I glanced into the last arcade on the boardwalk, there they were. A short row of skee ball machines. I was thrilled. I was digging for quarters when the sight stopped me cold. Andy.

I stood paralyzed at the entrance to the arcade as vacationers buzzed around me. Intent on his game, the PI's eyes never turned in my direction. I watched as he rolled the old wooden balls. The old scoreboard racked up the points fifty at a time. The old machine spit out long strips of tickets. Andy inserted another quarter and pulled the lever. Another supply of balls rolled down the gutter. Andy remained intent on the game.

It was only as I turned to leave that I sensed Andy's head swing to the left. Had his eyes turned in my direction? Had he known I was watching him? I glanced back but once again the PI's attention was focused on the alley. I thought of saying hello, but what would I say next? What would he say? I left the arcade.

As I approached the cottage it was Bascombe's home next door that held my interest. The house appeared black and still and menacing. I rushed by the building and raced up the steps to my cottage. For the first time I faced the night with a fear of the murderer—and the crime scene next door. I found the beeper that Detective Dupuy had given me. At least for one night, I would not sleep alone.

But first I had fudge to eat. After turning on every light in the house including the untouched lamp in the spare bedroom, I carried my fudge to the kitchen. When I opened the drawer for a knife, I cringed at the dirt caked on the blade on top. I pushed the offensive utensil aside, pulled out a dinner knife and grabbed a plate. Three steps into the living room I stopped. Could it be?

"It is." Detective Dupuy had responded to the beeper.

"Thank God." I was thinking how impolite and impolitic it would have been to disturb the detective if the knife were not caked with blood. But it was and there was a good chance that blood would be Bascombe's.

"You think that offering me the probable murder weapon is good." Detective Dupuy appeared confused—and amused.

"Well . . . yeah . . . sure . . . I mean now you have the murder weapon."

"Which was in your house."

"But not when you searched it. Don't you see? Someone planted the knife here."

"How do I know you didn't plant the knife yourself?" Detective Dupuy was studying me from under those heavy lids.

I sighed audibly. The detective and I would never see eye to eye. "Why would I plant the murder weapon in my own house and then call the cops?"

"To throw us off the track?" Officer Timmy Borden put in his two cents.

I eyed the young policeman with impatience. Wasn't he supposed to be a summer intern? Summer was ending. Didn't he have somewhere to be?

Nonetheless I had to admit that he proposed a pretty good plan. If I hadn't been so fast with the beeper, I might have reached that conclusion myself.

"Did you touch it?" Detective Dupuy slipped the misused utensil into a plastic bag.

"I don't know. I kind of pushed it aside." I recreated the motion. I didn't know if my prints would show on it or not.

"And tonight was the first night you saw the knife."

I had no idea when I had last used the kitchen. "Ooh. What if I cut something with it?"

Detective Dupuy held the plastic bag at eye level. "Wouldn't you have washed it?"

I nodded.

"No way you washed this." She passed the bag to Officer Timmy Borden. Together they headed for the door. I waited for her parting shot. The wait wasn't long. "You still have time left on your lease, right?"

I nodded my head.

"And you don't have any plans to leave town, right?"

I shook my head.

"Don't change your plans, but if you do, let me know."

I nodded and shook my head at the same time. I looked like an idiot.

Chapter 36

Now that I had retired from investigating, I tried relaxing. After all, I'd been on vacation for over a week; relaxing did not seem out of order. Unfortunately, I seemed to have lost the knack.

Maybe the problem was waiting for the test results to see if the knife was actually the murder weapon—or if earlier tenants had slain their own dinner. Or maybe the problem was knowing that I had jettisoned the man to whom I had given a piece of evidence intended to frame me for murder. Would Andy take the memo planted on my computer to the police? My hunch was that he would think about sending the letter to the cops. My bet was that he would decide against the vindictive move. It was the riskiest bet I ever placed.

Despite my preoccupation and in deference to my vacation, I dragged my towel through the dunes and spread my gear on the sand. Sunbathing seemed boring. The surf felt less than invigorating. Reading wasn't entertaining. Reading about someone else's investigation paled when compared to working with Andy. Without giving the sun enough time to tan my pale skin, I left the beach.

Not that the house offered much in the way of entertainment. I hadn't even turned on the old console TV that relied on bent and beaten rabbit ears. I had no radio or CD player. With no phone, I couldn't call anyone. I had no plans for the afternoon as I tromped up the steps.

I almost missed the card stuck under my door. It was Detective Dupuy's. Please call ASAP was scrawled on the back. When Detective Dupuy wrote ASAP, I read "now."

In the interest of speedy compliance with the policewoman's request, I drove the short distance to the phone booth. I viewed the casualness of her message as a positive sign. Surely, if the knife had proven to be the murder weapon with my fingerprints on it, the detective would have come to the house and found me on the beach. Nonetheless, my fingers needed three tries to hit the right buttons on the phone.

I was irritated by the length of time the detective kept me waiting. Remembering that this woman could put me away for a long time helped me keep my annoyance to myself. When she finally picked up, on speaker, my voice was pleasant. Detective Dupuy's wasn't. In dull, unfathomable tones, she explained that although she had no news on the knife she wanted me to come to a lineup. The police had identified a suspect in my mugging. She colored her final word with a touch of irony.

Detective Dupuy named a time an hour in the future. I promised to be prompt. Because the lineup was my first, I wasn't sure how to dress, but I was pretty certain a bathing suit and an oversized man's shirt were inappropriate. I doubted that black leggings and an oversized man's shirt were any more appropriate, but they were dry.

The lineup was not a success. I had the feeling Detective Dupuy knew it wouldn't be before she ushered me into a small room. She treated me with an overdose of courtesy, but I sensed her saying to herself. "You say mugging victim. Okay, I'll treat you like a mugging victim, but believe me I know better." She conveyed all that information via a slight smirk that marred her otherwise solicitous expression.

For the line-up the police had rounded up five young men who roughly fit the description I'd been able to give of my mugger. Given that sixty percent of the population qualified, I didn't imagine they had much trouble. I used lineups I'd seen on TV as a model for my behavior; there was nothing in the etiquette books. I eyed each of the men carefully. "As I explained, I only saw the guy running away."

Based on that comment, Detective Dupuy had the suspects turn. None of the posteriors looked familiar although one or two struck me as inordinately attractive. I apologized. I recognized no one.

"I see."

As usual, I wasn't sure what she saw.

"Oh, by the way." Detective Dupuy stopped me in the small lobby of the police station. My hand already gripped the handle of the glass door. I turned to find her in her Columbo mode. "You know, someone told me that you always wear great shoes."

"Yeah." What did she want? The name of the shoe store?

"They said you only wear one fairly expensive brand."

I shrugged.

"Do you know what kind of shoes Bascombe wore? As a rule?"

My face contorted and I made several attempts to answer before I spit out, "How the hell would I know what kind of shoes Bascombe wore? Are you . . . ?" I thought it wise not to finish my last thought.

"Did anyone ever make a remark to you about Bascombe's shoes?"

I stood with a frown etching lines into my face only for effect. I wanted the detective to think I was giving her question serious consideration. "No." I answered in a solemn tone. "I don't believe anyone ever did." I saw no point in asking why the detective was following this line of inquiry. I knew it had something to do with the mysterious "feet thing." I did not expect Detective Dupuy to share. She let the door she was holding fall closed; I pushed mine open.

As I left the police station, I felt jumpy. At sixes and sevens was the phrase I had learned when preparing for SATs. I didn't want to go home. I didn't want to eat. I didn't want to see a movie. What I did want, I had no idea. There had been a day when I'd found driving relaxing. Maybe I could recreate the day.

The recently redesigned Ford Taurus met all my automotive needs. I am sure that the engine was powerful and the electrical system reliable, but that wasn't why I loved my rental car. The Ford Taurus boasted of three separate cup holders—not one of which blocked the tape player which I could have used if I had packed any tapes. Using the armrest, I could, without fear of carpal tunnel syndrome, reach right by the medium soda I picked up at McDonald's and change the radio station repeatedly. The ability to get to the button quickly became more and more important as I realized that most songs played on contemporary radio addressed three issues: 1) the inability to find a romantic interest, 2) the pain caused by the romantic interest that is lost, and 3) the ongoing nostalgia for the lost romantic interest. I don't think I heard more than eight bars of any one song before switching stations. Eventually, I rode in silence.

The route I chose was one I had often driven when in a contemplative mood: south out of town on the Ocean Drive. After cutting across a stretch of marshland, the road deposited me, in return for a fifty-cent toll, in Strathmere, a town that although still small appeared to have grown exponentially in the last fifteen years. Everything in town looked bigger, crisper, cleaner—even the dilapidated old house whose living room floor did not survive a summer under my crowd's feet. The three-story building appeared spiffy with new paint, new landscaping and, I bet, a new owner. I was sure the changes made the residents of Strathmere happy, but they made me feel disconnected. Turn your back on a town for a mere decade or two and everything changes.

After Strathmere I looked forward to the most desolate, and comforting, stretch of road. I wasn't old enough to remember the Ocean Drive between Strathmere and Sea Isle City before a fierce hurricane hit in the early sixties. I did recall the long narrow string of beach that connected the two towns in later years when only a handful of original houses stood on stilts along the roadway. One by one in the seventies and eighties brave builders tucked houses into remote pieces of land among the grassy dunes. I didn't know if it was years of mild weather or advances in engineering that had prompted redevelopment of the area. The road still had a rustic feel and was far from overcrowded, but, in my bleak mood, I wanted a desolate spot. Still beautiful, the road was no longer deserted. I pulled over to make a U-turn.

As if my mood weren't bad enough, when I glanced in my rearview mirror I spotted a car like David's behind me. I knew my ex wasn't driving and not just because he had told me he was leaving town. David would never have put the top up on such a beautiful day. It wasn't that he was a nature lover. He believed having the roof down improved reception on his omnipresent cell phone.

Nevertheless, when the car passed I verified that David wasn't behind the wheel. Habit, I guess. The plates were New York, as were David's, but the tiny sports car was driven by a woman who, to judge by the scarf tied tightly around her head and large sunglasses hiding her face, had bought the wrong model. I couldn't discern if the woman was young or old, but I could tell that the sun and wind, the key benefits of driving a convertible, were not to her liking.

My mood had not improved when I returned to the old cottage. The sunlight felt scorching, not warming. The surf seemed agitating, not calming. Forgetting the limited water pressure in the old cottage, I climbed into the shower. The experience was not particularly refreshing. I wrapped a ripped cotton bathrobe around me, pulled out the fudge, and tried for the first time to turn on the old TV in the house. The technology might have been outdated, but, after extensive manipulation of the rabbit ears, the television worked—in a fashion I remembered from my childhood. The term flipping through the channels took on added meaning as I knelt in front of the TV and twisted the dial in search of entertainment. I passed shadowy images of soap operas and talk shows. I stopped at an NTS news show. Instead of Richard Rothman's dignified presence, I found the rolling image of a solemn young man who could not differentiate between happy and sad stories. I silenced the cackling sound, killed the snowy picture, and focused on eating fudge until a heavy knock interrupted my progress.

If I were to rank all the men I've ever met according to how much I would enjoy entertaining them in my bathrobe, Randall Wallace would have ranked dead last. But that's who I saw through the triangle of yellow glass in the front door. I had no choice but to respond to his persistent knock. I knew he could hear me. He'd stopped by at least once, maybe more. Not answering would only delay the inevitable. I held the door open only a few inches.

"Randall. How did you know where I was staying?" Without intending to be inhospitable I spat out my first thought. I blocked the entrance with my body.

"There were rumors that you were the roomer here." Luckily he guffawed, so I knew to smile in response to his pun.

"Can I come in?" Randall seemed doubtful.

"Of course. Of course. I'm sorry. I was just surprised to see you." I held the door open for my unexpected guest.

"I didn't mean to scare you."

I hated to tell him that aside from his taste in clothing he was the least frightening man I'd ever met. And that day Randall's attire was less horrifying than usual. Apparently, someone had introduced him to the Gap—and solids. There was nothing wrong with the blue jeans and white T-shirt he wore except the fit. Even at six foot six, Randall should have been able to find pants that reached his ankles. In the meantime, if calypso came back, Randall was ready.

Randall appeared nervous. Whatever had made him seem confident that day on the Atlantic City boardwalk had passed. "I read about the murder in the paper . . . I knew you were staying next door . . . so I knew . . ."

I interrupted to avoid listening to any further explanations. "Please sit down. Can I get you something to drink?" I waved him towards the couch and walked toward the kitchen area.

"No. No." He tried to inject his voice with jovial tones. "I was just in the neighborhood and thought I would drop by."

"In the neighborhood?" I asked with skepticism that I hoped Randall would interpret as surprise.

I failed. Randall heard the question as an accusation. "You saw me in Atlantic City with my mother."

"Sure, but I didn't know you were in Ocean City. Are you sure you wouldn't like something to drink?" I worked to appear hospitable while not feeling it. My vacation had been enough of a bomb without unscheduled visits from Randall Wallace.

When Randall said he'd like a coke, I realized that I'd pushed harder than I'd intended. My former co-worker looked a bit too comfortable for my taste as he settled on the sofa. "So you must know more than anyone about Bascombe's murder." He smiled broadly at me as I handed him a glass of soda.

"I am the last to hear anything." I explained that the Ocean City police didn't confide in me and the local press had downplayed the murder. "You probably know more than I do."

"I don't know anything." Randall's sentence sounded like a denial. I guessed I wasn't the only person feeling defensive. "I shouldn't bother you but I figured you must have seen or heard something—being here in town and all. I heard you were working with a detective."

"No. I know . . . " I paused. "I knew a private investigator in town, but I don't know anything about the case. Andy Beck, the fellow you met on the boardwalk, isn't working on the murder."

"I find it really interesting that you were right here, next door, when Bascombe was killed."

I shrugged. "Unlucky coincidence."

"That's some coincidence." Randall stuttered over the words.

I smiled and shrugged my shoulders. "If only I'd awakened, I could have solved the entire crime. Is there a reward?"

Randall ignored my question. "The cops believe you slept through the entire thing?" Disbelief seeped from his words.

"They believe me because I did." I didn't appreciate Randall's tone. What was the point of his visit anyway?

"That's hard to believe."

I chose to respond with another smile and shrug of the shoulders.

"Was Bascombe ever in this house?" Randall searched the room for traces of Bascombe's presence.

"Not while I was here."

Randall nodded. I didn't know what to say.

"Did you see him much?" In response to my confused expression he added, "When you were here. Did you see him?" His intonation clarified his meaning of "see."

"No." My tone told him that answer was obvious. "I didn't even know for sure he was next door until the day he . . . well, you know . . . died." I hesitated before adding, "Randall, if you want to know if I was having an affair with Bascombe, I can assure you that I was not. I know that's what everyone suspects. Of course, no one will spit the question out. They just pussyfoot around with not-so-subtle innuendos."

Randall watched me with wide eyes. "You are a pretty woman, Meg. People think that Bascombe would be lucky to have an affair with you. Any man would."

I felt my stomach execute a backflip. Oh, please, I prayed silently, do not let this be the reason for his visit. I was relieved when Randall returned to the topic of Bascombe.

"You must have seen his last visitors then." Now Randall sounded manic as if he found the possibility that I had inside dirt exciting.

"Nope." I didn't mention Miguel O'Shea and his girlfriend, Ella. I found Randall's grilling inappropriate.

Randall grew suddenly pensive. "I told them . . . the cops . . . that I wasn't involved in Bascombe's murder. They seemed to believe me. You didn't tell them you saw me, did you?"

"Why would I?" I was confused by his statement. "Randall, is someone trying to frame you, too?"

I bit my tongue but couldn't bite off the word "too." Randall ignored my slip. He showed his exasperation. "Did they ask you about me?"

"They?"

"The cops."

I hesitated long enough for him to reply to his own question. "I knew it. I knew it." He pounded his fists into his knees.

"Randall, Detective Dupuy asked about everyone. I bet she asked everyone about me."

Randall snickered. "Boy, did she. I thought for sure you were the one they were going to nail for this thing. She talked to everyone."

What had Detective Dupuy told them? "Really?"

I hoped Randall would elaborate but he wasn't interested in my problems. "What did you tell her about me?"

"I don't recall." My statement was true. I recalled Detective Dupuy asking about Randall but little else about the conversation. "I'm sure I told her you weren't capable of murder."

"When you told her I wasn't capable of murder, did she buy it?"

"What's to buy?" My voice grew concerned. "You're not a killer. Am I right?"

"Oh, God, yes. I couldn't hurt anyone. Even Bascombe. Even though he deserved to be cut down to size. Everyone knows that. Bishop was saying that at the funeral. But no one would believe I would I kill him. Everyone knew me so well." Randall sounded bitter. "Although he deserved what he got, didn't he Meg? That bastard. Didn't you want him dead?"

"Randall." I cut my trembling visitor off. "Don't talk this way." It occurred to me that Randall might be wired. Had Detective Dupuy sent him? Maybe I'd better make flattering remarks about the policewoman. "No matter what we thought of DK, he didn't deserve to die. No one had the right to kill him. The police will find the killer. I think that Detective Dupuy is extremely competent." I felt very satisfied with my comments.

"She'll never catch the killer. No one can. Anyone who killed Bascombe is too smart. Too wise." He focused on his hands as he wrung them. "Look," he said after a moment of nodding and mumbling, "I'm sorry to disturb you on your vacation." He backed across the room and out the door. After he disappeared down the stairs and around the corner of the house, I heard the roar of a motorcycle. I watched the alley but Randall must have headed in the other direction. I never saw him leave.

Chapter 37

When I next heard knocking, I didn't know whether to expect joy or horror. The potential for both lurked behind the door. Dutifully, I climbed on a kitchen chair to peek at my visitor. The hair I peered down on was that of a female, a shade of blonde I didn't recognize. When the visitor glanced up, however, I recognized the face. Lindy Sharpe. Apparently, the emphasis in her strawberry blond hair had shifted to blonde. I threw open the door. "Lindy, what are you doing here?" I was shocked to hear more surprise than pleasure in my voice.

Whatever the occasion was, she had certainly dressed for it. I'd spent the last week at the beach, but Lindy had the tan. Her golden skin tone appeared deep and lush next to the designer white shorts and loose sleeveless knit top she'd accessorized with silk scarf, gold jewelry, and more makeup than I owned.

The wide expanse of white teeth disappeared. "Boy, that's a nice greeting." Her oversized mouth accentuated her frown.

"Oh, I am so sorry. You're the best visitor I've had. I'm just surprised to see you standing there."

"It wasn't like I could call ahead or anything. Plus, mine was a last minute decision. I had some time. Everyone else has been

233

to the crime scene. It was my turn." Her wide smile reappeared. "Can I come in?"

"Sure." I stepped aside and waved her into the living room.

Her confident strides dissolved into tentative baby steps as she surveyed the interior. She came to a halt with her hands on her hips. "What a dump!" Lindy did a fair Bette Davis imitation.

"It's home."

"Luckily it's only a temporary situation." Lindy perched on the edge of a wood chair. Judging by the expression on her face, she wouldn't risk touching the upholstery. She strained her neck to check out the place before asking in a meaningful tone. "So, where's Mr. Right?"

"Andy?" I sighed. "Turns out he wasn't that right."

First I poured a glass of mineral water for Lindy. Then I poured out my heart. When I'd finished, Lindy was staring at me with wide eyes. "What is wrong with you?"

I didn't understand.

"This guy has lied to you. Used you. Deceived you." She was grasping for another word when I stopped her.

"Okay, okay. I get your point."

"How can you possibly miss him?"

I shrugged.

"Sometimes I wonder about your taste in men. I mean David was no prize either."

I wasn't going to argue that point.

"Really, I'm surprised Bascombe didn't fire him sooner."

"David resigned."

"Yeah. Right." Lindy's two words said it all.

I thought David had quit. While I was reeling from Lindy's revelation, she wandered onto the porch. Still dazed, I followed.

"This is a beautiful beach." Lindy leaned on the railing and gazed across the dunes and the wide expanse of white sand beyond. "I didn't know South Jersey had such beautiful beaches."

"And great surf."

"I can see." Lindy walked to the corner of the porch. "That Bascombe's place?"

"That's the spot."

Lindy stared in the direction of the Bascombe house. "So that's where he spent his last hours?"

"Yep."

"And where he . . . ?" Lindy didn't finish the sentence. I didn't think she could. She gulped hard. I pretended that I didn't see the tears glistening in her eyes.

Tears? For Bascombe?

Lindy continued studying the house. Her face suggested something I didn't want to know. Lindy and Bascombe? I shuddered. Not Lindy. I eyed her tear-stained face. Yes, Lindy.

She turned to face me. "You know?"

Now I did. "Did he promise to bring you here?"

The tears spilled from her eyes when she nodded.

I didn't know what to say. Finally, I asked the only question I could. "Lindy, what did you see in him?"

Lindy took several minutes to compose herself. When she spoke her voice was small and unsteady. "He liked me. I had no illusions that he loved me. I know he liked just about anything thirty years younger and reasonably attractive, but when I was with him . . . " She bit her lip hard. "He had this way, when he wanted something, of giving all his energy to get it."

That I could believe. What I didn't mention was that someone usually got hurt. "How long were you and he . . . ?"

Mercifully, Lindy didn't make me include a verb.

"Not even a month. But our affair was so . . . "

"Hot." I used Andy's description.

"Really, really hot."

I understood that Lindy needed to talk, but I hoped not too much. I was disappointed. She gave me dates, times, locations, and a few details that I wished had gone to Bascombe's grave with him.

I'd never feel the same about Markshell's main conference room, coffee room, reception desk . . . there appeared no end to the list.

When Lindy reached for her bag, I was afraid she was going to pull out pictures, but instead her hand emerged clutching a tissue. The honking as she blew her nose changed her mood. Suddenly Lindy grew playful. She nodded towards the house left empty by Bascombe's death. "Let's go inside."

Had Lindy lost her mind?

"You've heard the rumors, haven't you? They say there's a fortune, millions of dollars, hidden in the house."

Lindy knew about the hidden loot. I was really angry. Everyone had known but me. If it weren't for Miguel O'Shea blabbing in front of me, I might never have found out.

"Let's go. We can split the take." Her once tear-filled eyes were sparkling.

"Don't be ridiculous. There's no money in that house. The cops have been all over that place." I didn't mention that Andy, Miguel O'Shea, and unknown others had been through Bascombe's residence as well.

"Too bad." Lindy sank back onto the glider.

"Do you want to go get something to eat or something?"

Lindy declined with a shake of her strawberry blonde curls. She had an appointment—one she seemed pretty excited about. "I met this guy at the funeral. Really cute. You and lover boy should have stayed around for the post-funeral party. It was a blast."

I was incredulous. I guess my face revealed that.

"Meg. Life goes on. You can't sit around and mope."

Frankly, given her recent and tearful revelations, I felt a week or two of moping was in order.

"Who is this guy?" I asked although I had a feeling I knew.

"Bucky Whitelaw. Really cute. I'm meeting him this afternoon at the Seacrest Country Club. I'm taking a lesson."

"A lesson?"

If Lindy caught the sarcasm in my voice, she ignored it. "Tennis lesson, silly. He's the pro. What else could it be?"

I did not miss the lechery in her tone nor the excitement in her eyes as she rushed out. As I watched Lindy drive away, I recalled Bucky's performance on the diving board. I doubted that she would find her lesson disappointing.

With Lindy gone, I turned to the old TV, or at least the static it generated, for companionship. I was still in front of the TV when Rothman's news broadcast began. Rothman was off that night. For some inexplicable reason, the substitute anchored added "for personal reasons."

Personal reasons. I bet.

Detective Dupuy was next to arrive on my doorstep. "Did it ever occur to you to get a cellular phone?" The detective seemed annoyed that she had to drop by. I thought it wise to express my appreciation for her visit—repeatedly. Unless, of course, she had come to arrest me. She had not.

"I brought your linens and your clothes back." Without apology, she dropped a package wrapped in brown paper on the sofa. I thanked her profusely. Insincerely but profusely.

"Anything new on the knife?"

"No prints. None. Zero." In contrast to her calm tones, the detective's small eyes were darting around the room.

"Wiped clean, eh?"

The detective nodded but didn't look my way.

"Is it the murder weapon?"

"Maybe." She was studying the ceiling.

I followed her gaze but noted nothing unusual about what appeared to be the original plaster ceiling—one of the few features of the house spared renovation. "Will we know soon?"

She nodded with less conviction than indicated by her previous head gestures. I grew nervous as I watched her surveying the room. "How do you like this place?"

At last. An opportunity to bond. "Well, this vacation hasn't been the best of my life, so it might not be fair to judge the house."

"No." The single word said don't think that I'm trying to be sociable. I am asking for a reason. "I mean have you noticed anything odd about the house?"

I did not succeed in banishing the anger from my voice. "You mean other than my boss got murdered next door, I got mugged in the driveway, and the very people I went on vacation to get away from keep appearing at my door unannounced?"

"David Orlander, Randall Wallace, Bishop Winston. Have I missed anyone?"

I skipped mentioning Lindy and targeted the person who planted the knife.

"Well, that remains to be seen, doesn't it?" The detective was, as usual, cryptic. Was she saying I was not yet off the hook? Why ask? Communication with Detective Dupuy was uniformly one-sided.

"I can hardly wait."

Her sneer told me Detective Dupuy thought I was being sarcastic. I was offended until I realized I was.

Chapter 38

Rather than going out and having fun, I got dressed and sat on my porch watching other people have fun. And, everyone else seemed to be doing just that. The weather stayed clear and warm. With each day after Labor Day, the beach crowd diminished slightly as real life reclaimed the vacationers. I imagined I was the lone visitor whose real life had followed her to the beach—at least in such an emphatic way. With the possible exception of DK Bascombe. But then he didn't really count anymore, did he?

Sitting on the porch of the old house offered a pageant for the senses. For the eyes. Surf, wide expanse of white beach, and tall mounds of sand with waving dune grass. For the nose. Salt air, fresh breeze, and the occasional odor of sea life. For the ears. Sea gulls, heavy surf, and gentle wind rustling the tall grass.

And my name. Were the hallucinations starting again?

"Meg." The syllable took five seconds to pronounce. The word was sung more than stated. "Meg Daniels." Saying my full name took the voice a good ten seconds. I ignored the call. In response, the summons grew louder.

I could identify the direction from which the sound carried. Nonetheless, I checked over the rail to the east and the south of the house before I gave in and looked at the Bascombe house. What terrified me most was that I saw no one. Yet the voice continued—this time punctuated by a long "oooooh." I began to search the north side of the house in earnest. There was no one on the path that separated my house from that of my late boss. The Bascombe porch was empty—even the furniture had been removed. All the windows were shut.

"Up here." The ghostly voice offered a clue. Bishop's head peaked over the top of the solid second floor railing.

"Bishop," I affected a whispery quality to my voice that did little to hide the fact that I was screaming. "What are you doing there?" There was the second floor deck of the Bascombe house.

"Don't you just love this place." Bishop took a deep breath before lighting a cigarette. He tossed the match over the railing.

I didn't address Bishop's littering offense. In my mind, he had a more serious problem.

"Bishop, are you supposed to be in that house?"

"Door was open." Bishop took a long drag on his cigarette and polluted the air he praised. "This is a damn nice setting isn't it. This beach is beautiful. Only eyesore is that dump you're living in."

I didn't have time to argue the merits of my housing. "Bishop, get out of there."

"Why? DK isn't going be using the house tonight. You didn't tell me what a great place he had."

"Why would I? I've never been inside."

Bishop eyed me with an expression that said, "Right. I forgot that was your story" but remained mercifully quiet on the topic. "Why don't you haul your ass over here and dunk it in that big old Jacuzzi you know nothing about?"

"Bishop, I am not breaking into the house of a murder victim for a soak in the Jacuzzi."

"Honey Bunny, do you think the cops believe you killed Bascombe to use his hot tub?"

"Bishop." I spoke in measured, but very high tones. "I am not going to tell you this again. I did not murder DK Bascombe. Now get yourself out of there before you find yourself in big trouble."

I didn't mean "get yourself out of Bascombe's house and into my living room," but Bishop interpreted my suggestion as an invitation. When he appeared at the door, I still spoke to him in a faux whisper. "Are you nuts breaking into a crime scene?"

"I told you Honey Bunny. I did not break in. Door was open. The cops couldn't actually believe that a strip of yellow tape would keep people out."

I explained to Bishop that the tape did keep law abiding citizens out.

"I'm law abiding. Maybe not particularly literate but law abiding."

"The cops realize that you can read crime scene tape."

"Okay, so I'm curious." Bishop pushed by me. "Got anything to drink here?"

I used the last of the rum to make Bishop a pathetically weak daiquiri. If the drink tasted like dishwater, he didn't complain. But he did complain about aching muscles when he settled into the old rocker. "This health kick is gonna kill me." He sighed as he surveyed the scene. "This is nice. My hotel room has a balcony, but I like being down here closer to the beach."

"Yeah, it's funny isn't it. The view from up there is beautiful but you miss something."

I froze but Bishop didn't question my statement. He understood "up there" to be a generic evaluation of high rises. As if plucking the topic from my mind, Bishop volunteered that he had found his address book. "Just showed up in the rental car. On the floor. I must have dropped it. I guess a fast stop shook it free."

"Ummmh." I nodded as I studied the gulls. "See that one gull over there . . . "

"Honey Bunny, something big is wrong with your vacation if you can identify the individual gulls on your beach. My lady is working tonight. Whatta ya say we go out and I introduce you to a nice young man."

"You know nice young men in Ocean City already?"

"Hell no. We'll meet them."

I declined Bishop's offer. "I am enjoying a relaxing vacation."

"You don't look all that relaxed." He pointed to where the bruises were fading on my face and where the scabs were healing on my knees. "You get them fighting with Bascombe?"

Bishop's accusations were no longer funny—if they had ever been. "If you don't stop making those stupid jokes, I am going to ask you to leave. Now tell me whatever possessed you to go into the house."

Bishop took a long drink of daiquiri before he answered. "My new lady."

I shook my head to indicate that I didn't understand. Bishop explained. When he repeated what I had told him about the money to his new girlfriend, she suggested he check out Bascombe's house for the cash.

"And you did?"

Bishop nodded.

"Just because she asked?"

Again, he nodded.

What did women do to engender such devotion? I wished someone would let me in on the secret, but that was not a discussion to have with Bishop. I stuck to the topic of his actions.

"Shouldn't you have at least waited until after dark?"

That time Bishop shrugged.

I felt compelled to ask. "What kind of hold does this woman have over you? What does she have that makes her so special?"

"She got two of them." Bishop leered.

"You could hardly be more juvenile." I directed my gaze out over the ocean. The next time I turned his way, Bishop had too. He was waxing poetic about his new love.

"She cares about me."

Enough to send him off to commit a felony?

"Of course, I never lose sight of the fact that she can bench press me. That is one strong little lady. I'd better stay on her good side." The facetious tones slipped from his voice. "She takes care of me in a way my wife never did. She asks so little that when she does I can't deny her." He sighed. "She's like a finely cut diamond. She has so many sides. Each facet is more stunning than the last. When I go home I never know what, or whom, to expect." His far off gaze dissolved in a crinkled smile. "She has more wigs . . . ." He chuckled. "She has a whole new personality to go with each one. A whole new repertoire of . . . you know."

I did not want to know.

"How did you meet her?"

"She approached me. Said Bucky Whitelaw had pointed me out once. I gotta thank that guy."

My eyes narrowed. I was willing to accept it was a small world. But this small?

Chapter 39

The end of my vacation was to be marked by a full moon; looking at the sky made me realize that my time at the shore was growing short. The moon was already big and bright enough to lay a runner of light across the water to my feet. I fantasized about dancing down the path like Dorothy to an Oz where I wouldn't have to deal with dead bosses, avaricious co-workers, and suspicious cops.

I didn't know if it was legal for me to be on the beach so late at night. I didn't bother checking. A curfew violation paled next to the potential legal problems I faced. Plus, I wasn't the only one enjoying the moonlight. I was, however, the only one absorbing the ambiance alone. Alone, that is, except for the beeper that would, in case of trouble, summon Detective Dupuy. I checked the pocket of my denim jacket; the little black box was still there. I patted the beeper affectionately.

Dropping onto the sand, I lay back on the cool surface and stared at the stars. The beauty overwhelmed me. All my senses feasted on the overabundance of pleasure. Enjoying the sounds and smells of the cool breeze and the pounding surf, I focused on my search for shooting stars. I needed some luck. I specified good luck as I watched for motion across the sky. The heavens did not cooperate. Could I wish on a satellite? No harm in trying. I closed my eyes and formulated a complex yet mundane wish that catapulted me into my old life. I was envisioning myself back at Markshell when a waft of cigarette smoke intruded on the scene. I opened my eyes but found no one in the vicinity. I rolled onto my stomach for better observation. The red and blue flashing lights caught my attention immediately. Why wouldn't they? They surrounded my house—and Bascombe's.

I stifled my first urge—to run to the cottage to see what was wrong. "Stop acting like an innocent party," I murmured instructions to myself. For the first time, I cursed the wide expanse of beach. On a smaller strand, I might have been able to piece together what was happening. I lay too far away to determine whether my house or Bascombe's was the main attraction. I detected activity at both. I'd left my lights on, but at the Bascombe house lights flicked on and off. I stayed put in the sand and waited and watched. What was going on? I had no idea and made no effort to find out.

Not until the last police car disappeared from view did I rise to my feet. In a crouched position that looked far more suspicious than an upright stride, I ran to a hiding place behind the dunes. Both houses appeared quiet. Brushing sand from every item of clothing and part of my body, I considered the possibilities. There were a million reasons the cops might have come to Bascombe's house. A break-in? They hadn't detected Bishop earlier. A tip? Could be. Or had they come to my house? Why? To arrest me?

As I crawled through the cold and damp sand on my hands and knees, I learned something valuable. Burrs inflict as much pain in the hand as in the foot. I pulled the prickly sphere out easily and continued creeping towards the house like a soldier reconnoitering the enemy. I spotted no police cruisers. No suspicious unmarked cars. I heard laughter from a house down the beach but no sounds from either my cottage or the Bascombe house.

As I tried to figure out why the police had surrounded my house, I began to shake. From the cold? I wasn't sure. The urge to avoid the police was overwhelming—at least until I knew why they wanted me. I felt in my pocket. Fate had been kind. I had locked my cottage and taken my keys. The keys dangled from my tiny wallet. I had everything I needed for a getaway. Getaway. I repeated the word aloud. Two weeks ago, who could have imagined that I would be fleeing from the cops?

As I ran to the car, I expected someone to tackle me. As I backed out of the driveway, I watched for someone to block my way. As I rushed along the fastest route out of town, I waited for someone to stop me. No one did.

I chose the Garden State over Route 9 for several reasons. I was less likely to speed. The road would carry more traffic. The route was more direct. To where? I had no idea as I turned north.

On the drive, I listened attentively to the local radio stations. If the cops were after me, they weren't asking for the public's assistance. A couple of state troopers cruised by without taking special notice of my presence. I began to relax. Surely there must be a logical, and nonthreatening, explanation for the cops' visit to my house. I had to stop overreacting. I had been spending, far too much time alone. But just in case I wasn't overreacting I took the possibility that the cops could trace me through my beeper seriously. I rolled down the window and pitched the small gadget onto the shoulder of the road.

I drove until I couldn't stay awake; I traveled only five exits. Attracted by the only vacancy sign within a ten-mile radius, I pulled into the parking lot of what appeared to be a sleazy motel. As I checked in, I was happy to find the night clerk behind bulletproof glass—not for his safety but for mine. That was only the first of many clues about the nature of the lodging I had chosen.

The tension of flight coupled with the relief of escape knocked me out—until I hit the sheets in the olive drab and gold relic of the sixties. Immediately, I was wide awake. I lay in bed realizing that I was on the run. At least there was a good chance I was on the run. I didn't know how to find out. I couldn't call the Ocean City police and ask if they were searching for me. I couldn't go back to New York. The cops would find me there. The list of couldn'ts grew to be considerably larger than the list of coulds. At least until the puzzle of Bascombe's murder was solved.

The next morning, I awoke with the realization that what under the cover of darkness appeared to be a seedy motel was, in fact, an extremely seedy motel. By the time I opened my eyes, about two hours after I closed them, the insect guests, apparently exhausted from a long night of scurrying and buzzing, had dozed off. I didn't want to know what had tired out the human guests. Until I peeked through the crack in the soiled geometric print curtains, I had only listened to their nocturnal activities. The people I saw through the drapes were not as unsavory as I had expected. Even though I would not consider the guest list desirable, I wondered what had possessed those people to pull into such a dive? At least I had an excuse for winding up in the fleabag. I was hiding from the cops. I worried that I might have more in common with the other guests than I hoped.

In retrospect, the plan I formulated seemed so harmless. I would prove, or at least test, my theory. I would find a library and research Rothman. If I could find enough information, I could do a little nosing around. Maybe a little surveillance. After all, Andy had trained me. Sort of. My gut told me that Caroline Bascombe was hiding out at the newsman's house. I could confirm my suspicion. And then? I decided to take each step one at a time.

I'd executed the first phase successfully and found myself in the resort where Richard Rothman retreated each weekend. After searching the town, I identified the tall white stucco and glass house pictured in *People* magazine. Locating the Rothman residence hadn't been easy. The property was elaborately landscaped; heavy shrubbery provided the privacy a national celebrity needed. I had cased the property from all angles. The rear was as impenetrable as a fortress. The front of Rothman's house that faced the beach was a two-story wall of shaded glass.

Those inside could see out easily. Those outside could see in only with difficulty. At least until night fell and the lights went on. I could wait.

I parked my car at the end of Rothman's property in the surveillance position that I learned from Andy and sat. And sat. And sat. I was so intent on watching nothing happen at the Rothman house, I didn't see the patrol car pull up. Or the policeman approach the driver's side of the car.

"You'll have to come with me, ma'am."

I jumped. "Excuse me?"

The officer repeated his order with the polite tone of request. "Me?"

I feigned innocence.

"Yes, ma'am."

"Why? What did I do?" I stuck with my innocent act.

"Loitering, ma'am."

No mention of murder. Relief flowed through every muscle of my body.

"We've had a complaint."

I'd never even thought of loitering. "Sorry. I'll move."

"No. You'll have to come with me."

"No one asked me to move. Shouldn't that be the first step? Ask me to move. I will."

"Sorry, ma'am. You'll have to come with me."

"For loitering?"

"That's it ma'am."

"Wait a minute. You mean without notice or warning, I have to go with you? Where?"

"To the police station ma'am."

"What for?"

"Ma'am. Calm down. You don't want to end up in trouble for resisting arrest, now do you?" His phony smile was chilling.

"Arrest. What for?" My voice was an octave higher than usual.

"Loitering. I told you ma'am."

My gut told me to believe him. His visit was about loitering. Yet the approach seemed too severe. Maybe I would need to talk to the folks at the station to get the matter settled. "I'll follow you in my car."

"No, ma'am. Your car will be fine here. You'll have to ride in the cruiser with me."

I grabbed my jacket from the passenger's seat uncovering the magazine article on Richard Rothman. I knocked the pages to the floor and kicked the clipping under the seat. I yanked the keys with my wallet attached from the ignition and climbed out of the driver's side. I followed the policeman to his blue cruiser. The uniformed officer held open the back door.

"Back door? Officer . . ." I glanced at his badge. "Officer Healey, criminals ride in the back seat. I can ride up front with you." I didn't wait for a response. I walked around the front of the police car, pulled open the passenger door, and climbed into the front seat. Officer Healey slammed the rear door and slid into the driver's seat without comment.

The local police station was housed in a wooden Victorian dwelling that stopped just short of mansion. Although meticulously maintained, the building had been marred by the addition of a huge macadam parking lot. As soon as the officer stopped the blue police cruiser, I threw the door open, jumped out of the car, and ran up the narrow steps toward the entrance. I was several strides ahead of Healey when, after two tries, I yanked the modern glass door open. To my surprise, I slid across the linoleum floor of the bright reception area until a tall wooden structure stopped me. I smiled up at the female officer seated behind the elevated desk. "I want to see the person in charge."

The middle-aged woman fluffed her white teased hair as she studied me over her mother-of-pearl half-glasses. "Don't worry, Florence." Officer Healey caught up with me. "I've got her. Please follow me, miss." The policeman had a firm grip on my elbow as he propelled me through a door with wire mesh imbedded in the glass. I heard the lock click behind us. If this entire episode was about loitering, why was I being confined behind a secured door with an unbreakable window?

The police officer guided me into a large room with oversized, badly worn wooden desks arranged haphazardly on a battered floor. Although the classic exterior of the house was beautifully maintained, the interior had been completely mutilated.

"Look what you guys did to this floor . . ." Officer Healey's tightening grip convinced me not to elaborate. The cop dragged me across the scratched and scuffed wood before he dropped my arm and gestured toward an abused antique table in a corner. He pulled out a matching carved oak chair and told me to sit down. Captain D'Intino would be with me in a moment. In the meantime, Officer Healey sat on a brown metal folding chair staring at me. Or rather in my direction. No matter how hard I tried, the policeman would not make eye contact.

After fifteen minutes of ignoring my questions and comments, Officer Healey left the room. Alone, I mumbled remarks of disbelief. My jabbering was interrupted by a portly man who appeared at my side, from where I wasn't sure.

"Ma'am?"

"My name is Meg Daniels. No one has even asked me yet." I threw out my arms to express my dismay.

"Ms. Daniels. I'm Captain D'Intino. I'll need to ask you to fill out some papers. Your bail will be $500."

"Bail. What do you mean bail? I haven't even been arrested."

"Oh, I'm sorry ma'am. Didn't Officer Healey mention that to you. I'm afraid you have been."

"Have been what?" I asked incredulously.

"Arrested."

"For what?" I awaited his answer anxiously.

"Loitering."

"Excuse me, Captain D'Intino. But in a case such as this shouldn't the first step be to indicate there is a problem, ask the person to move, explain there was a violation of the law." My tone was polite.

"Ignorance of the law is no excuse, ma'am."

"So I've heard." I struggled to maintain a calm demeanor. "But exactly what law have I violated?"

"City ordinance, Ma'am."

"Which one?"

He hesitated. "242."

I swore he made up the number. To support his case, he added. "And then there's the noise issue." I stared at him blankly. "Your radio was too loud."

"I didn't have it on."

"Well, you'll have to tell that to the judge. We had a complaint."

If the Ocean City police were after me, shouldn't the cop have added their charge to his list. "Anything else?" I asked in the same annoyed tone I had been using.

"I think we have enough."

"You're sure. You're not going to hit me with another charge or anything?"

"You've been apprised of all your charges." He laughed. "And we checked to make sure there were no APBs out on you."

So the OC police were not after me. That meant the cops' behavior was as ludicrous as it seemed. The revelation also meant that my behavior was as ludicrous as theirs. I chose not to dwell on that thought. "What next?" I sounded, and felt, exasperated.

"You have to fill out a few forms for us. Post bail and then the officer will escort you out of town."

"Excuse me?" I regarded the detective with an unbelieving expression. "I hadn't planned on leaving town."

"I think it would be best, ma'am."

"You do?"

"Yes, ma'am." His flat tone matched his expression.

Had these guys heard of the constitution? They probably wouldn't believe the news from me. "Okay. Let me pay my bail and go."

"Mrs. Jeffers will take the information we need and then you can leave. After you pay your $500."

With that a disarmingly motherly matron rolled a creaky gray metal typewriter table through the doorway and across the room. Laboriously, she slid the table to a position next to me, pulled up a metal folding chair, and sat down. I gave Mrs. Jeffers the facts she wanted. Even though the requested information was minimal, the process took ten minutes. Mrs. Jeffers' typing skills were not at the expert level.

When the plump matron passed me the white sheets to sign, I smiled politely. As I scrawled my signature, I asked, "Do I give you the check for the bail?"

"Oh no." She patted her steel gray bouffant with a gesture reminiscent of the desk clerk.

"Who then?"

"You can give the bail to me but not a check. Cash only."

"Cash?"

"Yes. Cash." She glanced at her reflection in the window as she neatened her hairdo.

"Only?"

"Cash only." The woman was pleased with the adjustments to her hair.

I looked down to sign the second sheet. "Someone will have to drive me to an ATM. Is there a CIRRUS machine nearby?"

Feeling her stare I looked up at the policewoman. Her hand had dropped into her lap. She appeared shocked. "We can't do that."

"Why not?"

"You're under arrest. You can't go out to a bank machine."

"You take credit cards." My tone added certainly.

"Oh no. We don't do that."

"Well, if you won't take a check, or a credit card, and you won't take me to a cash machine, what can I do?"

"We let you make a phone call."

"Ma'am." I adopted the vernacular of the police officers. "Ma'am, I don't know anyone in town." Except Richard Rothman, and I didn't think the man who instigated my arrest would post my bail.

"You can make a toll call." She sounded impressed by the magnanimous offer.

"May I see Captain D'Intino, please?"

The portly woman shuffled out and the rotund detective in. I fought with the officer but to no avail. Finally, I followed the policeman to his office to make my one phone call. He pointed to a chair covered in a shade of vinyl that had not been seen since the summer of love—and only then by those who had taken the bad acid. He lowered himself into a large leather chair in a shade of green that was tasteful only by comparison. He passed me a clunky black phone.

I dialed Andy's number from his card. He seemed the obvious choice. Actually, he was my only choice. The PI's machine picked up. "Andy. It's Meg. I know this is hard to understand but could you get $500 and bring it to the Ocean Shores police station. The gestapo here won't let me out to get cash." I glared at the police officer. He ignored my slur. "Can I get calls?"

"He can call me."

I spoke into the receiver. "Call a Captain D'Intino. His number is . . ." I read the telephone number from the base of the instrument. "Thank you."

The receiver was less than an inch from the base of the phone when the captain asked, "Why did you give him that number?"

I yanked back my hand to avoid disconnecting my one phone call. I had seen movies about people in these situations. Stopped for a routine traffic violation . . . died in prison . . . of old age. I didn't want to be one of them. With a smug laugh, Captain D'Intino gave me the correct number. I repeated it for Andy's machine and hung up satisfied that I sounded cool.

"Chief?" Officer Healey stuck his head in the office. "We have to move her soon." He nodded at me. "Mrs. Jeffers doesn't work tonight."

"Florence?"

"We can't spare her from the desk."

"Move me? Where?" I glanced from the policeman to the detective and back.

The captain spoke. "We are a small town, Ms. Daniels. We have limited facilities here. And Healey is right. Mrs. Jeffers has a shower to go to tonight. And we can't transport you without a female officer. We'll move you within the hour if she's going to make it on time."

"Where?"

"To her niece's shower. Her cousin Nellie's girl, Emma. Nice girl. Pretty too."

"No." I spoke through clenched teeth. "Where are you moving me?"

"To the county jail. At the county seat."

Chapter 40

Officer Healey pulled the police car through heavy metal gates into a courtyard. I studied the huge walls in disbelief. I was about to enter a prison. And I wasn't on a tour. Slowly and with great effort, Mrs. Jeffers climbed out of the passenger's seat. She held my door, or my door held her, as I pulled myself out of the rear seat of the police cruiser. The only thing I'd found to be grateful for in this entire episode was that the cops didn't make me wear handcuffs. I suspected they knew that once cuffed I would need help to get in and out of the car. I also suspected they knew that Mrs. Jeffers wasn't capable of offering such assistance.

Walking three abreast we crossed the courtyard to a green metal door that Officer Healey opened so that Mrs. Jeffers could lead me across a narrow hallway into a small office. "Dorothy! Hi. Nice to see you."

"Tillie. I was surprised when I heard you were on your way over. I thought Emma's shower was tonight." Dorothy flashed a look that said "nuisance" as I stepped through the doorway.

"Well, that's why we're in a hurry." Mrs. Jeffers turned her attention to the large burly man behind the desk. "Hope you can get us in and out in a hurry, Harry."

That goes for me, too, I thought.

"No problem. Al called ahead. I got the papers all ready."

Mrs. Jeffers leaned down to sign the papers. Officer Healey signed in another place. After a bit of chit chat, my captors were gone and I was in the custody of the county jail. No one offered me a seat. I stood awkwardly in front of the desk as Harry and Dorothy discussed my fate. Despite my lack of familiarity with penal institutions, my instinct told me that I was not being confined in a state-of-the-art facility. Cell assignments were scrawled on a blackboard to my right.

"You're not going to put this one in with her?" Dorothy sounded horrified.

"She's the only female prisoner I got. No choice."

Without indicating who she was, Harry waved in the direction of an open book on the edge of the desk. "Sign here."

I leaned over, grabbed a badly chewed pen and signed my name as illegibly as I thought legal. After that I was in Dorothy's care. Without speaking, the woman led me to a small, old, and rusty locker where I deposited my wallet with my keys attached and the miscellaneous items from my jacket pockets in a manila envelope. Then, Dorothy asked me to step into a small green tile bathroom.

"Put your hands on the wall. High."

I turned and faced the wall and laid my hands against the cold, hard tile.

"Spread your legs."

I moved my feet apart and Dorothy began a thorough search of my person. I pulled away slightly as she groped my breasts. Despite her cold demeanor, she responded to my discomfort and finished frisking me quickly.

"Follow me."

I prayed that a delousing wasn't in my future. They could delouse the other prisoners but I didn't need . . . . Before I could complete my concern, Dorothy stopped at the end of a long corridor. She pointed to a stack of thin pads.

"Take a mattress." She used the term loosely. I dragged the

thin slab of striped cotton from the top of the pile. Dorothy then pointed to a collection of blankets that, whatever their original color may have been, were now gray. Again, I pulled one from the top of the heap.

As I followed Dorothy up a narrow metal staircase, our footsteps announced the new arrival to the other inmates. At the top of the steps, we faced a door that led down a long hallway with cells on either side. The residents of those cells, all male, had vacated their bunks to greet the new arrival.

"Wow, it's a babe."

"Whoa, honey."

"How about a little?"

A loud voice overwhelmed the others. "How about a lot?"

Through the bars, arms waved at me; hands grasped at my arms and my legs. I turned away from the obscene gestures and lewd remarks to watch Dorothy fumble with a lock in a solid metal door. Where was my bail? Going to jail was one thing but associating with criminals was another.

Dorothy struggled until the door opened. After we stepped through the heavy metal frame, Dorothy pulled the door shut, leaving the chaos of the cell block behind us. "Damn animals," she mumbled with a nod backwards. "Don't know why they had to bring you here." Dorothy opened yet another door. That one, all bars, led to a corridor identical to the one we had passed— except for the heaving mass of humanity. This hallway was empty. And quiet. And dark. Except for a single cell.

Dorothy halted at the lone bright cell, the first on the right. She selected a key from the huge ring she carried and stuck it into a door of bars with a single slab of metal across the center. The solid portion had a slot through which I imagined the jailers passed their culinary masterpieces. Luckily, I would be long gone before the first meal arrived.

Dorothy pushed the door open and gestured for me to go in. "No smoking in here." Her tone indicated there had been problems before.

I stepped inside and the matron pulled the door closed. As I turned, I heard the outside door slam. No instructions. No orientation. I was on my own. I stood motionless staring at the cell door.

"It ain't no hotel. No one's gonna show you around. You might as well settle in."

The voice came from a cot in the corner. The oversized woman who sprawled across the undersized bed leaned forward and spit into a paper cup on the floor. "Name's Lucille."

"Meg." I responded unenthusiastically.

"Well, Meg. Neither of them beds is taken." She nodded towards bunk beds in the center of the room. "You got your pick."

After studying the bare metal frame, I threw the thin mattress on the top bunk. That bed offered the only view—albeit a small one through a narrow window carved in the stone wall. I climbed up and checked out the panorama. Cement and brick. But lots of it.

I turned my attention back to the cell. Lucille's small cot covered the wall to my left. On my right a sink, a toilet and a shower were lined up. There were no doors or curtains. I noted the bare bulb in the ceiling. Simplicity was the order of the day except for the complex arrangement of trash strewn across the floor. "This place is filthy. Don't they ever clean it?"

"Sure. But the cleaning woman took this week off. I think she's in the Bahamas."

I ignored the inmate's sarcasm. "We have to live like this?"

"We don't have to. Thursday's the big day. They bring us stuff and we clean it. Clara, she left yesterday, she was pretty much of a slob."

"I can see." Old paper cups, a few upright, some overturned, most filled with coffee-stained cigarette butts, decorated the floor. I turned away in disgust. Avoiding the sight of the refuse was easy. There was no escaping the smell. What caused the putrid odor? After conducting a sniff test, Lucille became my prime suspect.

All I could tell about Lucille was that she was big, scantily clad, and could spit with the best of them. Her dark brown hair was profuse, everywhere except on her head. She remained horizontal; I couldn't tell if she was 5'1" and 250 pounds or 6'1" and 350 pounds. I hoped she took a liking to me. But not too much of a liking.

"So what's the drill here?" I worked at ingratiating myself with my cell mate.

"Pretty much like any other joint you been in."

"Oh." I nodded. "I see."

Lucille wasn't fooled but didn't taunt me for my lack of a prison record. "Next big event of the day is lights out. At ten. They're pretty good about that."

Obviously, Lucille had a point of comparison.

Lucille missed Clara—or at least a companion—and jumped at an opportunity to chat. Lucille could really talk. She rambled about her life in jail and out of jail. Shootings. Funerals. Domestic squabbles. Lucille had led a full and colorful life. She talked for an hour before it occurred to her to ask, "So what are you in for?"

"Loitering."

Lucille regarded me expectantly.

"And noise." I added proudly. After all, I was a double threat. Surely that carried some clout in the prison world. I pictured myself threatening Lucille. "Back off babe. I've got a radio—and I ain't movin'."

"Oh." For once Lucille had nothing to say. Obviously in the prison pecking order I wasn't her equal. She leaned forward and spit in her cup. I looked away.

"I am a suspect in my boss's murder." It wasn't bad enough that I was in jail; I was trying to impress my cell mate. Unsuccessfully from the smirk on her face. I embellished. "I didn't do it. I'm completely innocent."

"We all are, honey."

"No, I really am."

I wasn't sure why Lucille found me amusing or why I found her attitude insulting or why I kept trying to gain her favor. "I could have killed him."

"I'm sure." Lucille spit in her cup to emphasize her disbelief.

"He was a very annoying guy."

"Honey," she spit to punctuate her sentence, "if women killed every guy who was annoying, you couldn't buy a bed in this joint."

Clearly, I wasn't adept at prison chitchat but still I tried. "So what are you in for?"

Lucille leaned forward and spit again into her cup. "I cut up a woman."

"Where is she now?"

"Dead."

So much for prison patter. I crawled to the window and gazed into the courtyard longingly.

"Ain't no use looking, honey." Lucille's voice belied no sympathy. "Ain't nobody coming to get you before dawn. No one gets out of here at night."

I sighed and let my head drop to the filthy mattress. Reluctantly I covered myself with the equally vile blanket. My eyes had not yet closed when they detected the first rays of daylight.

Without a watch, I didn't know at what hour a matron, not Dorothy, slid two breakfast trays through the slot in the door. I hopped down from my top bunk eagerly and went to retrieve both trays. I passed one to Lucille and studied the other skeptically.

The dull metal trays resembled meatloaf pans divided in two. The right side held a sticky bun. The left side contained a foodstuff unknown to me and, I suspected, most residents of planet Earth. How did Lucille keep her weight up?

"What is this?" My face and voice registered disgust as I spoke.

"Keeps you regular. They want us regular." Lucille did not sit up to eat. She lay on her left side and shoveled a mushy, colorless lump into her mouth as she spoke.

With great effort, I wrestled my assigned spoon from the gluti-nous mess. Without tasting the food, I dropped the tray on the floor and climbed back onto the top bunk. Lucille stared at me.

"I'll eat on the way home." I explained. I said the same thing when lunch and dinner proved equally unappealing. Lucille found the comment amusing every time I made it.

"You'll be sorry." Lucille warned me when I refused dinner. "Ain't no twenty-four-hour room service here, you know."

"What's the latest I can get out of here?" I asked Lucille as the sun threatened to slip from the sky. After twenty-four hours in the county jail, I was certain I had served a life sentence. Next time I saw a mirror, I expected to see a grizzled old woman.

Before Lucille answered, I heard the matron coming—I assumed to collect the dinner dishes. But this time when the outside door clicked open, I heard a vaguely familiar voice.

"Meg Daniels?" The voice belonged to Dorothy. "You're out of here."

The matron pushed open the cell door. I leapt to the floor from my top bunk.

"Good luck, Lucille." I grinned at the woman who faced the possibility of thousands of nights in those or similar accommo-dations. My grin softened to a smile. "I hope it goes well for you." I headed for the door.

"Mattress and blanket." Dorothy nodded at my bed acces-sories. I grabbed them off the metal frame and followed Dorothy into the hall.

"Good bye, boys." I waved at white, black, and brown arms flailing from the neighboring cell block.

"Honey. Don't go. Not before . . ."

The comments couldn't bother me. Despite the load I carried, I skipped down the metal steps. After I exchanged my bed accessories for my own possessions, I rushed into the small office. I was disappointed to find Mrs. Jeffers and Officer Healey waiting for me.

"But who . . . ?"

"Some fella's waiting for you at the station."

Chapter 41

B ack at the police station, I was led to the office where Andy chatted cheerfully with Captain D'Intino. Frequent laughter punctuated their conversation. I stood in the doorway until the police captain acknowledged me.

"Well, here Maggie is now." The captain smiled at me.

Andy glanced over his shoulder and leapt to his feet. "Maggie. You ready?"

"Yes." I hissed through gritted teeth. More than a one word answer would have been dangerous.

"Well, listen, Al, we gotta go. Nice talking to you." Andy reached across the desk and shook the policeman's hand.

As I stared at Andy, anger crept into my face.

"Thanks, Al." Andy wrapped an arm around my shoulders and hustled me from the room. In the hall the PI smiled at Mrs. Jeffers in the hall. "Thank you."

"Thank you?" I spat the words at him.

"Shut up." He smiled at Officer Healey who was crossing the lobby. "Good-bye." Andy rushed me out the door silencing my attempts at speech. "Not now. I'll explain."

Andy guided me to his convertible. "Get in and stop acting so grumpy."

"Grumpy. Why should I be grumpy? I spend the last twenty-four hours in a jail where, I may mention, they do not even delouse the inmates, and find you yukking it up with the boys who threw me in the clink in the first place. What the hell was that about?" I nodded at the police station.

Andy smiled through gritted teeth. "Just get in the car."

I slipped into the seat and spun to face the driver's seat as the door slammed behind me. I was waiting for the detective as he slid behind the wheel.

"What was with the Mr. Nice Guy routine? Mr. Milquetoast is more like it."

"Meg." He used my real name. "I got the charges dropped, so you can let it go." His tone was curt.

"You what?"

"I got the charges dropped and any record of your arrest expunged."

"Why? I want to sue the bastards."

"Look, Meg." His continued use of my real name shocked me. "I had to use considerable charm to get Mrs. Jeffers to stay late. Especially since she was tired after Emma's shower."

I leaned back against the window and asked sarcastically, "And how was Emma's shower. I was awake all night worrying."

Andy ignored me and continued. "Not only did Mr. Nice Guy get the charges dropped but he found out what was behind them. Seems Richard Rothman was aware of your presence. He pressured the cops. You know they don't get many celebrities down here. So they're real impressed. They accommodate them."

"So I go to jail?"

"Well, yes. That. And," he paused, "here's the good part. They occasionally cut their local celebs some slack. Like when they get caught doing 85 m.p.h. on a two-lane back road at 4 A.M. On a Monday night. Or rather Tuesday morning. The morning Donald K. Bascombe died."

"Andy. I love you." I leaned over and planted a big sloppy kiss on the investigator's cheek. "I mean . . . not really . . . I mean not like . . . you know."

"I know."

"I assume Rothman was driving north."

"Northbound." The PI reached across the gearshift to pat my knee.

"So at last you believe that he might be involved."

"I never even considered the possibility before. I guess I was blinded by my relationship with Caroline and his prominence. Plus, he's such a little guy."

"He lifted weights in college—competitively. He still has a weight room in house."

"You went in his house?" His voice was full of admiration.

I hated to disappoint Andy. "Only in the pages of *People* magazine."

"You know I thought you were nuts when you suspected Caroline and Rothman. I hate to say it, but I was wrong. We've got work to do." He pulled his convertible away from the curb. "But first let's retrieve your car. We have to get back to batten down the hatches."

"Why?"

"Didn't you see the news?"

"The cable in my cell was out." I fought unsuccessfully to keep the sarcasm out of my tone.

"I thought you prisoners had it easy." A glance into my eyes prompted him to change tacks. "We've arranged another treat for your vacation. A hurricane."

"Did I miss the plagues and pestilence?"

"We're saving them for the weekend." He murmured as he pulled the old convertible away from the curb.

I directed Andy to the spot in front of Rothman's house where I'd last seen my rental car. "We could stop and see Rothman."

"And accuse him of murder? I have a few details to fill in before I'm ready to confront Rothman." Andy turned on the old Mustang's wipers. "Looks like the storm is starting. By the way, I told Detective Dupuy that we found you."

My stomach flipped. "I was lost?"

"Well, after you hit your beeper the other night . . . "

"I didn't hit my beeper."

"Well, someone or something did. The cops rushed over to your house and found out you were gone. They thought you'd been abducted. Especially after they found indication that someone had broken into Bascombe's house. They were even looking for your body for awhile—until old Mr. Downie told them he'd seen you drive off by yourself."

I went on the lam to escape people trying to help me. "I . . . I don't recall . . . I didn't mean to . . . the beeper was in my pocket."

"You might owe Detective Dupuy an explanation."

Great. How was I going to explain tossing the beeper out the window to Detective Dupuy—the last person on earth to whom I wanted to be indebted?

"You should check in with her after the storm."

I nodded. I was too tired to respond, to worry, or to drive. We moved the rental car to the highest land we could find. I doubted that the spot was five feet above sea level but feelings of fatigue outweighed feelings of concern. I climbed into Andy's car and fell asleep immediately. I had no idea how much time had passed before the PI woke me and led me to a door with his name on the glass.

"The beach is no place to be tonight," Andy explained, although I had voiced no protest.

The PI's office sat on top of some sort of store. I was too tired to note what the establishment sold but not too tired to notice the wind. If the PI hadn't supported me as he struggled to get the key into the lock, the gusts would have pushed my listless form over the railing.

When the key made its final rotation to open the lock, the door flew open and slammed against something in the PI's office that was apparently unable to resist its force. The object fell to the floor as Andy pushed me into the room. I found a hard-back chair and slumped onto it. Behind me Andy fought to push the door closed. He won the battle but it wasn't an easy match.

"Well, it's not the Ritz." Andy's tone was apologetic.

"But at least there are no bars." I nodded at the picture window. Beyond a huge masking tape X, I saw telephone wires engaged in a frenetic dance with the wind. What a vacation. The next day did not promise to be a good beach day.

Andy guided me past a desk and shelving into a small room that appeared to serve as both living and bedroom. I spotted a bathroom beyond.

"Oooh, can I take a bath?"

Andy didn't think I was in any condition to go near water. He thought I would drown.

"You can be lifeguard." I protested without perceiving the full meaning of my words. Andy, however, caught my drift right away. He perched me on the side of the bed and disappeared behind the bathroom door. As I fell back onto the soft mattress, I heard the sound of water running.

Andy reappeared. Actually, I heard him return. My eyes were closed—and not by choice. "Are you sure you can take a bath— and live to talk about it?"

"I've been bathing myself since I was a child. I'll be fine. Now help me up."

Andy grabbed my hands and dragged me to my feet. "I used bubble bath—for modesty's sake. I want you to go in and get settled. But then you have to call me. You are far too sleepy to be in the tub unguarded."

As I got undressed and climbed into the tub, I was too exhausted to question why the PI had bath bubbles readily accessible. The water, warm and inviting, made it easy to slip beneath the coating of pink foam. The warmth was lulling me to sleep when I heard a knock on the door. "Maggie, are you okay?"

"Sure." I mumbled.

"You don't sound so good. Are you awake?"

"Sure." I hoped I'd said the word aloud.

"I'm worried. I'm coming in."

I opened my eyes only briefly. The PI was fully dressed but not as I had last seen him. He wore sweats and an old T-shirt that indicated his predilection for a vacation spot in North

Carolina. He was folding the clothes I'd thrown on the floor. "All these washable?"

"Cold wash. Cold rinse." I specified. "Andy, I can't believe how awful jail was. How do people do it? No privacy. No stimulation. The boredom was incredible. They control everything. I couldn't eat. I couldn't drink. I couldn't . . . . Well, never mind." The PI was sitting on the floor beside the tub. I opened my eyes. He was not looking at my face. I glanced down the length of the tub. The best he could do was a glimpse of my toes; all else was bubbles.

I detected traces of a blush on Andy's cheeks when he realized my eyes were open. He dipped a washcloth into the tub. "Lean forward. I'll do your back."

Arranging bubbles over appropriate body parts, I sat up. I fought sleep as the detective rubbed the washcloth across my back above and below the waterline.

"You know the first time I ever saw you?" The PI's voice came from behind me.

I moaned a no answer.

"I let myself into Bascombe's a couple of times in the weeks before he died. I needed . . . well I needed to look around." He lathered the washcloth and began massaging my neck. "Then one night I glanced down from his bedroom and spotted you on the porch of the rickety old cottage. You looked so tiny in that big old wooden rocker. And so sad. You were crying. And drinking. From a pitcher yet. Your head would almost disappear each time you took a slug. I thought you were the cutest girl . . . excuse me—woman—that I had ever seen."

He pulled away, rolled up a towel and laid it across the rim of tub. "Now lay back, I'll do the front."

I opened my eyes and watched as he worked the washcloth down my right arm.

"When I found out who you were." He smiled apologetically. "That's my job. I wondered what Bascombe could have done to win you. You seemed so unlike him. Then when he showed up dead . . . "

He reached across for my left arm and repeated the action. "I'll admit I thought you had killed him, but all I felt was admiration. I figured if you killed him, he deserved it."

I was too exhausted to react.

Andy's eyes stared into mine as he ran the cloth across my collarbone and up my neck. He hesitated as he moved the washcloth downward. Watching for signs of resistance? I opened my arms wide to indicate he would encounter none. "That feels good." While I lay back with eyes closed, Andy dropped the washcloth and rubbed the bar of soap down my stomach. How far down I had no idea.

Officially, I think I passed out. I don't know how Andy interpreted my action or handled me. I awoke the next morning—dry except for damp tendrils of blond hair curling around my neck. I was in Andy's double bed wrapped in a large terry cloth robe. Andy stretched out next to me on the bed. Still dressed in the sweat clothes, he was lying under the comforter but on top of the sheet—a position I interpreted as a modest display of propriety.

I listened to the wind roar across the island; I watched the sleeping investigator. A slight smile showed on the corner of his lips. Every few moments a burst of air lifted a strand of his silky hair into the air. As the lock fell back on his cheek, he mumbled incomprehensible complaints and then lay quietly until the next eruption. Now that I was awake I wanted to discover where Andy had been headed before I'd dozed off but no matter how much I squirmed, the PI didn't budge. Andy was a heavy sleeper.

The next time I awoke Andy was gone from the bed. My need to sleep was being overwhelmed by my need to eat. As if psychic, Andy appeared at the door from the office with a donut in hand. "Sorry. It's the best I can do."

I thought the mass-produced pastry looked delicious. "What's that noise?" I was certain no subway ran under the house.

"Egbert." Andy nodded towards the other room.

"Who's Egbert?"

"Hurricane Egbert. You prisoners ought to stay better informed. What do you folks do with your time in the joint anyway?"

"Just let me have the food. And, would you do me a favor? Find that bag the jail gave me for my personal effects and get my lip gloss."

"You trust me to go into your bag?"

"Well, it's not really my bag, it's actually an envelope, and if I recall correctly, it won't be your first visit."

"Right." Andy blushed.

I tasted the donut. Vanilla iced. A favorite of mine. I never recalled one taking so long to chew.

I was still on my first bite when Andy returned to the room digging in the envelope that served as a makeshift purse. He pulled out loose bills, my tiny wallet with keys attached, and my Markshell security pass, but no lip gloss. He sat on the bed and rummaged some more until he found the small cylinder.

"Thanks." I reached for the tube.

Andy began to restuff my gear into the bag. "Hey, I thought you gave your security pass to John Mancotti when we were in New York."

That was how I remembered it, too. I took the card and checked out both sides. "Looks like mine but they all look the same." I yawned.

"Why did you have this with you on the beach?"

I didn't know. "I wore the jacket to work on the Friday I left."

"Don't you see what this means?"

"Maybe if I were awake." Taking another bite of donut was an effort.

"It means you got someone else's security pass back from the police when you were mugged. Someone dropped it on the night of the murder. We have to get John Mancotti to check the ID on that card. Then we'll have our murderer."

"Not necessarily, Andy. If that were true, why didn't the cops find it the first time."

"They weren't focusing on that area."

"Still, think about all the Markshell people who have passed through my house since the murder." I was too sleepy to name them, but I knew I could.

"But not before the mugging. Don't you see?"

"Just let me take a little nap. Maybe I will then." I was once again asleep.

The room was still dark when I next awoke. Andy sat at his desk working on his laptop computer. "You don't have to sit in the dark for my sake."

"As popular as you are here in Ocean City, the entire town did not decide to dim its lights in your honor. No power." In response to my confused expression he pointed at the computer and said "Battery."

"This hurricane . . . "

"Egbert." Andy filled in.

"Egbert still hanging on?"

"You slept through the worst of it."

After checking that the terry cloth robe was tightly shut, I rolled out of bed to check out the storm through the only dormer window in the room. It was early morning, but I couldn't tell that by the view. The sky was dark gray and appeared to have fallen perilously close to the earth. "Wow. Look at those trees."

"At this point they are being a bit melodramatic. They found themselves in that position overnight and haven't straightened up. The winds are dying down. The rain, too."

The storm still appeared formidable to me. I could hear rain beating against the window. The whistling of the wind, both around the building and through the weaknesses in its insulation, was loud enough to wake the dead—although apparently not me. Big puddles dotted the streets but the roads did not appear flooded.

"How long is this supposed to go on?"

"Long enough." Andy had taken a position behind me. Immediately behind me. He wrapped his arms around my waist and nuzzled my hair with his fine Roman nose.

I relaxed against him. Together, we watched the storm toss wires and tree branches about. We would not be going outside for many hours. The lights were off. There were few options as far as activities went. Seduction was inevitable. The realization rendered me both happy and nervous. Andy played with the sash to the terry cloth robe. He too seemed nonplussed by the certainty of what the afternoon would bring. "Do you need something to eat?"

Oddly enough the gnawing hunger had disappeared. "No, I'll eat after . . . " I caught myself before saying afterwards. "Later." I finished the sentence.

"You had a rough couple of days. How about I give you a nice backrub?"

I agreed. A massage provided a nice, easy segue to prevent my nerves, or brain, from kicking in and causing me to do something disruptive. Andy untied the sash and slipped the robe from my shoulders. Even though I had not actually witnessed them, I knew the activities of the previous evening precluded any false show of modesty. I took the few steps to the bed and lay down. Still in his sweats Andy straddled me and began gently rubbing my back. His strokes gained strength as he massaged my scalp and then my neck. I'd never realized how strong Andy was. Breaking my bones without breaking a sweat was well within his power. Luckily, I was on the good side of the muscular grip.

I was happy things were moving in this direction—at last. The timing seemed right. Especially after Andy's kind words the night before. Okay, he was breaking and entering when he spotted me for the first time, but his reaction was so sweet. I loved the way he described me sitting on the porch crying and drinking from a pitcher.

"What's wrong?" Andy felt the tension in my muscles as soon as I reacted to the recollection. From a pitcher. Andy distinctly said I had been drinking from a pitcher. I had drunk from a pitcher on only one night. The night Bascombe died. The night he was murdered.

"You feel so tense. What's wrong?" Andy repeated his question.

In place of the truth, I talked about those little jolts. "You know the ones you feel when you are just about to fall asleep."

Andy reacted not to my description of the involuntary movement but to the word asleep.

He stripped off his sweatshirt and rested his chest on my back.
He whispered in my ear, "You're not telling me that you are
falling asleep are you?"

"No. No." I tried to sound jovial despite the realization that
Andy had me pinned. There was no way I could escape. "But
what happened to my back rub? You're not finished are you?"

"I guess not." Andy groaned as he continued his massage duties.

I needed time to think. I couldn't make love to this man. Make
love. What a fool I had been to think that was the appropriate
phrase. How could I have been so blind? I realized Andy had
sought me out under false pretenses. How pathetic I must have
seemed to him. Alone and on the rebound. What an easy target.

"Hey, how much longer do I have to keep this up?" Andy's
strong hands were working on my shoulders.

"I hate to tell you, but I could go on like this all day." Even I was
surprised at how well I hid the fear in my voice. "Keep rubbing."

Andy was the one who understood that the person who
attempted to frame me had to know I was alone that night—
something he witnessed for himself. Andy knew who I was.
Andy had been to Markshell before. Andy asked about the keys
in my desk. Andy was there the night of the mugging. Andy.
Always Andy. So far, he had elicited information with kindness.
But what would he do when a kind approach didn't produce
the results he wanted?

I couldn't hold Andy off much longer. His hands were roam-
ing east, west and south into areas not usually visited by professional masseurs. What could I do? I was naked in his bed. I
didn't even know where my clothes were.

"Brrrr. It's cold out here." Andy slipped onto the mattress
beside me and pulled the comforter over both of us. While he
found his way out of his sweatpants, I searched for a way out
of my dilemma. At this point in the game, what excuse would
get me out of this man's bed without arousing his suspicions?

Andy pulled me close against him. I realized I'd better do something—soon.

He cradled my face in both his hands. "Don't be nervous. You look like you're going to jail again." Those eyes peered into mine. Did he understand?

I glanced away. "I am a little nervous. And, I just feel funny. Physically." His stare pulled my eyes back to his. "I am exhausted and I haven't really eaten. I'm sorry." As I gazed at that gorgeous face, I was sorry—sorry that Andy was a liar and a murderer.

"Relax. I'll make you feel better."

I guess Andy figured his kiss would do the trick, and I can see where he got that impression. Under other circumstances, I might have benefited from its healing properties. In fact, his kiss did relax me. All of me—including my stomach muscles. I pushed away.

"What's wrong?" Andy was talking to my back as I ran to the bathroom and vomited.

Chapter 42

"**D**on't worry about it." Andy reacted to an apology that I hadn't made. "I'll come back and we can go pick up your car. Now that the electricity is on, I'll run your clothes through the dryer and bring them with me." His smile was conspiratorial. "Maybe you'll feel better by tonight."

I nodded. Feelings of being small and defenseless were intensified by the oversized clothes Andy had lent me.

Andy kissed my forehead and left me in the living room of my cottage.

Before he brought me home, Andy verified that the old cottage was standing and the power restored. "That old house is amazing. If anything, it's stronger after the storm. You've got hundreds of pounds of sand as a new foundation."

Andy was right. The house withstood the storm with great aplomb—as it had so many before. The surf that had crossed the dunes was on its way back to its normal position. The waves rushed only to the middle of the wide beach. Before receding, however, the surf had packed sand around the pilings and the storage shed under the house. The unwanted landfill interfered with my plan. I had to get to a cash machine, take a cab to my rental car, load the Taurus, and get out of town before Andy came to check on me that night. The problem was that the first leg of the trip depended on liberating one of the old rusty bicycles from the shed. There was no time for a leisurely round trip stroll.

Without taking time to change out of the large sweatpants and huge Eagles jersey that Andy had provided for the trip home, I set about my task stopping only to tighten the belt Andy had fashioned out of rope. The makeshift belt provided the only guarantee that the clothes would stay on. As I dug, the wind was still strong enough to stymie my efforts. Loose sand blew on top of the heavy wet sand I worked to move with the largest measuring cup I could find, two cups. As I labored, I felt eyes on my back. I tilted my head ever so slightly to the right and tried to glance over my shoulder. No one appeared in my peripheral vision. I repeated the action to my left. Again, I could spot nothing. Yet the feeling persisted. In one motion I rose to my feet and spun around.

"Aha." I confronted the little boy who had watched me sneak up on Andy the week before. "Hello." I tried to camouflage my nervousness with a display of friendliness that included a broad wave to the child who stood six feet away. Considering the kid was five years old, my subterfuge succeeded. The child neither screamed nor ran. He waved back.

"I can dig." He said proudly.

I eyed the little boy suspiciously. Was this an offer? It was.

We negotiated a deal. I got the better end; the kid could really dig. "I work a lot with wet sand," he boasted. He maintained that wet sand was better for making forts. "I work on a lot of forts," he explained proudly. "I'm Matthew."

Matthew was as adept at conversation as he was at shoveling. He had a lot of hobbies and described them all. Finally, his conversation faltered. "You're not like the other moms." He eyed me nervously to see how I would react.

"Really?" I sounded pleased with the revelation.

"My mom never plays hide and seek with other grown-ups. She wouldn't jump off the porch. She always tells me not to."

"Well . . . it's . . . I think your mom is right."

"But everyone jumps off your porch."

"I only did it once. It was kind of an accident."

"But you let that other boy do it?"

"Other boy?" My casual question predated the feeling of concern that grew as I realized the implication of Matthew's comments.

"Yeah. When you were playing hide and seek."

I stopped shoveling and leaned back on my heels. "When was that Matthew?"

"One day. You came up the steps to find him and he jumped off of the porch."

Matthew stared at me. He seemed surprised to see me shuddering. "With the wind, it's cold out here isn't it." I lied. The air temperature was actually pleasant.

"Egbert made it get cold. I know all about hurricanes." What Matthew did know, he proceeded to share. I pretended to listen.

The news about the jumper on my porch compelled me to dig faster. I had to get out of that place—and fast. Matthew matched my pace. After he and I cleared the door with his two shovels, I sent him home with ice cream money and a promise not to tell the bad man in the red car that we had dug out the bicycle.

I had tucked my wallet into my waistband and was ready to move out when I heard a familiar voice. Randall was back. The nervous, downtrodden Randall. This Randall stood hunched over with his hands jammed deep in his jean pockets. His head dangled from his long neck so that looking at me required rolling his eyeballs high under his lids. It was hard to believe but Randall looked worse than I had ever seen him—but oddly prepared for the hurricane. His jeans stopped well above his ankle bones. Despite the storm, the pants remained absolutely dry.

I said "Where is your motorcycle?" I thought "why didn't I hear you coming?"

Randall didn't answer either question. "I worried how the house withstood the storm. I mean, if you were okay and all."

Oh, oh. Randall's interest in me had escalated way past my comfort level. "You drove here from Atlantic City to see how I was?"

"Sure." Randall seemed surprised by his own answer.

After that admission, how could I not invite him in? "Would you like to come in for something to drink?"

"Sure." Randall was more definite in that answer. He was actually ahead of me as we moved towards the stairs.

"I'm sorry it will have to be a quick visit. I have to go out in a few moments."

Randall stopped on a dime and spun to face me. "In that case, I'll go. You're busy."

I stopped myself from protesting. Any objection or request for a ride wouldn't have mattered. Randall's long legs carried him down the alley and out of sight in a flash. I climbed on the old bicycle with matching alacrity.

The rusty equipment moved better than I expected. The bike was easy to pedal in the only gear still working. Luckily the wind, while not actually with me, was not against me. I was not moving with the speed of the clouds that trailed Egbert, but I was making good time as I pedaled towards the cash machine. I had gone less than a mile when a van pulled up beside me. The car was close—too close. The wide street offered plenty of room to pass. Few cars were parked on Wesley. Yet the vehicle dropped back. The van's sitting on my tail made me nervous. I waved the car by. When it refused to pass, I slowed. The van was forced to move in front of me. I glimpsed the driver. A woman in a hat and dark glasses sat erect clutching the steering wheel with her hands positioned neatly at ten and two o'clock. Her eyes focused on the road ahead. Did she even realize that I was there?

Suddenly, the van braked and swerved into a deep puddle spraying me with dirty water and trapping me between the tail of the vehicle and the curb.

I didn't have time to curse the driver. I was too busy cursing David. My ex-boyfriend had jumped out of the back of the van shortly before the vehicle stopped.

"What the . . . ?" I repeated the same question using a few choice terms. Basically, I asked "what do you think you're doing" using more colorful semantics.

"Laurie and I want to talk to you." David was tugging on my arm.

"You never heard of the telephone?"

"Just get in the van and we can talk."

The guy always had an unnatural interest in Starsky and Hutch reruns.

"David, isn't this a bit melodramatic."

"Get in or I'll have to force you." He used enough strength to knock me off balance. While I was hopping on one foot he wrested the bike from under me.

"David. This is silly."

"Meg, I know that. Get in the van."

"What are you going to do? Throw me and my bike in the van and drive me to a secluded spot?" I laughed. David didn't. David grabbed the bike and threw it into the van.

"You're serious." I felt no fear—only amazement. "Don't be silly. We can talk here."

At that point, Laurie appeared around the front of the van. The hat and sunglasses were in her hands. "David, you wimp, can't you even handle a woman."

Judging by Laurie's tone, he couldn't.

Laurie faced me. "Get in the car." Her measured tones were frightening. "We can hurt you, Meg. If you get in the van, you'll be fine."

I didn't believe Laurie, but I did get into the van—although not voluntarily. While I was reacting to Laurie's bizarre behavior David swooped me up and threw me in the back. I landed on the bike. I felt sharp metal scratch my skin. "Now I'm going to need a tetanus shot. What is wrong with you?" David didn't answer. The door slammed shut. David was in the back with me.

Laurie hopped into the front seat and flipped on her turn signal. For a kidnapper, she was a cautious and law-abiding driver.

"This is silly." I protested as I checked for broken skin. "You're acting like a jerk." I directed my comment to David but the sentiment applied equally to Laurie.

"We wanted to make sure you knew we were serious."

"Oh, right. You two are really vicious criminals."

"Don't underestimate us." Laurie growled from the front seat. Suddenly, their threats didn't seem so ridiculous.

"Is this about the money?"

"I told you the bitch knew." Laurie spat the words over her right shoulder.

I looked from David to Laurie and back. "David, why didn't you just come to me and ask about the money?"

"I did."

"When?"

"Meg, you knew what I was talking about when I came to visit. You wouldn't cooperate so we had to get your attention. I'm sorry if we were a bit rough."

"A bit? That's an understatement."

"It's your fault. It wouldn't have happened if you had cooperated."

"Cooperate with what?" I stared at him with puzzlement across my face.

"What I asked when I came to your house."

I stared at him blankly.

"You didn't understand, did you?"

I shook my head.

"Shit." Now it was David's turn to shake his head.

"You dumb shit." Laurie was ranting from the front seat. "I told you not to break up with her until after vacation but noooo, you had to have your own way. Then I was disappointed you couldn't work a deal with her. Hell, you couldn't even communicate what the deal was!"

"You never were a good communicator, David." I had to agree with Laurie.

"Wait a minute, wait a minute. Let's think this over." David buried his head in his hands.

"What a jerk!" David's girlfriend was talking. "Meg, maybe I should have come to you in the first place. I made the mistake of thinking David was the obvious choice." She shook her head. "You know about the money. It's obvious you have it. David and I simply want our share. We aren't going to hurt you. We want to make a deal."

"I don't have the money. I only heard about the money from people searching for it. How did you guys know?"

"Explain it, David." She snapped.

And so he did. I figured David obeyed all of Laurie's commands. I was still wondering why he never acted that way with me when I realized he was deep into his explanation.

David had suspected DK was embezzling, but Bascombe got rid of him before he could prove anything or even make an accusation. He had forced the matter out of his mind until Laurie had called. She not only knew that the money was missing, she knew that the money had been converted to cash.

"Because she helped launder it?" I asked to Laurie's consternation.

"That's not the issue." David's retort was quick.

"And, the issue is?"

"Look, Meg, don't act so damn pure. Bascombe had that money in New Jersey. It isn't in his house. Where is it?" He was acting tough for Laurie's sake.

"David, you are really much more stupid than I thought." I might have been running around playing detective, but David had been out running around playing criminal. "I don't know anything about the money."

Laurie pulled the van onto the shoulder. I felt fear that David could not arouse in me as Laurie climbed into the back. "We'll cut you in, Meg. Just tell us where it is."

"Have you two given any thought to the matter that you are committing criminal acts?"

"We're not criminals." David dismissed my question as ludicrous.

"You just abducted me!"

"No. No. We just . . ."

"Abducted me." I pushed up my sleeve to display a red welt that was already showing signs of turning black and blue. "I've got bruises to prove it."

"You don't really see it that way, do you?" David sounded scared. I relished the fear in his voice.

How did this guy expect me to see the situation? I was knocked off my bike and dragged without concern for my safety into the back of a van. Did he think that because he was not a career criminal he could do whatever he wanted, and it wouldn't be considered a crime?

"You wouldn't . . . I mean the police . . ." David was sputtering.

"I will not press charges if you let me out right now. You might as well because I never heard a thing about the money except rumors that it exists."

David weakened. Dealing with Laurie, however, was something else. The two became involved in a hot discussion. Even I had to take David's side. Although both positions were illogical, David's thinking reflected a small grasp of real world conditions; Laurie's belied not a single trace of reality. Unfortunately, his was the losing side. I saw no point in waiting to confirm the outcome. My money was on Laurie.

With David and Laurie otherwise engaged, I edged towards the back of the van, figured out how to work the handle, and opened the door. I jumped out slamming the door behind me. I landed on the Ocean Drive where it cut through marshlands. What marshlands, I had no idea. I had run only twenty yards towards no particular destination when I heard the voice.

"Meg. Meg. I saw what happened. I was looking for you."

The voice, a familiar one, came from a sedan with black windows. In my enthusiasm to get away from David and Laurie, I yanked open the door and jumped in. The term out of the frying pan and into the fire flashed through my mind about the same time a heavy object smashed into my skull—before I had even pulled the door shut.

Chapter 43

I didn't really wake up; I regained consciousness. Slowly
and painfully.

I took an inventory of what I knew. I was on my side—
lying on a cold flat surface. I felt that I was still wearing Andy's
Eagles T-shirt and oversized sweatpants. My hands and feet
were bound—tightly enough that I couldn't have moved them if
I had the energy to try. Which I didn't. Every muscle hurt, and
I had far more of them than I had ever suspected. My hands
were tied in front of me but were looped to my foot bonds so
that I couldn't touch my blindfold. By whom I had been rendered immobile, I had no idea.

At first, I was too weak to feel frightened. As I came more
fully awake, I began to understand my predicament. After considering the lighter side of my dilemma, I concluded that there
was no lighter side. The situation was critical.

Working with all my senses, I focused on remembering every
detail of my environment to help the cops find my abductor—
an individual who seemed to be nowhere in the vicinity. No
matter how hard I listened all I heard was the hum of an air-
conditioner or a refrigerator. The surface I had been dropped on
was smooth, hard and cold but cleaner than several of the places

'd slept the past few nights. I sniffed hard. The pain wasn't worth the effort; I couldn't identify the ripe aroma that permeated the air. The absence of a gag surprised me. I contemplated calling for help but only a truly stupid assailant would bind and blindfold but skip gagging if it were necessary. I concluded noise would only summon my abductor.

I'd like to say I remained calm and collected as I lay curled up on my side—bound and blindfolded. I'd like to say that I methodically worked myself free of my bonds, removed my blindfold, and escaped out the window. I'd like to say that, but it wouldn't be true. Despite my best efforts to calm myself, I was shaking or shivering or both. Whatever the action, I was moving too violently to work the ropes lose.

My guesstimate was that I lay on the floor for several hours but probably only forty-five minutes passed before my captor arrived at my side. I didn't recognize the voice. How could I? The person's speech was altered outrageously—assuming the speaker was human. Each word was stated separately but in a similar guttural tone with a three-second pause before the next. I considered that subterfuge, along with the blindfold, a good sign. I was going to live.

"You can go home when you tell me where the money is." Waiting for the person to string together a long sentence was excruciating.

I explained that I didn't know.

"You know that there is money."

I explained that I had recently heard rumors.

"Where did you hear the rumors?"

I explained that the information was pretty much common knowledge.

"You can go home if you give me the money."

"Believe me if I could give you the money, I would. Contrary to any rumors you may have heard this is not my idea of fun time." I grew tired of arguing. "Could I have a drink of water, please."

"Very polite." My captive commented before leaving the area.

When the captor returned, I found myself being rolled into an upright position. I felt skin against mine. I couldn't quite figure out what body parts brushed my hands and face but there were enough of them that I calculated my jailer had traded the cheap polyester I'd felt on the way in for . . . nothing. Why was my captor naked? I could only reach the worst conclusion. However, after I had swallowed the last sip, the person withdrew to a position across the room.

"Talk to me."

"Why?" My captor grumbled.

"Let me help you." I volunteered. I ran through all the possibilities. "Did you search Bascombe's house?" I heard a snort.

"Dummy. Why do you think I killed Bascombe? Dummy."

I gulped. I'd felt a lot more comfortable before I knew my captor was capable of murder. I christened my abductor Mad Dog.

"Did you search his house in Brigantine?"

"Why do you think that bimbo wife of his went into hiding?"

"Did you . . .?"

Mad Dog cut me off. "Yes, I searched his office. Yes, I searched his apartment in the city." His tones dripped contempt. "You do not give me enough credit. I even searched his kids' rooms at his mother-in-law's. No matter what you think, I am not stupid."

Waiting for my jailer to pronounce every word disguised by a lack of cadence and accent was trying. But then again, I really wasn't going anywhere.

Apparently, Mad Dog hadn't thought to look for DK's widow at Rothman's. I considered sicking Mad Dog on Caroline Bascombe and Richard Rothman but couldn't bring myself to do it—at least until the torture started. My reasons were not altruistic. Better to have a card up my sleeve just in case things got rough.

"Do I know you?"

"If you do, why would I tell you?" Mad Dog made a good point.

I tried to think of other ways I could be helpful. "You can go search my cottage. I'll give you the keys." I made the offer even though I had no idea where they were; I no longer felt the bulge of the small wallet in my waistband.

I heard that snort again. For the first time I heard something familiar in the tone.

"I have visited that dump many times."

"How about my apartment in New York?"

"You think that I would miss that spot?"

"So you know I don't have the money."

"You hid it. Bascombe told you where he put it."

"No. I saw him only once. He didn't even like me."

At that pronouncement, Mad Dog giggled and left the room. At least, I assumed that was what happened. I heard a door slam. I heard no more chuckles or snorts.

I fought to bring my hands to my head—even though I wondered about the wisdom of removing my blindfold. Each time I heard the door open, I stopped my efforts and rolled into the fetal position.

The interview process repeated itself several times. I remained earnest, polite and scared to death. Mad Dog remained calm, condescending, and, from what I could tell, naked. When Mad Dog fed me water or bread, which oddly enough was freshly baked and absolutely delicious, I felt bare skin that was smooth except for an understandable display of goose bumps.

Mad Dog left me unattended for what felt like long periods of time. Where did he go? What did do? Why wasn't he in a bigger hurry? In my lowest moods, which was basically all the time, I envisioned my captivity lasting months, even years. No, I was wrong. Mad Dog would have to reconsider and kill me if this situation went on that long.

I was close to dozing off, really passing out, when I heard the sound of angry voices beyond the confines of the room. The voices were impossible to identify. The language was impossible to identify. The tone, however, was unmistakable. Someone was fighting—I hoped with Mad Dog. "In here." I shouted. "I am in here."

The voices quieted and moved away. I waited to be rescued, but apparently the visitor had no interest in saving me. Once again, the voices swelled with anger. I wasn't pleased with the tone. "Please don't upset Mad Dog." I prayed silently to the unknown visitor.

Suddenly, the door opened, slammed into a wall, and fell shut, at least that's how I interpreted the sound. Footsteps approached quickly, and my instincts told me, angrily. "We have to go." Mad Dog still took time for the measured tone but as the last word hit the air, I felt a shoe on my hip. The foot flipped me over, and a hand grabbed my rope belt. As Mad Dog picked me up I felt various body parts brushing against bare skin. If I pictured the scene correctly, Mad Dog, naked except for hard soled shoes, was carrying me like a purse.

Mad Dog dangled my bound body with one hand and fumbled with a lock with the other. Within seconds I heard a strong kick and a squeaky door opening. I could tell when we stepped outside. Mercifully, the air was warmer than the room's atmosphere but still cool from the hurricane. The wind had been downgraded to a strong breeze. Where was Mad Dog taking me? I heard a car door open, but Mad Dog didn't put me inside. Instead, I suspected, my kidnapper was walking to the back of the vehicle. I hoped it was a van. "Oh God. Not a trunk. I don't want to go into the trunk. I hope he knocks me out." Maybe I said the words out loud because Mad Dog did.

Chapter 44

The bed at the old house on the beach was uncomfortable, but its mattress hadn't been this hard in decades. The pillows had lumps, but the little balls of hardened rubber never seemed this sharp. And, although I'd confess to being a little sloppy about dragging sand into the bed, the amount I could detect was ridiculous—and damp.

With effort, I rolled onto what I discovered was a badly aching back and tried to open my eyes. When I finally got them open, they snapped shut immediately. What had I done to myself this time? I didn't remember drinking any daiquiris. Actually, I didn't remember anything. I lay on my back not moving and wondering if I still could move. My head ached; my back ached. Even my hair hurt.

I opened my eyes. Instead of the peeling ceiling I'd grown accustomed to in Ocean City, I was gazing at pine needles. Many, many needles on the branches of very, very tall trees. Although I saw blue sky and white clouds racing above the tree tops, the sun didn't reach me. I was cold and I was damp and I was pretty sure I had been abandoned at an unknown location within the huge area known as the Pinelands of New Jersey. There were similar topological areas on the East Coast but I dismissed them out of hand. Who would have bothered to transport me any distance?

How had I gotten to this desolate spot? And, more importantly, how was I going to get out? Getting up would be hard enough. I raised myself onto my elbows but dropped back onto a pile of sharp pine needles. All I wanted to do was sleep. A guttural sound in the brush cured me of that fantasy. I sat at attention and listened to the unknown beast move through the thick underbrush. Whatever the creature was, it had moved fast and, I hoped, far. Although I felt relieved at its departure, I knew the unseen animal was not the only problematic resident of the area. What kind of wildlife lived in the Pines?

From where I lay, I could see a sampling of the regional birds—or at least I thought the darkness that fell across me was the shadow of the bird that circled above. The creature looked more like a pterodactyl. Black except for its red head, the bird's wingspread resembled a 747's. The only consolation was that I didn't think the predator could fit between the trees to catch me in its beak.

Again, I heard a noise in the brush. I hoped the breeze was rustling the branches to my left. If the weather was responsible for the ruckus in the overgrown woods, the area was the target of a tiny but fierce squall. The surrounding trees and bushes remained quiet and motionless. I struggled to recall any knowledge of the local fauna. I was fairly certain I recollected all I knew—nothing.

At least it was daylight. I figured the worst critters—the creepers, the crawlers, the hoppers—were asleep. For the first time since the day of the final exam, I wished I had studied in biology class.

I knew, however, that the animals were the least of my problems. I'd always assumed that the lore surrounding the wooded areas was just that—lore. Lying immobile on the bed of pine needles, I certainly hoped so. Especially, the part about the Jersey Devil. The Devil, a strange twisted creature, half human, half, well, half something else, roamed the Pine Barrens wreaking

me that I would drop from a pine tree into the jaws of the Jersey Devil. Could the Devil really exist? What did it matter? Some fierce creature did—and directly below me. A decidedly real wild animal could do just as much damage as a mythical creature.

Suddenly the roars and growls rose to a higher pitch. Were there two Jersey Devils? Two incompatible Jersey Devils. The sound of the gentle breeze through the pines was no match for the roar of two animals involved in a fight for survival. How long did these things take? I couldn't judge by fight scenes on National Geographic specials; those scenes were probably edited heavily. I accepted the possibility of a long wait.

In a vain attempt to climb higher, I fell three feet. The slip apparently went unnoticed by the pugilists below; I heard no break in the horrid screeching. I fought to stay on my current perch. What felt like hours was probably only three minutes. The animals moved their argument elsewhere. I sat silently and waited. The beasts did not return.

With painstaking caution, I climbed to the highest branch that would hold me and directed my attention to the sky. I envisioned lying on the porch of the old cottage. I twisted my head until the sky appeared familiar. This was the way the sky looked when I rocked on the porch—facing the ocean. I thought. I hoped. I based my choice of route on that assumption.

As I hoisted myself into a climbing position, a smile spread over my face. Off to my left, just over the pointed tops of the trees, I saw a trace of light—the faint glow of the neon lights of Atlantic City. If I used that glow as a beacon and if I kept my limbs out of the mouths of the regional beasts, I could get home.

Thousands of trails must wind through the Pine Barrens of New Jersey. I didn't stumble upon any of them. I adhered to my route taking great care to avoid those slight shifts in direction that would return me to my starting position. Rather than walking towards Atlantic City, I chose a course perpendicular to the city's length assuming I would cross one of the roads that traverse South Jersey. Occasionally, I believed I had stumbled onto the beaten track but realized I had simply happened on a clearing in the thick vegetation.

I had no idea what plants I traipsed through and on. Egbert's recent visit left them cold and damp—characteristics they shared with me. I hoped none of the leaves were poisonous to the touch. Despite a growing hunger, eating any of the Pine's produce was out of the question. I couldn't see the plants clearly and couldn't have identified them if I could. I was more worried about dehydration than hunger. I had no idea when I had last taken fluid. I knew I'd drunk a bottle of water shortly before Mad Dog threw me in the car, but I had no idea when that occurred.

After an hour of strenuous hiking, I was regretting all the nights I had declined Lindy's invitation to the gym in favor of dinner. My legs rebelled; they shook uncontrollably with each soggy step. My limbs were not accustomed to such constant and rigorous activity. A nice run in Central Park was one thing; a trek over rough and uneven terrain was another. In addition to carrying me, my legs needed to serve alternately as a machete and a plow to move me through the variety of ferns, bushes and other unidentifiable fauna of the region. And, they had to do it all in wet sneakers. I sank onto a low branch and watched my legs vibrating uncontrollably. I wasted fifteen minutes waiting for them to stop—or at least slow down—before I started out again.

Not one of the varied terrains I traversed welcomed hikers. The ground was uneven as I moved from cushions of pine needles to shallow marshes to drying sand that proved the most difficult to negotiate. My feet slipped wide to the side jolting each joint from ankle to hip. My arms stung from pushing through sharp needles and thorny bushes. The adventure thing was getting real boring.

I ignored the berries that lined the path I'd chosen. They might have been edible; I would be the last to know. I was hungry and tired, but above all thirsty. Visions of tall, frosty coke bottles led me through low pines and tall ferns. Every now and then my feet would break through the foliage and into a puddle of very cold and very dark water. I was sure the fluid was pure and unpolluted. But was it potable? Black water did not seem suitable for drinking although I must have swallowed some accidentally on childhood trips to Sunshine Lake—a swimming spot I had visited with a friend each year. The lake before me (I called the body of water a lake but given its size it might have been a large puddle) resembled Sunshine Lake. Despite the evening chill I dunked my feet in the cold water in hopes of introducing fluid into my system through my skin, a proposition that at that point seemed perfectly logical. The idea quickly lost its charm as the reptilian and amphibian residents of the lake came to check out the intruder. I looked down.

"What are you doing there?" Actually, the question should have been "what are you?"

I hadn't the foggiest idea what the tiny frog-like creature clinging to a hole in Andy's sweat pants was. Perhaps a miniature frog. The amphibian didn't answer but stared at me with eyes that would have been far more attractive on a much larger animal.

Apparently, the frog was looking for a free ride. "Okay, you can come with me, but if I were you, I'd think the idea over. You believe you'd like a change of venue. A relaxing vacation. Trust me. It's hell out there. You'd be better off staying home. You'd better believe I wish I had." The frog paid no attention. The tiny amphibian clung to my pants despite, not because of, my attempts at friendship. I ended all efforts to bond and turned my thoughts inward.

I recalled conversations with friends who had brushes with death. They claimed that at the threat of a fast, violent death, their lives flashed before their eyes. As I sat on the rough, cold, damp log, my life began to play out in excruciatingly slow motion. Did this mean I was in line for an excruciatingly slow death?

How did I ever end up in this position? Of everyone I knew, I was the least likely person to die from exposure. I never hiked. I never camped. I never even barbecued. What kind of cruel fate subjects a person like me to such a demise. For the first time, I addressed the possibility that I might not get out of the Pinelands.

Suddenly, the situation struck me as incredibly sad. I began to weep and, after eliciting a promise from the tiny frog to keep my behavior to himself, even whimper a bit. "I'm only thirty-three." I sniffled. "Why is this happening to me? Why do I have to die? Why didn't it happen to David? Or Laurie? I'm a lot nicer than either of them." I took a few moments off from talking to myself and sobbed.

"Who's going to miss me?" I knew my sister would, but she was working in Prague. She might not even notice I was gone for several months. Markshell employees would notice I was missing but largely because they would wonder if my job was open. Within days my tenure at the company would be no more than a faint memory; my accomplishments, errors to be corrected. My landlord would evict me. All my personal belongings would be stolen from the sidewalk in front of my apartment. Within months, it would be as if I'd never existed.

"What will it matter to you? You'll be dead." I wiped my nose on Andy's shirt. After all, there would be no witnesses to report the breach of etiquette. By the time some hunter stumbled onto my bones the shirt would have long since decomposed—if people even hunted in the Pines. I might not be found until the world population grew so large that the Pinelands would lose their protected status and the spot were I died would be turned into a housing development.

With a silent apology to the Philadelphia Eagles, I bunched up the green cloth and blew my nose. I imagined Andy, months in the future, mentioning to Charlene. "Have you seen my Eagles jersey. I haven't seen it in months. I wonder what I did with it? I really liked that shirt." At the same time would he wonder what happened to me?

Suddenly an eerie calm descended upon my spirit. I'd lived a good life. At least I had no regrets. I had done a lot—had a lot of fun. Well, okay, I never learned to speak Japanese, but I wasn't a complete failure. I did know a little. "Ohayo," I shouted to the Pineland creatures. If they understood, they didn't respond or maybe they didn't want to hear that it was morning. I tried again.

If the animals in the vicinity cared that five bound red books were on the small black table, they didn't let on. "Who needs you guys anyway?" I yelled into the woods. "At least you're reliable." I spoke to the tiny frog still lodged on my pants. "If I have to go, at least I've lived a full life." The assurance seemed to mean little to the tiny amphibian.

Given the frog's indifference, I comforted myself aloud. I'd wanted to work abroad and I had. I wanted to live in New York and I had. I wanted to learn to ski and I did, although even I had to admit I was a really bad skier. I could do better. I knew I could. If I ever got out of this godforsaken predicament, I would make the most of my talents, just as soon as I figured out what they were. And I would do good.

I made a deal with the same supreme being who never let me win when I gambled. "If I get out of here alive, I swear I'll do something meaningful with my life. Please let me find a road." I negotiated. "I never ask for much. I mean all those parking spaces that emptied when I pulled down the street, all those checks that didn't clear before my deposits, all those questions that turned up on final exams . . . I never specifically asked for those favors. This one I'm asking for . . . and I am prepared to pay for a positive outcome." I'd live and work with the poor. I'd never be motivated by money again—especially mediocre money. I felt a determination growing inside me. I had to get out of here. And if I didn't?

"They'll pin this murder on me." I grew suddenly angry. I pictured the news broadcast. "A New York woman who allegedly followed her boss to the beach (the Philadelphia station would say shore) to murder him, has disappeared with millions. The police ask your help in locating this woman." My picture would flash on the screen. Oh God, I didn't have a recent photo. What shot would they use. Not my college graduation picture. That hair! Those extra chins. On the bright side, maybe no one would recognize me.

But everyone would believe I was a murderer. The inequity of the situation angered me and energized me. Mad Dog wasn't going to get the best of me. I was going home. With great hope I returned my feet to the squishing sneakers and plunged through the trees.

Hours later I was rethinking my plan when I heard a beautiful sound. Somewhere through the dense woods ahead of me a police siren blared. Although I rushed in that direction with renewed vigor, my speed wasn't going to put me in any record books. The sun was rising when after an hour I heard the occasional whoosh of a car advertising a highway in my future. When the last branches relinquished their hold on me, I fell to the ground as if propelled by rejecting arms of woods that regretted the intrusion. No more than I had regretted intruding, I was sure.

I lay on my stomach relishing my safety and enjoying the rays of the new sun, even if they did lack the warmth to vanquish the chill. Without fear, I laid my cheek on the bed of pine needles that lined the road. Just as I was drifting into unconsciousness it occurred to me that I hadn't heard the whir of traffic on the road above me. I'd check later. First, I just needed a little nap. I wondered how the tiny frog on my slacks was doing. But not for long. I was out cold.

The sun was hot, and I could tell that the back of my legs were badly burned when my catnap ended. I'd been wakened by the sound of youthful motorists who had apparently stopped to take advantage of the privacy of the roadside location to relieve a basic biological urge most likely related to the beer bottles they tossed into the woods. Luckily the two men stopped twenty yards ahead of where I lay. Unluckily, they didn't spot me. By the time I pulled myself into relative consciousness and onto my feet, all I could see of the chattering motorists was the taillights of their pick-up truck disappearing down the long black stretch of macadam that extended as far as the eyes could see—in both directions.

Within a minute, I had noted with dismay that the road on which I found myself was not heavily traveled. Fifteen minutes later, I knew that it was rarely traveled. Occasionally, I detected vehicles on the horizon, but they repeatedly proved to be mirages courtesy of the waving band of heat that danced above the hot black surface.

I was determined that no car would get by me. According to my calculations that next vehicle was headed toward Pennsylvania, but I didn't care. I stood in the roadway waving both arms frantically. I grasped the equally frantic expression on the lone woman's face as she veered around me with her foot planted firmly on the gas pedal.

"Must have thought I was the Jersey Devil." I chuckled. The joke struck me funny only because I had yet to see a mirror.

I heard the next vehicle before I saw it. I hoped the Jeep was both headed in my direction and able to take extra passengers. The good news was the driver seemed willing to stop. At least, rather than stepping on the gas and steering around me, he slammed on his brakes and brought the car to a halt in the lane I stood blocking.

Even I had to admit that limbs smeared with blood could be off-putting to potential rides. I stared down at Andy's tattered sweats. Once they had been gray pants. Now they were orange shorts stained by my repeated rests in the South Jersey clay. Not only was the frog gone, most of the pants were. My exposed legs were smeared with red blood as well as the orange dust that overlay a wide array of black and blue marks. Their overall appearance complemented the black, blue and bloody appearance of my arms.

The woman that I assumed to be the wife of the driver was definitely concerned and pretty gallant. Fearlessly, she jumped out of the car and ran up to me, screaming over her shoulder, "Can't you see she's hurt, you idiot." My assumption had to be correct; this had to be his wife.

The husband surveyed the woods to determine if I were the bait in a car jacking. I couldn't blame him. He drove a very nice car—albeit considerably nicer before they picked me up than after I climbed into the backseat.

If the driver worried about blood or soil on the beige seats, the man's wife did not. She wrapped a comforting arm around me, guided me to the back door, and helped me settle onto the plush leather, despite the protestations coming from behind the steering wheel.

"Tom. We can fix the things. Let's hope we can fix this nice lady."

If I can judge by the muscles in the back of Tom's neck, he wasn't convinced, but luckily he seemed a bit henpecked. On his wife's advice, he turned the car around (I was wrong about the directions) to take me to the nearest hospital in Somers Point.

"I don't need a hospital," I protested. "I'm fine."

"I don't think so." The woman responded firmly.

I wasn't about to let my savior know that I resented her using the same attitude on me as on her husband. If there was ever a time to remain polite, this was it. I pulled myself upright and assumed a position reminiscent of car trips with my parents. I pushed my knees between the two front seats and pushed my head between those of the couple.

I eyed the woman's bottle of Evian jealously. For the first time in my life, I actually smacked my lips. The wife took the hint and passed the bottle to me. Without regard for medical advice I'd heard about in such situations, I guzzled the water. The couple was kind enough to stop when I lost the water and generous enough to provide a second bottle, which I drank slowly.

"Just drop me at a bus stop." Why I thought bus service was offered within miles of the location was hard to fathom. At the time, however, the request seemed perfectly logical. I felt in my waistband for the wallet I'd stuffed there the day before. The wallet with my keys attached was long gone. "Maybe you could lend me five dollars. I'll take your address and send it back."

"You'll do no such thing. We are taking you to the hospital. Look at yourself."

With that the woman shifted the rear view mirror—revealing my face and a possible mean streak. Reflected I saw, a third at a time, what had become of my face. It was not a pretty sight. The dirt and the quilting pattern left by the pine needles I understood. I had no idea how I had gotten the black eye or why my jawline was now considerably larger than it had been the day before. Dried blood from numerous scratches laid a web of dark red over my face. A wad of caked blood in the corner of my lip completed the image.

"I hope you don't mind my asking, but what happened to you?"

The woman's question didn't seem out of line, although her tone did. I sensed that no matter how I answered, she had already concluded that I had brought this on myself. I started the story a lot earlier than she wanted me to—I could tell by the annoyed expression on her face. Her impatience only prodded me to provide more detail. When I got to the events of the previous night, I realized I was filling in the gaps as I spoke. Slowly, the memories were returning.

The woman watched me with narrowing eyes that indicated understanding. She began to take the journey with me. Her husband, however, seemed to be growing increasingly uncomfortable. He kept his eyes on the road and his face tilted towards the side window.

"I'm sorry. I should introduce myself. I'm Meg Daniels."

That news really made the driver uncomfortable.

I understood his discomfort when his wife introduced them. What were the odds of being rescued by my prom date—and his wife. By my prom date, who made the evening special by announcing that he was in love with Suzanne Lisette Rossiter. Not that after fifteen years I could still remember every detail of how he slipped my prom key around my neck, gave me a wan kiss, confessed to being a hypocrite, offered to take me home early . . . well okay, I did remember the details. Certain occasions tend to stick in your mind.

If Tom knew who I was and I was sure he did, he didn't mention it.

"Tom, did you go to LaSalle High School?"

Tom cleared his throat before answering. "Yes."

"Oh." I paused. "I knew a Tom Kennedy. I think he would be younger than you." Why not take the opportunity to attack. "As a matter of fact, I think I went out with him a few times." My voice indicated I was straining to remember, as if the nights spent in the backseat of his sports car or on a blanket along the East River Drive were of such little importance that I moved them out of my ready memory. "Yes. As a matter of fact, he was my prom date. Boy, was he a jerk."

Tom's response was quick. "I look better than you do." The guy still had a flair for interpersonal relationships.

His wife looked from her husband to me with wide eyes.

"Today, of course, but my bruises will heal. What are they doing with male pattern baldness these days?" I didn't add that I, like many women, found bald men attractive. Why would I? I'd waited fifteen years to pay Tom Kennedy back.

Chapter 45

A ndy arrived at the hospital when I was still in the emergency room describing the events of the night before to the local police. The nurse made the PI wait outside while I told the young policemen what I remembered. I watched Andy's feet under the curtain; he paced back and forth in a fifteen-foot-long area. Although I had pretty much abandoned my fear that Andy and Mad Dog were one and the same, I did note that the PI wore sneakers—not the hard-soled shoes I last heard on Mad Dog's feet.

I didn't have much to tell the cops about my abductor. The phony accent. The great strength. The synthetic fibers. "The guys clothes felt really icky while he was wearing any." That comment led to another round of questions. Only at the doctor's urging did the cops say good-bye with a promise to keep me posted.

When the nurse with my agreement finally gave him the okay, Andy sauntered in casually. His appearance and demeanor suggested that he had been up all night—fighting. He admitted both.

"Who hit you?" I asked the first question of what I knew would be many on both sides.

"I established . . . I thought . . . I determined conclusively some unexpected relationships that I thought . . . believed . . . that Bucky Whitelaw was hiding. So I confronted him."

"And he hit you?"

"No. Turns out his student was eavesdropping. She hauled off and hit me with her racquet." A smile toyed with the corners of his lips. "Bucky said it was the best shot she ever took. You know that Bucky is a really nice guy."

"So you were in the hospital all night?'

The PI shook his head. "At the police station."

"You got arrested?"

"No. In case you hadn't noticed, I had a certain degree of interest in a missing persons case."

"And the cops can confirm this?"

Andy appeared incredulous. "Of course. Did you think that I . . . ? You took a harder hit on the head than we imagined." He reacted to my accusation without rancor or reproach. Was this guy for real? I'd just suggested that he might have abducted me, and he was still smiling. I didn't mention that yesterday I believed he'd killed Bascombe.

"Where have you been? They ripped your house apart. We didn't know where you went."

"Oh God, did they demolish it before I got my stuff out?" How long had I been in the woods anyway?

"Not the demolition team. David and Laurie. They got them."

"Who got them?"

"The Ocean City cops."

"For what?"

"Kidnaping for one thing. Those idiots grabbed you in broad daylight. Cops found your wallet and keys in the back of their van. There's a whole list of charges. Breaking and entering. Destroying your property and the landlord's."

I nodded.

"I didn't think they had it in them to do this to you although that Laurie . . . I don't know what David sees in her." Andy spoke as matter-of-factly as if he had met the couple at a cocktail party.

"When the cops brought them in, all she did was berate David. Apparently she was the mastermind. He suspected the money was there. She made the confirmation."

"Tell me more about how awful she is."

Andy related what he had heard around the Ocean City police station. Apparently, my disappearance put the PI and Detective Dupuy on the same side of the fence. "Laurie blamed David that they had to resort to scaring you. She sent him to talk to you time and time again. She said he was a buffoon. I think they might break up. On the bright side, David is in the cell next to Bishop's."

"What did Bishop do?"

"Basically the same things with the exception of abducting you. Bishop claims he didn't know anything about the money until you mentioned it."

I shrugged. The motion required great effort. "I mentioned the cash because I assumed he knew. When did they arrest him?"

"Sometime during the night when he finally showed up at his hotel. I feel kind of sorry for the guy. Seems that Miguel O'Shea's girlfriend, Ella . . . " The PI stared at me to see if I remembered her.

"From the casino?"

He nodded and continued. "Seems Ella figured that Bishop had to know so she developed an interest in him when he came down to take tennis lessons with Bucky."

"You mean Bucky was in bed with Ella?"

Andy shook his head. "Actually, Bucky was one of the few who wasn't. That guy is a real innocent . . . in his way. Ella used him. By the way, she said she was sorry she lied to you."

"I gave her a twenty."

Andy's face contorted to tell me he was confused.

"The only time I met her. We didn't even talk. She made change at the casino. Correct change."

"No. You met her one other time."

Then my contorted features asked for clarification.

"The reporter. She came to your house."

Now I understood why Ella had been so nervous in my presence. Needless worry. I never would have connected the flashy blonde at the casino with the earnest reporter. "Is she in jail, too?"

Andy nodded.

"Have we identified anyone who wasn't ransacking my house?"

"Actually, Ella hasn't been charged with that crime. She was arrested for hiring a guy to get information from you—the guy who mugged you."

"And I thought Detective Dupuy didn't believe me."

Andy looked sheepish. "She didn't, but she believed me."

I eyed him with a quizzical lip. "Why is that?"

Andy's expression turned even more sheepish before he moved on, ignoring my question. "The police aren't finished yet. They found John Mancotti nosing around your house, but he didn't break in. Most likely the cops questioned him and sent him home. He was still at the station when I left—in a holding cell on his two hundredth sit-up. I think the only thing that really bothered him about jail was the absence of mirrors."

"Anyone else?"

"The day is young."

I mulled over what Andy had told me. "Laurie and David didn't put me in the hospital."

"Who did then?"

"The guy who grabbed me when I ran away from David and Laurie."

Andy appeared more than a little confused. "Are you telling me that you got kidnapped twice in one day?"

"Apparently, I am a very desirable woman."

"That I knew. However, two abductions in a day is still rather unusual."

I nodded. "Kind of unlikely isn't it. Especially when you figure that I've never been kidnapped before and wouldn't be able to raise any ransom."

"I would have led a fund-raising drive." Andy seemed embarrassed by his show of concern—no matter how facetious. He changed the subject. The PI wanted the details of my experiences.

Without mentioning why I was pedaling frantically to a cash machine, I explained how I had sneaked away from David and Laurie and found myself in Mad Dog's car.

"And you didn't see the driver's face?"

I asked Andy to recall horror movies he'd seen. "Remember how the young innocent girl is hitchhiking. Then the car stops and she runs up to it with a big smile. She opens the door and only after she is all the way inside does she turn to look at the driver."

"Then she screams, right?"

"Well, I never got that far. I got knocked out during the climbing in phase."

"I never believed those scenes."

"Believe them."

"And you never saw . . . ?"

I regretted shaking my head. The pain took several minutes to settle down.

Andy rubbed his chin in an exaggerated display of thoughtfulness. "Maggie, three different people thought you had enough money for ransom. Does that suggest anything to you?"

I shook my head once, but it hurt too much. "Not really."

Andy just made a hmmmm noise. I was too tired to care what these developments suggested to him but not too tired to share the coincidence of my rescue.

"Wait until I tell you what happened to me." I related that Tom Kennedy and his wife had rescued me from the Pines. "My prom date. Can you believe it? It was fate. No other cars came down that road."

I was still talking about the unlikely turn of events when I snuggled against my pillow in the room I'd been assigned for 24 hours of observation. A real bed. I relished the feel of the sheets. They were too crisp—almost rough. I loved them.

"You know I never thought about Tom Kennedy much, on a conscious level, but I think on a subconscious level I did. And now, I've had the chance for closure." My eyes were closed, but a smile played on the corner of my lips. "I looked much better than he did."

I thought I heard Andy mutter something about that being hard to believe before he mentioned that he didn't do closure. "I want to know what happened to you. We were all worried about you."

"Who worried about me?"

"What?" Andy's annoyed tone was somehow endearing.

"You said everyone was worried about me. Who's everyone?"

Andy shook his head. "The cops." He paused. "Okay, I was worried. I was. I admit it. I was worried."

"That's nice." I answered just before I dropped off to sleep.

Andy was sleeping in a old vinyl armchair by the door to my hospital room when I awoke. Once again the moon was high in the sky. My body clock seemed to have been knocked off kilter for good. The middle of the night and I was ready to go. "Andy."

The PI responded with a snore.

"Andy."

It took three more tries, each with increased volume, before the PI stirred. He shook his head and struggled to consciousness—actually semi-consciousness.

"What are you doing here? Shouldn't you be home in bed?"

"Gotta protect you." He mumbled and fell back to sleep.

Feeling safe I tried to follow his example. But after lying unconscious in bed all day, sleep didn't come easily—even though this was the first night in many when I has the opportunity to fall asleep on crisp, clean sheets spread across a soft bed.

Even though Andy had filled me in, I still didn't have the total picture. I searched my memory for the events of the previous forty-eight hours. I was glad David and Laurie were in jail, but that was strictly personal. What woman wouldn't enjoy seeing her ex and his new flame incarcerated—even if only for a few hours until they made bail? But something felt wrong. I had gotten away from them. Did they have a third partner? David and Laurie had gotten a bit heavy handed in trying to talk to me, but they weren't criminals. Okay, they were criminals, but they didn't have the guts to throw me in the middle of the Jersey Pines. For one thing, they would have had to mess up their outfits.

I was close to sleep when I realized a trespasser had entered the room. It wasn't that I heard the intruder; I sensed the desperation that had evolved into evil. I didn't open my eyes but I knew who I would see if I did. The person who killed DK Bascombe. If I lifted my lids, the killer would have no choice but to murder me too.

Chapter 46

As I feigned sleep, I envisioned the entire thing. DK's killer trying to smother me with the pillow from the next bed. Hearing my cries, Andy leaping to my rescue and wrestling the perpetrator to the ground. A proud Andy delivering the culprit to the police. But that's not how it came down.

"Meg, are you awake?" The killer spoke in a natural voice. I recognized the tones immediately; I assumed the killer knew I would. "Now you're toast." I informed myself silently.

I wasn't sure whether or not to answer—or what to say. The perp would notice a move for the call button. After the soft voice repeated the question, I opened my eyes and met the intent gaze of the visitor who bent over my bed—without clutching a pillow I was relieved to see.

"Don't be afraid. I didn't come to kill you again."

Now that was a sentence I never thought I'd hear.

"I'm going away where no one can find me. Before I go, I wanted to say I'm sorry. I'm glad you're out of the woods. Trying to kill you was wrong. I never meant to hurt you."

I'd heard that one before.

"I bet all your cuts and bruises and things will clear up okay. You're a very pretty girl. I mean woman. You'll meet someone.

I hoped maybe we could . . . you know . . . but I guess not now."

My standards were low, after all I was on the rebound, but I drew the line at dating people who tried to kill me.

"I could have gotten away with it, you know." The voice surged with criminal pride. "Except I got greedy. I wanted the rest of the money. Actually, I need it. Turns out I have a problem with gambling. Who knew?" The next sentence revealed the real point of the visit. "You have the rest of the money, don't you? I went through your house. Ripped the place apart. It wasn't there. That means one thing. You moved the cash. All I need you to do, and then I'll be gone from your life forever, is to tell me where you put it."

Andy snorted aloud and shifted position. I waited for him to rescue me—I only had the killer's word that I was not the next victim—but soon the PI was again in deep sleep.

"I don't know anything about the money. Why are you so sure you didn't get it all?"

The story of how Bascombe had begged for his life gave me no pleasure, but neither did it arouse feelings of sympathy. "I felt so powerful. Sometimes the sensation returns. When it does I am a whole new person."

I had witnessed that phenomenon myself.

"I'm not going to hurt you tonight. Sorry about the meat locker." His sentence explained the smell. "It seemed a good place to locker up. Get it?"

Given the circumstances I thought it best to say I did.

"I came here to give you a chance to make your life easier. You give me the money, I'm gone forever. You don't? Well, you will never sleep well again. I'll come back for my share."

"If I knew where the money was, wouldn't I have told you last night?" Persistence is a virtue but this was one impractical, implacable killer. I would have been long gone with the money I did get.

"Did you know all along that I killed him?"

I rolled my head from side to side on the pillow. "I never dreamt you killed DK. I still find it hard to believe."

"I didn't kill DK Bascombe." The emphasis was on the word kill. "Didn't you ever hear of downsizing? Bascombe wasn't killed. He was downsized." In the light that came through the window, I saw Randall smile. "Trust me. Someday, wherever he is, he can look back and think it was the best thing that ever happened to him." Randall pulled himself to his full height. "I tried to cut his feet off. I thought I could literally downsize him. Get it?"

For the first time in my life I tittered and understood the roots of tittering: the need to laugh hiding fear and disgust. I tried tittering more loudly, but whatever noise I made didn't disturb Andy's sleep.

I might have learned more about Randall's rather unconventional viewpoint but Detective Dupuy chose that moment to burst into my hospital room. The Ocean City police had been a little faster to figure out that Randall was the man than I was. They just couldn't find him. My great service was in smoking him out.

Randall appeared bewildered as he was handcuffed and advised of his rights. "I don't see why it should be a crime to kill a man like Bascombe." He protested before I suggested he talk to a lawyer before he expressed any more opinions. On the vinyl chair Andy mumbled and shifted position.

Officer Timmy read Randall his rights from a card. Didn't the kid ever watch television. I could have Mirandized Randall with less effort. As Randall indicated that he understood, Andy released a single snore.

Before Detective Dupuy escorted Randall from the room, she awakened the sleeping PI. "Yoah, Beck. Beck." She shook his shoulder and yelled loudly. "You can go home now. We got him." She smiled at me. "Guy sleeps like a log, eh?"

I couldn't determine if she was speaking based on current or previous observation.

Before Andy was fully awake, the entire entourage, criminal and keepers, had vanished out the door. "What happened here?" The PI watched the hospital room door fall closed.

"Go back to sleep. It's all over. It was Randall. I'll tell you about it in the morning."

Andy glanced out the window. "I think it is morning."

"Which one?"

The PI struggled to a sitting position. "Saturday."

I sighed. "Oh no. I was supposed to be out of the house by noon on Saturday. And I mean out. I think the bulldozers were coming." I shook my head best as I could given my supine position. "What a vacation. I'm more tired than when I started, and if I don't get out of this hospital all my clothes will probably end up somewhere in a landfill."

"Don't worry. You should get out of here today. If not, I'll pick up your stuff." The PI brushed a stray hair from my forehead. "You haven't had a vacation."

"I had an adventure but no vacation."

"Why don't you stay at the shore a little longer?" The detective laid his arms along the bars that guaranteed I wouldn't fall out of bed. "Given the circumstances, I'm sure your company would give you more time."

"I told you they're bulldozing the house. I've got no place to stay."

"Well." Andy waited thirty seconds before he proposed a plan. I was beginning to think he wasn't going to take the hint when he finally spoke. "I have a place. You know that my apartment isn't fancy . . . it's more of an office . . . as you know . . . but I would be willing . . . I mean . . . you know you're not in such good shape . . . you need someone to take care . . . I mean just because of this thing in the woods . . . you could use a rest." He stopped and glanced into my eyes reluctantly.

"Before I make a commitment, would you answer a few questions for me?"

"Well . . . sure . . . yeah . . . you can ask me." I could tell he was worried.

"The first time you saw me. You said I was drinking from a pitcher. That means you were in Bascombe's house the night he died."

I judged Andy's sheepish expression to be genuine. "You didn't tell the cops?"

"They never asked and besides it would be hearsay. You're the one who let it slip. I never saw you."

"Bascombe went out on the beach for awhile that night. You must have missed that. I thought he might get a little sloppy when he was in residence. I used to let myself in every so often. I lifted a key when I was in Bascombe's office. So I let myself in that night. The only thing of interest I saw was you."

I wasn't ready to succumb to Andy's charm. I had more questions. "Why did you drag me along to break into Bish Winston's room?"

"Break-in is such a severe word."

"Okay, okay. This isn't about semantics. Answer."

"Maybe just that once, I used you. I worried that if I walked through the lobby alone, a hotel employee would spot me and stop me. If I were with a guest, like you could have been . . ."

I nodded. His explanation made sense.

"Why did you drag me along to see Bucky Whitelaw at Seacrest?"

He cleared his throat. "Maybe just that one time, I was kind of testing you. I wanted to verify that you and Bucky did not know each other. You could have easily ignored each other at the funeral . . . but meeting one on one . . . I didn't think the two of you had ever seen each other before." His voice perked up. "I could also verify that he wasn't the guy who came to the house the night Bascombe died."

"I can live with that."

"You can?" Andy seemed surprised—and relieved.

"Why did you take me along when you went to Atlantic City?"

That question was the first to cause Andy real discomfort. "Well . . . " he hemmed and hawed. "Maybe just that one time, I really wanted your company." The words were so hard for him to spit out that I believed him. "Did I pass the test?" He kept catching my gaze and glancing away.

With my encouragement, his fleeting look grew into a steady gaze and then one of his penetrating stares. "Maggie," he wrapped his hand around mine careful to avoid the intravenous needle. He leaned his face close to mine. "Maggie, I'd like you to come and stay with me for a few days." Prompted by the confusion on my face, he clarified. "If you catch my drift."

Andy released the bar and, in clear violation of hospital rules, slipped onto the bed beside me. We tried to kiss, but touching was too painful for me. Tentatively, Andy wrapped his arms around me and cradled my head in the crook of his arm. The mood was sweet. I felt myself drifting into the first gentle sleep of my vacation when I felt a jolt run through Andy's body.

"When you said 'it was Randall' you didn't mean . . .?"

"Yep."

"Randall 'Don't-Call-Me-Randy' actually killed someone?"

"Yep."

"He actually stole all the money?"

"Nope."

"What do you mean, nope?"

"He stole half. If he'd been content with that he never would have gotten caught. For some reason, he became convinced I had the other half, or at least knew where it was. If he hadn't been so greedy, he probably could have gotten away with it."

"So half is still missing?"

"Andy, give it up."

"What time do the bulldozers come today?" The man was nothing if not persistent.

Chapter 47

Andy grilled me more thoroughly and more openly than ever from outside the curtain as I climbed into the clothes he'd laundered after I got out of jail.

"I want to talk about Randall."

"Hey, don't forget, this is a hospital and I am a patient." I flung the curtain open.

The PI checked his watch. "Not for long. Let's try to get through these questions while we have the time."

"How do I look?"

"You can change as soon as you get home. About my questions . . . "

Andy had a long list. All I knew was that Randall had confessed to murdering DK and not much more.

"How did he get rid of the body alone?"

I related watching Randall moving his motorcycle. The guy was powerful. "Who knew?" I responded to Andy's skeptical expression. "When he carried me out to the trunk of his car, he just slipped one hand into my belt and carried me like a briefcase."

Although I could tell from his expression that Andy was shocked to hear that I had been tossed in the back of a Hertz rental car, his words stayed focused on the money. "But he only took half the cash."

"His story was that he ran into Bascombe when he was leaving to make a payoff to his ex-wife. To get her off his case."

"Wait a minute. She knew?" Andy was trying to figure out if Caroline Bascombe had sold him out.

"How would I know? I do know something else."

Andy gestured for me to spit it out.

"I know how Randall figured out that he only had half the booty." Andy did not appreciate my dramatic pause. "Bascombe tried to buy Randall off." I explained how Randall had rejected his first offer. "According to Randall, Bascombe really begged. Randall got off on that part." Andy's sigh told me to move on. "That's where Randall got the ridiculous idea that I was involved. Bascombe kept saying let's go over and get it. Randall got fixated on that word 'over'—and I lived next door."

Andy also became fixated on the word "over." "That makes perfect sense. After all they found Bascombe's prints in your house."

"They what?"

"The cops didn't tell you?"

I recalled a cryptic conversation with Detective Dupuy. In a way, I guess she had told me. I just hadn't heard.

"But why didn't Randall simply take all the money from Bascombe and then kill him?" Andy asked.

"All the money wasn't there to take, according to Bascombe anyway. Apparently things got out of hand. Bascombe ran."

Andy interrupted. "Is that why he tried to cut Bascombe's feet off."

I shook my head only briefly. The effort left me dizzy. "No. Didn't I ever tell you that Randall liked puns but he didn't understand good ones. Randall was the king of the truly horrible pun. He thought it would be cute, that's his word, if when they found Bascombe he had been downsized—i.e., brought down to size."

"He was trying to cut off Bascombe's feet to make him shorter?"

I nodded. "That was the feet thing."

"But it's not funny." Andy feigned earnestness.

"None of Randall's puns ever were."

Chapter 48

On the drive home, Andy kept preparing me for the condition of the house.

"What do I care? I'll just grab my stuff and clear out. The next people in are the demolition crew members."

"I hope you can find all your stuff. When I say it's a mess, trust me, it's a mess."

As I walked in the door I realized that Andy was in no way prone to exaggeration. Mess hardly described the array of destruction we found. The furniture had been overturned. The upholstery had been punctured and ripped open. Balls of hardened foam rubber littered the floor as did the linoleum squares that once covered it. Pieces of paneling had been torn from the walls and strewn about like match sticks. Holes had been punched in the ceiling so that plaster powder coated the entire mess.

"David and Laurie did this?"

"That's what the cops think. You doubt it?"

I shrugged. "I just can't figure out what Ralph Lauren sells for household demolition."

"Seems you overestimated your old boyfriend."

"Or underestimated."

"Oh my God." I hadn't spoken. I was watching Andy so I knew the words hadn't come from his mouth. Together Andy and I pivoted to face the source of the sound. A fortyish man of ordinary appearance stood in the doorway with the most extraordinary expression of horror on his face. He was trying to speak. At least his mouth was moving. However, no sound was coming out.

"Can we help you?" I thought my tone was pleasant.

"What have you done to my house?"

Even if it was his house, I thought he was overreacting given that it was scheduled to be demolished within hours.

"You . . . you . . ." The man was sputtering again.

I was too angry and defensive to speak. Did Andy and I look like the kind of people who would trash a house? Apparently the stranger thought so.

He pointed from Andy to me and back. "What kind of people do this to a house?"

"Not our kind." Andy defended our honor. "Vandals broke in and left their mark."

"Besides, calm down, the house is getting ripped down." I threw in my two cents.

"No. No. The sale fell through." The man's voice was full of horror.

I surveyed the room and understood why the man was near tears. Who would want to discover that they owned this disaster area? I metamorphosed into a solicitous hostess. Although I had no traditional amenities to offer, I did find a can of soda.

"I think he needs something stronger." Andy rummaged in the kitchen and emerged with a bottle of beer. "It was in the dairy drawer."

The visitor took the beer eagerly but, after an initial gulp never raised the drink to his lips. The dazed homeowner sat on the metal couch frame with his head bowed as he listened to Andy's explanation of what had happened or rather what the police thought had occurred.

"It's just such a shock to see Mom and Dad's house this way." His words made him realize he had yet to introduce himself. After introductions were made all around, Bob Beacom, son of Robert and Dorothy Beacom, continued. "My parents owned this house for over fifty years. Mom stayed here when Dad went to war. My brother and sister and I spent all our summers here." He surveyed the room with sad eyes. "The house wasn't gorgeous; we wanted Mom and Dad to rebuild or at least renovate. We talked them into it once in the late fifties and Mother always regretted it."

I nodded. I agreed with his mother.

"When they died we sold it to a group of investors but then the main investor died. Actually it turned out the group was a sham and he was the only investor. So here I am. The proud owner of . . . of . . . "

I couldn't fill in the blank. What would you call this crumbling and violated structure? I wanted to ask if I were going to lose the security deposit, but then I remembered David had paid it.

Andy seemed energized by the man's latest statement. "The guy died?"

"Yeah. You probably read about it in the paper. He got murdered. Lived right next door."

"Yeah. We heard about it." Andy was not prepared to say more.

"Well." That was the man's entire statement. Andy and I waited almost two minutes for his next utterance. "I'd better stop by the police station. And my insurance agent's. And my real estate agent's." He put his hands on his knees and pushed to move to a standing position. "Have a good day." He said dejectedly as he headed for the door. There was no point responding in kind.

When Bob Beacom stopped for a last look, an item in the rubble attracted his attention. "Do you mind?" He bent to pick up one of the seascapes. The frame was broken at the corner, but the painting was intact. "My mother was so proud of the way she placed these pictures. She wanted it to appear that the sun was streaming into the picture." He chuckled ruefully. "As if anyone would notice."

My eyes met Andy's. He winked. The PI followed the dejected homeowner to the door and watched until he drove away. Then he turned and rubbed his palms together in anticipation. "We've got work to do."

"Andy, short of rebuilding, there is no possibility of making this place right before I go. Besides, David paid the security."

"You don't see?"

Apparently, I didn't.

"Bascombe was going to own this place. He needed a hiding place. Maggie, the money is in here." Excitement surged through his voice. I could see it surging through his muscles.

I surveyed the destruction. "Maybe the cash was here, but if so, some lucky person beat us to it."

Andy's view was more optimistic. He cut open tiny balls of foam rubber. He peeled off the few remaining panels of wall covering. He poked his head into the holes in the ceiling. He examined each room with the same care. I sat on the porch and waited for him to complete the search.

The PI was dejected when he stuck his head out the door. "I know it's here. I can feel it."

He leaned against the doorjamb and stared back into the living room. I watched as he twisted his head first to the right and then to the left. "Eureka!" The screen door slammed shut as the PI disappeared inside.

I took my time pulling myself out of the rocker and following the investigator. When I caught up with him in the kitchen, his head was under the sink. "Is the money there?"

"I need turpentine. Is there any in this place?"

"Maybe in the storage closet under the house."

Andy was gone and back in a flash. I'd never seen him move so fast. I wasn't sure I had ever seen anyone move that fast— and I'd gone to the Olympics. Andy had brought turpentine and rags with him. What he was doing with them I wasn't sure, but he was kneeling beside the dark and heavy painting of the forest that we had ridiculed. The back had been sliced open reveal-ing a huge open space. "Was the money in there?"

"Maybe some."

Andy would not be distracted from his work—wiping the rags across the face of the painting.

"Yes." His scream sounded like a prayer of thanks.

I peeked over his shoulder. He'd wiped paint off the canvas to reveal a shiny surface. When he moved the canvas and the glare faded, I saw faces. Lots of faces—all belonging to dead presidents I had never encountered in my wallet. "Bascombe created the canvas out of the bills. Then he painted over it. This canvas is made of money. Lots of money. It's solid money." Andy's behavior was highly animated. He appeared to relish saying the word money over and over again. "Can you believe it? He painted over the money."

How had Bascombe accomplished this? "I didn't know he was that handy."

"I didn't know he was that smart." Andy's voice was full of admiration.

"Or that artistic." Granted the painting was ugly, but it showed a rudimentary, misdirected talent.

Andy stood up and planted a big, sloppy, happy kiss on my forehead. "I knew we could do it."

We? "What do we do now?"

Chapter 49

I sat with Richard Rothman behind the dark glass that was, as I suspected, transparent only from the inside. We enjoyed the view from white leather sofas identical to the ones in Caroline Bascombe's house in Brigantine. As far as I could detect, taste in furniture was the only thing the twosome had in common. Yet, Caroline and Rothman appeared to be a devoted couple—although at the moment Caroline was in another room hunched over the canvas with Andy.

"You know, I am terribly sorry about the arrest episode. It's just that I thought you might have bad intentions—towards Caroline. After she returned from the funeral and that intruder in her house . . . ." The newsman let his voice trail off. "You can imagine how scared she was. And even though we felt favorably towards you when we met you, we really didn't know you, did we?"

I had to accept his apology. For one thing, it sounded so sincere when delivered in his dulcet, anchorman tones. And after all, he was right. I had been harboring ill will towards Caroline that day. I was out to prove she had killed her husband. By the end of the adventure, I had even suspected Rothman himself.

I didn't have to ask about his traffic ticket on the night of Bascombe's murder. Rothman volunteered that in a fury at

Bascombe's failure to arrive for his meeting with Caroline, he had driven down to "drag him up there" because he "was sick of the way that bastard treated her." I probably wouldn't have believed him except for two things. Randall had already confessed to Bascombe's murder, and Rothman was the one who had reported Bascombe missing before dawn.

With apologies out of the way and suspicions put to rest, Rothman and I chatted amicably over tea. We discussed the weather, the surf, and other innocuous topics while Caroline and Andy huddled in the library figuring out what to do with the money. Legally. The last stipulation was Caroline's. I didn't know if Andy would have been so insistent on adhering to all laws—local and federal.

The first dilemma the two faced was removing the bills from their storage place. Bascombe had planned well. The task was time-consuming, but few of the bills below the top layer were damaged. Eventually, Caroline grew tired and suggested hiring a person to strip the canvas. Andy applied for and got the job on the spot. He was not about to let the cash out of his hands. So, while Rothman and I relaxed, the twosome worked, Andy peeling and Caroline counting.

"How much?" Rothman asked when Andy and Caroline took a break.

"Over half a million and counting. We're not even halfway there. Unless Donald put all one dollar bills on the bottom. He did have a bizarre sense of humor." She paused. "But not about money." Caroline's eyes became riveted on me. I squirmed under her scrutiny. "Maggie, dear. You look like you could use a vacation."

"This was my vacation."

Caroline eyed me from head to toe. "In the future, maybe you should avoid holidays."

Caroline plopped on the arm of Rothman's chair and wrapped an arm around his shoulders. "After all this work, I sincerely hope I get to keep this money. I broke a nail." She seemed genuinely disturbed.

Andy on the other hand was elated. He had the plan all laid out. The painting belonged to Caroline—not that they intended to tell anyone exactly where they found the painting. If the issue arose, however, Caroline would swear the artwork was one of the assets that Bascombe had hidden from her. "I really did see him working on that monstrosity one day." Since the two were married at the time of his death, the claim seemed likely to hold up. "As long as I return what he stole, declare the rest and pay taxes on it, I should be fine. And that applies to you too, Andrew, my lovely."

"I think I'll be fine with the legal amounts." He slapped my knee.

I grimaced. There wasn't really a spot on my body that could handle a gentle touch let alone a jovial slap.

"So I was right about you two. You are . . . " Caroline's lascivious tones finished the statement.

Andy and I glanced at each other. Each of us sported a smile tempered with confusion—and doubt. Waiting for an answer, Caroline glanced from one to the other.

"Not exactly." Andy fielded the question.

Caroline turned to me with wide, questioning eyes.

"It's complicated."

"We'll get back to you, Caroline. Soon, I hope." Andy's tone was optimistic. "Right now I've got to get back to work." That time he slapped his own knees before rising.

He had barely disappeared when Caroline spoke. "So, what's the problem?" Her tone was teasing.

"I don't know what you mean." I lied.

"Andrew is awfully cute and keep in mind that shortly he'll be . . . well, if not rich, at least no liability."

"Caroline, please." Rothman interrupted. "Let nature takes its course."

Caroline directed her words in my direction. "If he only knew what would happen if I let nature take its course." She dropped her voice to a whisper. "Frightening."

"As if I would care." Rothman pulled a giggling Caroline into his lap. I read his actions as my exit cue.

Given my physical condition, I needed several minutes to reach Rothman's library where Andy bent over his work with fanatical zeal. When I peeked over his shoulder, he spoke without turning.

"You know, Meg, I owe you an apology."

"Ooooh, you called me Meg. Must be serious."

"That's it. I'm sorry I insisted on calling you Maggie. Meg is a lovely name, but you seem like a Maggie to me."

"Like Maggie the cat?" I was thinking Tennessee Williams.

"How did you know I had a cat named Maggie?"

"I didn't."

Andy straightened and turned to wrap his arms around my waist, careful not to let his soiled hands touch my clothes. "I was twelve. I named her after Elizabeth Taylor in *Cat on a Hot Tin Roof*."

"So you think I look like Elizabeth Taylor?"

"No, you resemble the cat."

Before I could explain to Andy that was the wrong answer, he added, "And, I mean that as a compliment."

I accepted his word. "I actually like it when you call me Maggie, but maybe if you could just reserve that name for private times. I have my own name and an identity to go with it. So when you introduce me, if you could use Meg, I would appreciate it."

"I'm just happy to hear you are planning some private time." He planted a tentative kiss on my lips.

I played with the buttons on Andy's shirt. "What are you going to do with this money after wanting it so long?"

He wiped his hands and pulled his wallet from his back pocket. He leaned near as he flipped the billfold open. In the spot where I would have expected to find his driver's license, I saw instead a picture of a sailboat.

"How big?" I asked.

"Thirty five. Big enough to live on. And," he smiled at me meaningfully, "to entertain on."

In response to this steady stare, I asked, "Is that an invitation?"

"You could use a holiday. After your period of recuperation."

"No vacation time left." I couldn't make the statement without guilty recollection of my promise to find meaningful work. I silently vowed to honor the pledge.

"No problem." Andy explained that by the time he got the funds, bought the boat, and got it in the water, a new year would have begun.

"Sailing in January? BRRRRRR. I don't think I'm that rugged."

"The temperature should be in the eighties."

"Where?"

"A little island in the Caribbean I especially like."

"Where you'll be living?" I tried not to sound dejected.

"Not for a few months. I'll hang around here while things get settled. Take a few tennis lessons from Bucky Whitelaw. As a way of compensating for calling him a thief and a kidnapper." The PI shook his head. "That guy has the most incredible disposition." Andy returned the wallet to his pocket and bent over his work. "So what do you say?"

"About what?"

"About January."

"You aren't going to make me polish and scrub and all that sailing stuff, are you?"

"You'll be my guest. It will be your vacation. I promise."

"Why don't we see how this week goes first?"

Andy glanced in my direction. A sly smile curled the corners of his lips as he bent back to work. "If we both stay healthy and if you can stay awake, I think this week will go just fine."

We did. I did. It did. I returned to New York as pale as I'd left. I didn't really care. I would work on my tan in January.

Other Titles of Interest About New Jersey

A Field Guide to the Pine Barrens of New Jersey
By Howard P. Boyd

This book is a 420-page volume containing descriptions and illustrations of over 700 species of flora and fauna that inhabit the area of New Jersey known as the Pine Barrens. Throughout the book the author reviews how the Pine Barrens was developed and used by man for such things as agriculture, lumbering, iron mining, and glass manufacturing. The majority of the book focuses on the species descriptions, along with illustrations.
1991/420 pages/hardbound/ISBN 0-937548-18-9/$32.95
1991/420 pages/softbound/ISBN 0-937548-19-7/$22.95

Natural Pathways of New Jersey
By Millard C. Davis

Natural Pathways of New Jersey describes in eloquent detail over 100 natural places in New Jersey along with directions on how to find each of these amazing natural places for your own enjoyment. The book also includes over 100 original watercolor illustrations, by artist Valerie Smith-Pope, to display landscapes and creatures native to New Jersey.
1997/262 pages/softbound/ISBN 0-937548-35-9/$19.95

Old and Historic Churches of New Jersey Vol. 2
By Ellis L. Derry

This inspirational book of history tells the stories of how our forefathers established their religious communities and houses of worship, often with great hardship and sacrifice. Striking photographs bring each church alive, enabling the reader to visualize the exciting history as it unfolds. This is a book not only for those interested in New Jersey history, but also for those interested in church history as well as the history of our country.
1994/372 pages/hardbound/ISBN 0-937548-25-1/$29.95
1994/372 pages/softbound/ISBN 0-937548-26-X/$19.95

A Pine Barrens Odyssey: A Naturalist's Year in the Pine Barrens of New Jersey
By Howard P. Boyd

This detailed perspective of the seasons, meant as a companion to Boyd's previous title, *A Field Guide to the Pine Barrens,* continues its comprehensive look at this region in New Jersey. Included are descriptions of plant and animal life as they pertain to the chronology of the seasons in the Pine Barrens.
1997/275 pages/softbound/ISBN 0-937548-34-0/$19.95

Pinelands
By Robert Bateman

In this novel, set in the New Jersey Pine Barrens, the integrity of the area has collided with what some would call progress. In a compelling blend of history and fiction, *Pinelands* examines the seductive legacies of the past and how they are used by many to resist the abrasive realities of modern life.
1994/248 pages/hardbound/ISBN 0-937548-27-8/$21.95
1994/248 pages/softbound/ISBN 0-937548-28-6/$12.95

Whitman's Tomb: Stories from the Pines
By Robert Bateman

This book is a compilation of 13 fictional short stories, set in the unique area known as the "Pine Barrens" in Southern New Jersey, which examine the mysteries of everyday life and the chaotic world we all live in. Bateman uses a variety of different characters to examine the personal struggles we go through on a daily basis and the previously untold truths that we discover throughout our lives.
1997/215 pages/hardbound/ISBN 0-937548-32-4/$21.95

To order directly from the publisher, include $3.00 postage and handling for each book ordered.

Plexus Publishing, Inc., 143 Old Marlton Pike
Medford, NJ 08055 • (609) 654-6500